## What Doesn't Bend

"I can't play anymore. You know I can't."

"My dear," Loyd sighed, measuring out his breath and his voice carefully. He sounded as I suppose a father might. "Do you think you can quit?"

I said nothing. He wouldn't yield to me, and I would say no words that admitted defeat.

He measured his silence as he had measured his words. Then he pulled a drawer in his desk and took an envelope from it. "Clear your things from the dormitory," he said, laying the package on the desk, not near me. "You have two days to find accommodations." He rose from his desk and left me in his office.

Could I have resisted? Could I have walked out as quickly as he had, with nothing in my hands? The envelope contained some money, a little, not enough to live on for long. A letter as well, with the usual details. I crumpled it without reading it and thrust it back into its wrapping. He knew I would take it.

# CONFIDENCE GAME

## MICHELLE M. WELCH

**BANTAM BOOKS**
New York • Toronto • London • Sydney • Auckland

CONFIDENCE GAME
A Bantam Spectra Book / October 2003

Published by Bantam Dell
A Division of Random House, Inc.
New York, New York

ISBN 0-553-58627-0

Manufactured in the United States of America
Published simultaneously in Canada

OPM   10 9 8 7 6 5 4 3 2 1

# Acknowledgments

My thanks to all who helped this book come into being.

The obvious: Nanci McCloskey and the Virginia Kidd Agency, Juliet Ulman and Bantam.

The not-so-obvious: Lejon for his proofreading and for putting up with me; Brian for his reading, criticism, and subversive comments; and Jen, Jen, and Jeff for their suggestions.

And most of all, to Kim, who created this world and gave it to me in 1986. It's changed quite a bit since then, but someday Adina will burn her room down, I promise.

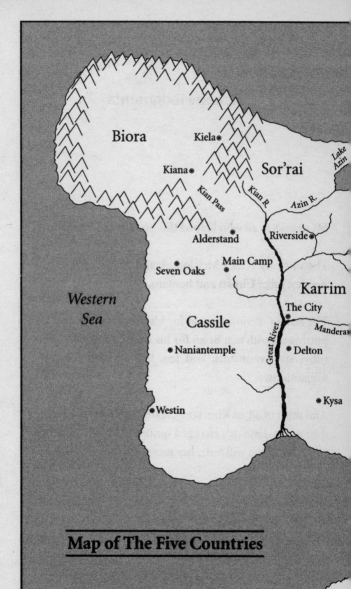

## Map of The Five Countries

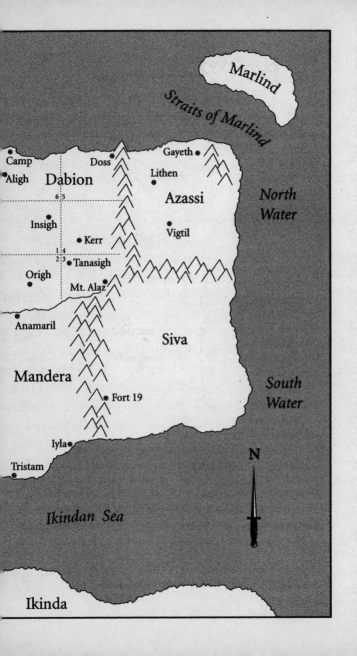

# PROLOGUE

*Spring, 764 C.C.*

❦

I WAS QUITTING THE GAME. I WOULD NOW, FINALLY, after all the years I'd played it for them. I would now, after losing a year of my life in Siva, a year burned up by that sun like water dried out of your skin. I lost pieces of my life in Mandera, in Karrim, in cities whose names I cannot speak. I would be done with it. The game was never mine. I had played it, yes, and played it well, but I tired of it long ago. I grew old and they were still children.

He was waiting for me in his office. His hair was white; he was still bareheaded. Others in his class had taken to wearing wigs, and soon he would as well. He would never do anything to make himself conspicuous. He could walk down any street and no one would know who he was. Some old man, a clerk perhaps. Never the most powerful man in the Five Countries. He wrote the game, and he played it best.

I thought I might beat him at it, or I would have, once. I was arrogant as a child. "I'm quitting the game, Loyd."

Did he react? Did his eyes betray anything, one

flutter, one damned twitch? I called him by name, without any polite title. It didn't matter—it wasn't his name anyway. "Are you?" he replied, mildly.

"I was your best, Loyd."

These words, simple, foolish-sounding, they were all moves in the game. Questions answered with questions, remarks that did not follow, words that plumbed for information but gave away nothing. Loyd turned them back on me with an easy smile. "You still are."

I had tried quitting once before, last winter. He hadn't listened to me then. But things were different now. They had to be. "I can't play anymore. You know I can't."

"My dear." He sighed, measuring out his breath and his voice carefully. He sounded as I suppose a father might. "Do you think you can quit?"

I said nothing. He wouldn't yield to me, and I would say no words that admitted defeat.

He measured his silence as he had measured his words. Then he pulled a drawer in his desk and took an envelope from it. "Clear your things from the dormitory," he said, laying the package on the desk, not near me. "You have two days to find accommodations." He rose from his desk and left me in his office.

Could I have resisted? Could I have walked out as quickly as he had, with nothing in my hands? The envelope contained some money, a little, not enough to live on for long. A letter as well, with the usual details. I crumpled it without reading it and thrust it back into its wrapping. He knew I would take it.

# 1

TOD WAS GOING TO BE LATE. THE WOMAN'S MESsage said that she would come to see the flat precisely at noon. Keller didn't have a clock in his shop, but Tod was sure it was getting close to noon, and he still had to walk through Origh and two miles out of town to get to his cottage.

"It's all right Keller," he whispered to the older man, trying to hurry him along. "I'm sure they're fine, I'll take them now."

The printer looked up from the pages he was proofing, raising his face only a little bit, not relieving the weight that the low hang of his head put on his tired shoulders. He didn't say anything, but Tod heard his answer very clearly. Keller never cut corners on a job, even when he'd been swamped by three law revisions in one day, even when the Justices threatened him with shutting down his press if they didn't get their orders in rush time. Every page had to come out perfect, even if it meant that Keller didn't sleep. The printer was doing

Tod's job and he was going to finish it. Tod would just have to wait.

Finally, Keller's dry voice uttered, "Good," and he gathered up the last of the barely dry sheets and filed them in a battered leather portfolio. "It's done, now get on your way. Although," Keller added, looking through his cracked window, "you'll have trouble hurrying anywhere."

Tod had been thinking the same thing as he paced anxiously past the window of the shop. Walking into Origh this morning, he'd seen troops of Public Force guards marching toward the center of town. Not that that was unusual—the pounding of their boots and the creak of the short heavy sticks and pistols swinging at their belts was something he heard every day he was in the city. When he'd first moved to the cottage on the outskirts he'd been shocked at how quiet it was without that sound. But there seemed to be more guards today than there usually were, and as Tod stood at Keller's window and waited for the printer to finish with his job, their numbers grew. Tod lost count of them; he didn't know there were so many in the whole District. Then they stopped moving and backed up in the street. Something was happening in the center of town and Tod's way was blocked.

"You there, back inside," a guard barked as Tod inched through the doorway. He startled and froze, but the guard was shouting at a clerk who'd stepped out of the chandler's shop next door. The clerk, his arms full of boxes of candles bound, no doubt, for some Justice's office, stepped up to the man in the gray uniform and began arguing. A moment later the chandler was out in the street, adding his booming voice to the argument, complaining about how this mess in the street was harming his business.

"Better run for it while you can, lad," Keller said at Tod's ear.

He only had a glance at what was going on as he darted out of Keller's door. The Public Force had filled up the street as far as Tod could see, preventing anyone from moving forward, pushing anyone who stepped out of their shops or houses back inside. Tod clutched his portfolio and hurried away in the opposite direction of the roadblock, and found himself in the middle of a thin crowd that was doing the same, escaping out of a bakery and away from the guards. From behind him, in the thick of the blockade, Tod thought he heard shouts and the distant sound of breaking glass.

For a second he stopped short. Breaking glass. Then it was himself he saw in the crowd, in the center of town. Shouts all around him, the press of bodies nearly sweeping him off his feet. Bricks were thrown, rocks hurled through windows, matches touched to whatever would burn. Where they had gotten the debris, Tod couldn't remember and couldn't imagine. He couldn't imagine because the streets of Origh were kept so clean, not to offend the Justices with the sight of waste. He couldn't remember because he had been drunk. He couldn't remember what

the riot had been about—what had so angered the towns-
people that they had scraped rocks from the ground to
destroy whatever they could before the Public Force
came—because he had been drunk. That was enough of a
crime on its own, even without the rioting. Tod had no
idea how he'd gotten out of it, but he had, and he'd ended
up at home, free and frightened and sleepless and sober.
Sober enough to dream.

That had been four years ago. He had no taste for gin
now, almost. Only when he remembered the dreams. He
clamped his eyes shut, hard, as if the face of his nightmare were in the street in front of him, and stumbled,
his hand flung out for balance. Someone met his hand,
grasped it, and steadied him. Then something was
pressed into his hand, buried deep in his palm. That
someone was gone before Tod opened his eyes.

Behind him shouts were cut short, dull cracks sounding on bone or flesh. In front of him those people who
had gotten away were hurrying toward the edges of
town. For a moment he stopped to look at the wad of
paper in his hand. It was a note, scribbled hastily.

*Follow Nanian, not the law.*

Tod dropped the paper like it was a hot coal. Being
found with it in his hands would be enough of a crime.
Those were the rioters, then. Mystics, Nanianists. Tod
had never heard of people like that outside of Cassile.
Dabion wasn't a country for religion. He kicked the note

into the gutter—a strangely dirty gutter—and started running.

Somehow he got out of Origh, onto the road home. When he was some distance away he finally felt it was safe to turn and look behind him. No gray uniforms had followed him out of town. He sighed with relief. Then he started thinking, confused, and looked behind him again. No one else was on the road, either. Where was his visitor? She must have been coming out of town, too. He started running again, hoping she hadn't beaten him home.

The little mechanical clock on the mantel read just a minute before noon when Tod rushed through his door. With a faint smile he dropped his package on his table, took a breath, and lowered himself into a chair. He would have time to rest, he thought as the clock's tinny bell began to ring. Then there was a rap at the door. Tod jumped wearily to his feet. She must have a watch, he thought. That was foolish, though. Only clerks had those things, officers in the Halls of Justice. His feet hurt from his long run and this irritated him so much that he forgot about wondering where his visitor had come from.

Tod opened the door. Elzith Kar stood outside. He regarded her for several moments, thinking she did not see him. She was looking away, her head dropped casually to the side as if surveying the herbs in his neighbor's box, and she said absolutely nothing to him. Any greeting Tod might have given seemed more and more ridiculous as time went by, and so he only looked at her in the silence. Clothed in the manner of Dabion's working class, she wore a loose blouse of a mute gray color, with a bodice laced over it to fit a slight figure. Wealthier women now wore their bodices inside their dresses—so Tod had heard—and had servants stitch the gown to the undergarment each morning. Elzith Kar was a washer-woman, perhaps, but she seemed too thin to haul loads of washing. Was she a lady's maid, forever stitching her mistress into her clothing? Then Tod continued his inventory and halted. The woman before him wore breeches. Stranger still, the breeches ended not at white stockings like his (though his were rather yellow) but at boots, blackened leather pulled up to her knees. Boots like those worn in Mandera, the seaside country to the south, or by the guards of the Public Force—

"Your neighbor's a thief," Elzith said suddenly.

Tod opened his mouth but not even a ridiculous greeting could come out this time.

The woman was regarding him now. "Has he ever stolen from you?" Her voice was even and clear, her words sharp at the edges. She spoke in a command, though quietly enough that no one beyond his doorway would hear her. It was like the voice of a Justice, but no women worked in the Great Halls.

She was watching him still. Tod felt himself flush; he had not yet answered. "No," he gasped. Elzith's eyes were green, steady, leveled on him in examination. Then, suddenly, she nodded. "Good," she said, only half to him, a motion of dismissal, and then, "Shall I see the flat now?"

The flat was the lower floor of Tod's cottage, half-buried in a hill. Here outside the city the land was filled with smooth rolling hills and valleys, blanketed with rich velvety grass. It was beautiful land, peaceful, and almost empty. The cities of Dabion were scattered, built around the branches of the Great Halls of Justice that were posted throughout the country: Insigh, Tanasigh, Kerr, Origh two miles away, and others. Almost all the remaining population had been ousted from the country generations before, leaving the hills and valleys nearly barren. The few commoners who remained lived in cottages half-buried in the slopes like the burrows of moles.

Tod stumbled a little as he started down the steps that edged the slope of the hill, rough-hewn shards of flagstone placed irregularly in the earth. Tod's cottage was one of a row of three burrowed into this hill. All three had lower floors with doors that let out at the bottom of the slope. The inner stairwell that accessed the lower floor in Tod's cottage had been blocked to form a separate flat. The neighbors did not use the outside steps; Widow Carther's lower door, at the far end of the row, was even boarded over.

"These steps need fixing," Tod said, his voice tripping, still a little breathless from his frantic rush out of town. "I'm afraid they were let go for a long time—I just started trying to fix them up a few years ago. I try to keep them clean, but the rain, you know, and mud, and then in the winter they get icy, then snow covers them up, and once it melts in the spring…" Tod cut himself short. The riot, the note, they had made him lose his wits, and he was babbling like a fool. He usually only spoke much in the company of someone quieter than himself, and his great-aunt had been the last person to fit that description.

No taste for gin except when he remembered the dreams, his great-aunt's ghost face in them. He almost lost his footing completely. It was too much to remember in one day. He swallowed hard and looked around, searching for something else to see. Behind him Elzith was navigating the steps, not stumbling at all.

"I need to replace the stones, at any rate," Tod said thickly. "It's so hard to contact the landlord, though. He's a Lesser Justice, of course."

Tod did not expect his companion to finish his thought. "Of course," said Elzith dryly, surprising him. "And what do they care for us?"

Tod's hand shook and rattled the keys in the lock. Speaking ill of the Justices was enough of a crime. He had a mad, sick sensation that the woman's voice was carrying over the fields, where the guards massed in the streets of Origh would hear it and come for her. For a second he was also sure that she knew exactly what had happened in the middle of town. He fumbled the door open and rushed Elzith inside.

The basement flat was tiny, cold, low-ceilinged. Morrn, Tod's former renter of six years, hadn't cared.

Morrn had been perfectly happy with the flat, until he'd been carried off to the Great Hall for keeping a distillery there. Three years later, the smell of gin was almost out of the floorboards and plastered walls. The renter Tod had had during those three years since Morrn left hadn't seemed to mind, either, but that man had been a Healer. Healers were a race so strange, so mysterious, that Tod could say little about his previous flatmate at all.

In the flat now was another mystery. Elzith made a circuit of the room in a few strides, peering at the walls, checking the skinny mattress for fleas. She spent more time at the chest, opening its drawers and looking inside them. Tod's imagination tried a string of explanations for her strange actions, then gave up. Abruptly Elzith straightened, fixing him with that gaze that weighed him like a balance. "Is it available today?" she asked.

Tod floundered.

"You have no other inquiries?" Elzith restated.

Tod shook his head. "No. You could move in right now."

"Good," she answered, nodding as if she had known already. She drew a fold of notes from a pocket in the breeches, confirmed the flat's price, and paid Tod for a full season. He failed to find another single word. "The key," Elzith prompted him after waiting silently for a moment.

"Yes," mumbled Tod, fussing it off his ring. "But your things—"

"My things," the woman said. She ushered Tod out of the flat that was now hers and locked its door. "I will have to get some." Then she climbed the irregular steps up the slope and vanished behind the green rise of the hill.

# 2

"A TART, IS SHE?" SHAAN WHEELWRIGHT PULLED AT his pipe and let out the smoke in broad rings of laughter. "Strolled in here in her knickers, did she?"

Tod felt himself redden and tried to keep his concentration on his work. "Not in her knickers," he corrected, telling himself to keep his voice steady, keep his knife steady. "She was wearing breeches." The knife slid through the paper smoothly.

His neighbor laughed on another puff of smoke and started coughing. "Well there's only one reason a woman's wearing breeches, chap, and that's so we'll look at them legs." Shaan's round face was pink with merriment. "So did you see anything you like?"

Slash. Tod's knife skidded off the fold in the paper and cut through a whole line of text. Tod gulped. The book had ninety-six pages. Now he would have to cut apart the quarrels, unnest the stacks of folded paper, get the ruined sheet printed again, and start over with his stitching. He tried to breathe evenly. He would not lose his temper, he told himself. No riot scenes in his house.

Shaan was bigger than he was, anyway, and could probably squash him under a thumb like a bug. "You saw her yourself, Shaan," he forced himself to say coolly. "See anything *you* liked?"

"Aaah," the man grumbled, "I only saw her as she was leaving, through my window, and her halfway down the road to town." Shaan shook his head, looking sad as a marionette. Then he winked, grinned, and said, "But I'll be seeing more of her soon, eh, mate?"

Tod turned his head aside to avoid the smoke flooding out of his neighbor's face. He found Shaan overbearing but couldn't ask the man to go away. Tod was familiar with the feeling; he felt the same way about his own brothers. He found himself eyeing Shaan suspiciously. *Why is he sitting so close to my desk? Did I see him open a drawer?* His eyes half on Shaan, Tod brought the nested quartos close to his face, inserted the knife under the thread that held them together, and prepared to slice.

"So you don't know where she's from, and you don't know why she's moving in." Shaan leaned in and tried to get Tod's attention by winking suggestively. "And you don't know what her business is."

Tod frowned. "Nothing unlawful," he uttered through closed teeth, trying hard to avoid Shaan's suggestion. "Not after Morrn."

"Poor Morrn," Shaan was saying, shaking his head. "A good chap, he was." Then his color came up again and he leered. "Shame if that's true about the girl, though. You'll have lost your chance to get deflowered."

Tod put his knife down before he could damage any more of his book. A protest lodged in the back of his throat, that he was twenty-seven and well past the deflowering age, but he wasn't really willing to start cataloging his experiences for Shaan's amusement. Now Shaan was on his feet, strolling around the room as he continued to bark stale laughs at his own dull joke. Where was he going? What was he looking for?

The mechanical clock started chiming.

"Damn and blast," Shaan muttered, "is that thing right?"

Speechless with relief, Tod nodded. Shaan's workday was as irregular as his own. While Tod did most of his bookbinding work out of his home rather than going into Origh, Shaan didn't go into town until the end of the day. Like most of Dabion's commoners, Shaan's family had never strayed from the work that named them. The Wheelwrights did their business in the late hours, mending and fitting the Justices' carriages with wheels at times when the carriages were not needed, so as not to disturb the process of the law.

"Good luck on the roads," Tod put in, glad to change the subject. "They were all blocked up this morning. Something going on in the middle of town. Public Force all over." They cracked the chandler's skull, he thought but didn't say. There were mystics there, the guards arrested them, they're sure to be executed. Tod felt ashamed, using them to shut up Shaan. But there was nothing he could do.

Shaan tapped out his pipe onto Tod's hearth, muttering under his breath. He was overbearing and he had no love for the Public Force, but he would never take the risk of saying what he truly thought of them aloud. "Well, if there's something to be found out, I'll find it out. I'll miss your renter's arrival, though. Give her my regards!" He winked and raised his hand in cheery farewell as he let himself out.

Tod lifted his hand and smiled tightly.

When Shaan was gone he took a dustpan, swept up the ashes from the man's pipe, and carried them out to dump in the street, in front of Shaan's door. "No wind?" he challenged the sky, expecting a gust to blow the ash back into his home. He looked up the street and saw no thin silhouette approaching opposite Shaan's thick one; Elzith was late enough that she would not have to deal with the man yet.

But where was she? Somehow the excuse of riots and guards in Origh did not feel like the answer.

Tod looked down to check that the ash pile was still lying quietly in place. As he turned back toward his own door his eyes grazed over the herb boxes that were arrayed along Shaan's front wall. Beside them lay a little pile of tools: trowel, spade. And concealed along the length of one of the boxes, a long, heavy-handled rake. It was too large for such small gardening. Shaan might have used it for keeping the grass on the hill, but Tod knew he did no such work. Under a casual sprinkling of dirt, the tines were rusty with disuse. Tod stood before his door, where Elzith had stood that afternoon, his head tilted at the same angle hers had been as he looked at the partly hidden rake.

He'd felt uneasy with Shaan in his house this afternoon, but then he'd had no more than a suggestion that the man was a criminal. He hadn't been able to imagine glass breaking under a heavy wooden handle, or the brittle sound of it shattering and the shower of glassy shards. *Your neighbor's a thief.*

Tod shivered and darted into his house.

It was too late for any more work. Tod would go to the printer's tomorrow to replace the quarto that he'd damaged. He still had more to do; he'd fallen behind, but that would wait until later. In the last hour of his day, he would turn to matters of his own.

He did not follow the usual tradition. Tod Redtanner was a bookbinder. His family—father, aging grandfather with hands gnarled beyond use, two elder brothers following in the business of tanning—had all ridiculed him. A foolish trade, bookishness. Weak and unmanly. Only the Justices were so learned, and he had no reason to act so proud. Tod had tried to learn the family craft; he'd been no good at it. He had failed at everything from dressing the skins to mixing the dyes that gave the leather its characteristic red tone, a family heritage handed down like an inheritance. He, the youngest, had received nothing. At eighteen, after four fruitless years of apprenticeship, Tod had left his family.

It had been Morrn's suggestion to lease the cottage, to block the inner stairs and make two separate flats, to sublet the lower one to him. Tod had gone along with everything, these plans fed to him by someone he hardly knew. If Tod hadn't been so blind with shame and anger at his family, he might have realized how bad a plan it was. Morrn already had a criminal record—only petty crimes, he'd assured Tod, but enough to blacklist his name with all the Lesser Justices who owned the tenements of Dabion. That was why he wanted Tod's name on the lease. If Tod hadn't been so blind, he might have recognized the trouble in store when he found Morrn's still, but he fooled himself into using it to his own advantage. He had already started drinking, two years earlier, when his brothers had taken him across the border to Karrim, where distilleries and other illegal businesses operated out of the sight of the distant Dabionian government. If he'd had less temper, Tod might have quietly cast aside his brothers' influence. But he had things to drown out, shame and dreams, nightmare faces, so he went to Morrn more than willingly.

Noise from the street shook Tod from his unhappy thoughts. He went to the window. In the distance, a cart rolled by. He ran to the back window, thinking Elzith might have walked past the door and was headed down the steps, but he saw no one.

He sat down at his table again. It was no good to

resurrect old guilt, he knew that. He should think of other things. It did no good to fret over his new renter, either. She would be like the Healer who had lived in his downstairs flat for the last three years. Like him, she would come and go as she pleased, with no ties to Tod's life. He had no reason to hope for anything else, no reason to feel sorrow over it. He sighed, trying to convince himself, and reached for his needle.

Keller had taught him the bookbinding. Tod had gone to the printer looking for some sort of work shortly after leaving his father's house, on one of the rare mornings when he woke and remained sober long enough to realize he had no money. He had wandered into town, knowing there was a wall in front of the printer's shop where public notices were posted and hoping that he would find advertisement for work. When he found the shop, he discovered that it had rained the night before, a rain he had not heard or remembered, and with his head still muddied he was unable to make any sense of the smeared script on the crinkled scraps of paper. Desperation kept him from leaving. He stared at the notices, counting them over and over, trying to tell himself that he'd be able to read them once the pain in his head went away. Tod didn't realize how long he had lingered at the printer's doorstep until he heard Keller call out to him, in a gruff, rattling voice like wheels on cobblestones, "Well, if you're just going to stand and block up my door, come give a hand here."

Tod at first became a runner for Keller, delivering the

printer's wares to his customers. He had been at the doors of every Lesser Hall of Justice in the town of Origh, every clerk's office, even the Great Hall—just once, when he stood at the mouth of the servants' tunnel, at the foot of the enormous flight of stairs reaching upward to the giant hallowed doors. It had been a simple job, and he'd had almost no delays, even when gin-lost. He never betrayed his illegal habit by failing to deliver an order. Then Morrn was arrested and Tod could no longer pay the landlord.

He went to Keller's shop to ask his employer's leave, expecting he would have to return permanently to his father's house. But the printer did not give his leave. Tod had waited as Keller walked about his shop, sorting through drawers and boxes of type, clinking metal letters together as he searched for something. Finally he drew out a pouch, upended it, and dumped its contents in a shower of scattered words, and tossed the pouch to Tod. Tod caught it, barely, not understanding.

"Were you sober when you made that?" Keller asked.

Tod looked at the pouch, vaguely remembering having stitched it from a scrap of irregular leather. It was badly matched, poorly colored, but the stitches were even and straight. "More or less," he answered.

The printer had approached him then, crossing the room in long strides, and he grasped Tod's head with his inky hands. He looked at Tod, holding his head so Tod couldn't look away, and examined his eyes as he might examine a page he'd printed. "Are you now?" Keller had asked.

Tod had nodded solemnly.

"Then try this for me," Keller said, releasing Tod's face and hunting out some thread, a glover's needle, and sheets of paper he had discarded for stains or errors. He folded the sheets into fourths and made quarrels by nesting them inside each other. "I did this once, years ago," Keller told Tod, in the broken speech he lapsed into while working, words strung out like the metal letters scattered on his worktable, "but it takes time. A lot of time." He threaded the needle and stabbed it through the sheets at their fold.

"I think I have time," Tod replied.

Keller had worked for the Justices all his life; he knew how to manage them. He marketed Tod's services to them for less than their own bookbinders were paid, and when Tod's work became known for its quality, Keller raised his rates. What Keller hadn't known was that one of the displaced bookbinders was a relative of Tod's landlord, and the landlord raised his rent. Tod found a new tenant to sublet the lower floor to and went on with his work.

What he worked on now, late at night, was not a job for hire. It was a book of his own, an unusual book, ir-regularly bound, made up of notices and sheets of dif-ferent sizes, leaves saved from a journal he'd written as a child. He was almost ready to cover it, but now he thought he wanted to add more pages. It was not yet finished.

How did he know? Tod shuddered. There was an image in his mind again, a faint thought, a snatch of dream suddenly remembered. It troubled him, this shade calling to him from the shadows at the corners of his eyes, hiding when he turned, swelling when he closed his eyes until it was swallowed by other, darker dreams.

His eyes snapped open. It was late, and Tod knew he should take these wild thoughts as signs that he was short of sleep. He put his book away, folding the pages gently and storing them in a box, then he went to the window, which he'd left open to the late-spring air, to shut it.

There was someone outside.

Tod jumped a step back, shook his head, rubbed his eyes. He was seeing things, making shadows out of fatigue, he told himself, that was all. There was no one on the street, nothing out in the foothills. Even Shaan wasn't due home for hours, safely at work—if he'd made it there—and away from his rake and its illicit threat.

But there *was* something on the street, lurking at the side of the hill that curved away from Tod's door. A figure, cloaked. It broke away from the hill and approached. Tod could not move. He might have been trembling, his heart might have thudded and his breath might have raced, but he could feel none of it. The figure came near, facing Tod outside the glassless window. Tod's hands tightened on the shutters but he could not close them. The figure's cloak was colorless in the dim light of a half-moon, and from within its hood he faced Tod. Lamplight from inside the house illuminated the shadowed visage, the skin that seemed too pale, snatches of hair braided and bound in streaks of color, and the piercing eyes. They were not simply penetrating like Keller's, those eyes, or secret like Elzith's. These were eyes that did not belong in this world. Tod had seen such eyes before.

In a startled rush Tod found his arms and slammed the shutters closed. He felt his heart hammering with such force he was sure his body couldn't contain it. He felt the breath that he couldn't catch, his hands numb and trembling. He fastened the latches on the shutters. And waited. And, reluctantly, unfastened them. He looked out on the street again. No one was there.

# 3

THERE WAS A KNOCK AT THE DOOR. IT WAS LIGHT
and quiet; Jereth might have mistaken it for a
mouse or a servant or some other inconsequential noise
in the old Hall. Certainly any passerby was meant to
mistake it as such. It was as Jereth expected, the summons to this most secret of meetings.

It would not do to call out to the messenger. Jereth
would have to go to the door, open it silently, and be prepared to accompany his guide. First he would finish his
preparations, though. He examined his reflection in the
narrow, smoke-colored mirror a final time. Only fifty-
eight, yet Jereth felt like an old man, aged past his time,
his face gray and wizened like withered fruit, his eyes
dark with unfocused dampness. He scowled at the image
that looked back at him with weak jaw and drooping
brows. The somber black of his clothes—plain jacket,
long vest, breeches—washed out the olive coloring of his
skin and made him look like an invalid, pale and wither-
ing. Not that he would wear anything else, of course. The
garments were the uniform of the Justices. Anything less

would be like the weeds of a commoner. Anything bright of color or rich in decoration was unthinkable; such garments were Manderan, from the time before the economic collapse twenty years since and the recovery that had been led by Dabion. Jereth was an heir to the power of Justice and he would, finally, come into it.

With a reflex of self-consciousness, Jereth ran his hands through his close-cropped hair. His head felt strange and cold with no covering, its hair shorn to bristle lengths. In the glass he caught a glimpse of an ancient creature, hairless with age or disease. Quickly he turned away, resting his eyes upon the wig on its stand.

The peoples of Dabion and her neighboring countries of Karrim, Mandera, and Cassile possessed a uniform coloring of olive skin and dark hair. Azassi, the fifth of the Five Countries, was marked by the red hair and ruddy coloring of her people. The wig, however, a new and elaborate ornament fashioned of long, curled locks, was blond. Such coloring was to be found on a foreign people, in the land of Biora, secluded by distance and mountains in the extreme northwest. So Jereth was told; he had not been to Biora and had never seen her people. Yet he now found himself the guardian of Bioran culture and its gateway to the Five Countries, a new role, a powerful one. Jereth set the wig upon his head and adjusted it blindly, with only his fingertips guiding its position along his temples, so that it was set in place when he turned back to the mirror. The face confronting him was a new and foreign one. It was not weak, not an invalid, not withered, but strange and secret and strong. It was not the face of a Lesser Justice whose career was pocked with failure and who had little to do in his long remaining years but wait to die. The knock sounded again. Jereth blew out the candle and opened the door to his summoner.

The man outside, cloaked in shadowy garments and utter silence, led Jereth through the corridors of the Great Hall. The Great Hall of Justice in Insigh was the center of Dabionian law, the home of its governing body in the land's capital city. It had been the seat of power throughout the past two centuries of Dabionian Civil Rule, but the building had been erected even earlier, and the great cornerstones bore the mark 200 C.C., the date of the establishment of the Common Calendar in the Five Countries. Bioran, Jereth thought. The Common Calendar was Bioran, brought to the Five Countries by early traveling scholars, five hundred years ago, in the time that no books recorded and no men remembered.

And I, the old Justice breathed to himself, imagining his voice to be deep and resonant as a foreigner's might be, I shall be the one to bring the secrets back to them.

He listened to the striking of his hard-heeled shoes on the ancient stone stairs, heard it echo in the deserted air of the descending passageway. Jereth had never been in this part of the Hall. Lost in his thoughts, he had failed to note the direction he'd come from or when he'd started descending. Surely he was below ground. Abruptly his guide brought him to the foot of the stair, and Jereth found himself staring at a blank wall. He turned and saw the faint light of the last lamps, above them, fifty yards higher up the stairway. Then the guide opened some secret door and Jereth was swept into blackness.

"Take my hand," uttered the guide, and as the door swung shut behind him, Jereth was just able to see the man's hand stretched out to him in the last light. He clasped it, a young, strong, sure hand, as he felt his own grow shaky with an old man's palsy. Jereth stumbled, certain he would trip, plunge down a stairway or an unseen precipice. He could not hear his footsteps; the floor was earthen. How was the guide finding their way? Panic scattered all of Jereth's thoughts. He would be lost, an old, forgotten pebble beneath the feet of important men, trampled in a dirty pathway in some cavern. Nervous, hopeless blood pounded in his ears; he thought he might have heard himself cry aloud. He strained to hear. Lost and humiliated—that was his fate. But as he listened he did not hear the cry of his voice, only a rough slipping noise, something dragging, a gloved hand on a rope, like a laborer pulling some heavy load.

Jereth's heart jumped. This memory horrified him more than the threat of falling into an unseen chasm. The laborers, the rough, dirty men who had fathered his family, would be discovered under Insigh's scrutiny. Jereth would be discredited, not only lost and humiliated. Vainly he reached for something, anything, to pull himself out of this terror, and his free hand flew above

him. It skidded coarsely into the dry twine of a rope
strung over his head, tied with many knots and merged
with branches that might divert intruders into blind
paths of a maze. It was only a rope, with which the guide
was finding their route, that was all. Jereth was not lost,
not hopeless. His heart began to slow. He had nearly regained his composure by the time his guide opened
another door before him, and he was blinded with light
from within.

"Ah, my lords, here is our Advisor." A voice rang in a
strangely echoing chamber. Jereth blinked, unable to
clear his vision, and he heard the voice grow closer. "I
trust you were brought here safely. The passage is, ad-
mittedly, disconcerting. Each of us was somewhat troubled, you might say, when we first came here. You do
understand our need for secrecy."

Through a film that stubbornly clouded his eyes,
Jereth saw the face that matched the condescending
voice come into focus. The speaker was dressed in the
same uniform that Jereth wore, yet his had none of the
weathered and funereal look of Jereth's. He was not
many years younger than Jereth, but his wrinkled face
had the quality of fine leather, and his brushed chin-
length hair had the sheen of silver. He smiled smoothly
into Jereth's watery eyes. Jereth despised him at once.

"My lords," the smooth man said, turning elegantly
toward the room. "May I present Justice Advisor Jereth
Paloman." Jereth stiffly mimicked the man's turn. The
room he stood in was circular, walled in polished wood

that reflected a ring of lamps hung below the incline of a domed ceiling. Eight men regarded him from around a U-shaped table. The smooth man led Jereth toward the opening between the arms of the U, where a podium stood stacked with the man's neat papers. A second podium stood beside it, vacant, waiting for Jereth. He had nothing to place on it; his hands felt awkwardly empty.

Jereth was startled from his nervousness by a regal and weighty voice. "Welcome, Justice Advisor," said the man at the center of the table, "to the Circle."

There had been no monarchy in the Five Countries since before the Common Calendar, except in Azassi, where the people persisted in their barbaric structure of clans and chieftains. Such tribalism could hardly be called royalty, though. The man at the center of the table, however, was as nearly a king as any figure from the peasant lore of Jereth's childhood. His appearance was even more perfect than the first man's, his face finer and his silver hair bright with an ethereal shine. He seemed taller than the other men, as much because of his demeanor as his higher chair. The richness of his garments and the manner in which he wore them belied their black simplicity. Jereth felt as if he'd shrunk to the size of a barefoot peasant child.

"Allow me the honor of presenting to you," the smooth man intoned, "Lord Councilor Muhrroh." Jereth caught his breath and bowed minutely. The Lord Councilor was the head of Dabion's ruling body. The Lord

Justices who led Dabion's six districts and to whom the
local Justices reported were under the direction of the
Lord Councilor. Jereth guessed that the other men
seated around the table were the six Lord Justices; indeed, when he looked at the faces he recognized that of
Hysthe, head of Jereth's home district in the northeast
corner of Dabion. Hysthe wore a wig, as Jereth expected,
and he watched Jereth with the attitude of a proud
father, though the man was barely forty. Jereth looked
away from his own Lord Justice, and he noticed with
something like joy that two more men wore wigs as well.

The introduction continued. "Lord Justice Frahn of
District One, Lord Justice Jannes of District Two." The
two men bowed flax-crowned heads. District Two was of
little note to Jereth, a rectangle of land in the southwestern corner, wedged between agricultural Karrim and errant Mandera. District One, however, was the seat of the
capital. Frahn's support was encouraging.

"Lord Justices Timbrel and Nosselin of Districts
Three and Four." District Three was more innocuous
than Two, bordered by the Azassian mountains on the
east and on the south by Siva, a land so foreign beyond
its isolating cliffs that it was not counted among the Five
Countries. Timbrel had the sort of face that was forgotten as soon as it was out of sight, and Nosselin, whose jurisdiction sat above District Three, was known as a
stubborn cynic even to those who had never met him.

"You know Lord Justice Hysthe, of course, and finally,
Lord Justice Varzin of District Six." Varzin's jurisdiction

was on the banks of Lake Azin, which separated the northwest corner of Dabion from Sor'rai, another land not counted among the Five Countries. The entire region was shadowed in rumor and enigma, and Varzin, with his dark eyes and inscrutable expression, was nearly as unnerving as the land from which he came. Jereth's eyes darted back toward the man standing beside him. "I am Secretary to the Council, Justice Bint. We are the Circle."

"We are pleased to have you here in Insigh," Frahn said. "With all respect to Lord Justice Hysthe, of course, who will be losing you."

"Of course," replied Hysthe, in the same liquid mercury voice that Bint used. Jereth smiled appropriately. Hysthe had never supported him before, not until he learned that Jereth had collected a library of Bioran writings, and that the Bioran influence was beginning to be felt in District One.

"We are anxious to share in your learnings of Bioran philosophy," said Jannes. "All we have yet seen was brought to us by merchants. It will be preferable to be directed by a Justice."

"Yet Insigh opened a school of Bioran philosophy seven years ago, on no better word than that of merchants." This was voiced sourly by Nosselin.

Lord Councilor Muhrroh responded with an ageless calm. "And with the assistance of the Justice Advisor, this school and other schools that will follow it shall be enriched. There is great support for Bioran thought in our land, and its rationality will undoubtedly help in the resolution of conflicts in Mandera and Cassile. Varzin, what are your thoughts?"

All eyes turned toward the end of the table nearest Jereth. Varzin was the eldest man in the room and thereby accorded the most respect, but his demeanor would have commanded awe at any age. He was silent for several breaths before replying, and the room waited on his words as if time had stopped. "Rationality," the Lord Justice began, in a voice as quiet and commanding as Muhrroh's, "is certainly to be desired. It will give us the weapon we require finally to subdue the mystics."

"We will be closing the monasteries in Cassile, of course," agreed Frahn.

A murmur of accord filtered about the room. Jereth nodded obediently. The mystics were dangerous—everyone knew that. Their threat had to be eliminated. If asked to articulate that threat, Jereth would stumble, reaching fruitlessly for words to describe it. This didn't matter, though. It was not Jereth's duty to understand.

"And how many of these monasteries are there?" Nosselin demanded. "How much longer will these lessons delay their closure?"

"The process has already begun," another voice said. Jereth realized he had neglected the final man in the room, a small, white-haired, nondescript man standing at Muhrroh's shoulder. He had not been introduced. He still was not.

"Let us allow our guest to prepare his lessons, then,"

Muhrroh said, putting the discussion at an end. "We will consult with you when you are ready. Bint."

At the Lord Councilor's beckoning the Secretary directed Jereth to the door. Jereth paused for a moment to bow again to the assembly, then he spoke. "Thank you, my lords." His voice was surprisingly even. He almost felt optimism at his rising fate. Then Bint opened the door and ushered Jereth into the darkness.

# 4

TOD STARTED AWAKE WITH A VAST PAIN IN HIS neck. He tried to move his head but it was stuck, and when he tried to stretch his limbs he found his body was numb. He had fallen asleep folded into his doorway.

It was late afternoon and the air was starting to carry a chill. Tod felt it on his face although he could not yet feel it on his hands, and he realized how much of the day he had lost. The morning had been productive, until he found the book he'd botched the day before and blissfully forgotten about, and at noontime he'd gone to Keller's to have the damaged sheet reprinted. There were no guards blocking Origh's streets this time, but people gathered in scattered clumps all over town, and it took Tod long enough to dodge through them. He tried not to linger and listen to their gossip as he passed. "Twenty of them arrested," one voice trickled out to him. "No, only six," said another, "but all of them shave-headed monks." "Of course they weren't shaved, but they did have those papers, those mystic writings."

"No, they didn't!" a clerk with a shrill voice shouted

to no one in particular as he pushed around Tod and into Keller's shop. "And if there were such papers," he added, with a threatening look at Keller, "they had better not have been printed here."

Tod blanched, and his fist clenched involuntarily as if he were still holding the forbidden note that had been passed to him the day of the riot. Keller, though, ignored the clerk's words and went straight to the cabinet where the finished jobs were stored. The clerk changed tack and started complaining about the state of the prints, ink too dark on one page and too light on another, margins too wide or too narrow. Tod knew he wouldn't get Keller's attention for a while, so he went to the window to look out while he waited, and found himself watching a squad of the Public Force as they strode through the streets. They were a formidable sight, these keepers of the Justices' laws, buttoned stiffly into their steel-gray jackets that were crossed over the shoulder and around the waist with black leather belts, sticks and lethal pistols buckled at their sides. They marched as evenly as soldiers in childhood stories of war, the sound of their steps ringing in the streets. War was a thing of old history and children's tales, doubtful to be seen again in this age of order and the Public Force's gunpowder. Trouble like whatever had happened yesterday was cleaned up in the blink of an eye. Tod recalled watching a troop of Public Force guardsmen dismantle the downstairs still and carry Morrn away in shackles, from the window in Shaan's flat where Tod was lucky enough to have been when the Force came. He was also lucky to have been unconscious when they returned later to question Morrn's neighbors.

As Tod tried to brush these things out of his mind and get his breath to slow, something caught his eye. A narrow female face among the Public Force? Elzith? Tod opened the door slightly and peered out for a better view. He did not see Elzith, but there was an irregularity among the rank and file of the Public Force: a line of guards clad entirely in black, without the sticks but retaining the heavy pistols and their accompanying sacks of powder and shot, a silent threat of strength.

"Out of my way!" snapped the clerk at Tod's back. He had to abandon his observation of the guards in the street to step aside for the clerk, who somehow managed to look down his nose at Tod even though he was a good head shorter. "Commoner!" the clerk added unpleasantly. For once, Tod did not have to check his outrage at being insulted. He was too preoccupied with the realization that he hadn't seen Elzith that morning. He hadn't seen her at all since she moved in the day before.

It was an hour's walk between Origh and the hill where Tod lived, and in the steadily warming afternoons, the walk home was growing more and more tiring. Arriving at his door, Tod knew he should get back to work. He wanted to watch for Elzith, though, and didn't want to miss her return. Tired, he sat down in the doorway, where he had a good view of the road from town. He only planned to rest for a moment. It wasn't long before he dozed off. He was half-aching, half-numb, and entirely annoyed with himself for wasting the day by the time he woke. When feeling finally returned to his fingers he ran them through his hair and rubbed his eyes. "Fool," he muttered softly to himself, but he felt no anger. For a moment he was proud of himself.

Then he felt that he was being watched.

The memory of last night's prowler shot into his head forcefully. It wasn't dark, though, and Tod was utterly unable to imagine that otherworldly face in the light. Cautiously he raised his head and found Elzith standing above him.

"You shouldn't leave your door open," she said.

Tod had intended to say "You're back" or "You've been gone so long," but now such remarks seemed silly. Uncomfortably he looked over his shoulder at Shaan's door, at the rake under his box, and edged himself to the inside of his doorway. "I shouldn't?" he echoed.

Elzith nodded, peering critically at Tod. By the time he looked back up at her she had turned and started toward the steps down.

"Elzith!" Tod cried suddenly. "Can I invite you to dinner?" He paused in his own surprise, feeling his face redden. "Hospitality, you know. I'm not so good at it but I think I should try."

She watched him for a moment. He couldn't tell whether she was considering his offer or considering him a fool. But then she nodded. "Yes. Yes, you may invite me."

Not that Tod had much to offer. He hurried into his
flat and cleared a stack of paper and boards from the half
of the table that had seen no guests since the Healer
who'd lived downstairs. That seemed like ages ago, the
one and only time that Tod had entertained his enigmatic former renter. Now he dragged a chair away from
the fireplace where Shaan liked to sit and pulled it to the
table opposite his chair, then cleared more partly finished books from his half of the table and stacked them
on the steps of the unused staircase. He looked at the
space on the table and couldn't remember what to do
next. It had been too long. Plates, bread, cheese. He
thought he had apples in his pantry. "I think I have
sausages, too," he thought out loud, searching through
that little closet.

"Don't put yourself out," Elzith said, sitting calmly in
the chair, which she had canted a little at an angle. "I'll
have plenty here."

Tod backed out of his pantry, a skillet in his hand,
confused. Unsure what to do with the skillet, he set it on
the stove and began to fry the sausages anyway.

"Oh, please don't wait," he said a few minutes later,
noticing that Elzith had touched nothing while he was
cooking. He also noticed the angle of her chair. It occurred to Tod that if she'd left her chair straight, facing
his, it would have put her back to the door. Why would
she be so concerned? And what made him think of it?
She reached for an apple and Tod turned back to the
stove.

Elzith had finished her apple and was starting on a bit of bread by the time Tod came to the table. He became aware of the silence but could think of nothing to say, so he busied his mouth with eating. Elzith was casually surveying his flat. He watched her eyes make a circular path from the door, across the front window, the mantelpiece with its clock, the stove and pantry, himself across the table, the door behind him that led to his bedroom, the desk cluttered with paper and boards and rectangles of leather and pots of glue, the downward staircase. The clock chimed the hour and Tod jumped slightly at the sound. Elzith's eyes drifted back to the timepiece but she did not react. She finished the morsel of bread, and as Tod hadn't taken an apple, she reached for a second one.

"Don't you like sausages?" Tod asked meekly.

She chewed calmly, undisturbed by Tod's asking her a question at the moment she'd taken a bite. "I can't eat them," she said at length.

"*Can't* eat them?" said Tod, puzzled. "You mean they make you sick?"

"In a manner of speaking." She took another bite and left Tod despairing of further information. He gave up, sighed, and went back to his meal. As if this were a cue, Elzith continued. "I had an injury to my gut. The Healer who mended me told me I could no longer eat anything but what came out of the ground or the water. I wonder sometimes if he could have mended me better but left me this way to play a trick on me."

Tod frowned. The lawmakers ascribed such trickery

to the Healers, of course, but Tod found it hard to believe. Elzith watched him frown, her eyes half-interested, watching for something. Tod didn't know what to say.

"I'm sure he would tell me he did it to teach me a lesson," she finally concluded.

Tod took a breath and sighed it out in relief. He didn't have to reveal his thoughts after all. He tried to remember what he'd served the Healer who'd come to dinner that one time. "I don't have any turnips, I'm afraid. Or carrots."

"Don't worry yourself." Elzith looked straight at him as she spoke, and Tod let her hold his eyes for a moment before the contact became too disconcerting and he looked away. He looked up again a moment later and found her still watching him. Her mouth was slightly open, caught almost unawares in a long breath. On another person it would have been an expression, it might have betrayed surprise or some other emotion, but on Elzith's steely face it only made Tod uncomfortable. He retreated back to the view of his plate. When he looked at her a third time she was again glancing casually at the clock.

"This—this Healer," Tod asked, "how long ago did you see him?" That must be it, he thought reasonably. The man who had stood outside his window the night before had the desperately strange eyes, gray green blue and always changing, of a Healer. That must have been what he was, Tod soothed himself. Simply a Healer asking after Elzith's health.

"Why?" Elzith asked flatly, facing the fireplace.

"Someone was by last night," replied Tod, trying to sound as casual as she, and not doing a convincing job of it. "He looked a bit like a Healer. Might have been looking for you." He decided not to mention slamming the shutters in the man's face. Looking back, it seemed rather rude.

When Elzith looked back toward Tod, her face had resumed the expressiveness of a wall. "I can't imagine he was. But I'll keep an eye out for him." She placed the second apple core on the plate. "Thank you for dinner, it was most kind. Now I hope you'll excuse me."

Tod watched her stand with his mouth full, and hurriedly he rose to open the door for her, only catching up to her as she was already halfway through it. He wasn't good at hospitality, he thought glumly, not at all. But Elzith wasn't an easy guest. He caught a last glimpse of her before she disappeared around the hill and down the steps: black shirt, black breeches, black boots. No jacket, though, and no belt or pistol. But she looked very pale, out there in the shadows. Too pale, and a bit too tall. She didn't look back or wave good-bye. Tod's stomach tightened, the food cold in his mouth. She was really gone, he thought, and he should close the door. But she'd never answered his question, really, about when she'd been to the Healer.

# 5

COINCIDENCES MOCK ME. MY LIFE IS CHAOS, OF course, repetitive though it may be in its grinding endlessness. Everything is the same, but nothing is the same. I was traveling again, to some new place, somewhere I've never been before but a journey like so many others, step after endless step. There should be no coincidences.

There would be no reason for the Healer to come. It was only twelve days ago that we parted company, when I left the north coast with his bill of health and a nearly empty belly. Healers don't wander around following their patients. They finish their business and go on. The same is true of this one, except he goes nowhere. He is blind. I've never wasted time wondering why he's never healed himself; Healers are strange that way. Loyd got him, certainly, dug him out of some prison or asylum where he'd been locked up because he couldn't get away. He's part of the camp there now, on the north coast. He can't leave, can't follow me if he wanted to, or if he were able to see the way.

But it had to be him.

Coincidences mock the game. There's no sense in them, no reason, no evidence that can be pieced together to solve them. There's no reason the Healer should come. I could look for the evidence that would explain it and find nothing.

No, it couldn't be him. These thoughts were useless. I kept marching, urged forward in thoughtless ranks with the other guards. We were suited up in black, to match the Justices we were assigned to watch. They were leaving Dabion, going out into the wide wide world on their important business, and they needed us specially to take care of them and do their dirty work. And not to ask questions. We followed our orders and we marched, our boots pounding the earth as if the Justices wanted it punished for the insolence of existing. None of us looked at one another; none of us wondered what mad thoughts we entertained ourselves with as the rhythm of the march vibrated our senses out of us.

Mad thoughts are all I have left. I've a hole in my belly and one in my mind. Cracks, scars, like the pockmarks of coincidence. They're points of weakness, breaches in my armor. If I let them through they'd break me. I'd lose this way. I knew better. There's no way the Healer could have come, no reason he would have, so it's doubtful it was him. It was someone else, then. Someone else. I didn't have enough information to speculate who. There was nothing to be done for it now. We were marching to Cassile.

They were sending us to close down the monasteries. The mystics were dangerous—that was Dabion's official word. Unarmed, unskilled, half-starved, these men and women whose eyes were more on the invisible beyond than this world somehow had the power to scare the Justices as much as any army they'd ever fought. Now we were going to disband them, arrest them, kill them if they didn't submit. Because the eyes of the mystics were not on Dabion, not on the law. Nanianism had the nerve to suggest there was something beyond the law, and Dabion couldn't tolerate the threat.

Years ago I went to Cassile, back when I was still playing spy for them, before they decided I wasn't good for the work anymore and they handed me over to the military. Back then—that was twelve days ago. But it's been years since it was a game. I went to one of the villages in Cassile, those clumps of humanity that stab the landscape between monasteries, inhabited by people who haven't become monks yet. Once the villages were full of mills that made velvet for Mandera, in the days when Mandera had money. Now they make velvet for Dabion, for the Justices who pretend they don't have money. But the Justices thought there were men in that village who still had dealings with Mandera, ties to some criminal cell that was plotting the demise of the Five Countries. I went to that village and watched all the people, the managers of the mills, the weavers bent over their looms. I watched them tear their fingers as the cloth crept out inch by inch, watched them argue with the clerks who came to collect the taxes, watched the few who had an idea to resist get thrown down on the ground. I collected every one of their words and reported them to the big men. That was my first coincidence: The man I gave my report to was one I'd met before, one I'd never expected to see again. Not one of those words I gave him had anything to do with Mandera. The Justices were wrong. But those words I collected said something else, something about Nanianism. The villagers had religion, and they were telling others about it. Nanianism was spreading. It had to be stopped.

So now I was going to fight the big men's battles for them, as I always have. I went into Siva for them, got attacked by my second coincidence, and came out with a hole in my mind. Then I tripped over the third coincidence when I went to Mandera for them, and left with a hole in my gut. I dropped through that hole and out of the spy trade—they can't use me now with such a visible scar, one that even the Healer with all his magic couldn't mend. Or wouldn't mend, I'll never know. The big men can't just let me go, of course, so they put me away in the Black Force where a thousand men with guns can watch me, make sure I don't give away any secrets, make sure every step I take is straight and tedious, with no coincidences. But I've dropped into another coincidence anyway. What will I leave with this time?

But it might have been nothing, no connection, not the Healer at all. Tod might not have known what he'd seen. He hadn't seen the rusted rake at his neighbor's box, a tool his neighbor would never need for any legitimate reason. Tod wasn't the sort to question. He didn't push me when I baited him with half answers. He's the sort I might call trustworthy. If I could trust.

Then there were his eyes—so widely, truthfully open. He offered me hospitality, not a bribe, not a trick. Real generosity. He was honest.

I wouldn't pursue this lead, though. Tod could give me nothing. I would have to wait until I saw more myself. I've never hated waiting before. I've spent whole winters waiting, tracking my subjects and biding my time until I had the chance to catch single words, ice flakes of information. I would never before have been upset by the smell of damned sausages when I couldn't eat any. Cracks, scars, points of weakness.

The bridge across the Great River was in sight, and Cassile on its west bank. The commanders were calling us to a halt, and we, two hundred black gnats in four obedient files, stopped to pitch camp. We would wait until morning to thrust the law down the monks' throats. More waiting. We bundled into the triangles of our tents and waited for our rations to be deposited, into tin bowls that we held out like orphans. The salted meat I couldn't eat. The hardtack I sucked on tastelessly. When the Justices called the end of the day, I lay down on the ground with my hands folded over the scar of my last coincidence.

# 6

I T WAS SUMMER IN CASSILE. THE COMMON CALEN-
dar dictated that the season was only just turning, that
the heat of summer wasn't due for weeks. Cassile was
one of Dabion's stubborn children, too late in abiding
laws, too early with the weather. The Western Sea that
washed against the country's long coast drenched Cassile in humidity, and the southern half of the land was
miserably hot in the summer. In the wilting dampness, a
crowd of black was gathering on the heavy grass around
a monastery's dark and aging stone walls.

A Dabionian Greater Justice stood before the door.
He lifted the wig that sat uncomfortably on his head and
ran a hand over his wet, bristle-haired scalp. Struggling
to fill his lungs with the saturated air, he reached a hand
out to one assistant for a flask of water and to another
for a speech etched on a scroll of paper. The tall wooden
doors of the monastery were barely open, a few thin
faces peering out at the strange sight of foreigners on
their grounds, but to this meager audience the Justice
began to read his statement.

"On the order of the High Council of the Five Countries, this first day of the second season in the year Seven
Hundred Sixty-four by the Common Calendar, this
institution is declared mystical, subversive, and unlawful..."

The foreigners who were ranged on the grass shifted
and panted in their heavy black garments. Some of them
watched the monastery doors warily, hands at their
sides, fingers twisting sacks of powder as they made
ready to prime their pistols. Others tugged restlessly at
the buttons of their high-necked jackets. The Black
Force had been assembled in the past year, trained to
guard the Justices as they traveled to Cassile to close the
monasteries. It was the first time in twenty years that the
Justices had gone personally into the foreign lands under
their jurisdiction. The rebellion in Mandera had finally
been controlled, and it was now time for Dabion to
bring Cassile into line. All the Five Countries would
soon be perfectly under Dabionian order, with no wasteful commercialism or dissident religion, once the Justices had their way. The guards who escorted them had
been drawn mostly from the Public Force, and had been
trained to expect resistance.

"The doctrine referred to as Nanianism is hereby
censored. Those acknowledging themselves as followers
of the sixth-century mystic Nanian will be duly prosecuted..."

"Look at that," murmured one bored guard to his
shuffling fellow. Their eyes were diverted away from the

monastery, where there was still no activity, and turned toward a female guard they did not recognize from their training barracks. "Letting women on the Force. Madness. And look how thin she is. She can't fire that weapon, the kickback will throw her a dozen yards." The woman in question, though in the range to overhear these words, displayed no reaction, but gazed calmly at the narrowly opened doors.

The Justice finished reading his proclamation and stepped away. The front ranks of the guards moved in to force open the doors. Inside the stone walls there was some rustling, some cries of protest, but overwhelmingly there was quiet. Then from a slit of an opening in the rear of the monastery a young ascetic began running madly toward an outbuilding.

The guard who had spoken in boredom a few minutes earlier snapped to attention, drawing his pistol, priming it hastily, and aiming its heavy barrel over his forearm. The female guard had reached the escaping boy first, though. She ran alongside him, blocking the aim of the other guard. Then she clapped her hands in a sharp rap. The boy stumbled, darting his head in the direction of the noise. His eyes were wide in shock. And then he froze.

More guards were storming the outbuilding, a smoking shack hung with the monastery's scant supply of meat and hot with fires. It was deemed a rash and hasty attempt at defense, an ill-thought plan to use the fire as a crude weapon. Or the boy may have been trying to evade

arrest so that he might warn other monasteries. The
guards could not question him, though. He was senseless, eyes wide-open in a corpse-stare, hunched near the
ground. The guards were called to round up the other
ascetics in the monastery. The woman stayed in place,
standing a few feet from the boy, never breaking her contact with his wide, shaking eyes. "I'll bring him," she uttered to the withdrawing guards. As they whispered
among themselves that the boy must have tripped, must
have been so terrified he couldn't move, they didn't notice that the female guard spoke through clenched teeth.
When they were a distance away she let her breath out
with a gasp. The boy dropped flat to the ground.

He did not stop shaking as the woman approached
him. His eyes widened impossibly farther as she knelt
beside him, and he shrank into himself as if he were trying to get away but was still trapped. He craned his neck
away but his eyes were fixed to her still. "What—did
you—do to me?" he stammered.

"Hush!" the woman commanded, seizing the collar of
his robe. "You tripped."

The boy shook his head furiously, trying hopelessly to
struggle out of her grip. "You—you did—" He sobbed
through uneven breaths. He clenched his head in his
hands and finally closed his eyes, his face creased in pain.
"It hurts—still hurts!"

The woman shook him until his eyes snapped open
again. "I did nothing," she hissed. "You will say nothing.

If you go quietly they'll take you quietly. If you try to fight they'll kill you."

Through a deep, racking gasp, the boy cried, "*You* could have killed me!"

It was the woman who wrenched her eyes away this time, breaking a contact that made her face even harder than before. She stood, dragging the boy to his feet behind her. She averted her eyes from him as she led him toward the other prisoners.

# 7

THE PUBLIC FORCE WERE OUT AGAIN, AND TOD couldn't even get to Keller's shop. He had to wait almost half an hour, he guessed, for them to move on. Only when he finally got close to the door did he realize they'd been in Keller's shop itself.

He sneaked through the door just as the last guard came out, shrinking away from the long-barreled pistol at the man's side, ducking his head so he wouldn't be recognized. He was afraid to ask Keller what was going on, so he only widened his eyes and hoped to catch the printer's gaze, but Keller didn't look up. The older man was exhausted, it was obvious, his shoulders slumped and his face dark and shadowed. Tod finally gave up trying to get his attention and wandered over to the cabinet, to rearrange the bound and finished books.

"What are you doing here?" Keller said eventually, coming toward him with a box of type in his hand, sorting through it noisily with the other hand. "Don't you have something at home waiting for you?"

"No," Tod said absently, his arms full of books. "Elzith's gone three more days. She left a note this time."

"Oh, is that it?" Keller chuckled, clinking his metal letters as he teased. "Somebody's lovesick."

Tod turned toward him, still distracted. "What?"

Keller laughed again gruffly and shook the box of type. Tod frowned, knowing he wouldn't get an answer. "What were *they* doing here?" he asked quietly, gesturing with his chin toward the Public Force guards that could still be seen through the window, making their way down the street.

The printer shook the box harder. "Investigating," he said shortly, drowning himself out. "Making sure I'm not printing contraband. Again."

In the noise of Keller's withdrawal Tod almost didn't hear what he'd said. He turned to watch Keller shuffle back toward his worktable. "Again?" Tod asked, but Keller would not answer him, because at that moment there was a great banging at the door. An instant after this cursory announcement, the door was flung open and a dozen guards marched in, new guards, foreboding in black uniforms and pistols. Tod turned shakily and Keller came out from behind his table, his face severe but his voice silent.

"Keller Blackletter," announced the black-clad man at the front of the troop. It was not a question; he looked directly at Keller and waited a few seconds for the man to acknowledge him. Then he turned and said, "And this is Tod Redtanner."

Tod nodded, dry-mouthed. These guards knew him. He hadn't escaped the riot four years ago after all, or they'd found the note he'd dropped in the gutter a few days earlier and knew it had come from his hand. He looked nervously at Keller. The printer was examining the guards with narrowed eyes, too weary to keep the mistrust out of his expression. But the guards did not make any moves toward them, and no fingers moved at any pistols. The two lines they stood in formed an aisle from the doorway, and a figure was moving through the aisle into the shop.

It was an old man, withered-looking, hunched around a parcel that he grasped against his chest like a child's toy or a madman's fetish. A wig was perched on his head, slightly skewed. At the head of the aisle he stopped and looked around the printer's shop, like a tortoise peering reluctantly out of his shell, his eyes dim and watery.

"Justice Advisor Jereth Paloman," the foremost guard announced flatly.

The old man blinked as if the light hurt his eyes, or as if he didn't recognize his own name. "You're the printer," he rasped to Keller.

"Yes, your honor," Keller replied. "You have an order?"

The Justice moved forward with halting steps, clutching his parcel tightly as if he didn't want Keller to take it after all. He looked up at Tod suddenly, panicked at this intruder he hadn't noticed before.

"The bookbinder," assured the guard, emotionless.

"Ah, yes," the Justice murmured, "the bookbinder."

Finally he released the package from his arms and tenuously extended it toward Keller. The cloth that concealed it slipped awkwardly away, and Tod saw a sheaf of papers, wrinkled and scrawled with rows of ink, bound with a leather cord. "I will—here is..." The old Justice licked his lips and bit the end of his tongue. "My lessons." He drew a deep breath and seemed emboldened by it. "A book I will be teaching from. I will need seven copies." His hands shook slightly as Keller took the papers from them.

"And you'll need it when?" Keller's words were never laden with niceties, and less so when he was fatigued.

The Justice's words were far more confident as he replied, "I start the lessons in one week."

Tod's jaw dropped. "Seven copies in a week?" he gasped, before he could stop himself. The old Justice's eyes turned on him, wide and stunned. Justice Paloman might have been shocked at having his words questioned, but it was not simple offense that smoldered in the old man's eyes. Not righteousness, not superiority, but desperation, a fever, a madness.

"Will you send a clerk or do we deliver it?" interrupted Keller.

The Justice turned slowly back to the printer, his discomfort obvious again. "Have it delivered," he answered, "to Lord Justice Frahn."

There was a stomping and creaking and clattering as the guards withdrew with their guns and their Justice. Tod thought he saw the old man turn and cast a look back at him, but before Tod could examine that look and guess at what it meant, the Justice was swept out in a wash of black.

"Well," came Keller's voice, hard and short, "I'll be starting on this now." He circled around his worktable and untied the bundle of papers.

Tod peered at the uneven hand that covered the pages. The Justice had completed his notes hastily and messily. "Hell!" gasped Tod. "How can you read that?"

Keller said nothing, shook his head, and rubbed his eyes.

Tod knew better than to ask what would happen if they didn't finish the job in time. He also knew Keller would lose more sleep to finish the printing in a hurry and give him enough time to bind the books. And then he'd have to deliver them—"Wait!" Tod cried. "They're going to Lord Justice Frahn. Not Jannes, not our Lord Justice. They're going to . . . to . . ."

"District One," answered Keller, still leaning over the difficult script.

"But that doesn't make sense," Tod protested. "Why would he come all the way to Origh from District One? There's got to be printers and bookbinders in Insigh. Why would he come here?" Tod realized he was rambling an instant before he realized Keller had looked up from his table and was fixing him with a deeply serious look.

"Don't ask those questions," the printer said. "Don't read these laws when you sew them up. I never do when

I print them." He leaned back toward the table, slowed by the fatigue in his body. "Knowing what's coming won't help."

Still Tod lingered by the table, trying to read the hand-scrawled notes with a wrinkled brow, until Keller sent him away to pull a composing stick and a box of type.

Five, maybe six days later, Tod lost track of the date. All he did was count books. He had four left. Keller had taken three days to finish printing the quartos, and Tod had spent those three days anxiously watching the clock. He'd worked himself into a frenzy about the deadline before Keller even got the pages to him. It almost made Tod nervous enough to drink, if there had been any gin around. When he finally got the pages from Keller, he took the mechanism out of the clock. It no longer mattered what time it was. The job would get done no faster than he could do it.

The sun was going down. Tod had thought several times over the last hour or so that he needed to close the shutters and light the lamps. He wondered if he'd eaten dinner already or if that had been yesterday. Looking up from his work, he noticed it was darker than he thought. He was finished stitching his current book; he had only to fix it into the boards and glue the cover on. He could allow himself a break, he thought. His legs were stiff as he clambered out of his chair, he rubbed his eyes and his aching fingers, and he began hunting in the dimness for matches.

"I left them somewhere," he murmured to himself as he sorted blindly through a desk drawer. "Did I leave them on the mantel?" He shuffled toward the fireplace, his foot grazing over something crumpled.

There was a noise from the street. Tod leaned toward the open window, still too preoccupied to remember his fear of the outside. Suddenly he realized that in losing track of the date, he no longer knew when Elzith was due to return. He went into his bedroom to look out of the back window. There was no one on the steps that skirted the downward slope of the hill. The sun was gone and the bottom of the hill was in shadows. Tod leaned out as far as he could to see whether there was light coming out from Elzith's window. Then, among the shadows, he saw movement.

"Elzith!" he shouted. But he couldn't hear his own voice, because the air within his head was filled with a shattering sound like glass.

There was no glass in his windows, nothing that could have broken like a shop window in a riot or a wealthy man's pane under the handle of Shaan's rake. Tod started to run back into the main room, but he was halted by a twist of fear. The shutters were still open. Had the intruder returned? Through the doorway he saw light. He hadn't lit the lamps yet. No, he hadn't found the matches. The glow drew him. It pulled him out into the room, a lure around his neck. He was through the door, at his table. Light emanated from be-low it. The light crept out at his ankles, pulled him closer. He was on his knees. He was at the source of the light. A tile, a square of clay. The red earth of it shone from within. It was hot, he felt the heat on his face. His eyes were drawn along the carvings of it, three curved lines, the shape of waves. Waves, the water. He could hear water in the heat. The heat, the light, washed over him like water, pulling him, pulling him downward—

Tod—Tod—Tod—"Tod!" A voice in the waves. "Tod! Get away from it!"

Away. He couldn't move, couldn't turn his head. His eyes were too heavy to lift away. "I can't."

There was noise above the waves in his ears. Pound-ing, shaking, boots on the floor. Elzith was running toward him. He saw her boots at the edge of his vision. A foot moved under the table, blindly. Then her boot met the tile and covered it. The water washed out, the light was gone. Tod could move.

"What was it?" he stammered. He backed out from under the table, brushing his head on it as he moved. Elzith did not answer. As Tod looked up he saw that her hand was splayed over her face, her eyes shut tight. She drew her foot backward, scraping the tile from beneath the table. Not taking her foot off it, she leaned over it, holding the edge of the table and supporting her weight on her arms. Her eyes were still closed. "Elzith?"

"Stay back," she said, her jaw so tight it did not move.

She was working the tile under her heel. "Close your eyes, don't look at it."

Tod crouched in the doorway of his bedroom, his eyes averted, his hands covering his face, but he could not resist looking, turning his head back just a fraction. Elzith was standing in the same posture, frozen, head bent and hands on the table. Tod could see her silhouette in the moonlight from the window. She lifted her foot, very slowly. The light began to bleed over the floor. Her eyes opened, for a second. Then she smashed her heel on the tile, grinding it to dust.

Her figure sagged against the faintly lit window. "You have a lamp in here," she said, unquestioning. Tod clambered to his feet and searched again for the matches, finding them in his bedroom. He lit the lamp there and brought it to the main room, where Elzith was still bent over the table. Her fingers were clenched, her knuckles white. Her hair fell down around her lowered head and shadowed her face.

Tod noticed himself shaking, throwing the light in eddies over the floor. He put the lamp down on the table. "Elzith," he said, hunting for his voice. "What was it?"

She raised her face to him then, a face drowned in the utmost fatigue. Her voice was no longer flat and casual. "Do you have a blank page?"

"You didn't answer me." The dregs of fear kept Tod from curbing his voice.

"I know," Elzith said. She drew a breath, straightening very slowly. "I can't answer you." When she fixed his eyes with hers this time, her gaze did not carry so much power. "I will find out what I can. Someone will come for you. Wait for them," she said, a command, a plea. "Talk to no one before then. Please, Tod."

He nodded, very solemnly.

"Do you have paper?" Elzith repeated, and Tod scrambled in his desk for a blank leaf. Elzith took it and knelt down, scraping the dust from under her boot into the paper and folding it into an envelope. "You should keep the shutters locked," she said, absently.

"But it's getting hot." He said it without thinking. It was a ridiculous thing to say. He started laughing, irrationally, a dry laugh that split his lips, and he gasped to swallow the air that would stifle it.

Elzith glanced up at him. There was a slight wrinkling around her eyes that might have been a smile of irony or derision. "Wait," she murmured, and, sliding the envelope into her pocket, she let herself out the door.

# 8

TOD WAITED UNTIL IT WAS ALMOST DAWN. HE
didn't think of trying to sleep; it took him an hour
even to sit still in a chair again. He fastened the shutters,
replaced the clock's parts, set it for a time he thought
might be right, and wound it. He refilled the lamp with
oil and finally sat at his table. The work strewn across the
top was pushed back slightly from the edge where Elzith
had been leaning. Tod found he was afraid to stretch his
legs into the space below the table, and he timidly collapsed to hands and knees, carrying the lamp with him,
to examine the floor. He watched the clock move forward, slowly. At length he went back to work, careful, de-
liberate work. He finished only a few pages before the
knock came at the door.

The razor point of the glover's needle sank into Tod's
fingertip. The book dropped from his hands. He was
frightened. But an intruder who meant him harm surely
wouldn't knock. He thrust his finger into his mouth before the drop of blood welling there could spill on his
papers. The knock came again, quiet but sharp. Tod

looked at the clock, wondering if Shaan would be on the streets, returning from work, or watching from his window, eager to spread the gossip.

The knock sounded again. It had to be after four, and Shaan would be in by now. The men outside knew that, Tod guessed. He went to the door.

Two men stood outside. Clerks, they might have been, dressed inconspicuously in their typical black suits. They weren't black guards, and they weren't armed, as far as Tod could tell. They wore no insignia, no special markings. Not even the placid expressions on their faces gave any indication of their secretive purpose. Nothing was notable about them but their presence here, well before dawn.

"Tod Redtanner," one of them said. His voice was quiet and smooth, a whisper of velvet. He could have been receiving a delivery, some dull papers Keller had printed, in a plain office in town. Tod hesitated before answering. It was a rhetorical question, probably; he was sure they knew exactly who he was. The clerks waited, polite in their calm silence, perhaps. The slats in their lantern cast grids of shadow on their faces, lighting an eye, a corner of a mouth. Then one spoke again, which one Tod couldn't tell. "Are you ready? Your door needs locking."

Tod knew he used to walk to town after dark, when he was making Keller's deliveries, in winter months when the sun went down early. Since he began binding books, since he stopped drinking, he'd had no need to be out at night. Though he walked the road into Origh almost every day, in the darkness it was unrecognizable. The clerk with the lantern held it out to the side so that it lit Tod's path as he followed, but the skirt of the man's jacket flapped over the light, and each time it did Tod seemed to find a rut or a stone in the road. The men did not speak; Tod had little to concentrate on but the black-ness of the clerk's hand. At some length he worked out that the hand was black because the man was wearing a glove, to protect him from the heat of the lantern.

They were headed for the Great Hall. When Tod looked up from his feet, he saw the mass of it against the faintly lit sky, a building so large he could feel it, even though the setting moon cast too little light to make a silhouette. They went around to the east side, to the tun-nel entrance, where Tod had been before. Soon there would be servants at this door, readying the Hall for the day of business, and then clerks, deliverymen, and others would flock here. Even at this hour the tunnel was not deserted. It was as brightly lit as day, already, and Tod squinted at the few servants who were about, their eyes averted as they began their duties. It was an ordinary day in the Great Hall of Justice, the center of law, the center of light. As if there were no secrets.

The tunnel under the Great Hall was a labyrinth. Tod was utterly lost in the many turns, and there was such a number of doors and side passages that he couldn't be-gin to imagine what went on behind them all. One of them certainly led to the kitchens, Tod thought with an aching stomach. It was crazy, he scolded himself, being hungry at a time like this. He was led around another turn, and his disoriented head kept turning. He couldn't imagine what was at the end of the passage.

Suddenly they were there. The end of the passage was a flight of stairs that ascended into a closet. The guides lit their lantern again, as there was no other light, and Tod was surrounded in confining shadows. The walls of the closet were crammed with shelves and dense with books, eating up even more of the tiny space. Tod looked behind him and couldn't find the opening he'd come through. They waited for a few moments in silence. Tod was about to clear his throat and ask his escorts what was going on when another door, hidden among the dusty volumes, swung outward and open.

He was led out into a courtroom. He had never seen one before, never having been admitted past the outer doors of the Hall with his deliveries, never having been dragged farther by his own faults. From material in the books he had bound, he was able to piece together an image in his mind, though the scraps of description that he found in court records and law statements were hardly picturesque. He had wished for a novel—another piece of contraband he'd seen in Karrim—a story, rich in description, set in a courtroom, to bring to life the dull papers he bound. The image he'd made in his mind was not quite accurate. Tod would have devoted his first words, had he been writing the novel, to the hugely arching ceiling that made a cavern of the courtroom, opening before him, enormous as justice and eternity. The room was lined in wood, floor, walls, vast ceiling, polished and impenetrable. The Table of Justice was a massive marble block set on a dais. Tod entered the room from a door to the side of it and it loomed before him, high over his shoulder, taller than he was. He was torn between dropping his eyes in humility and staring in awe at the Table and the Justice who would be sitting behind it. There was no one there, though.

"Is this the break?" a voice asked, echoing in the room. Tod's attention was drawn toward a man sitting at one of two tables that stood facing each other along the sidewalls, perpendicular to the dais. Tables where the prosecution and the defense sat, Tod guessed. He wondered which side this man was sitting on. It must be the prosecution's side, he thought. Of course, it would have to be. There was no reason he would be brought here except to be prosecuted. Tod swallowed coldly, a lump catching in his throat.

"This is him," one of the escorts answered.

The man at the table angled his head down slightly, surveying a number of papers that were ranged in front of him. "Hmm," he uttered. Tod wondered how much more intimidated he'd feel if this man were clad in Justices' robes and sitting behind the marble. "Tod Redtanner. Twenty-seven, bookbinder, Barrow-under-Origh." The man looked up from the papers he was reading from, judging for his impact. Tod could do little more than blink his dry eyes mutely. The man's already thin mouth drew into a tighter line. "I suppose," he said, and for the first time Tod noticed that there were other people sitting at the table, "your operative has the complete information on this security break."

Immediately beside the intimidating man was a large man in a Black Force uniform. He wasn't the one being addressed, though, and he sank back in his chair. At the end of the table sat a small, old, inconspicuous man. He looked as if the wind would blow him away, but he did not shrink from the intimidating man's sarcasm.

"Yes," the old man said calmly, "I suppose she has, if one wished to test her."

The intimidating man narrowed his eyes, then cast them toward the far corner of the courtroom. Standing there, arms crossed, in the familiar black guard's uniform, was Elzith. She met the man's critical gaze with eyes just as sharp, but the rest of her face was emotionless as ever. "Is the local director asking his superior for authority to conduct such a test?" Elzith asked, with exacting formality. Tod thought she sounded a little bored.

The intimidating man, the local director, snarled silently. "Your damned report, Kar."

Her eyes didn't even twinkle in victory over the man's rudeness. She started speaking, then Tod woke up enough to be shocked.

"Tod Redtanner," Elzith began, "born 737 in Origh to Warith Redtanner, occupation obvious, still in service at Thirtieth Street. Youngest of three, unremarkable youth. The eldest brother was noted in illegal establishments in

Karrim between 752 and 753, distilleries, brothels, and the like. One citation also notes the middle brother. It can be deduced that Tod was also present at some of these incidents, but there is no formal record of such. In 760 he was witnessed on the scene of a street riot, but the witness was discarded as unreliable and no evidence was brought against Redtanner. In 761 Morrn Weaver, who was subletting a room in Redtanner's cottage at the time, was arrested for operating a still in this sublet. Redtanner was summoned for questioning but excused due to illness; he was sent to a Healer after an excess of alcohol. A cousin, who was a clerk under Greater Justice Umbrin, had the summons dismissed, as well as the charges of using alcohol, and Tod was released to his family. In three years there have been no further incidents on his record. The only Justices I found who had any remarks about him noted prompt and competent work." Elzith smiled thinly. "Is the damned report complete?"

The local director looked sourly at his papers. "Complete, yes." Then he looked up at Tod.

The shock Tod felt deteriorated into fear. They knew about the riot. He hadn't escaped—they knew about the riot. And the illegal establishments in Karrim—suspicion of being there was enough of a crime, even if he hadn't actually been there, which he had. The lamps in the courtroom made spots in front of his eyes. He'd completely forgotten why he'd been brought to the Great Hall.

But the local director turned away from Tod, looking

unconcerned. "So, nothing more than common follies of youth?"

Elzith answered, "Nothing."

"No ties to Mandera, Cassile, Siva, or off continent?"

"None."

"No further ties to Healers or other suspicious parties?"

"None."

"And he is the only break?"

"The only one. There were no others present."

The local director nodded and collected his papers into a stack. "Are you satisfied," he asked dryly, turning to the old man at the end of the table, "sir?"

The old man nearly smiled. There was something like pride in his eyes. "Of course," he replied. For a moment, an odd thought passed through Tod's mind, that the old man was Elzith's father. But somehow he didn't think that was true. "Administrator Traite," the old man continued, "would you introduce your guard?"

The uniformed man in the middle got to his feet, obviously relieved that the conflict between his companions had cooled. Once on his feet, he looked like nothing could shake him. Administrator Traite was an enormous man, as tall as a Healer but broad as well. If it weren't for his coloring he might have been accused of being a foreigner.

"Redtanner," the Administrator addressed Tod, sharply as an order. "My Black Force Guards. Kar," he said, gesturing precisely toward Elzith's corner, "and my other Guards are a special force, arranged to escort the Justices in their business to foreign and hostile areas. We are a division of the Public Force. Our assignments, Redtanner, are of the greatest importance. But Kar comes to us from beyond the Black Force."

"From my organization," interrupted the local director. "And let me impress upon you, Mister Redtanner, the severity and importance of *these* assignments." The two men drew themselves up stiffly, like generals of opposing armies. Tod wished he could drift back toward the door of the closet, away from the battlefield. "And," the director insisted weightily, "the utter secrecy of them. The information you will receive is minimal. You shall not divulge it." The man leaned toward him, ever so slightly. "Do you understand me, Mister Redtanner?"

On either side the clerks who had brought him drew perceptibly closer to Tod. He hadn't seen that they were armed, yet their nearness still felt threatening. Reflexively he raised his eyes toward Elzith. She was attired for work, a pistol belted at her side. Cold rumbled in his stomach. He couldn't imagine Elzith doing harm to him, though. Filled with fear and not fear, he looked at the local director and nodded.

"Good," answered the director. "Now understand that Kar was previously an operative in the Secret Force"— he looked pointedly at the Administrator of the Black Guards—"*my* Secret Force." The Administrator's face fell and he stared at the old man at the end of the table. Even Elzith raised an eyebrow and looked at the old man for a reaction, but the old man merely smiled, ambiguously, and said nothing. The director continued. "The work she has done for the Secret Force is most critical, and most dangerous. We believe that last night's attack may have been in retribution for activities that she was involved in previously."

"Retribution?" echoed Tod faintly.

"You saw someone outside your flat some time ago." The director demanded, turning toward Tod. "You said he looked like a Healer."

The old man spoke now, patiently cutting through his subordinate's interrogation. "Tod, can you describe him?"

"He—looked like a Healer," Tod stammered, the intruder's face having evaporated completely from his mind.

"What did he wear?" the old man pressed gently. "Healers wear simple undyed wool robes. Is this what he wore?"

Tod felt as forgetful as if he were drunk. He wanted to look at Elzith but felt ashamed. "I don't know."

"What time was it?" The voice was Elzith's.

"It was night. It was dark. I couldn't see him." Then he caught it, the memory. "No—he had on a cloak. I couldn't see his clothes, they were covered with a cloak. It had a hood. I could see some of his hair, it was braided, with things braided into it. And he was pale. Very pale."

The old man smiled lightly. He nodded and seemed

about to speak, but the local director spoke over him. "A madman," the director pronounced sourly. "Escaped from his asylum. The incidents are unrelated."

The others in the room seemed unconvinced. The old man asked, "Elzith?"

She shook her head. "I don't know. I told you the impression I got from the rune."

"Take him out," the director ordered sharply, waving at Tod without looking at him. "He's enough of a break as it is."

"I still have words for him," said the old man.

"Then send him out to wait!" insisted the director.

There was a silence as the men regarded each other. Then, with utter calm, the old man made a small gesture and directed Tod and his escorts out. A look of victory glowed on the director's face, but it was the old man who smiled, as if he knew a secret.

They did not go back into the closet, but instead went through the courtroom and out the main doors into a broad corridor. Through a distant window light was beginning to break. Tod realized his heart was pounding. Retribution. Elzith was in danger. Tod was in danger. Secret Forces. Things he knew nothing of and could not control. His hands were shaking. There was nothing he could do.

No taste for the gin, except when he was scared. He'd never been more scared in his life. Outside the Great Hall, down the street, was a depot where he could get a wagon to Karrim for the money in his pocket. He could get oblivion by nightfall. But as soon as that image came into his mind, he had a picture of Elzith there as well, leaning over his table, her hair obscuring her tired face. *Please, Tod.* And he could not go. The window was full of light now. It was morning and he had work to do. Quite a lot of work.

The courtroom doors opened. It was Elzith. She passed Tod by a few paces and looked out the window, arms crossed, the emerging sun lighting the long gray barrel of her pistol. Then she turned back toward him, a crooked smile painted on her face. "So, welcome to the place. How do you like it?"

Tod let out a breath of laughter.

"I know you have things to do," she said. It sounded like an apology. "They'll send you out through the tunnel again, like you're one of their servants."

"Will you find him?"

Elzith stopped, her eyes fixed on him. There was a flaw in her calm. "We will try," she said, looking away from him. Then she uncrossed her arms, and when she looked at him again her expression was perfectly contrite. It was rehearsed, Tod had to believe, but still he felt it was truthful. "I have to apologize for this, Tod. I can collect my things tonight. Will you need a fee for the flat until you can rent it again?"

It was a moment before he realized what she was asking. "No!" he said hurriedly. "No, I don't want you to move out."

"Tod, you understand you may be in danger."

The urge to escape had passed. "From what you told me, I could be in danger anyway." And once he said it, he was no longer afraid of Shaan. The worst his neighbor could do was rob him, as if Shaan wanted his books. There would be no surprises.

Elzith nodded. "Thank you," she said. Then she turned and headed down the corridor, disappearing around a corner.

The doors opened wider; they had not shut. "Tod," issued a mild voice. "You may wait without, gentlemen." Tod's escorts held back and Tod slowly pressed forward.

The old man was alone in the courtroom. There was a bench along the wall at the back, next to the outer doors, and he gestured for Tod to sit beside him.

"So severe, don't you think?" the old man said, musingly, looking around the courtroom. "These dark, empty walls. All wood, no ornamentation. Bioran architects. The old style, fifth century, when the Biorans were travelers in the Five Countries, before we sent them back. The old style, severe. Believing austerity is a measure of truth. Have you been to Azassi, Tod?"

Astounded, Tod shook his head.

"You may call me Loyd," the old man said, smiling. "Painting on the walls. Frescoes. Very elaborate, artists, those Azassians. It's their heritage, folk art. Mandera was highly decorated as well, of course, but that was obviously a sign of wealth."

Tod was reminded of his grandfather, his rambling stories and ancient red-stained fingers. He smiled, felt himself relax. Then Loyd changed his words, suddenly, without warning.

"Are you sure you understand, Tod, the danger you could face? Of course you do, Elzith knows you do. But why would you take the risk?"

"What..." Tod began to realize that the man had been listening through the open door. "What do you mean?" But he knew what the old man meant. Of course he did. Dabion had an army of spies and this grandfatherly old man was its commander. Tod felt light-headed, grasping at the edge of the bench.

Loyd did not challenge Tod's feeble protest but went on as if he hadn't spoken it. "She has assured me of your sincerity, but neither one of us can deduce a cause for it. Now listen, Tod, this line of reasoning is important. Reason is all we have. We are given this man—you—who is a crucial link in the chain, though he may not realize how crucial he is. We must test that link. You could be—now I don't think you are, though that popinjay in there called you one—a break in the chain. I do not think you are one, but you could become one. That's why we must learn what this link is made of."

Tod had to be half-asleep. The old man's words washed together without making sense. Tod blinked, wordless.

The old man softened, laughed a bit. "I know you're in love with her, but that's hardly an explanation. Such infatuations pass. It won't sustain you through this danger. Ah—you're going to deny it!" Tod felt that his mouth had dropped open, though his voice was still out of working order. "My boy, I've had a lifetime of reading expressions, and you are not what one would call a closed book. I could see it in your first glance at her. I am surprised, though, that Elzith said nothing of it to me herself. She told me of your invitation to dinner, but she only took that because she wanted to see whether you were a counterspy." Loyd's eyes were drifting around the room, as if he were not giving a debriefing, as if he were simply a rambling, dotty old man. But a man in his position wouldn't be carelessly spilling secrets, Tod thought with slow difficulty. He must be doing it intentionally, trying for an effect, trying for something. To win his trust? Tod was very tired.

"You passed her test, of course," Loyd continued. "You didn't pick up any of the leads she threw, didn't ask her any suspicious questions. She judged you truthful, but she never went back to analyze the real reason for your invitation. I believe she does not realize you're in love with her. Our dear Elzith has a blind spot, it would seem."

Tod felt his face burn red. Then the old man turned again to look at him directly, shifting into a new role as easily as a traveling actor on an illegal stage in Karrim, but the role he played now was ten feet tall and frightening.

"Which brings me to my true concern, Tod. With an ordinary girl you would hear this speech from her father. I am the nearest Elzith has to one. She is our finest agent; even dismissed, there is none better than her on the

Force. She is a keen observer, absolutely emotionless. I admit that I have taken advantage of these strengths. But she is human, and as such she must have weaknesses. I will have," Loyd said, his voice falling, slowing—"*no one* take advantage of those. I will not tolerate it if you trouble them unwittingly. If you hurt her with intent I will sacrifice my position to come after you."

"But that's why I want her to stay."

Silence followed the eruption of Tod's voice. He was so surprised to hear himself that he floundered for a moment, wondering how to finish. "I want to help her."

The man calling himself Loyd watched Tod for a long minute. Even when threatening, his face was not unkind. Tod didn't know whether to feel assured or worried by this. Then the old man nodded slowly. "I believe you," he pronounced. Then he stood, motioning Tod toward the doors, and just before he shut Tod out, he said, "Now tell it to Elzith and we'll see if she does."

# 9

A WAGON ROLLED THROUGH THE STREETS OF IN-sigh. It was a familiar sight to the commoners who lived on the outskirts of the capital, these wagons that looked like the weekly refuse collection but were guarded by a detail of Public Force. They came infrequently but steadily, and more often when there was unrest somewhere. They rolled in from the west, through the thinly peopled Dabionian villages, from Karrim, having begun their long circuit in Mandera. When faces appeared at the windows of the shops and tiny houses, drawn by the noise of heavy horses and rolling wheels and the clattering guns of the guardsmen—if not their pounding fists on the doors of those who dared sleep too late—those guards reached into the wagon to put its contents on display.

This wagon carried a colorful assortment. Dabion's guardsmen had found a treasure. Clothing was lifted on pikes, a bright blue shirt, a red petticoat. Such illicit dyes were banned in the Five Countries, not to be sold, not to be made from secretly cultivated plants. Those who subverted the Dabion-authorized fabric trade would not go long without punishment. Strings of beads were held out on tongs, glass baubles, precious stones, gold chains. Mandera could not hide the last of its wasteful riches forever. Papers were held up in the gloved hands of a guardsman, chapbooks full of poetry, that Karrimian distraction born of Manderan excess in the last century, and letters that carried other forbidden words. The guard did not deign to read any of it before throwing it back onto the trash heap. The Justices would not let the words be spoken—the very sound of them might cause corruption.

The Justices ordered the people to follow the wagon through the city and beyond its eastern limits, where the fire would be set and the takings in the wagon burned. News of the recent riot in Origh had traveled, and Insigh's people were restless. A calming influence, a corrective, was necessary. Arresting rioters and removing them before their actions could attract any more disruption was effective, and confining the masses while the criminals were taken away preserved the order, but these procedures did not educate. A demonstration was needed, and fire was always a good aid to instruction. The fire would not burn in Insigh, of course. The ash would dirty the streets.

The Lord Justices Frahn and Jannes stood at the side of the road, waiting for the wagon to pass, their hands held lightly in front of their mouths and noses as they watched it roll by. To the people, the peasants, the dirty, shuffling pedestrians who tracked dust in its wake they turned their heads and presented the backs of their carefully fashioned wigs. "A vile necessity," one muttered to the other from behind the shield of his hand. What the men truly thought—that Jannes regarded the parade through the streets as a disgusting display, and Frahn condemned Jannes for shirking his responsibility by allowing District One to do all the work of collecting contraband—neither said.

Frahn did not allow his irritation toward his colleague to disturb him much, though. He had every reason to be pleased. The lessons in Bioran philosophy, brought by Muhrroh himself to the Circle, were nothing less than an official endorsement of Frahn's school. When he had opened the School of Bioran Science seven years earlier, the other Lord Justices had not been supportive. Tuition brought to the school by students from throughout the country would raise revenue for District One, they complained, but it would be a loss to all the other Districts. They tolerated the school only because Muhrroh gave them no instruction to oppose it. But then evidence was brought forward: the mystics were dangerous and needed to be subdued. Bioranism could subdue them.

That followed, Frahn thought with a satisfied nod. The rules of Justice may have originated at the time of the mystic Nanian and the religion he created, both movements born in response to conflict among the early Bioran scholars, but at this late date there was little resemblance. Dabionian Civil Rule had been shaped by the rulings of the great Justices in those early centuries. Those patriarchs wrote their own interpretations of Nanian's doctrines, to be sure, but their interpretations were grounded in logic and rationality. They had nothing in common with the mystics. The mystics were past their time, overgrown, like weeds to be rooted out. Bioran learning was the ancient foundation upon which the rational movement was based, and it was the logical tool to use against the mystics. The Circle was convinced. The Insigh School was given approval. Frahn was vindicated.

As for Jannes, he did not care about mystics. He had no interest in going to the Circle and listening to the lecture. He had finished school years ago and had no interest in going back. But he had even less interest in going to the Circle and hearing Varzin's accusations of the evils of the mystics. The lessons, at least, would be a change. A pointless change, he thought, and a waste of time, like the dog-and-pony show he was subjected to nearly every time he came to Insigh, the contraband cart and its parade of clowns. He wrinkled his nose as he watched it disappear down the street. But this was what Justices did, the act they played, every day, throughout the years. It was all pointless. 200 C.C.: Biorans come to Dabion, all the world becomes Bioran. 495: conflicts break out, the Light Controversy, scholars come to blows over the shape of a ray of light, all the world goes to hell. 523: Dabion makes laws against Biora, following the words of

some mad mystic. By 541 Biora is shut up, all the world
is Nanianist. Two hundred years on Nanian is legislated
out of existence and all the world is Bioran again. And
Jannes would send his son to the School of Bioran Science when the boy reached the proper age, sending his
money to District One, because that was what Justices
did. He patted the wig on his head to make sure it was set
correctly. Why Lord Councilor Muhrroh supported the
suppression of the mystics, Jannes could not guess. It did
not matter. Jannes would go to the lecture and learn the
rules of logic, then he would go back to his office in
Origh to do a few things Justices did not do. He needed
to find the money to pay tuition to the Insigh School, after all, so that his son could grow up and learn the rules
of logic as he was supposed to. Otherwise, he might turn
into a contrary nuisance like Nosselin.

"My lord," Jannes said in perfect form, and as if on
cue, to the very nuisance he had been thinking of, as he
passed through the arched entryway at the top of the
stairs of the Great Hall and across the paths of Nosselin
and Timbrel.

"Hmph," Nosselin grumbled, ignoring the dips of the
wigged heads that greeted him.

"My lords," Timbrel uttered weakly toward Jannes
and Frahn, trying to catch his breath. He was running
late. He hated traveling, he hated the Great Hall and its
mountain of stairs, he hated meetings with the Circle.
He hated being a Lord Justice, for that matter. He was
in over his head. Each step, up the stairs, through the

marble corridors, down into the distressing labyrinth that led to the Circle, was like trudging through quicksand, every one sinking him a little deeper into a mire he couldn't get out of. The administration of District Three was too much for him on its own: the masses of paperwork, trial records, laws, and the uprisings of rebellious communities in the District's southeastern reaches. Now he would have to study. He was never a good student; ideas were like a flood and he couldn't swim. He never really wanted this job, Timbrel thought desolately. When he was younger, an aspiring clerk, a promising Lesser Justice, he had regarded the seat of Lord Justice as the highest achievement, the prize at the end of the race, the coveted accomplishment. Now he knew better. There were rumors about the seat of District Three, rumors he had somehow never heard until after he was appointed, after his feet were in the quicksand and there was no getting out. They said that his predecessor had been assassinated. They said that Timbrel had been chosen for the appointment because he was inoffensive to the hands responsible for the predecessor's murder, but it was those hands that held the reins, and Timbrel did not know where he was going.

Nosselin glanced over his shoulder as Timbrel shuffled along behind him, not bothering to disguise the scowl on his face. He wished the man would grow a backbone. In front of him the ridiculous blond wigs bobbed on the heads of Frahn and Jannes. Leeches before, insects behind—Nosselin was surrounded by

vermin. The entire Circle was nothing but a gang of
sycophants pandering to Muhrroh, and Bioranism was
just another example. Dabion had outlawed those
white-headed northern scholars two centuries ago, and
that was one of the few sensible things ever done. The
Light Controversy was just the start of the troubles that
Biorans had brought. When their wooden-brained lessons got to Azassi, the barbarians took them over and
started a war over who would be in control of the
schools. One of them, Byorn r'Gayeth, even tried to attack Biora in 510, hoping to conquer the whole
damnable country. Getting rid of the scholars was what
let Dabion get hold of power, and now they were throwing it away, reversing everything, so that a few political
vine-climbers could scarf up some crumbs.

Nosselin fumed as he and the other Justices assembled at the door of the council chamber that held the secret mouth of the labyrinth, waiting for the guard who
would open it for them and lead them through. He
frowned around at his peers, Hysthe who was already
there, the others shuffling into their places, looking like
bratty schoolboys. Timbrel didn't have the personality to
show an opinion, and Frahn, Jannes, and Hysthe had
donned wigs the second they heard Muhrroh supported
Bioranism. Nosselin would let himself be turned onto
the streets to starve like a beggar before he would put on
a wig. He wondered if the breath of sycophants would
poison the air in the corridors of the labyrinth, and he
plugged up his nose as the guard arrived to lead them

into the dark tunnel. It occurred to him that this was the most absurd ritual he could conceive of. He dreamed briefly of quitting his post, a lovely image that vanished too quickly in a shot of annoyance. He couldn't possibly leave his hateful position. There was no one else who could run District Four right.

Hysthe would not have been disturbed in the least by Nosselin's accusations that he was a sycophant. He let go of the rope guide above him for a moment to straighten his wig, which he had, in fact, acquired as soon as he'd heard his subordinate Jereth had been appointed to teach lessons to the Circle. Not that he had read any Bioran books at that point, or had even been interested. He learned in a hurry, though, memorizing the titles and the dates of the classic texts: *Rationality and Logic,* 238; *The Art of Dialogue,* 274; *Structures of Thought,* 312; and then the secondary source, Dal'Nilaran's *Classics of Bioran Learning,* 491. That inferior text was the one upon which the Insigh School was founded, brought by traders to Dabion when the borders of Biora were reopened. Jereth Paloman, Hysthe's Justice, had in his possession the three primary documents. His lessons would be authentic. Hysthe did not miss any opportunity to remind the Circle of this fact. He had to take every opportunity that came his way; there was little enough of it on this continent. Hysthe often wished he had been born a generation earlier, a century earlier, when the Ikinda Alliance was at its apex and the ships of the Alliance could carry a man away from the Five Countries, into worlds he could not imagine in his landlocked life. When the Alliance failed the whole continent had become depressingly myopic, and it had not yet recovered. Hysthe had little to do but deal with Azassians, traffic going into Azassi and traffic coming out of Azassi, the same day after day, year after insufferable year.

When the Justices came out, squinting, into the circular room, Muhrroh and Secretary Bint were already there. Bint was laying out books, their new textbooks, each one neatly bound, shiny like a schoolboy's new primer. The Secretary was the guardian of order and never seemed affected by the worries that plagued the others. Muhrroh never seemed affected by anything. The Lord Councilor was inscrutable, sitting at his place in the center of the table, placid and wise and impenetrable. So few people had ever seen him away from his seat at the table that one might imagine he never left it. No Lord Justice would speak such irreverent words about Muhrroh, though; they would hardly even think them, no matter what they thought of one another. They would follow his word unquestioningly. So they had been taught to do. History may have been a curse, and the faults of men may have plagued the Lord Justices, but the law was sacred—perhaps the only thing that was, the only standard and strength—and Muhrroh was the embodiment of the law. Muhrroh gave the command that the mystics were to be subdued, and so they would be. His motivation for this command was unknown and irrelevant. Muhrroh's word was as unmovable as his place at the table, from which few had ever seen him rise.

The Lord Justices were disturbed by a late opening of the door to the chamber. Justice Advisor Paloman was entering, and with him Lord Justice Varzin.

"Ah, yes," Varzin said smoothly as he slipped a book out of Bint's hands. "Your work. Most impressive, is it not?"

Jereth nodded nervously, trembling and grasping at his podium. "Impressive, yes, my lord," he managed to utter. "I hardly recognize it."

"Your words are destined for nearly the same greatness as the classics from which they are drawn." Varzin smiled as he paged through the volume. "Such a fine job. A fortuitous recommendation, don't you think? The bookbinder in Origh?"

"Yes, yes, the printing. A fine job." Jereth fumbled for the glass of water that sat upon the podium. Printing, he thought—did Varzin say printer? What did he say about the bookbinder? His hands shook again and he had to put down the glass, afraid to spill the water.

Varzin took his place at the table. "My lords, Lord Councilor," he said. "I beg your pardon for my tardiness, but I have had the pleasure of escorting our Justice Advisor to the meeting today. With your leave, he will begin his first lecture."

Jereth blinked at the faces around the table, smeared in his blurry vision. Only Varzin appeared clear to him. His breath quickened with a hint of what he almost recognized as enthusiasm. He seemed to have a powerful supporter. Looking at the book that Bint placed before him, he opened the cover. His words—these were his words, pressed into paper and bound, like the words of his precious books. He raised his shaky voice and read from the first page. *"Rationality and Logic,"* he began, "was the first codification of Bioran thought. It laid out the rules for logic. These rules are listed in the first chapter..."

The Justices followed little of the first lesson, though they remained dutifully hunched over their books. Any impulse they might have had to flip through the pages or inspect their fingernails was quelled by the presence of Varzin. That he was the eldest of them and his seventy years demanded respect was only one reason for them to emulate his studiousness as he attended to the lecture with conscious gravity. He had the same wise and in-scrutable aspect that Muhrroh did, and when that placidity was disturbed by uncharacteristic stridency, it was reason to take notice. Varzin had brought a matter of great import to the Circle, and he was determined that it be acted upon. He had found evidence of the dangers of mysticism, evidence that was strong enough to convince even Nosselin that Nanianism should be eliminated. Even now, as the wagon filled with contraband rolled by on the streets above them, bound for the fire that burned outside the city, it carried evidence: letters, treatises, writings about Nanianism. Prayers from the subversive faithful. Admonitions to follow Nanian instead of the law. Assertions that Nanian was greater than the law. Everything in the wagon had been gathered from outside Cassile. The rumor that the rioters in Origh two weeks ago had had mystical writings in their possession had not been confirmed even by the guards who arrested them, but the contraband wagon proved that such an unimaginable thing was truly, terribly possible.

Mandera was in ruins. Without the money that had given it life, it had fallen, this giant that had once been the greatest force on the continent. If Mandera could fall—every Justice in the chamber knew as he bent his head over his book, whether that head was wigged or not—then Dabion could fall. That the people would disregard the law was as unimaginable as a Lord Justice holding Muhrroh in disrespect, and yet evidence of that disregard had been found. Varzin had brought it in with his own hands. The one last standard and strength that supported Dabion was in danger of crumbling. The men below ground would fight to hold it fast with words, and with the arms of the Black Force, and with the fire that cast its smoke over the roofs of Insigh.

# 10

TOD HAD GONE SO FAR AS TO BUY THE CARROTS and peel them before he decided it would be foolish to invite Elzith. From the mess on his desk he pulled a pen and an ink bottle that was not dried up, then opened the box where his own book was stored. He took out a fresh quarrel, a packet of pages that were still blank. He'd decided to begin a journal.

> *No reason E should come to dinner. First time was test. Now I've passed, no reason for her to accept. Feel silly if she says no. Wasted carrots.*

He felt a need to put Elzith in his book. She would be part of his life now, one way or the other. Some unknown danger had decided it. Strange, he thought, that the unknown was deciding the course of his life. The problems he knew about had always been quite enough for him.

There was a page in his book that he had forgotten

about, one he saw now as he was turning through the pages. It was near the front, and had been one of the first he'd sewn in. It was a small square, thin, and nothing was written on it. It was a sheet woven of delicate fibers, made by the first Healer he'd met, the one who'd tended him—in Elzith's tidy words—"after an excess of alcohol." Tod remembered little of that encounter, and had forgotten about it entirely until Elzith reminded him with her report. Of course, he'd been unconscious for much of that time, and had missed whatever powers the Healer had worked on him. When he'd woken up, lying disoriented within the canvas walls of one of the tents that Healers normally lived in, the man had been sitting harmlessly beside him on a stool, working intently on weaving this sheet. Tod had peered at it through blurry eyes. Flax? Straw? Tod still didn't know what the sheet was made of, but it was so fine that the light shone through it when he turned it.

Now Tod remembered something else. The Healer had spoken to him, a few words in the seconds before departing and leaving Tod to his consequences.

"I've mended you, but I've not cured you. That work is your own. Not yours alone, though. You will find help for it."

Tod picked up his pen again and continued writing on the new pages.

*Help—Keller. E also mended, not cured. My turn. Should've told Loyd.*

Of course, he hadn't remembered it when he talked to Loyd. He hadn't remembered the Healer's words until he found the woven page.

"Why are you doing that?" he'd asked the Healer.

The man had smiled. "Patience."

"You've been doing it since—since you . . ." Tod hadn't wanted to mention the healing, and even though he hadn't felt any magic in him, it still bothered him to think of it.

"I've been doing it since I knew you," the Healer had replied, his voice secretive as mist. "A Sage told me I should make it for you."

Tod had wondered about that. He'd made himself dizzy with wondering, really, and now that he recalled this conversation, he was amazed that he'd forgotten it for so long. Sages were what the wandering madmen called themselves.

There were hundreds, maybe, of the wanderers, traveling alone and in packs. Tod had seen one himself when he was younger. The wandering woman had been sitting beside the road, halfway between Origh and the Karrimian border, talking to herself. She was pale and bony, with wild eyes and wilder hair. Tod remembered it had been stained in streaks of color, braided and strewn with feathers and leaves, and he felt foolish now for not recognizing the same hair on the intruder outside his window. Tod's brothers had thrown rocks at the old woman—he thought she must have been old, but there was really no way to guess her age—and she hadn't moved. Tod had been stunned, and had hung back as they passed. "They'll arrest you if you stay here," he'd tried to warn her. The woman had continued to talk in some sort of bizarre poetry, uninterrupted, as if he hadn't spoken, but she'd looked right at him. Tod searched his mind to see if his recollections were pulling back any of those strange words, but he couldn't remember even one of them.

The wanderers were all utterly mad, so mad that the lawmakers succeeded where they'd failed with the Healers. Every wanderer they got their hands on was locked up in an asylum. The madmen apparently made no attempts to escape or evade capture, which was odd, since they claimed to have magical powers. There was a folklore among the Healers that attributed powers to the wanderers—Sages—that were even greater than their own abilities to heal. If the madmen ever showed any of these powers, Tod thought, it might keep them out of prison. The Healers' powers earned them respect, at least; even if the lawmakers didn't like them, they left the Healers alone. Maybe the wanderers had no magic after all, and they'd just gotten mixed up with fairy tales and myths about witches and magicians.

There was no reason to take the Healer's words seriously, Tod thought. *A Sage told me I should make it for you.* A Sage could just as easily have told him he should sprout wings and fly. Tod tried to scoff but he couldn't. He couldn't bring himself to ridicule the wanderers, madmen though they were. The same lawmakers who

wanted to shut them up in asylums wouldn't be any
more merciful to Tod if they knew about his dreams.

Tod gripped his pen tightly and stared hard at his
journal. He wasn't going to think about the dreams, the
shadowy faces he saw in them. He had to get his mind
back to where it had been before. He'd been thinking of
Elzith. He wanted to see her. He was in love—according
to Loyd—and the only way to solve the problem was to
be realistic. He'd talk to her. He wouldn't invite her to
dinner; she had no reason to accept. If he wanted to talk
to her, he should just go down and do it.

When she opened the door to his nervously tardy
knock, he saw that she was holding a book. He wanted to
see it, but as his eyes drifted toward it they passed her
pale face, the black shirt unbuttoned to its center seam
and untucked from her breeches, her bare feet. Within
the shadowy plunge of her shirt her ribs were visible,
stark against the fair skin between her breasts. So fair, so
pale, because of that black shirt, he told himself. She
only looked that pale. The scar he couldn't see terrified
his imagination from somewhere below. Tod swallowed
and looked down at her feet. They were small, the toes
almost childlike, like her hands with their small fingers,
hardly seeming able to grip a pistol. Tod shook himself
and focused his eyes on the book.

"What are you reading?" he began.

Part of a smile twisted the corner of Elzith's mouth.
"Have a look," she said, casually handing the volume
to him.

He was captivated. The book was exquisite. The leather was of a texture he'd never felt before, even in his father's best work, more like fine fabric than animal skin. The corners were edged with caps, delicately wrought of metal and jewels. The embossing on the covers was pigmented brightly, and the edges of the pages were gilded. Tod opened the covers, examining the endpapers and their painstakingly detailed illumination.

"It's something, isn't it?" Elzith said. "Manderan, obviously, of the last century."

Tod finally looked at the book's title. *A History of the Glorious and Sovereign Country of Mandera,* it said in ruby-colored letters. He searched for the printer's mark in the flyleaf. *P L Rathsen 643.* The numbers and the printer's initials were crafted into fanciful animals. "It's—it's beautiful," he gasped, looking up at Elzith.

The chill struck him without warning. It happened when he met her eyes, dark and black and deep as water. But her eyes are green, a piece of his mind said. It was drowned by the chill, the deep cold, so far down in the core of him that he could not feel it on his skin. It froze his mind in a last image of fear.

And just as suddenly, it was gone. Elzith had turned to attend to something on her diminutive stove. Her eyes would again be green, Tod was sure. He had imagined it, he told himself, his daydreaming had gotten the better of him. But he recognized the fearful image he'd been left with, and it wore his great-aunt's face, and it smelled of death and dreams.

"It was hard to find that book, as you can imagine," Elzith was saying, idly, her face to the wall where the stove was propped.

Tod realized the volume was still in his hands, the cover turned upside down. He righted it. *A History of the Glorious and Sovereign Country of Mandera.* "You read history?"

There was the sound of laughter. If Tod hadn't known better he'd have looked for someone else in the room. "I have an interest in reading history, yes," Elzith replied. "Finding it is another matter. That book in your hands calls itself history. It's a fine little story meant to flatter its author's patron. Those merchant leaders liked to make themselves look good, and they were more than willing to hire other people to do it. That was written at the height of the Ikinda Alliance, when Mandera was ruling trade overseas and pulling in money like water. You'd think they were every name of god. It's something else entirely to read Dabion's history of the same period. All the Dabionian histories were written after the Ikinda Alliance failed and the economy collapsed. The evil, wasteful Manderans were doomed to misery and subjugation, to hear the Dabionians tell it. It's hard to find out what Dabion wrote before the collapse. The Justices are always rewriting things." Elzith turned from the stove, back toward Tod. "Do you remember your grammar school classes?"

"Ah…" Tod tried to think back. Childhood was another lifetime, before the gin, before his great-aunt's death. "Something about benevolent law, Dabionian Civil Rule, the Manderan economic collapse, 742. The law saving us from chaos, that sort of thing."

"Just what they wanted you to hear," Elzith said. She began to eat out of the pan in her hand, something mashed and bland-looking. "Forgive me for not offering you dinner," she told him, "but you wouldn't want this anyway."

Tod felt himself laugh, and felt the weight of the book in his relaxed hands.

"But I never thought that was enough," Elzith continued. "I always wanted to know more. Certainly my employers told me all I needed to know about modern politics, but I wanted to know why things are this way, what made them this way."

She paused to take another bite. Tod looked at the book again. The detail on the endpapers was a series of interlocking fish wearing crowns. *Sovereign Country,* Tod thought. That claim must have driven the Dabion lawmakers mad. Imagining it made him feel overwhelmed.

"Do you wonder?" Elzith asked him. "Do you wonder what made things this way?"

Tod nodded. History fascinated him in the same way that the books of the Justices did, great secretive tomes read by other people. He could ask Elzith about history and he had no doubt she could answer him, but it would be as if she were speaking a different language. Another idea was in his mind. "It must be lonely work."

She ate silently for several minutes. Her brow did not wrinkle the way Keller's did when he was deep in thought. When she spoke it was in a drier voice than before. "I've never given much thought to loneliness," she said. "That is all there is."

Tod could think of no reply. Whatever polite conversation he'd hoped to have was fruitless. Elzith asked whether he'd seen anything unusual around the flat, another stranger, any suspicious movement from Shaan. Tod had not. He'd been sleeping in the afternoons for the past few days, trying to replenish the sleep he'd lost while working on Justice Paloman's job, so he had not seen Shaan at all. Elzith assured Tod she'd seen nothing in the last few days that suggested a threat. She wished him a good evening and showed him the door.

He did not work on his book anymore that night. He sat by his window for some time before he fastened the shutters, watching the empty road that led into Origh. Tod wasn't thinking of Shaan, though, and he wasn't worrying about anyone coming down that road. He found it easy to imagine he'd never see anyone on that road again. Loneliness is all there is. It was the first time in three years that he'd realized he was lonely.

# 11

I COULD PLAY HIM, I COULD PLAY HIM SO EASILY. BUT
it wouldn't be fair.

The classic confidence game is this: Make your subject place his confidence in you, even despite his best
judgment. The greater the risk, the more he has to silence his doubts to believe in you, the better the game.
You only need to take a token from him in order to win.
There are men who call themselves confidence artists
who prey on widows or wealthy spinsters, helpless
women keeping afloat on old money, and these men seduce the women to gain their fortunes. That is no game.
Such men are nothing more than common thieves—
worse, since even thieves have their honor. The helpless,
the fragile, will give their confidence to anyone who
looks strong enough to pull them out of their misery. It's
no game to win it.

I did play him, it's true. I made the first moves. This
book, have a look at it—I said. It's something isn't it?
Manderan, of the last century. History is something
I know a little about. I can deduce Tod does not.

Bookbinders rarely have time to read what's in the pages they put together, and they revere them like some sacred mystery that buys them life. That book in your hands, a fine little story meant to flatter et cetera. Let me tell you about it. It's something I know that you don't. I can give you a little of this knowledge, I can share a little of this secret, if you trust me.

The next step, encourage your subject to relax in your presence. Never mind that you've seen me with a gun, or that your life is in danger just by living in the flat above me. I'm going to tell a little joke—mashed turnips, ick, you don't want any—and you're going to laugh. You don't want any. Trust me.

Now make your subject think he's in control, think it's his game. Rouse his curiosity, get him to ask questions. Questions you'll feed him, of course. Here's a little bit about me, haven't you wondered what I'm like? I know you have. I'll share a little with you. I like history. Isn't that interesting? Here's a secret about the big men, the ones without names—they won't teach me history. Now I've given you something that other people don't know. You should be excited, you're in on the secrets. The big men won't tell me how things got to be the way they are. But I want to know. Don't you want to know? Aren't you curious? Why don't you ask me? I know things. I'm an expert. You can trust me.

That is your last move; you only have to wait and see if you've won. Listen to what the subject says now, see if he asks for your knowledge, see if he gives you his trust. But he doesn't say what I expect.

*It must be lonely work.*

He turns the game around on me. He demands the answer. He wants me to give him my confidence. He's playing me now, as I suspected all along. Why did he come down here, if not to play me? What is he? A counterspy? An agent of Mandera or Azassi? Or an even longer shot—does he know that intruder, that Healer or madman, that Sage, whoever cast the rune, whoever was trying to spell me?

But it's all ridiculous. Tod is no agent, no counterspy. I've read him before, I know he's honest. I've trusted the power all my life, and it's never failed me.

It's what makes me Loyd's best. Among his associates he'll speak of my detachment, he'll tell the abandoned child story, he'll speak of the lack of mother love that made me hard and unemotional, an ideal observer, excellent for espionage. Even the big men have a taste for melodrama. But of greater value to Loyd is my ability to read truth. Poets and others have called the eye a passage to the soul. Their figure of speech is real for me. I can read that soul through the passage, see if it is truthful, and do more, sometimes. There are a few others of us in the Secret Force. Some years ago we were called Sor'raian operatives, a precious nickname bestowed by the big men. The Healers have been traced to Sor'rai, although you'll never hear them speak of their homeland, and the madmen seem to come from there as well. We operatives

may all be descended from that sort. Then the insurrec-
tions in the other countries intensified, and Dabion's
lawmakers stepped up their hatred of all things not
themselves. The suggestion that there were foreigners in
their own Secret Force was unthinkable. The nickname
vanished. If I ever met any of these other operatives, any
of my distant kin, I didn't know it.

I have no reason to doubt the power. I read Tod and I
know he's honest. I only doubt because I've cracked. My
performance is flawed. I trembled when I found the
rune, and I hesitated when Tod asked if I could find the
man who cast it. Even someone as naïve as Tod could
have seen through my act. The hole in my gut took my
composure with it. I've lost my perfection. I wanted to
play Tod to prove I could still win a game.

But it would not be fair. I know more than he does. I
dove into his eyes, looking for a reason why he'd come to
my door, and he saw me do it. He recognized it without
knowing what it was. I felt the chill of that recognition
sweep over him. He has felt power, something other than
the invisible hand of a Healer, who would have left no
memory of his work. Tod has felt power and he does not
understand it. This makes him vulnerable, like the helpless widows. I could play him, it would be an easy game,
but it would not be a fair game.

The rune is the real game. This is what I should think
of, rather than wasting my efforts gaming with Tod. The
rune was a spell, an attack of mind control. Whoever cast
it, I can guess, knows who I am and knows my powers.

In the instant that I allowed it contact I felt that it was targeted to me. That is not a sound deduction, though, as clay has no eyes and no thoughts, and there is no other evidence to explain its source. If the intruder Tod saw was a Sage, as he described, there is no way of connecting the rune to him. Not enough is known about the Sages. I can deduce nothing until I learn more.

I did not report all of this to the local authority or the Administrator. Only Loyd knows of my power. I told the others only that it was a spell of attack. Most of the big men would be just as happy to blame it on Cassile. There are rumors that those mystics in their monasteries are wizards. It's a ridiculous rumor. I saw in the eyes of that boy I bullied in Cassile that he's never touched anything like magic. I can't explain to the big men how I got my proof, though. As if it would matter. Proof means nothing to them when they have wars to wage.

What, then? What do I do now? I have no choice but to wait, again, wait for something to come to me, some bit of evidence, some explanation. Or something else, another spell, another attack. Another invitation from Tod. Will I play him again? Will I find out what that thing in his mind is, that recognition of magic, that bizarre honesty? Or will I keep my promise not to be unfair? Even thieves have their honor. I wonder if old, broken spies do.

# 12

LORD JUSTICE VARZIN WAS RETURNING HOME. HE spent as much time as he could in Insigh, preferring it to his home offices in Aligh in District Six. The weather was better, he told his retainers; the food was finer and the service more competent, he admonished his household. Then he would vanish into his chambers, not to be seen again unless his Greater Justices required him for counsel.

The men in his stables claimed to know him best. You could tell much about a man by tending the horses he's ridden, they said. The Lord Justice's horses were always spooked. A nervous man, some of the stable hands claimed, lowering their voices lest an eavesdropper report them for subversion. Beneath the calm and despite his seventy years, they said, Varzin had the quaking heart of a terrified infant, and the horses knew it. But others— those who were more likely to have relatives in the Halls of Justice to watch them—said it was because he rode the horses close to Lake Azin on his route back from District One.

Lake Azin, in the northwest, divided Dabion from Sor'rai. An odd property of the lake was that it could be seen from any point in District Six, even at the farthest corner, as if the borders of the District had been established by determining where this effect ended, and the other Districts' lawmakers had put themselves firmly outside of that line. That was not the lake's only strange property. Azin had resisted all attempts to be crossed. Exploration vessels had been turned back, their crews befuddled, their captains reluctantly and tersely declaring the body of water unnavigable. Cartographers had been confounded in their attempts to map what could be seen of Sor'rai across the lake. Their sketches, done one day, never matched what they observed the next. No one seemed willing to cross the rocky land bridge that separated the lake from the ocean in the extreme north, yet there were often reports that people were camped there. They were the only people who could be described as citizens of Sor'rai, and even they were only observed leaving it. No humans had ever been seen across the lake, although children's stories placed fairies and elves there, dancing on the shore on the Sor'raian side. The nomads were usually described with the physical characteristics of Healers or madmen. That was what led the authorities to declare that both groups were of Sor'rai. Healers never identified their homeland, but they were not native to any of the Five Countries, nor could their lifestyle or unusual gifts be linked to what was known of the peoples of Biora or Siva. The wandering madmen called themselves Sages and claimed to have magical powers, which they never displayed even when captured, tortured, and locked away to starve in asylums. No evidence outside of those rocky straits could link the nomads more conclusively to Sor'rai, and by the time the authorities of District Six reached the camps to investigate, the wanderers had always disappeared. The lake and the land across it remained an unsolvable mystery.

Lord Justice Varzin's retainers verified that his homeward route passed close to Lake Azin. It was part of his jurisdiction, they defended, and he was going to enforce the law there. The region's enigmatic nature made it an ideal attraction for the lawless, who might lurk there hoping to evade timid authorities. The Lord Justice was not so timid. If no one else would bring order to the land across the lake, he would. Let no one jeer that Varzin often halted his party's progress, leaving them to wait on the grass as he urged his nervous horse ever closer to the banks of Lake Azin, his eyes combing the forested distance, searching for signs of evil among the unpopulated trees. He was the prime agent of the law and such vigilance was his prerogative.

In time this agent of the law withdrew, turned his horse away from the water, and led his relieved retinue back toward their homes. As the travelers left the lake behind them, one remained. He watched as they drew away and grew small, breathed deeply as their scent faded, narrowed his eyes as the Lord Justice dissolved out of sight.

The man on the shore was not part of Varzin's party, although he was dressed like any one of them. He could impersonate them easily, if he wanted to. He would give his name as Magus if he thought it was necessary. If he wanted to not be seen, though, and he usually did, he would not be seen. But he could not do one thing, and that was to leave the shore. He watched this party of intruders withdraw with as much resentment as relief, but he remained silent. When a young and incompetent clerk scurried back to the lake to retrieve some document or piece of rubbish that had fallen out of his hands, he would not know the man called Magus was there at all.

# 13

TOD WAS SERIOUS THIS TIME, HE WAS GOING TO ASK Elzith to dinner. He was going to make her carrots and invite her up for some company. He could encourage her to talk about history—she seemed to like that. He didn't spend time imagining the ways she could decline. He went straight down the steps and knocked on her door.

There was a moment when he was ready to abandon his resolve, when he heard all those imagined refusals tardily echo in his head. He was standing in her doorway, watching her look at him, her head slightly tilted in that attitude of carelessness. But she didn't refuse. "All right," she said neatly, and ducked behind her door to fetch the key to its lock.

Tod's worktable was more cluttered than usual, but most of it was on one side. He pushed the lighter half clear and dragged both chairs to that side. Elzith slid into one chair with the grace of a cat, a large cat like the ones that came from Siva, a tiger. There were stories of tigers from Siva; people used to see them in circuses in Mandera. Tod decided his comparison was too much. "I haven't looked closely at your work," Elzith was saying, her voice notably polite. "Do you mind if I do?"

Tod answered that it was fine, as he turned to busy himself at the stove. In the time that followed he noticed the quiet. Elzith wasn't saying anything about history, nothing about books, and she had no questions for him. There was only quiet, and the occasional whisper of turning pages.

Tod cleared his throat lightly. "Have you found out who the man at the window was?" he asked in the silence. There had been no sight of him since the first night, and no sign of threat at all since the strange rune. Tod found himself not caring much who the man at the window was.

"They're still investigating. They have some leads, and they've already addressed some parties who might have proven dangerous. We shouldn't be bothered by intruders anymore." Elzith sounded as unconcerned as Tod felt, and a little rehearsed. Tod was happy when she finished her answer and the easy quiet returned. He sighed, feeling contentment. Quaint, he thought. A quiet evening at home. Given the choice, he could get used to it.

"You certainly have patience," Elzith remarked as Tod brought the food to the table. She ran a thin finger along the many rows of stitching in a half-finished book.

Tod sat, less gracefully than Elzith had. "It can be learned," he answered.

Elzith nodded very slightly, a trace of a smile on her face. Then she put down the book, thanked him as she served herself, and there was quiet again as they ate.

Everything was peaceful, Tod thought, until there was a furious rapping at the door. His fork dropped with a clatter and his face wrinkled up. Elzith did not react, waiting until she'd swallowed before asking, smoothly, "Expecting someone?"

Tod went to the door and opened it to Shaan's ruddy face.

"Evening, chap," he said, hissing urgently while attempting—badly—to sound casual. He was hunched in such a way that his shoulders filled up the doorway. "I can come in for a second, right?" He blustered in without waiting for an answer. "Need you to hold something for me." He drew a small sack out of a voluminous pocket and thrust it into Tod's hand, hurrying toward the window to latch the shutters.

Elzith continued to eat, looking unsurprised. Tod was at a loss. He started back toward his chair, untying the sack to see what Shaan was so worked up about. An instant before it fell open, he realized he should have misgivings about this. As with letting Morrn and his still move in, Tod realized it a bit too late.

Inside the sack was a dagger, an ornamental weapon, ornately carved, studded with finely faceted gems. It was sheathed in impressively tooled leather. Tod realized his eyes were huge before he thought about how he was gawking over Shaan's theft. He snapped his eyes away and sank the loot back into the sack. Then he looked at Elzith. Her face was emotionless as always, but her eyes were trained on the sack. She had seen the dagger. And then Tod looked across the room. Shaan had seen Elzith.

"Ah, chap!" laughed Shaan, losing all his nervousness in a mass of leering. That, at least, was convincing. "Interrupting something, am I? Ha-ha!" His eyes bulged at Elzith.

Tod tried to distract himself by dropping back into his chair, taking another bite of his dinner, and turning toward Elzith. Then he saw something very strange. Elzith was returning Shaan's look, even more convincingly.

"What have we here?" Shaan was drawling. "Haven't met this pretty one," he said, or something like it. Tod was used to ignoring Shaan's words. He was not, however, used to Elzith giggling, batting her eyelashes, or fawning on his own arm. She seemed to be enticing Shaan by clinging to Tod. Shaan was adoring it.

Elzith draped herself on Tod's arm, drawing up her knees in a way that was coy and artificially naïve. Her fingers brushed the back of his hand, he felt her breath near his cheek. "Oh!" she cried in a most foreign voice, "can I see it? Please!" Tod found himself suddenly glad to be sitting down, and behind a table. Having lost his voice, he handed over the sack, which she opened with an attitude of rapture. The gold of the dagger's hilt reflected in her wide eyes. She can't be serious, Tod insisted to himself, watching Shaan continue to leer. Tod started to giggle.

"It's bea-u-ti-ful!" Elzith crooned, as Shaan hung on each syllable. "Where did you get it?"

Shaan laughed throatily. "Ah, now, little miss!" he teased. "I can't tell you that, but, well, maybe I can boast a little." He seized the chair from the corner of the room and dragged it to the table, sitting on it in a rakish sprawl. "Let's say I—ah—*borrowed* it, from a certain chap in the city. Big house on Scrivener Street, walls all around it, and full of guards. Not very understanding, those guards, sods! But—yes, old Shaan got around them, yes I did!" He laughed again and Elzith echoed it. Tod thought Shaan was a fool, Elzith being an agent of the law, but he noticed she was out of uniform, and Shaan probably had never seen or recognized her in it. What she wore now was like the clothes that Tod had first seen her in, the gray shirt untucked, the breeches baring her legs below the knee. Shaan went on about the house and guards, barking dogs, and his incredible skill at picking inconvenient locks. Elzith went on fawning. Tod started thinking about illegal establishments in Karrim and how long it had been since he last visited them. He flushed. Get back to the moment at hand, he tried to tell himself. Shaan was a thief. The evidence was in front of him.

"Well then," Shaan said finally, "I hate to leave, but can't stay in one place too long!" He laughed and winked, as if he were talking about sweeping the street rather than committing a crime that could make him disappear. He got out of his chair, not bothering to return it to its place near the shuttered window, and sauntered toward the door. "See you again, chap." He winked at Tod. "Sometime later! And you too," he dropped his voice at Elzith, as if arranging a tryst without Tod's knowledge. He was laughing still as he went out and closed the door behind him.

The instant it settled in the jamb, Elzith was on her feet. The mooning look had vanished; she moved quickly and straight, with no more of the flirtatious and easy posture. She latched the door, and as she turned back toward the table she was tying up the sack in her hands. "I'm sorry if that made you uncomfortable," she said to Tod, her voice low and serious, "but I think this will be safer with me."

Tod cleared his throat. His face felt cooler but his hands were now starting to shake. "What is it?"

"Nothing important in itself," she said smoothly, "except for the man Shaan stole it from. And the man who had it before him."

"But Shaan wouldn't tell you who he got it from."

Elzith sat down again. "He told me enough," she said. "With some information my employers have, we can determine who the owner was. The answer can be put together," and here Elzith raised her eyes and fixed them on Tod, "but I would advise you not to. You don't want information that could prove dangerous to you."

She turned her attention back to her plate, resuming

her meal as if there had been no interruption. Tod picked up his fork but found he'd lost his appetite. His attempt at being a host was failing again. "You've done this before."

"Oh, that act?" A wry smile crossed her face, briefly. "It's been a while since I've done that, but I did a good enough show. Not that it was a challenge. He was too easy a game."

"You were wonderful" tumbled out of Tod's mouth.

Elzith abandoned her plate this time, turning to face him fully. The posture did nothing to create a connection between them. Her voice was as cold as an empty courtroom. "Tod, I won't play you," she said. "I won't manipulate you, I don't have anything to gain from it. You're in danger here, but I won't put you in any more if I can help it. Keep out of it, Tod. Keep your distance."

She rose then, the sack in her hand, and headed for the door. "Lock it behind me," she said, and waited there until he got to his feet. She was out of the door before he could try to say anything to her. He'd asked her up for company.

It's her training, he told himself as he began to clean things up. The sun, which had only started to set when he'd started dinner, was entirely down. He'd let it get dark again and had to search for matches. She has to be cautious, he told himself. She has to keep secrets, to keep her distance. *Forced withdrawal,* he scribbled on a page of his book, which he'd left out of its box. *Must be lonely.*

He put the fold of papers back in the box and put it away. It might take a long time, he thought, to help her. He'd wanted a drink every day at the start, but in time that thirst had lessened. He had practice at patience. He would wait.

# 14

THE OFFICE WAS UNDERGROUND, NOT HIGH IN THE towers of the Great Hall, where crystalline windows looked down on Insigh. It was not in the concealed barracks where the Secret Force operatives were trained, a building tucked among the repetitive façades of lesser courts, guarded by a clerk indistinguishable from the hundreds of others. Loyd's office was buried in a maze of storage rooms under an old, lesser court building, where inferior clerks without the status to work in the Great Hall scurried like mice to retrieve records for the important men. Loyd, in his nondescript clothing, was not noticed by the clerks, who never raised their eyes from their weary feet. When the woman arrived at his door, she was in the uniform skirt and bodice of a cleaning woman, a basket at her hip, nodding with lowered eyes in answer to a passing clerk who gave her an order to mop a dirty floor several doors down.

"They won't let you rest, will they?" Loyd said.

Elzith let out her breath shortly through her nose. Loyd didn't expect any more of a laugh from her.

"Although I must say *I* was intending to give you a rest, taking you off the Force. I certainly never expected two formal reports from you within your first season away."

"You took me off the Force because I have identifying scars, Loyd," she replied, refusing, as usual, to be humored. "And you can never expect coincidences. Especially not this kind." She reached among the dirty rags in her basket and pulled out a small but heavy sack.

Loyd untied it with no show of curiosity. He recognized what he saw inside, though, from reports that had described it, reports that could not be admitted into court to prosecute the man who had allegedly owned and wielded it. "This is what I think it is," he said, the characteristic question-not-question.

Elzith nodded. "From the Smyth assignment. Let me tell you how I got it." She related the visit from Shaan and repeated his description of the house he stole the dagger from.

"The house of Smyth's connection in Dabion," Loyd said, confirming Elzith's deduction. "Well, with that description, and knowing which of the Justices would have had the ability to suppress the criminal reports against Smyth, we should be able to narrow it down." Loyd smiled lightly, the proud father smile. "Good work, Elzith."

"It wasn't my good work," she answered. "It was dumb luck. Coincidence, that dagger falling into my lap, two years after the assignment."

"But we can identify Smyth's insider now," Loyd soothed. "That is the point. It hardly matters what means were used."

This time Elzith laughed aloud, and bitterly. "Of course. It hardly matters."

In another life, Loyd might have felt guilty about leading Elzith on like this. The guilt was eased by his realization that she knew exactly what he was doing. She was his best. "But it would be hard for you to think so, wouldn't it? You endured quite a bit on the Smyth assignment."

She met his eyes, judging his words for only an instant. "Yes, Loyd. Why do you mention it?" Flat, unemotional, unyielding, but those eyes had a weariness in them. There were wrinkles beginning to form there, and gray strands in her chestnut hair. Elzith was twenty-eight.

"It can't be far from your mind," Loyd said, "especially with this reminder. The stress of it must be remarkable." He turned the dagger over in his hands. "Elzith, you are tired."

She did not reply. There was no reply.

"You asked me yourself for a leave from the game."

"I asked to *quit* the game," Elzith corrected, expectedly. "Obviously I was under some delusion. I can't just walk away from it, knowing what I do. But at the time I'd just recovered from nearly having the life stabbed out of me. I was not entirely rational."

"But you were in need of rest. I was wrong to give you another assignment so soon."

Elzith's eyes narrowed. "What are you telling me, Loyd?"

"I am offering you a rest. Two weeks off from your assignment."

"So you won't let me leave, but you'll let me sit at home and wait to be called in again. A dog waiting to hear his master's voice." She shook her head. "You wouldn't play me like that, Loyd. What are you up to?"

Loyd sighed and patted Elzith's unresponsive hand. "My dear, so diligent in her work."

"I hate my work. I have no respect for these men and their games."

Loyd dropped his kind paternal attitude. "But you have respect for me," he said. "And I am ordering you to take leave of your assignment for the next sixteen days."

She would not argue. Loyd knew she would not. There were aspects of her that he did not understand, although he'd tried to find a cause for them in her past. He had to accept these aspects as given, like the hours on the clock. He knew them well: her loyalty, her obedience, her trust—almost—of a very few. He was among that number whom she had inexplicably found worthy, and Loyd knew her loyalty and obedience would not fail him. Elzith stood and took up her servingwoman's basket, nodded a curt acceptance, and exited his office.

He was indeed a father figure to her, he supposed. Why she should have a need for such a figure, given her history, was beyond him. Others with similar childhoods had no recognition of authority. But if environment was not the cause, perhaps it was in her blood, like her rare gifts. He prized Elzith for these, as he did for her detachment, as he did for her utter loyalty to him, which surpassed the blind patriotism or hatred of other countries that drove most of his other operatives. She was more reliable, more effective. The best player at a game she despised. She would play it for him until it destroyed her.

Loyd rubbed his eyes. Age was beginning to affect him, he thought, watching his hands shake. He needed a rest himself. To quit, perhaps. But to whom would he go with his threats to quit? It was as foolish a fantasy as Elzith's had been. Still, he would protect her as best he could. He needed her safely away from the Black Force, out of public view, for a short time, while he conducted some investigations. One of his other Sor'raian operatives was missing, and he did not know why.

# 15

---

"IF *PRIME* IS TRUE AND *SECOND* IS TRUE, THEN *PRIME or second* is true."

Jereth was reading from a page in his book, his transcriptions of *Rationality and Logic*. The Lord Justices, arrayed in their ring before him, pored over their copies like schoolchildren.

"If *prime* is true and *second* is false, then *prime or second* is true."

It was his third lesson with the Circle. Jereth had utterly forgotten the first one, and only Bint's meticulous notes reminded him where he'd ended it. That planning proved useless, though, as Nosselin was absent from the second meeting, sending an assistant who recited a lengthy formal complaint and sparked several hours' worth of objections and injunctions and legal arguments of a complexity that Jereth had only ever read about in his long-ago years of schooling. The session had dragged on into the late hours, long after Jereth was dismissed, so he did not hear its outcome, but when he arrived today he saw Nosselin sitting morosely in his

place. Jereth was directed to his podium and began the
lesson where it should have started on the second day, by
enumerating the rules of logic.

"If *prime* is false and *second* is true, then *prime or second* is true."

Jereth paused to moisten his throat. As he raised a
glass to his lips, he glanced around the Circle. Frahn was
nodding but his brow was wrinkled. Timbrel's face was
crumpled in utter confusion. Hysthe's wig lay in a heap
beside his book, and he ran his hands over his cropped
hair. Jereth wondered, in a moment of levity so rare he
nearly choked on the water, whether Hysthe was trying
to massage in the information. He put the glass down
quickly and looked away toward something else. Jannes
was scribbling intricate notes on a sheet of paper, periodically crossing things out. Nosselin stared at his book
and had not objected once. Lord Councilor Muhrroh
watched Jereth and nodded in what seemed to be approval rather than understanding. Varzin was doing the
same.

"If *prime* is false and *second* is false, then *prime or second* is false."

Jereth had always been enchanted by the words of his
precious books. They whispered their secrets in their
rustling pages, carrying him back to an ancient time.
When he read them he was in the presence of the ancient
Biorans. When he spoke the words aloud it was with
their ghostly voices. They changed him, possessed him
with their wisdom until he was a wise man. But there

was something else about the words of the ancient scholars, something he realized as he watched the faces of the Lord Justices. The words of his books were not only powerful, they were his alone, a secret language only he understood, a magic only he possessed. The other men in the room, for all their temporal power, could not grasp it.

"If *prime* is true and *second* is true, then *if prime then second* is true."

A giddiness filled Jereth. It was a feverish feeling, a fear that what he saw was false, that his senses were deceived, that he was dreaming or possessed of fancies. The thought that it was true was even more feverish. They did not understand and he did. His star was rising. He was coming into a power of which his fifty-eight years had been deprived, until now.

"If *prime* is true and *second* is false, then *if prime then second* is ..."

"How much more is there?" cried Nosselin, finally looking up from his book.

There was a general sigh around the chamber, as the Lord Justices gasped for breath at this unexpected reprieve from their difficult lesson. Then Frahn said, wryly, "We appear to be halfway down page eight. It would seem we have half a page left of the rules."

The wooden room echoed again with a breath of uncomfortable laughter. Nosselin, though, chose not to take the bait. He turned to Muhrroh for an appeal. "What use can these rules possibly be to us?" he pleaded. "They mean nothing."

"No rule has meaning in and of itself," the Lord Councilor decreed. "It is the significance of the rule which is meaningful."

"And if I might add," Varzin said softly, from the end of the table, "the significance of these rules is the new paradigm which they represent."

"A paradigm can be summed up in a sentence," growled Nosselin. "The Cassilians are mystics. The Azassians are warmongers."

"But if we do not wish to be as simple as this, we must have a deeper understanding." The room was finally quiet at these words of Muhrroh's. Even Nosselin would not dispute him a second time. "These rules are the foundation upon which Bioran thought was based. To understand that paradigm and to convey it to our people, we must begin at the start. Justice Advisor Paloman, please continue."

"If *prime* is false and *second* is true..." Unlike the second day, when Jereth had watched the legal battle in cold agony, today he was unmoved by this conflict in the Circle's chambers. For all their temporal power, these were only men. Their quarrels were petty. Their words were harmless. Jereth had knowledge beyond their understanding. "...*if prime then second* is true." Varzin nodded. Jereth had his support. Nosselin rubbed his eyes and dropped his head over his book again. Varzin smiled. Jereth had nothing to fear.

"I have some materials which may interest you," Varzin said to Jereth when the lesson was finished and the chamber was emptying. He took from the satchel he carried a number of papers scrolled in a leather binder and unrolled them for Jereth. The sheets displayed grids that were filled with symbols. "A summary of your rules, which they use at the new Bioran school here in Insigh. They are not as fine as your work, certainly, yours being taken directly from the original words of the scholars. These tables were drawn from Dal'Nilaran's book, which you mentioned before, the secondary source, which is all the Insigh school has had. They simplify the rules in graphic form, and there are some among us who may find the simplification useful."

Jereth allowed Varzin to put the scrolls into his hands, murmuring gracious thanks at the compliment. He was gaining practice at that gracious murmur.

"The next meeting of the Circle and our next lesson will be in three weeks," Varzin added. "Time enough for the printer in Origh and the bookbinder I recommended to you."

"Certainly, my lord," Jereth said. "You have my great thanks. I am indebted to you."

"Of course," Varzin intoned, and left the chamber.

Not as fine as my work, certainly, Jereth thought as he bundled the Insigh school tables to carry them back to his rooms, and he thought it again later, when he unrolled them to examine them. But Varzin's encouraging voice had faded by then. The tables were incomprehensible. The

symbols were gibberish to Jereth. Those inferior scholars
with their battered copies of Dal'Nilaran's plagiarized
book had concocted a language so far beyond him that
Jereth could not recognize it as human.

I am a fool, he thought. His reflection stared, wrinkled and rheumy-eyed, from its mirror across the room.
Jereth seized the leather tube that had encased the scrolls
and threw it at the offending mirror. It missed shattering
the glass, which was what Jereth had hoped for, bounc-
ing off the frame instead and rolling under the chest of
drawers.

He sat for a time staring at his failure. In the past,
he'd spent hours each day staring at piles of records,
amended law certificates, his decisions overturned by
higher authorities. He'd watched them stack up while his
docket of new cases went neglected. As to be expected,
he'd told himself. Paloman wasn't even his name. His
father was a Ploughman, the last son of a despised family of farmers, the only one allowed to stay in their part
of District Six when the rest of them were displaced to
Karrim. There was dirt in his blood and no mind in his
head. He wasn't suited to justice. The waxen seals of
other authorities that were stamped on his court records
were proof of that.

The tube moved under the chest, most likely pushed
by a wandering mouse. Jereth painfully pulled himself
out of his chair and crouched on the floor beside the
chest of drawers. He could not reach the tube, though
the sight of his hand sent the mouse scurrying. He had

to pull the lowest drawer out of its frame completely to retrieve the leather case.

He almost replaced the drawer immediately. It was the drawer that contained, wrapped carefully in layers of fabric, his books. I do not deserve them, he thought, but once he laid his hands upon them he was under their spell, just like the first time.

The books had come to him four years ago, the eightieth and final day of the first season, the year 760 by the Common Calendar. Jereth still had the court record preserving that date. The new Insigh school had been open for three years, and Jereth had read a copy of Dal'Nilaran's *Classics*, which one of his clerks had confiscated from a son too rebellious and full of scholarly aspirations to follow quietly in his father's footsteps. The book had been idle reading for Jereth, but it had sparked a strange curiosity, causing him to daydream like a child about the mysterious mountains of Biora. A warning of senility's onslaught, Jereth had thought.

His final case of that day had involved three merchants attempting to smuggle undeclared goods into Azassi. Such incidents had been common since 748, the year Jereth had finally ascended from a clerk's office to his seat as a Lesser Justice, and the year that the borders of Biora were reopened after two centuries of embargo. The old conflicts inspired by Bioran learning were forgotten, the collapse of Mandera's economy drove merchants to find other sources of trade, and so the peacekeeping forces that had been stationed at the narrow mountain pass that

connected Biora to Cassile and the rest of the Five Countries were disbanded. Not that the merchants found
much in Biora. The country had fallen into ruin in its two
hundred years of isolation. The merchants who had crept
out of Biora, crossed the Great River, and made their trail
across the northern passage and into Jereth's hall, were
practically empty-handed.

"Devil's Advocate," Jereth had called, summoning the
merchants' nominal defense.

"These men were only carrying books, your honor,"
the clerk who played devil's advocate had said, gesturing
to the pile of illegal goods that was stacked on his table
before the accused men.

"Was it with intent to sell?" Jereth had asked the
guardsman at the opposite table, who had led the arrest
of the merchants.

"Of course!" crowed the guard. "Doesn't matter what
it is. Azassians don't know their purse from their sack—
they'll buy anything. It's contraband, books or bricks!"

"Books are hardly contraband," the devil's advocate
had protested. He grasped one from the top of the pile
and carried it to the Table of Justice behind which Jereth
sat. "Boards and paper. There is nothing in the law that
assigns value to them. Only what is valuable can be
judged as smuggled goods. These men will testify that
even the Biorans saw no value in them. Shall I call upon
them, your honor?"

Jereth had not responded.

"Your honor, shall the accused men speak?"

Jereth had shaken himself and nodded absently, ignoring the merchants as they stood one by one and told of run-down shacks in Biora, starving women surrounded by sunken-eyed children, emptying out battered trunks and pulling dusty boxes from basements, searching for any scrap or trinket that would fetch a penny from the foreign merchants. Jereth did not care. He had just deciphered the archaic letters that spelled out *Rationality and Logic*. He recognized the title from its reference in the confiscated schoolbook. A foolish dream had suddenly been transformed into reality.

"Contraband, obviously," Jereth had ruled. "These men shall be imprisoned for the requisite time. The books shall be seized." Let a Greater Justice overturn his decision and set the smugglers free. Few would make an attempt at the lengthy and convoluted process required to release the goods from seizure. The books were Jereth's.

# 16

"WHAT ARE YOU DOING HERE?" TOD ASKED, STOP-ping halfway down the steps. Elzith was at the bottom of the hill, on her knees with a hand rake.

She didn't look up as she answered, "Raking. Watch the fourth step, it's still crooked."

Tod looked at the stones under his feet. They were swept clean, and though they were still old and cracked and in need of repair, the dirt had been molded under them so that they were more stable. "You did this?"

Elzith sat back on her heels. "Yesterday. Early, before you went into town. Didn't you notice?"

Tod laughed a little at himself. It had been five days since Elzith had left with Shaan's dagger, and during the first day he hadn't been able to keep himself from check-ing out the windows, looking for her return. Then he'd calmed himself. Patience, he remembered. She'd be back. He'd gotten so patient that he hadn't even looked out the window for the past few days, and he'd missed her work. "I'm sorry, I didn't. It looks wonderful."

She didn't drop immediately back to work, as Tod

expected. She actually stayed there, sitting on her heels, surveying the steps and the hill and the earth in front of her door. She nodded slightly, not quite smiling with pride or contentment.

"But why—" Tod ventured. "What got you started on this?"

"I'm bored as hell," answered Elzith. She brushed damp hair out of her eyes, rubbing a trail of dirt across her brow.

"Can I offer you a drink?"

It was less surprising that she accepted the invitation this time, since it was warm and Elzith was understandably thirsty. She sat at his table without dispute, drinking the water that he offered deeply, and thanked him for the damp cloth he brought so she could clean her face and hands. Tod sat across from her calmly, without tripping over any of his furniture. He was learning. "You don't have—what do you call it—an assignment?"

"I'm on vacation," Elzith muttered from behind the cloth.

"This doesn't sound like a good thing."

She lowered the cloth, eyed him quizzically. "Would you like a vacation? Shall I do your work for you?" Tod realized she was joking with him. He laughed.

"Well, I have a large rush order coming in a few days," he started. Keller had just received another job from the Justice from District One, and Tod would have to bind it. "But I have a few things to wrap up before then." He reached into the pile on the table, drew out a partly

stitched quarrel, and searched for the needle at the end
of the tail of thread.

Elzith pulled her chair in closer and leaned toward
the work.

"You nest the quartos like this, and then you stitch,
over and under." She watched him make a few stitches,
and when he held the pages out toward her, she took his
suggestion and grasped them. Quickly she continued his
chain of stitches, small and even. "Careful of the needle,"
Tod warned, needlessly, since she was so precise. He
doubted she would put red spots on her pages. "You're
better at this than I am."

"No," Elzith said, speaking evenly in time with the
needle. "I couldn't keep it up for long."

Tod sorted through his papers to find something to
work on himself. "Not very exciting, I guess."

Elzith finished out her quarrel. "No. Much less exciting than getting stabbed or shot at." She twisted the needle between her fingers. "What's next?"

Tod searched for the next pages, found them, checked
that they matched the right book, and started folding
them into quartos.

"Amazing," Elzith said. "How did you find the right
page? Order out of chaos."

Tod laughed again. His table was cluttered, but he
knew where everything was. "I don't have much to keep
in order, not as much as you do, I'm sure."

"Order?" Elzith scoffed, sounding more mournful

than sarcastic. "Bringing order to the big men's game is beyond me." And then, "Why am I telling you this?"

"You're bored as hell?"

Elzith nodded, and the edges of her mouth turned crooked. It was, Tod realized, a smile. Then she pointed her needle at the folded pages that Tod was handling, and said, "Are you done with that yet?"

They worked until the light ran out. Tod was grateful for the help, of course, but he was much more pleased about something else. Out of boredom, maybe, or loneliness, Elzith spoke.

"There's a city in the south of Karrim," she said, so absently that Tod was paying more attention to the rhythm of her voice than her words, until he realized what she was saying. She was telling him a story about the city where she was born.

# 17

THERE'S A CITY IN THE SOUTH OF KARRIM, AT THE junction of two rivers, the Manderan River at its southern border, and the Great River that cuts it all off from Cassile. The City, unique in a country of scattered villages and endless farmlands, was established in the last century. Manderan trade was strong overseas then, and the heads of industry extended their reach into their northern neighbor. The City was a clearinghouse for Karrim's produce; farmers went there to unload it, Manderan businessmen went there to trade it, and workmen from all over went there to collect it and ship it across the Five Countries.

Another curiosity of that time was the traffic from Cassile. The land of religion happened to breed a class of wandering poet-musicians, the minstrels, who sang the most earthly of songs and were adored by Mandera. They crossed the river, often passing through the City because—yet another curiosity—a good bridge had been built across the Great River at that point. There were many Manderan elite who took minstrels into their patronage and started them on the road to immortality right there in the City. So with the minstrels' salons, the corn exchanges, and the inns and taverns and shops necessary to serve such mobs, the City was quite a thriving metropolis. Until 742. Good news always floats a while before it takes shape, but bad news is wildfire. Within days of the failure of Mandera's alliance with Ikinda, the City was a shambles. It didn't die, though. Generations had been born who had never touched the plough. There was no going home to the farm for them, so they stayed in the City. Its position was still the crossroads to three countries, though the travelers were no longer wealthy businessmen but stiff-faced lawmakers. The City survived.

We always called it the City, that's all. The Manderans, men with their important business, had another name for it, and the Dabionians had another one for their law books. Say one of these names to a native of the City, and he'll say "Where?" He needs no other name. He'll never go anywhere else. His vision is small. Mine was too, once.

The place where I was born was small. Ten feet across. It was a circle, ringed by a four-foot-high wall of brick, a trash heap. Merchants once threw their chaff and scraps there, giving scavengers the opportunity to pick it over for anything useful before it was torched. More recently, a wider and less useful assortment of refuse was thrown into it: bones, rags, dead animals, the occasional small child. I couldn't have been born there, actually, though I know nothing of my birth. I couldn't even have been there long, or I'd have been caught in one of the not-so-frequent blazes as the trash was burned. I might have been in the heap for a year or so before the day I was dragged out of it.

My first memory is screaming. I believe it was the first time I had done it. My infant brain had the sense to keep quiet to elude discovery, and I must have done so for some time. My unknown early life probably involved a great deal of hiding, from angry mother or drunken father perhaps, from the feral dogs I competed with for food. It was quite a shock to be pulled into the cold, empty air, held by the ankles, helpless, discovered. My discoverer claimed it was a shock to find I was alive, a fact he'd been doubtful of when he first saw me among the refuse, but which was proven adequately by my screaming. That was how I met Big Geordie.

Big Geordie was a man of many talents. He was a clever scavenger. He could find the chance last piece of silver in a rubbish heap—or the chance lost child. He was a talented thief, never so greedy that he took foolish chances and got himself caught. He was a smart man, much smarter than anyone gave him credit for. By my size he judged me to be three years old, then he raised it to four, to account for the malnutrition I had no doubt suffered. And he was the best con man in the city. Big Geordie was scarcely five feet tall and made of bones. He would threaten people who didn't know him in his own name, and offer them protection from himself at a prime rate. He could tell people lies to their smiling faces, with them knowing it all along and believing it anyway. Big Geordie was the man who raised me and taught me his trade.

My second memory is watching a man's throat cut. The City survived, in spite of itself, in spite of its people killing each other off for hatred or a few coins or because there was nothing else for them. A day, maybe, after I'd become aware of other people in the world I was watching them die. It hardened me, Loyd and his local authorities would say, made me a good operative. Damned good operative. One of their best.

I was four years old and could not speak. When Big Geordie—he being a clever man—tried to piece together my life before his entrance into it, he said I must have been abandoned. Children learn to speak by mimicking their elders. I must have had none. Then he altered the story, since until I was weaned I must have been fed by someone, fed but not cared for. A castoff, a pariah, despised by someone with just enough humanity to not let me starve, until they tired of me or became so overwhelmed with hatred that they threw me away.

Geordie could not imagine what would stir such hatred toward an infant. Even if I'd been Azassian—which I couldn't be, since I lacked the red hair and ruddy coloring—someone should have cared for me. I had an idea. I wouldn't have told him, though, or anyone. Only Loyd worked it out.

(*Tod doesn't ask the question. He lets these provocative*

*words go without pursuing them, almost as if he hasn't
heard them at all.)*

It was also Loyd who worked out my absence of emotion. With no elders to teach me to speak, I had none to
teach me to laugh or cry, either, and while language can
be learned, the lack of familial bonds in infancy can
never be compensated. A strength of mine, Loyd called
it. Damned good operative. Geordie would have agreed.
Emotions were a liability. People who left themselves
open got stolen from, raped, their throats cut. I could
tell, mute at four years, that the man I watched bleed out
from his throat had reached out in friendship to the man
who killed him.

# 18

A T A WINDOW IN A SMALL, WHITE-WALLED, WOOD-floored room, a woman sat at her needlework. She was dressed plainly as a widow, in unadorned black silk that had no shine on it, the cut of the dress simple, the corset to which the bodice was stitched rigid and straight, the neckline square and not low. Her sole ornamentation was a collar, white lawn a few inches wide, pinned to the neckline and falling lightly over her shoulders and modest bosom. There was no lace on the collar, and none of her industrious needlework appeared anywhere so conspicuous as her clothing. Decoration of that sort was an extravagance of times past, before her birth, times that came to an end when she was a small child, too young to be aware of them. Yet despite the severity of her dress, one who guessed she was a widow would have been incorrect. She was the wife of Lord Justice Jannes.

The home of Jannes and his family in Origh was small, all things considered, for the personal home of a superior member of Dabion's ruling class. Newly built in the rational style, it was compact and well proportioned. It was not decorated with the expensive paintings and sculptures or inlaid floors and ceilings seen in Mandera at the extremes of its wealth, or the strange ethnic painting seen on the walls in Azassi. The rooms of Jannes's house were square and smoothly plastered, and decorated with nothing save in Ciceline's room, where he had allowed his young wife the fancy of putting up bits of needlework on the walls.

Ciceline was surrounded by flowers. There were no flowers in Origh; errant weeds that were so bold as to poke their heads up among the halls of law were quickly exterminated. But Ciceline had grown up at the outskirts of town, where the Lesser Justice who was her father owned a very old house on a sprawling expanse of property. As a child she had spent long hours among the rolling green hills and fields of flowers. She grew out of her childhood, though, and eleven years ago she dutifully left her youthful fields, married the Lord Justice, and bore him a son. It was by the grace of her birth and the law that she was not a woman of work, and that she had the leisure to spend such frivolous time making mementos of her childhood, stitching roses and violets and wisteria branches.

"Madam," a servant said quietly at the door.

The Lord Justice's wife sighed, popped the embroidered cloth out of the hoop in which it was stretched, returned the work to the basket by her chair, and bade the servingwoman enter.

Ciceline's only personal servant was a woman of middle age, the brown in her hair already lost to gray, her face heavy with wrinkles. In the eleven years Ciceline had known her, she had changed very little. She'd spent her life as a servant, so far as Ciceline knew, although she spoke little of herself, or indeed of anything. There were no marriages or births on the records, as Jannes had scrupulously investigated. When a kitchen servant once spread a rumor claiming otherwise, Jannes had ordered the kitchen girl thrashed and turned out, and threatened the same to anyone who repeated what he had proven untrue.

"The master is home, madam," Pera said as she entered, bobbing tensely in an arthritic curtsey. She did not meet Ciceline's eyes when she spoke. Efficiently she walked about the room, smoothing a bedcover, straightening a window shutter, seizing up Ciceline's basket of needlework to shut it away in a cupboard. As she passed Ciceline she reached into the pocket of the apron that she wore over her plain, gray dress and bodice. "A message for you, madam," she said, at half voice, and handed her a carefully folded paper.

Ciceline did not read it, but tucked it among the folds of her skirt.

"And your son is expected within the hour," Pera concluded. Having finished her ordering of the mistress's room, she bobbed again and passed silently through the narrow door.

She never expected a friend, Ciceline often reflected.

Friends were a fantasy from childhood, like the flowers, except that the flowers had been real. It no longer mattered, though. Ladies' maids were sometimes companions but often only servants. Ciceline had other duties. Her son was home for the break between sessions at the grammar school where he boarded, and her husband was home as well. Managing them both would leave no time for daydreams. She rose and went to her husband's study.

Filanar Jannes's chambers were the largest in the house, spanning half of the ground floor: study, library, and bedchamber, interconnecting squares in immaculate white and polished wood. Jannes himself was seated at the desk in his study, writing calmly in a ledger. Ciceline never asked what he wrote.

"Good day," Ciceline said to her husband, waiting properly in the doorway.

Jannes continued to write until he was finished, then he put up his quill, corked the ink bottle, preened the already perfect wig on his head, and finally looked up to acknowledge his wife. "Is the boy home yet?" he asked her.

He was answered by a crashing noise from the foyer and the shouting of a child's voice. The page he had so carefully written crumpled in his hands.

"Shall I have the cook prepare you a drink?" Ciceline suggested. She did not turn to watch the chaos going on behind her, down the hall. Jannes's manservant was already there, trying to restrain Aron and carry him to his room upstairs. "Perhaps a cool restorative?" Her husband answered her with a tight wave of his wrist and she withdrew to the kitchen.

Aron had bawled himself into exhaustion and silence by the time Ciceline returned with the drink, so there was no further noise to disturb the household. She passed the manservant at the door of the kitchen, holding a compress to a bruise on his wrinkled face, and she discreetly bowed her head to avoid eye contact. When she reached her husband's study, she found him gazing out the window, his face set in a wooden placidness. A pile of crumpled and torn paper was scooped neatly into a bin. "Your pardon, my lord," Ciceline said to announce herself, and carried him the porcelain tankard.

After taking several long, slow draughts, Jannes turned away from the window and, for the first time since seeing her, smiled at his wife. "Heavenly," he said. "Nectar of the gods, if the heathens of our continent ever had gods that deserved such a fine drink." Then he reached out his hand and touched Ciceline's wrist, a rare gesture of fondness. "And no other man deserves such a fine wife."

Ciceline dropped her eyes demurely. "It is my pleasure, Filanar." She lingered for a moment beside him, feeling the intimacy of using her husband's given name, not looking directly at him lest she overstep her bounds. Then the need for her there was finished, and she left the study.

Her son was sprawled on his bed, his head thrust under a pillow. "Go away!" he shouted, muffled, as he heard the door open. Ciceline closed the door behind her and took a chair by the bed. Aron grumpily took the pillow from his head to glare at the intruder, then subsided into erratic sobbing. Ciceline reached out a hand to soothe her son's dark hair.

"Your hair is long like your uncle's," she murmured. It came to his chin and was spread over his tear-streaked face. "You may have it cropped, if you like. Are they wearing wigs at your school?"

"I hate that school!" Aron sobbed. "I never want to go back!"

"Let me bring you something to eat, you'll feel better."

Aron wound his mouth into a frown. "I'm never eating again if you send me back there!"

"We all have our duties, child," Ciceline whispered. She handed him the pillow that he'd dropped on the floor, and he thrust it over his head again. "Let me bring you some cakes. Lemon ones. They're your favorite."

Aron sniffed loudly from behind the pillow. "With sugar icing?"

On her second trip to the kitchen she found the broken pottery. The sole decoration in Jannes's home was a sculpture of the scales of Justice, the symbol of his position. It had stood on a shelf in the foyer, until Aron had knocked it down this afternoon.

"Can you find another one of these, Dal?" Ciceline

asked the manservant, careful not to look at the purple mark on his chin. "Whatever the expense. Bring it by nightfall."

The old man nodded, wearily. "As you wish, madam." He went to the rear door and let himself out.

Before it closed, Ciceline caught a glimpse of a figure outside, on the narrow road that ran behind the Justices' houses, dressed in gray like a servant but wearing a metal plate on a chain around his neck. She hurried to gather the food for her son and darted upstairs.

Much later, the man on the back road left, accompanied by a second figure concealed in a light cloak. "Why were you so early?" the cloaked woman admonished in a whisper. "I was supposed to signal you with a lantern from my window," she said, pointing at the plate that the man wore to catch such a signal light.

The man hurried his companion along through the darkened streets, taking quite a few strides before answering. "Are you always so chattery?" he finally replied. "Quite unlike the dutiful wife of a Justice. One would think you were a fisherman's shrew instead."

Ciceline set her mouth in a line and hurried on, silently.

They came to the Great Hall in the center of Origh, and descended into its lower tunnel. Ciceline ducked her head and pulled the hood of her cloak farther over her face. Her guide seemed to be walking faster, to spite her. At one point she thought she had lost him, but suddenly a door opened before her and she heard the guide's voice. "The woman is here." Ciceline stepped forward and entered the room, letting down her hood. The guide closed the door behind her. She looked up into the broadly, boldly smiling eyes of another man, well dressed, sitting on a lounge in this secret chamber.

# 19

"HONOR AMONG THIEVES, THAT'S NOT ONLY A SAY-
ing."

Elzith was leaning back in her chair, her booted feet
crossed at the ankles and resting on a tiny uncluttered
spot on the table. Piles of stitched quartos covered the
table's surface. With Elzith's help, all the copies of Justice
Paloman's rush order were stitched, but Tod had to catch
up on pasting them into their boards. A needle dangled
easily in Elzith's hand. Tod looked up as she spoke,
caught by her voice and the light glinting on the needle
that swung like a pendulum.

"You might not call them honorable, and the Justices
wouldn't, of course. It's their own honor. Not poaching
another man's territory. If there's too many in one block,
you move. If you can't move, you make an agreement
with him, divvy up the streets, the days you'll hit. Anything else is starving him; it's dishonorable. Not draining your quarry, that's another one—not hitting the
same shop over and over until it's dry, not decimating
your resources. That's starving yourself. Dishonorable.

We're thieves, not jackals. Not Justice tax collectors. You see. It's perfectly sensible."

Tod laughed a little. As mad as it was to hear such things, he'd heard stranger. There were theatres in Karrim, boards set up in inn yards where players in shabby costume acted out scenes from folktales and corrupted history. Tod used to watch them in groggy fascination. Those plays, though, had been just stories with little truth behind them. Elzith's monologue about thieves was disturbingly real. Still, her voice was more captivating than an actor's, and Tod listened as she continued, rapt.

"Big Geordie was a thief, that was his trade. The confidence game was his avocation, his dream, but there was no money in it. He was a thief to put bread on the table. Not that we had a table, of course. We lived in the streets, slept in alleys when the weather was mild, in tents under eaves of abandoned buildings when it turned cold. A few times Geordie conned our way into some rich man's house, playing himself as a misfortunate father and me a dear suffering daughter. I was tiny then, people thought I was darling. Until I stole from them, of course.

"Geordie taught me his trade as well as his dream. I, too, had to eat. I was good enough at it. The City had waifish children by the cartload. The butchers and fruit sellers were always on their guard when the noisy ones were around, but I was quiet so they didn't watch me as closely. That was my in. Thieving was dull. I wanted to see what else I could get. I made it into one grocer's own home, he told me he liked me, wanted me as his assistant. He wanted me on his table, more likely; he was a dirty bastard. But he was a fool—the game wasn't what he thought it was. I pinched his favorite bottle of cordial off his shelf and slipped out the window. It was cut glass, fancy like diamonds, more excessive than a Manderan banker. I showed it to Big Geordie. He cried for an hour out of pride."

"He was proud of you," Tod said, squinting at glue fumes as he bound a sheet of leather to the boards of a book. "Like a father." The leather wasn't the least bit red; he never used that coveted color, trying not to remind himself of his failure. "You must have been happy to get his praise."

Elzith shook her head. "I didn't care. No emotions, remember. I played the confidence game because I won at it. I stayed with Geordie because I respected him. He was good. I couldn't play him."

Tod looked up from gluing down an endpaper. "You didn't care?" he breathed. He felt his eyes widen.

"No," Elzith answered. "I just played the game. I was good at it, wasn't I?"

Tod nodded.

"I was good. I still am." Her face sharpened more, if that was possible. "I'm playing you now. You're drinking up every word I say. You believe every bit of it, I can tell. You're gullible, Tod. I could be telling you anything."

He shrugged his shoulders, capping the jar of glue

and rubbing his irritated nose. "Why would you lie to me? I don't expect you to."

Elzith laughed shortly. "Ah—truth. The Justices' game. Everyone plays by the rules of discourse. You ask a question, I tell the truth." She dropped the needle on the table and the sarcasm from her voice. "Haven't you ever been lied to?"

Tod closed the book and turned it over in his hands. It was something, this book he'd made, an accomplishment. Like winning, maybe. He was good at it. The truth wouldn't blot out what he'd accomplished, not even if he told it. "Yes, I have," he said. "By my brothers."

He started on another cover. He'd have to keep busy while he talked about it. "I apprenticed to my father when I was fourteen. My brothers—I have two, they're older than me, Wen and Lor—they never hesitated to tell me how awful I was at the work. A few years into it, though, they started complimenting me. Half compliments, you know. Good work, Tod, it's almost right. I should have noticed them snickering. They started going away then, days at a time. It was to Karrim, I found out. One day they asked me to go with them."

There were straps of leather laced under the threads that held the quartos together, and he'd carved grooves in the boards to paste the straps into. They set in place easily, comfortingly. "Why don't you join us, little brother, they said. Just like one of us. I had to go. I was going to match them, for once. I was going to keep up with every dram they swallowed, every tavern they visited, the bawdy houses—well, illegal establishments in Karrim." He opened the glue jar and let out the fumes. It gave him the chance to rub his eyes and half hide his face.

"I had a temper then, it was the gin that did it. Temper got me in trouble, not with the law, not yet, but almost. I was in fights all the time. I think my brothers put me up to them, got me drunk and put me in the way of big angry men. I remember them sitting back and laughing. I don't remember much, of course. Once they told me I'd roughed up one of the girls, but I think they lied to me. I don't remember doing that. I hope I didn't. It's hard, though, with all those holes in my memory." He looked up, took a breath from his ramblings. Elzith watched him closely with her inscrutable gaze. "Well, you know that, about the illegal establishments, Wen and Lor getting in trouble. It's funny, they put me in the middle of all that, set me up so they could, I don't know, laugh at me, and they're the ones who got in trouble. I always tripped and fell down, or someone punched me in a fight and I was unconscious, but Wen would be the first one by the door when the Public Force came in." Tod let out his breath in a laugh, one he'd never before given to this story. "It was justice, I guess, from fate or the gods or whatever."

Elzith nodded very slightly, and said, "If you believe that sort of thing." Her words were clean and hard, like stones or rare pearls.

A little dizzy from fumes or confession, Tod closed

the glue jar. "So that's my answer. Yes, my brothers lied to me. Conned me, I guess. Corrupted me for their amusement."

Elzith's face turned as hard as her words, as if assessing a dishonorable thief. "Not a good game," she declared. "You were a child, a vulnerable one." Then she met his eyes, and her expression changed subtly, as if reading something new. "But you weren't a foolish child. You had a mind in you. Yes... and you knew what they were doing." She shook her head. "Why did you let them?"

There was only a moment's pause before Tod answered, "I wanted to let them."

He realized he was seeing something that few people had seen before. Elzith's eyes widened slightly, and her mouth opened almost imperceptibly. She was surprised. "That's the truth," she murmured, with slow and heavy certainty. But the surprise lasted only an instant before her voice went quick and sharp again. "You were willing to buy their attention at the cost of your life."

"Very nearly," Tod agreed. He had not felt the touch of the Healer who brought him back from his gin-drowning after Morrn's arrest, but he was certain he would have died without it.

Elzith's eyes were drifting toward the window, over her shoulder, as she sat at an angle so her back wasn't to the door. "I never wanted attention so badly," she mused. "I never wanted it at all."

"Is that a good thing?" Tod asked.

The sun was invisible, fallen past the windowsill. Tod often found himself looking out that same window, watching the last of the day's light die before getting up to light a lamp so he could continue his work. Elzith's face was shadowy, dimly silhouetted against the window. "Yes," she said.

"My lovely little vacation is at an end now," she said afterward, quickly, a bit too quickly. "The master has called me to heel again. I'm going to Cassile tomorrow, off to do the work of the honorable Justices."

Tod asked, "Why do you go back?"

"Why?" Elzith repeated, reaching for one of the finished books. "These choices aren't mine." She opened the book and peered at a page filled with strange symbols. "What do you think it means?" she asked him.

"Keller tells me not to ask," Tod answered.

"And do you?"

Tod opened another copy for himself. "I'd like to know what it says. $T$ is true, $F$ is false, $v$ is or, I don't know what this is." He poked a square on the chart, running his finger over the foreign symbol as if his touch would translate it. "All the truth in the world could be in here, if I could read it. I'd be the smartest man of all time." He smiled to himself, laughing at the idea. "I'd like to go to the school in Insigh, if I could."

"Would you believe what they told you?" Elzith asked, tossing her book on the table.

Tod turned a few pages, looking for the few sentences written in a language he knew. "Maybe."

Elzith stood. "Don't." She went to the door. "Keep your own mind. But don't tell anyone." Then she was gone, as abruptly as ever, and Tod rose routinely to latch the shutters and lock the door behind her.

What stayed in his mind, repeating itself as he tried to fall asleep, was a word—*attention*. Images followed it, his brothers looking down on him, sneering, but it didn't matter. Then Elzith was saying that she never wanted it, that attention. *Is that a good thing*—he heard in his own voice, and Elzith answered—*Yes*. If he could judge her the way she'd judged him, if he could proclaim her words true or not, he'd have said she was lying. Elzith knew things, things he could never know, and she had a skill at it that he couldn't imagine, but he knew things also. For once, maybe the only time, he thought that he knew better than she did.

# 20

THE SCHOOL WAS TOO NOISY. ALL THE STUDENTS sat in neat rows, never speaking out of turn, and the lecturer's words were so clear and ordered that Jereth could have drawn a diagram of them, but still it was noisy. The walls of the lecture hall were high, white, hard, and reflected sound like mirrors. Jereth fought the urge to cover his ears.

"Dal'Nilaran shows us throughout the importance of rationality," the lecturer was saying. "Rationality is the only force that can combat chaos. Give me Dal'Nilaran's three genres of chaos," he ordered his students, pointing to them one by one, straight across the first row. The young men stood obediently, the heels of their shoes clicking on the polished wood floor, their voices echoing painfully in Jereth's head. He knew nothing about Dal'Nilaran or his genres of anything. He closed his eyes, wished the headmaster hadn't invited him, and hoped he would not be asked to speak.

The School of Bioran Science in Insigh was nothing like the school of Jereth's childhood. Behind his old closed eyes he saw the sprawl of low buildings across the empty hills in the northeast. The school grounds had been quiet, not surrounded by the busy streets of any city. The buildings were dark, thick with bricks and rugs, cold even in summer. The boys walked from their dormitories to their classes in silence, and in the classrooms the voices of the professors whispered their lessons low and heavy.

A boy called Piers had been Jereth's roommate in the boardinghouse. They were assigned to the same room because their names fell next to each other in the roster, or at least that was the official reason. They had shared other common ground, though; they shared a great secret, and they spent their first three years at that grammar school in fear that it would be discovered.

They went to their classes, Jereth and Piers, listened to the words of their professors, recited them in the cavernous quiet of the lecture halls. "This is the law," whispered the professors in Jereth's memory. "These are the truths, the teachings of our masters, the old Justices." Then one day Piers spoke in class. He stood timidly, having waited all morning to be recognized, and cleared his throat. "The Justices interpreted Nanian, professor?" Piers said, trembling as the old teacher in his black robes nodded to verify the boy's puzzling statement of fact. Then Piers asked the question that could not be allowed, the challenge to authority and truth that would make him disappear from the school.

"Why don't we read Nanian's words?"

When Jereth returned to his room, Piers and everything belonging to him had vanished. The secret had been discovered, no doubt, and Piers had been sent back to the family of Karrimian farmers he'd left to sneak into the Dabionian school. Jereth would be more careful than ever before, never speaking out of turn, never saying a wrong thing, never giving his superiors reason to peer too closely at his own family, his father dutifully working the Lord Justice's lawns, the uncles tilling the dirt in Karrim. No one would learn his name was Ploughman, no one would make him disappear.

"Power, wealth, and superstition," the lecturer echoed in the white room. "Name the process by which rationality eliminates each of these three genres of chaos."

Jereth's eyes started open and he swayed in his hard wooden chair, stumbling out of his memories. He was the Justice Advisor to the Circle, and a guest of the headmaster at the Insigh School, yet he still felt like a timid boy holding his tongue in a dark classroom, afraid someone would find him and cast him out as an intruder.

"We must use these lessons to fight the forces that oppose us," the lecturer was concluding. What forces—Jereth wondered, ashamed at letting his mind drift. The word *superstition* lingered in his head, one of the genres of chaos. That meant mystics, Nanianism. We don't read Nanian's words. Somehow the lesson was the same, after all these years, even though Nanianism had been accepted then and was prohibited now. The law was truth. The mystics were dangerous. All that was not Dabion was dangerous. The professor dismissed his students and they stood in a body, preparing to be ushered out of the lecture hall, and behind this shield Jereth ducked out of the white room.

He didn't care about the mystics, really. The realization of it pounded in his throat as he hurried out into the streets. He didn't care about the Justices' truths. He wanted to get back to his rooms, back to his books. He had followed the Justices and their orders for years, and all it had earned him was mediocrity. The books were all he had. If he could climb between their boards and disappear, he would.

As he lunged headlong across a street and toward the Great Hall, he narrowly missed being run down by a public transport, too smothered by his own thoughts to see or hear the pounding horses or the creaking wheels rolling toward him. He failed to notice the cursing driver or the faces that peered out at him. He did not recognize one of the faces as that of the unnamed man who had stood with the Circle in the round room, the first time Jereth had been admitted, and whom Jereth had not seen since. He would not have questioned, had he or anyone else known, why the leader of the Secret Force was riding public transport southward, out of the capital, toward Origh.

•   •   •

An hour later, his heart pounding, Jereth was running through the Great Hall, through ancient hallways and stairwells, lost. He passed other Justices who kept quarters in the upper floors of the Hall, blurred faces contorted in confusion as they regarded his mad chase. He did not know who he was looking for, but he had to find someone. The bottom drawer had been pulled from the chest, and *Rationality and Logic* was gone.

The Great Hall in Insigh was not like Dabion's newer buildings, with their gridlike order and square, white rooms. The Great Hall was a labyrinth, full of twisted passages, some of which Jereth had never been down. Some one hundred Justices, men of importance in the workings of District One, lived in the Great Hall, above its rows of courtrooms. Jereth normally tried to avoid his neighbors, never looking into their eyes as he passed them, lest they recognize his weakness. Now he wished he knew even one of them, one of the doors he rushed by, so he could call on someone's assistance. Finally his lungs were taxed to their limit and he sank to the floor.

With his head bowed to his knees, he did not see a servant—drably dressed, plump, elderly—pass at the end of the corridor. It was the same servant that Jereth had failed to see enter and exit his room that morning, as he was leaving to visit the school. He wouldn't have questioned a washermaid's presence, though, as she gathered his linens. Servant women were never questioned, and hardly even noticed. The woman turned a corner and met a man in a black suit. She passed the man quickly in the narrow hallway, not raising her eyes, only pausing long enough to allow him to retrieve a bundle from her basket.

The footsteps that Jereth was too weary and distressed to hear parted, the woman's decaying into the distance, the man's turning in on the corridor and approaching. Jereth heard them then and began to raise his head, in blind supplication to whoever it might be, hoping beyond hope that the stranger might help him.

"My lord!" cried Jereth, stunned.

Varzin stood before him.

"I beg your pardon," Jereth stuttered, trying to force arthritic and uncooperative knees to raise him to a standing position.

"Do not trouble yourself," said Varzin smoothly, extending one hand in a halting gesture.

Embarrassed, Jereth abandoned his attempt to stand, and instead gazed up dumbly, like a monk to the mythical heavens. Then he saw something that could have moved him to conversion then and there. In the other hand Varzin held his book.

"My—my—my—lord!" Jereth was beyond words. "You—found..."

Varzin smiled ethereally. "I feared it was yours, stolen by some ruffian. It was not enough to cast the inferior classes out of the land and into Karrim's fields. We still depend upon servants, and so we will always be surrounded by the dregs of mankind. The lawless are among us even in this most lawful of cities. I shall have the superintendent install a better lock on your door." He held the book at arm's length, admiring it as a holy relic, but keeping it outside of Jereth's desperate reach. "*Rationality and Logic*. The cornerstone of the great philosophers' thought. A shame, a dreadful shame it would have been, had this vanished from our sight."

Jereth nodded mutely, reaching for the book like a parched man for water, dizzy with thirst.

A cool smile still on his face, Varzin tucked the book under his arm, offering the other arm to Jereth. "Allow me to escort you to my Insigh quarters, Justice Paloman. They are very near, and I believe you must be in need of a rest after this shock."

Varzin had been given sizable quarters in the Great Hall, a suite of rooms outfitted with heavy furnishings and thick rugs and tapestries. Jereth was seated on a massive chair near a tapestry that depicted a hunt scene. He'd had no idea such decorative hangings still existed.

"Allow me to pour you a drink," Varzin said as he deposited his guest. "Will you take water, nectar, or another restorative?"

The suggestion of alcohol was lost on Jereth. He wanted his book. "Water is—good—fine—satisfactory," he stuttered, "my lord. Thank you."

The Lord Justice disappeared into another room to fetch the drink. He must have taken the book with him, surely forgotten, still under his arm. Jereth sighed, hearing a childish whine in his voice, and he muffled it by turning his face to the tapestry. The hanging concealed a window. Jereth pulled the tapestry away from the wall, its dust stinging his eyes, and saw that a whole series of plate-glass windows ran along this wall of the room, affording an excellent view of the city. Varzin had it entirely covered.

"Here is your drink," the Lord Justice announced, entering the sitting room again and setting a crystal tumbler on a petite table near Jereth's chair. "And here is your precious volume." Varzin drew up an ottoman and perched on it, at Jereth's knee, opening the book and turning the pages, inches away from Jereth's fingers. He murmured appreciatively. "What a treasure. Impeccable. These are the hands of the masters, as clear as if they were written yesterday. You are a fortunate man, your honor."

Varzin closed the book, extended it subtly. Jereth snatched it back. In the curtained dimness the Lord Justice's mouth turned slightly at the corners.

"M—most fortunate, my lord," Jereth uttered in an attempt to salvage his manners. "I am lucky that you were able to rescue it from that thief." He continued to clasp the book close to his chest while Varzin watched. I must look like a batty old man, Jereth thought. He hardly cared. The book was back with him; its very presence in his hands soothed him. He felt the racing of his heart slow.

"Every father feels such joy when his most precious child is returned to him." Varzin spoke in a lyric tone. He smiled placidly. "And this, not only yours, but the child of time. You are ecstatic. I am most happy to bring you this relief."

Jereth could finally breathe normally again. He loosened his grip on the book, letting it rest in his lap. Varzin motioned him to take a drink from his glass and he did so.

"Remind me, your honor, what is the date of that book?"

Jereth swallowed. He could act knowledgeable once more, if only he were up to it. "Two thirty-eight," he said, doubt creeping into his mind, as if he hadn't memorized the year like that of his own birth. "Only a few years after the advent of the Common Calendar, and the arrival of Biorans in the Five Countries."

"Of course," smiled Varzin. "Your other books are of the same era?"

"Yes, within a hundred years. *The Art of Dialogue*, 274, and *Structures of Thought*, 312."

"The volumes are undoubtedly similar, physically. Same construction, size, binding?"

Jereth knitted his brows. He knew the pages as if he had written them himself, the shapes of the letters, the arrangement of ink on each page, but he had paid little attention to the boards that bound them. As he thought about it he realized he couldn't even remember what colors the other two books were. "I—yes—certainly they must be—they are."

"I should explain myself," Varzin said. "I am in possession of a number of old books. They were given to me by an associate, many years ago. The books have suffered a great deal of decay, unfortunately, and in some cases the printer's mark is damaged. My associate claimed that these books date from the third century, but I have my doubts about the truth of his assessment." Varzin leaned forward, confidingly. "I am afraid that I have little knowledge of old books. It is a deficiency of mine; I wouldn't know an ancient book from one bound yesterday, but for the dust."

Varzin smiled more widely at his joke, showing his teeth a little. Jereth's mouth was tugged up into an echoing smile, as if the corners of it were on puppet strings.

"But you certainly have more knowledge than I, your honor," Varzin continued. "You have handled these exquisite volumes intimately. You are the master in this field. Generations will remember you for your expertise, as the man who brought Bioran learning back to the world. I trust I can rely upon your superior knowledge to help me authenticate my books."

Jereth didn't know whether to revel in the praise or to cower in the back of the massive chair. The water in his glass was splashing. He shakily put it down on the table. "Thank you, my lord," he rasped through a suddenly dry mouth. He knew nothing about authenticating books.

Varzin stood, replacing the ottoman and towering over Jereth again, no longer a saving vision.

"Your recent series of lessons has been excellent," Varzin said, the words sounding hollow and distorted in Jereth's ears. "I believe the Circle is becoming enlightened by your teachings. Even Nosselin is absorbed with your words. I knew that once support for your work was felt, the others would see the value in it."

"I have you to thank, my lord," Jereth whispered.

"It has been my pleasure, your honor," Varzin replied, drifting easily toward a heavy cabinet, which he opened with a profound creaking noise. "I am bound for Aligh in the morning, very early," he said as he unearthed a volume from within the cabinet. "I will return for the midsummer meeting. That will be time enough for your evaluation, will it not? It is a shame we will have to wait for the verdict. But it will give me something to look forward to, in addition to the reading of the year's law changes." He showed his teeth again in a joking smile; the midsummer law reading was reported to be never-ending, guaranteed to put the most impassioned of Justices to sleep. Jereth did not know how to laugh. Varzin held a fragile book out to him, a loose wrapping of gauze holding together its dry and flaked binding, and reluctantly Jereth took it.

"Thank you, Justice Paloman. I know you will not disappoint me."

Jereth's heart was thundering in his chest again. He

was a charlatan, he was a fool. He would be found out and sent back home, proven a failure by the very man who was his greatest supporter. He thought he could feel the book disintegrating in his hands. His own book was forgotten on his knees.

# 21

CASSILE WAS UNBEARABLE. MAIN CAMP HAD BEEN established in the north, at least, at one of the evacuated monasteries, the second largest in the country. It would figure that the Cassilians would build their largest monastery, Naniantemple, the closest thing that these ascetics had to a capital city, in the infernal southern half of the country, near the western seacoast, where the humidity made breathing nearly impossible. No sense, these monks.

Justice Geremain frowned. He would be in Naniantemple as soon as the closures reached it, and it would likely be before the season was out, while summer still held Cassile in its stifling grip. It would not be an easy closure, either. That monastery was reported to be the burial place of Nanian, the prophet and madman who was responsible for starting the entire monastic movement two hundred years earlier. Some of the ascetics seemed to think that he had been assumed bodily into the heavens, and so Naniantemple wasn't literally a burial place, they claimed. Still, the site was full of relics and

peopled by the most faithful and impassioned of followers. That closure was sure to be a violent one.

Geremain hadn't been summoned to hold court at
Main Camp because of violence, though; just the opposite, in fact. Dabion had given him the assignment of
overseeing the monastic closures, and he made a circuit
of the sites to verify that the acting Justices and their
troops of Black Force guards were doing their jobs adequately. He was holding today's court in the refectory,
the only sensible structure that the monks had ever
built, a long and low room, kept dim and cool, ventilated
with a series of opposing windows that allowed a blessed
cross breeze. A disobedient guard was being called to
account.

"The guard failed to fire upon an insurgent," Geremain read aloud from the report that he held. The acting
Greater Justice who had been on the scene and who now
stood before Geremain nodded, causing his wig to slip
down his sweaty forehead and into his eyes. Geremain
thought they were fools to wear wigs, especially in this
heat. Biorans were blond-headed from living in that
tiny, cold, sunless, mountain-wreathed country. Dabionians weren't blond. It looked absurd, and they claimed
it was a symbol of rationalism. Geremain shook his head
and kept reading the report. The guard was a female,
he saw. Well, that explained it. Dabion promised to
employ the women as well as the men in countries like
Karrim and Mandera, to keep those populations out of

starvation and poverty. There was no need to carry the practice to extremes. He was surprised that failing to fire was the worst this female guard had done; he would have expected wantonness and scenes of hysteria.

"Oh, well, bring her in," Geremain said. He had to administer justice fairly, after all. "Devil's Advocate!"

"The guard has been assigned one, your honor," an unfamiliar voice called out. A young clerk, red-faced and panting from recent travel, rushed to step in front of the Lesser Justice who normally filled the role of devil's advocate in Geremain's court.

"Who the hell are you?" asked Geremain, with narrowed eyes.

"I've been dispatched from Insigh, your honor," the man panted, stretching out a hand full of papers. Geremain scrutinized them. It was true; the clerk had been assigned to the case of Elzith Kar by Administrator Traite, head of the Black Force, and the document had been signed by Lord Councilor Muhrroh.

Geremain's hand dropped. "Let her come forward."

The woman was maddening. The heat did not affect her. While everyone else in Main Camp walked with bent shoulders and a gait slowed by heat and fatigue, Kar stood ramrod-straight. Sweat dampened her face and neck, but her expression was so sharp it was insolent. She bowed briefly and stood before Justice Geremain.

"What does she have to say for herself?"

The devil's advocate mopped his face with his sleeve

and began reciting. "Administrator Traite has acknowledged years of satisfactory service by Guardsman Kar,
your honor. He appeals to this record to excuse her recent error."

"It wasn't an error."

The papers slipped out of Geremain's hand. The
woman had interrupted. "What did you say?"

"It wasn't an error," Kar repeated. "I was part of an
advance guard that was flushing out a group of resisters
who had escaped monastery number twenty-six. One
monk was standing on the road in front of some brush
and forest cover. I anticipated that more of the resisters
were hiding in the brush. Had I shot the single monk,
who was certainly a decoy, the others would have been
alerted. They would have come out and overwhelmed
us. There were only two of us. The resisters could have
attacked and gone into hiding again before the rest of
the party got there. I did not fire, I walked through as if I
did not see the monk, giving the rest of our party time to
catch up. We had the numbers then to subdue and capture the resisters without violence."

"And the other guard in the advance unit?" Geremain
managed to ask, through his astonishment.

"I took his pistol."

The acting Greater Justice had had enough. "You dis-
obeyed orders!" he shouted. "And you influenced
another guard so that he was unable to obey orders!"

"The orders were senseless," Kar said calmly.

The Greater Justice threw his wig down on the floor in a rage. "The order was to shoot resister ascetics on sight! You have no authority to question that order!"

"You would rather let the rebels pick us off one by one?" With all the heat and temper that filled the room, Kar did not even raise her voice. "That's what they would have done. They may preach peace and mysticism as a sect, but there are some of them who'll fight when you back them into a corner. Those are the ones who have escaped. They're smart enough to hide. If you want to stop them you'll have to be smart enough to flush them out. Your order can't stop any more than the one or two that let you see them. It's a senseless order. Do you know why it was even given?"

Geremain could almost hear the blood pounding in the Greater Justice's temples in the silence. "I know why the order was given, Kar," Geremain said to the infuriating woman. "And it is your duty to follow orders. As it is my duty to reprimand you."

"If it please your honor," the devil's advocate pleaded in a helpless-sounding voice, "Administrator Traite had already recommended punishment for the guard." He gestured toward the papers that Geremain had dropped. Another clerk hurried forward to gather the papers and put them back into Geremain's hands.

"Reassigned," Geremain scanned, "off active Black Force duty...installed on household guard for Lord Justice Jannes...personal guard to Aron Jannes."

Geremain snorted. "I've met the Lord Justice's son. He's as obnoxious as you are. It's a fitting punishment."

Then, irritatingly, Kar snapped her heels and bowed efficiently. With a growl Geremain raised a hand to dismiss her. Before he could make the pronouncement, she spoke. "A boon of the court, your honor."

Geremain rolled his eyes. He had to administer justice fairly. "What is it?"

"Why was the order to shoot on sight given?"

The order had been given in confidence to the acting Justices. It was not a matter of public record, but it wasn't under terms of secrecy, either. It would be a good instruction to this arrogant guard, who thought she knew everything. "Send Kar to my chambers in ten minutes," Geremain ordered his assistants.

It was not a shamed or contrite guard who left Geremain's chambers fifteen minutes later. "You're mad," she'd said in response to official revelation. "You have no idea what you're talking about. And you don't even know what the source of the order is." Although her attitude as she turned and left without the Justice's leave was all anger, not smugness, Geremain felt the humiliation of having been shown up again, because she was right. He had no idea who had originated the order or why.

"She knew you sent me."

"Of course she did," Loyd said, somewhat distracted by the news his operative had brought and hardly listening to the man's words.

"That's why she told me about the order. She wouldn't have otherwise."

Loyd blinked and turned to face the young man. "You've done good work, Collin," he assured the operative. Collin was superbly talented at playing roles, even more so than Elzith herself, but he was young, and required the frequent reassurance that children did. Elzith had needed no such coddling, even at half Collin's age. "But I will need you again for an immediate assignment."

Collin's eyes sparkled like an eager puppy's. Loyd turned away to busy himself with papers that he didn't need. Having lost his father at fifteen—and a cold, drunken, loveless father at that—Collin had bonded to Loyd instantly when Loyd rescued the boy from a prison cell where he sat for stealing bread. Loyd was assured of Collin's loyalty; the young man would gladly risk death to earn Loyd's praise. There were benefits to recruiting operatives when they were youths, fifteen or sixteen, or even younger. A quietly interfering part of him wished he had never done so and never would again.

"I need you to get into the clerk's offices of each of the Lord Justices. The shoot-on-sight order must have come from someone with their authority, but it wasn't given in the Circle or I would have known about it. Someone has bypassed the Circle to his own ends. I need to know who."

"I can get into their retinues," Collin offered, "each one of them."

Loyd nodded. Collin could serve as personal secretary to all six of the Lord Justices and they would never know he was the same man, even if they did compare notes.

"When I find out who gave the order," Collin asked, with the confidence of youth, "should I attempt forging a counterorder?"

"No," answered Loyd. "I don't want to risk his discovering it and knowing we're watching him." The lives of rebel ascetics, in this unfortunate case, were not worth what Loyd suspected was at stake.

"But it's not as if he'll run if he finds out we're on to him," Collin protested. "If he's a Lord Justice, where would he go?"

Loyd shook his head. It wasn't a matter of the quarry running. It wasn't a matter of discovering who it was, either. Not precisely. Loyd *knew,* but he needed to *find out.* He also knew what would happen when the quarry learned they were on to him. But in the meantime he said, "It's not where he might go so much as what he might do. So use caution, Collin."

The young man nodded obediently, and once Loyd drew up the necessary documents, he went on his way to assume his next disguise.

Sometimes he wished he had a window, Loyd thought as the operative closed the door behind him. If he had a window, he'd be looking out of it now. It would have to be in a tower high enough to see past Insigh's neatly ordered streets, though. He'd want to see past the grid of the city and the law it represented, that thing he'd pledged his life to protecting. He'd want to see Dabion's green hills and the lonely peace he was enforcing upon them, and the rest of the Five Countries beyond that, bending under the rule that he was responsible for sustaining. That would not be all, though. Somewhere beyond that, in the hazy horizon, would be the scarce-remembered mists of home, untouched by his hand. He dwelled on the image for an instant before turning from it, to put on his jacket and make ready to leave.

He'd failed to find his missing Sor'raian operative, or any sign of him or explanation for his disappearance. It was not surprising, though, since the man was a shapeshifter. Loyd had an intuition that Elzith was somehow endangered by this, and although he hadn't resolved the problem in the time he'd allotted, he'd had to send Elzith out of safekeeping and back to duty. He could not keep her off the Black Force any longer without attracting attention and suspicion. The news Collin had brought him indicated even greater danger. Someone wanted the mystics of Cassile dead. Escaped or resister ascetics were to be shot on sight on the chance that they were magic workers, gathering in the woods to launch an attack against helpless and unmagicked Dabionian authorities.

It was preposterous. There was no evidence that the monks had any possession of magic. Not even their legends spoke of magic, and Cassile had no records of

Healers or wandering madmen in excessive numbers. Nanian was nothing more than a man possessed of wild ideas and charisma. There was no connection whatsoever between mysticism and magic. Elzith could verify that, if there were any doubts. But someone disagreed. Someone hated magic enough to destroy it, and as the mystics were easy targets, someone believed the mystics were close enough to being magic to justify their deaths.

Loyd could not help but suspect that the Sor'raian operative's disappearance was somehow connected to the order to kill mystics. And if someone wanted holders of magic dead, then the danger that the operative's disappearance posed to Elzith was greater than Loyd first imagined. It threatened his entire network of Sor'raian operatives. It threatened Loyd himself.

At least Elzith had gotten herself back out of Cassile. Something wasn't right at Jannes's house, though. Loyd had had information on it for some time, although he'd never considered it serious enough to act upon. Now he was afraid for Elzith. He almost wished he didn't need to send Collin away; he didn't have another operative he trusted well enough to watch Elzith. Fear was irrational, though. Elzith herself would tell him that. So was intuition. The irrationality of it didn't stop him from having it. He'd had the intuition all his life. He'd seen the moment of his own death.

Elzith was there, in his vision of that moment. He died before he saw what happened to her.

Once he'd had passion, he remembered as he exited

and locked his little door, blending silently into the shuffle of drop-headed clerks in the tunnels beneath the Hall. As a young man he'd been driven by dreams and ambitions; he'd fought for his causes without heeding the cost. Preserving Elzith's life would have inspired the most amazing efforts in him, at the age of twelve. He was much older now, though. He had looked at the limits of his ability for years, and he'd gazed at his hazy dreams beyond those boundaries with an aged and jaded eye. But he knew what he was able to do as well.

When he reached ground level he sought out a public transport station, scuffing his shoes in a pile of dust from a gutter that had escaped cleaning so far that afternoon. He would look unimportant enough to escape all notice. The Justice Advisor, Paloman, did not see him as he walked in front of the wagon that Loyd rode in; of course, he hardly saw the wagon, either. Imperceptibly, Loyd shook his head. He'd considered putting a shadow on Paloman, to make sure the man didn't accidentally kill himself. In the end, though, Loyd knew, Bioran learning would hardly be important. The words that men in power exchanged among themselves in public places never were.

It was not such a long ride to Origh. There was a stop overnight, and Loyd slept almost comfortably in his seat in the wagon, alongside those commoners who could not afford to rent a room. It was adventurous; it reminded him of his childhood, the years when he craved danger.

Knowing when he was going to die was liberating. He could walk unarmed into the house of enemies and fear nothing.

No one noticed him walk into that house, as he expected. A nondescript old man dressed like a clerk walking down Scrivener Street to the door of some Greater Justice or other was hardly unexpected. The servant who let him in led him to the Justice's private study without question. The Justice looked up from his papers with nothing but mild irritation on his face as Loyd handed him a rolled sheaf of papers.

"What is this?" the Greater Justice asked blandly.

"Something I wanted to return to you, your honor," Loyd replied. "You should open it over your desk, though. I would hate for it to fall on the floor."

The Greater Justice was too stunned to do anything but follow the old clerk's order. Wrapped within the papers—reports from Secret Force operatives about the actions of a Manderan criminal known by the name Smyth, if the Justice had stopped to look at them—was a jewel-hilted dagger.

"Where did you get this?" the Justice stuttered.

"Where did you?" Loyd returned. "Wait, I know already."

The Greater Justice stood in an outrage, drawing a breath to shout for his servants. The servants would never hear him, though. They would not hear his body fall on the floor, either. Loyd caught him.

Good work for an old man, Loyd thought as he left

the house, as unobserved as he'd come. He'd avenged the harm done to Elzith by the Justice's associate Smyth. It would not make up for the things Loyd had failed to do, years he'd lost in an untouchable past, but it was something.

# 22

A RON JANNES WAS EVERYTHING THEY PROMISED
me: obnoxious, disobedient, maddening. One
thing the clerks and retainers missed in their description
of Lord Justice Jannes's son, however, was intelligence.
Not surprising; it had been left out of my description as
well. Aron appeared at his door scrubbed, neat, and
quiet. I took my place at his side as the party made its
procession to the Great Hall, and through that long
march there wasn't a peep out of him. He waited until
we were up the stairs, into the Hall, into the huge atrium
where his father was to make some official speech, where
the old marble dome made every word echo infinitely.
That's when Aron started screaming at the top of his
lungs.

Two burly men cut short his string of insults at the
stupidity of everyone, hefted him out of the atrium, up a
narrow set of stairs, and into a small chamber. I followed
and was shut into the room with the boy. The men, who
had sustained a good amount of damage to their shins
and knees from Aron's kicking feet, regarded me with

the doom-filled look of executioners as they limped out and locked the door.

Aron kept screaming and kicking at the walls for ten minutes or so. I sat in the chair next to the tiny, deep window, and looked down at an alley. Aron finally quit shouting so he could catch his breath.

"How come you're not looking at me?" he whined.

"Are you more interesting to look at than this alley?"

He was quiet for a minute, trying to figure it out. Then he decided the window was a means to escape and lunged for it.

We're trained to withstand torture. Early on in the Force I spent a season getting pins stuck in my hand every day. My nerves were burned out in the year I spent in Siva. The last of my capacity to feel notable pain was used up when someone put a hole in my gut. It was never completely healed, so every day it hurts, a fact I know without bothering to feel it anymore. Aron did his best to kick his way out of my grasp as he tried to get through me to the window. He kept kicking even after he realized it was no wider than his head. I kept hold of him around the waist, not flinching and not fighting back. When he was tired I dropped him in a heap on the floor, where he stared up at me with his mouth hanging open.

"You've got blood on your nose," he said.

"Do I?" He'd elbowed me in the face. I took a handkerchief out of my coat pocket and daubed it at my nose. He stared at me while I let the blood staunch, waiting for me to do something. After a few minutes I bunched up the handkerchief and put it back in my pocket. Aron started rocking restlessly on his heels. Soon he was back on his feet, kicking and shouting at the door. Every few minutes he'd stop and look over his shoulder at me. "Are you done?" I asked him once.

He chewed on his lip. "Yeah," he answered, flopping onto the floor again. Then he started messing with the buttons on his jacket and vest. "I'm hot," he complained.

"Would you like to open the window?"

He looked at me like he thought I was trying to trick him. With my foot against the wall I pushed myself away to give him room to get around my chair. Skeptically, he stood and inched forward, then bolted to the window and pushed it open.

He stuck his head as far out as he could and let it hang there for a few minutes, then said, "It's hot out there."

"That happens in the summer," I replied.

"You're stupid," he muttered from outside the window. "Am I?"

He sighed loudly enough for me to hear him from inside the room. "It's too narrow," he finally announced, pouting as he pulled his head back inside.

"I tried to jump across a latrine ditch once," I said, as soon as he was bored enough to listen, before he could start throwing tantrums again. "Do you know what they are? They don't have them in Origh."

"They have them in the provinces," Aron answered, twisting his nose in fascination with all things gruesome. "They're nasty."

"You're right, they are. Someone put a board up as a bridge over it, but it was a quarter mile down the road, and I didn't want to walk that far. Big Geordie—he was like my father—and the Thin Man—he was like my uncle—they were going on down to the bridge, but I told them I could jump across it. They said it was too wide. I backed up, as far as that wall is from that window, and I ran at it. I jumped. I didn't make it. I dropped my foot in and twisted my ankle. They had to pick me up, one under each arm, and carry me around."

I watched Aron's face as he thought about it, curling his face as he imagined the smell, then frowning as he recognized being carried around by a man under each arm as a mirror of himself that afternoon. "Do you have a scar," he asked, changing the subject thoughtlessly as children can. "You know, on your ankle?"

"No," I answered.

"Oh," he frowned. Then, "I'm Aron."

"I know, I've heard."

He waited. "Who are you?"

"I'm Elzith."

"Oh, you're my new guard." He stretched out on his back on the floor. "I'm supposed to shake your hand. I hate that. It's stupid."

"Why?"

He thought. "I don't know, I just don't want to do it. My father says I have to do it all the time."

"Then it's a good thing I'm not your father," I said, and kept my hands to myself. Aron was chattering

placidly about the scars he had on his knees and the ones
he'd given other boys at school by the time his father's
party came to retrieve him.

"I want to walk back with Elzith," he announced, as if
that wasn't already the plan, and that was all he said to
them for the rest of the day. The entire party, not the
least of all Jannes himself, stared at me in astonishment,
and said something I would never expect. They pro-
claimed me good with children.

It's odd they would make that claim, I said to Tod
when I told this story to him later. I've had virtually no
contact with children, even when I was a child myself in
the City. The clever thieves among them were kin and
competitors; I stayed out of their territory. All the rest
were alien to me. I knew nothing of their tears and
tantrums, fears, nightmares, laughter. Big Geordie had
no children. The Thin Man, who took up with us the
year I was—supposedly—eleven, had about thirty of
them, but disowned them all.

The Thin Man wasn't a confidence artist, only a thief,
and an audacious one. He was almost as thin as Geordie,
but close to seven feet tall. We thought he was a Healer
or a madman cut off from his tribe, except that he spoke
normally and had no powers, even for subtlety. He did
absolutely nothing to disguise himself as he broke into
buildings and picked pockets. He had a voice that carried for blocks. He got at least five children in the year
that I knew him. The first thing he did when he met
me was to search the front of my dress to see if I had

breasts yet. Geordie threatened him thoroughly, but the Thin Man protested his innocence. "I don't do the young ones, not anymore," he said, "but there's some that does, and the lass could make a fair piece of silver for a little piece of skin." Geordie never trusted him, and after the Thin Man took me to meet some of the talented women he knew, anger was his first expression every time he saw the Thin Man.

I was never angry at the Thin Man. I was never angry at all. I recognized the repulsion on the faces of other people who looked at him but felt none of it. I neither loved nor hated him when he joined us. The day he helped Big Geordie pull me out of a latrine ditch I felt no embarrassed rage at him, no desire to call him or myself stupid. I recognized my mistake as if someone else had done it. I regarded the Thin Man as I did the dirt in the street or the poxy beggars who slept in the alleys, or even the sun, always present, a part of the world, and that was all.

I watched emotions, of course. I had to learn to mimic them in order to play an effective game. I watched those children although I didn't understand them. Learning from them was all I needed to do. I learned well, too; I convinced a whole herd of fools to take me home, feed me, give me coin and shoes and the coats off their backs, by squeezing out a few tears and a good story about a dead mother or a starving baby sister. The tears weren't real, though, and I knew I lacked the thing that generated them, the thing my peers understood but that I had no grasp of.

Less than a year after he joined us, the Thin Man was arrested. They carried him off to the square to have his head chopped off, since this was Karrim and executions were festive public events. Dabionian Justices were scarce and so were their hypocritical claims to cleanliness and order. Thieves and miscreants didn't simply disappear in Karrim; they were done away with in the full light of day, and the spectators in the first row would have the blood on their clothes and their faces to testify.

On the day the Thin Man was executed, I lied my way into the old guard tower and watched the affair from above. The crowd was full of taunting, cheering, noisy people, and two wailing women near the front. I recognized them as two of his dalliances. One held a messily swaddled infant in her arms, and the other was still pregnant. I watched their bizarre displays of emotion and concluded that they had fallen in love with the Thin Man. Wretched fools. The one with the infant was hoisting that squalling bundle up above her head, crying to the man on the platform to give his son his name. The other one seemed to be pledging her love, promising to follow him to the underworld, and some such. I knew the Thin Man well enough to have heard him scorn all women and their thoughts of love, and to commend all children to hell. In fact, he mounted that platform with a sneer on his face. Once the black-hooded man with the axe stripped his shirt, though, cutting it off him with a pass of a knife up his chest and hacking the sleeves off his bound wrists, and then pressed him to his knees in front of the block, the Thin Man changed. His face went white, his bony shoulders shook. Just before his neck went down to receive the axe, he stretched that doomed throat and shouted out his real name, the name that would survive in his son.

*(But he did not die by that axe. I did not tell Tod that; I let him think whatever he wanted about the Thin Man's death. But when he looked up with that white face, the shock of seeing death opening his eyes wide, I found my way into them. Not only into his mind where I could see the truth of him, but into the center of him. I could reach in and stop his heart before the executioner's axe, which he hadn't bothered to sharpen for such a common criminal, met the Thin Man's neck.)*

I still remember the name that the Thin Man shouted out, as if it matters. I've always had a head for names. Another thing Loyd values me for. I also learned, that day as I watched the Thin Man look on his own death, to take all evidence with a grain of salt. The cavalier attitude with which he'd lived had been thoroughly convincing; he'd even convinced himself. Then he saw the end of that careless and arrogant life, and the whole act crumbled as a sham.

# 23

THE LETTER F WAS MISSING. TOD HAD LOOKED ALL over the shop and couldn't find its box. He had fourteen F's that he'd taken out of the press and nowhere to put them. He could hardly wake Keller up to ask him, though.

"They must have some young printer they're breeding to take my place," Keller had said when Tod walked in, once the door had closed completely behind him. He didn't say what he meant, although Tod could guess at the meaning: The Justices were working him to death. A fresh job lay drying on the tables, and others still hung from the ropes above them. The job that Tod had come for wasn't done, though, having been pushed aside again.

"I'll finish it for you, lad," Keller said, in a voice cut in half by fatigue, "just give me a minute." He slumped into a chair and dropped his head onto an inky hand.

"No you won't," Tod said on impulse.

Keller looked up with sleepy surprise on his face. Tod never talked back to him. "I won't?"

"You've been up all night again," Tod stumbled.

"Of course," Keller began, and took a breath. After the breath he would say, "Not like I haven't done that before," or some such thing, as usual. Tod cut him off before he got there.

"Well, you're going to bed now."

Keller stared at him, speechless.

"Come on, off with you," Tod prompted, boldly taking Keller by the elbow and leading him to his own room at the back of the shop. Keller was seated on his bed and had his shoes off before he could even start muttering about ink and sleeping and irritating binders. Tod closed the door on the printer with a smile on his face.

This was how Tod found himself putting the type away for Keller, and at a loss to find the F's. There were boxes of letters scattered all over the shop, and Tod was sure he'd checked all of them twice already. He went to the crooked set of shelves behind the front door to check there again. When the door was flung open it nearly hit him in the head.

"You—Redtanner!" It was Justice Paloman. He was shaking, his wig was askew, and his face was damp with exertion and the heat. He let the door slam on his guards, leaving them in the street. He reached out a hand and grasped Tod's arm. "You're here!"

It was only the second time Tod had seen the old Justice, since he hadn't been at Keller's shop when Paloman's last job came in. Tod remembered the desperate look, though. If anything, the Justice was more desperate, more frantic. He was a drowning man and Tod was the only one who could save him.

"Help me," the Justice pleaded.

Tod reached out, as if to lift him out of the water. What could he do? He sought the man's face for answers.

"I have this," Justice Paloman stammered. Under his arm he held a parcel, wrapped in layer after layer of cloth like swaddling. "I have to authenticate it. The—the Justice—the Lord Justice," he was struggling to say, unwinding the wrapping in strips that began to pile up around their feet. A small, very old book was revealed. "I don't know what to do," the old man nearly sobbed. Then he lifted his eyes and met Tod's, with a look that was shameful and imploring. "You can help me," he whispered, "can't you?"

Tod stared at the book. He took it carefully in his hands, while Paloman seized him by the arms, and Tod turned the book gently, peering at it through the layer of gauze that was still tied around it. That activity kept him from having to speak. It took him some time to figure out what he was being asked. Paloman had this book, and he needed to authenticate it. He didn't know how. He thought Tod knew how, being a bookbinder. He wanted Tod to authenticate the book.

But Tod didn't know how to authenticate it. He considered telling Justice Paloman this; the words almost slipped out of his mouth. He caught them back, not wanting to make the Justice any more frantic.

The old man's hands tightened on his arms. "Can you do it?" he rasped.

Tod looked up. The Justice's teeth were not so yellowed as his grandfather's, although Tod had guessed they were of an age. Maybe the Justice wasn't as old as Tod had thought. Looking at his teeth, Tod said, "Yes, I think so. Let me see it." Then he was able to pull out of the man's grip and walk away, turning toward one of Keller's tables to set the book down, to open it, and to think.

He had an idea, actually. He thought he knew what to do; he was fairly confident, in fact. The thing that truly bothered him was something else entirely. He'd have to leave the shop, and since Keller was sleeping, the shop would be unattended. Tod wondered if he could get the door locked, but he was afraid it would hurt Keller's business to have the shop closed up in the middle of the day.

For a minute it occurred to Tod that he was playing Justice Paloman. He wondered if Elzith would think he was playing a good game. He felt a twinge of self-consciousness, a slap of guilt. Then he realized suddenly what he could do to solve his problem, and he forgot that twinge in an instant.

Jereth Paloman couldn't wait until he reached Insigh to write the letter. It was late, and though the coachman offered to drive all night and get the Justice back to District One by morning, Jereth refused.

"Find me an inn," he commanded the driver. A few minutes later, he pounded the roof with a walking stick and brought the rolling coach to a halt. "First, find me a stationer's." The coach obediently took him there. When he climbed back in a few minutes later, his arms full of purchases and his head full of uncommon victory, he was shaking with something like ecstasy.

"My lord," he dictated to himself, not able to wait for the table that a room in a proper inn would bring him, "I have fulfilled your command."

The answer had been hard-gained. It was an hour before they had even departed the printer's shop, as Redtanner told him he had to wait for a printing job to be finished. The press used special ink, Redtanner said, and it had to be monitored as it dried to be sure it set properly. Then the bookbinder went next door to the chandler's shop, telling Jereth that Keller had not yet returned from an errand, and he had to borrow the spare key that the chandler kept to lock the shop. Finally, Jereth waited as Redtanner penned a note for the door directing customers to the chandler. "He's probably in there sleeping, the sod," joked the fat, sweating chandler. He was as waxy as the candles he made, he had an ugly, black bruise on his forehead that he had not covered, and Jereth turned away from the man in distaste. "He's fooling you, lad!"

Redtanner blushed, obviously in embarrassment at the chandler's teasing. "Well," the bookbinder answered, "if he sneaks home without your noticing, you might just find him doing that."

At last they were on their way, and Redtanner led him to the archives building. "This book has a partial printer's mark," Redtanner told Jereth as they walked. "In the archives, there are rolls listing all the printers for the last five hundred years or more. Keller's shown it to me. I can match up the mark, and then we'll know who printed the book."

"You're certain you can match the printer's mark?" Jereth asked, having looked at the title page over Redtanner's shoulder. Half the leaf had crumbled away. But Redtanner had nodded enthusiastically and quickened his pace.

> I can tell you with all assurance, my lord, that your book was produced between the years 450 and 480 by the Common Calendar, in Dabion, by the printer Dalanis Black.

Jereth felt utter calm as he wrote these words, finally sitting at a table in the inn, carefully tracing letters in new ink on fresh paper. His hand did not even tremble. It was as if another hand was writing, as if he inhabited another body entirely. He was a scholar again, a man of power. He had not been this calm before, when Redtanner was scanning page after page of historical rolls, turning leaves endlessly as the light began to die out of the high, narrow windows. A clerk came to turn up the wicks on the lamps above their tables. Jereth became so nervous that be began seeing his own fear in the bookbinder's face. Then, suddenly, another page turned, and Redtanner exclaimed, "I've got it!" Jereth nearly cried out with joy. The only part of the mark that remained was the top of some creature's head, wearing a seven-pointed crown. In the rolls of printers, a stamp of a rampant horse was annotated with the words: "This is the only mark bearing an animal crowned with seven points. The standard crown has six."

I wish to thank you, my lord, for your invaluable recommendation of . . .

Jereth stopped himself short. Varzin had expected Jereth to authenticate the book based on his own knowledge. Even if the worthy bookbinder had come to Jereth's attention on Varzin's recommendation, it would certainly be shameful to admit that Jereth had relied entirely on Redtanner to complete the task that Jereth had been assigned himself. Jereth's hand began trembling; he could almost feel himself shrinking back into his old, tired body. It would be better not to mention Redtanner at all.

. . . this task. It has given me the greatest of opportunities to demonstrate my loyalty to

you. You can trust that I will be always at your
service.

He signed the letter and dropped his quill before the
shaking of his hand could mar his penmanship any further. He sighed deeply and unevenly. He believed he was
now safe.

# 24

A RON HAD FOUND, CICELINE LEARNED, A NEW WAY of harassing the servants. She could hear him shouting downstairs. Her husband was quartered away in his rooms, burning things in the fireplace that was unnecessary in this season and drinking large quantities of restorative. Ciceline waited to hear the pounding in the stairwell that always came at the end of Aron's tantrums, when Dal would finally get his hands on him and wrestle him up to his room. It would be her cue to go in and soothe him, and she had to be ready for it.

"Look at me, Mother!" she heard near her door, her son's voice drowned by loudly pounding feet. "I'm a guardsman!" There was a click, a snap, and a brief yelp of pain from Dal. Ciceline tried to imagine what had snapped, curiosity driving her to open the door before her cue. Her son was outside, brandishing a pistol. Ciceline froze. Her body was torn, wanting to hide from the danger her son held as much as she wanted to cover him and protect him from it. The clicking happened again. Ciceline knew nothing about firearms, but it clicked again and again as Aron pointed the pistol at various targets. Nothing happened. The weapon was disabled. For effect Aron pulled a marble out of his pocket and threw it at Dal, who ducked to avoid being hit again. "Bang!" shouted Aron.

Then there was another voice, from below, echoing up the stairs. "He's done what?"

Ciceline stepped backward and shut her door. The guard had arrived. Ciceline sat down and went back to her stitching with as much concentration and calm as she could muster. The woman was in her house. The needle pricked Ciceline's finger and she gasped, dropping the stitching into her lap. She thrust her finger into her mouth so that the blood would not stain her work. She had to regain her composure. It was her husband's house, and he had hired the guard, to mind Aron while he was home from school. It was not for Ciceline to doubt her husband's orders.

She resisted the temptation to stand behind the door and listen. Ciceline would do nothing unsuitable; she would simply continue her stitching. The tiny flowers had been ruined by the noise, her hand having shaken so badly that she stuck the stitches all out of place, but she could alter the petals and make them into large blooms. Roses, perhaps, which she hadn't seen since her youth. Flowers were not allowed in the city of the Justices, yet this woman-guard was, wearing her men's clothes and a pistol at her side. There must be some wisdom in it, something the Justices saw that she did not. Even in

Karrim women worked alongside men in the fields. It increased productivity and made use of the ignorant masses; it kept peace and order in the lands under Dabion's guardianship. Filanar said as much himself. Perhaps they needed to make use of the lower-class women in Dabion as well. There were villages, weren't there, outside the cities? Such places had to be full of peasants who needed to be brought to order. That was it; this woman was no threat. She was a peasant.

"What are you doing?" the woman's voice said in the next room.

"I'm a guardsman," cried Aron. "Bang bang!"

"Why are you doing that?" The woman was talking to Ciceline's son.

"I'll shoot you! Point your pistol at me!"

"I will not, and you will not, either."

There was a crash. Aron must have dropped the object. "You're no fun at all."

"It's not my job to be fun. Where did you get this?"

"Why should I tell you?"

"Only the Public Force has weapons authority. That means I already know where you got it from. No one would give you a weapon, so you must have stolen it. Why did you do that?"

"Ask me how I did it."

"No, I want to know why you did it."

"They were taking a rubbish cart through the streets this morning. It was early, it was so early it was still dark! The kitchen door was open 'cos cook was taking out some rubbish. I went outside and looked, and there it was. They had old uniforms in there, too. They'd just come from the barracks, I'm sure. I could've stolen a uniform!"

"So you're crawling around in other people's shit and scraps. How charming. You still haven't told me why."

Then, suddenly, Ciceline was at her son's door. She could no longer sit quietly. "I will not have you speak to my son in this manner."

The guard was silent immediately, and she turned to face Ciceline. It was obvious the woman-guard did not think of herself as a peasant. She did not lower her eyes, or bow her head below the level of her betters. Ciceline trembled a little and reached her arms out toward her son, who was standing on a chair. "Aron, come here."

The boy clambered off the chair and went to his mother, scuffing his feet. Ciceline grasped his shoulders and held him in front of her until her shaking subsided. Aron tilted his head up to look at her backward. "Is Father going to punish me for going outside without permission?"

"No one's going to punish you," Ciceline said, looking straight at the guard, trying to look equally strong. "Your father wasn't there, so he won't know."

If the guard took her words as a challenge she did not show it in her face. She clasped her hands behind her back and bobbed the short bow of a servant. "It was not my intention to undermine your authority, madam," she said. "I shall await the order of yourself or your husband." Then she left, and Aron began squirming like a snake in Ciceline's hands.

The guard persisted in arriving every morning shortly after dawn and staying until sunset. Ciceline watched her calendar, counting the days as they moved toward the end of the season and grew shorter. She looked with anticipation to those occasions of state that drew her husband, her son, and the guard out of the house. When they were at home, Ciceline listened carefully but inconspicuously to the woman's lectures, and knew when she could find Aron alone and petulant in his room, ready for Mother to bring sweets and wipe tears. Ciceline would do nothing so obvious as steal the guard's keys or defame the woman in front of Filanar; those things would be inappropriate. A wife was bound to protect her family, but she did it with the stealth of a Sivan cat.

Then one day, in one of his fits, Aron broke the mirror in Ciceline's room. Ciceline had been inspecting the cleanliness of Filanar's study, and arrived upstairs in time to watch the guard drag Aron to his own room by the collar.

"Why did you do that?" said that maddeningly calm voice from behind Aron's door. Her son's answer was muddled and distorted, and Ciceline could not hear what he said as she drifted, shakily, into her room.

"What are you so angry about?" the guard's voice went on, clear but far away.

Ciceline sank to the floor amid the broken glass.

Methodically she began to pick the pieces up, one by one. Her breath caught in her throat. She closed her hands on the biting edges of the shards. She could cut them up, her hands, her clothes, the linens on the bed, scratch the clean white paint from the walls. She sobbed, cast the shards away from her. Her hands stung in streaks of blood.

There was someone at the door, and Ciceline jumped. It was the guard. Ciceline turned her face away, wanting to wipe the foolish tears, but unable to do so without smearing blood on her face.

"I took these out so he wouldn't break them. There's still water here, if you want it."

Turning only a little, to see from the corner of her eye, Ciceline noticed that the woman was carrying the pitcher and basin from Aron's room. "Aren't you going to stay there and watch him?" Ciceline asked, trying to keep the tears out of her voice.

"There's nothing he can do now but finish crying, and he can do that without me." The guard set one foot in the room, to set the basin and pitcher down next to Ciceline's—which were empty, perhaps? Ciceline couldn't remember. The woman noticed what Ciceline hadn't; she must have seen the cuts on Ciceline's hands as well. Then the woman turned to leave, saying nothing else about what she'd observed.

"A silly thing to fret over," Ciceline found herself saying. "This mirror. It's only glass." She stood, shook out her skirt, and tried to walk smoothly to the basin to wash her hands.

The woman had paused in the doorway. Ciceline would have the chance to demonstrate her composure, after all. Then the guard spoke, unexpectedly. "You don't believe that."

Ciceline looked up, splashing water out of the basin.

"The mirror was important to you." The guard was watching her intently, looking into her with eyes that were, Ciceline noticed, quite disturbing.

Ciceline looked back down at her hands, at the water. She had a towel, but where was it? She searched her bureau blindly. "My father gave me the mirror. But he got it from a Manderan trader. It was a symbol of wealth and vanity. It's just as well it's broken."

"But it was important to you," the guard repeated, "and your child broke it. And you let him get away with it. You always let him get away with misbehaving. Why?"

Ciceline tried to counter the accusation with anger. "I am his mother and I will not stand for this—for your . . ."

"I know how you feel about me," the guard interrupted, not rising to the attack. "How do you feel about your son?"

Ciceline had to stop to breathe, and fresh tears dampened her cheek again. "I would do anything to protect my family," she whispered.

The guard had no other argument. She read Ciceline's eyes for a moment, then nodded, and left the room.

Two days later Aron slipped a note under his mother's

door. Ciceline picked it up gingerly in her scratched fingers and read: *Dear mother sorry for the broken mirror youre son Aron.*

"Did you put him up to it?" Ciceline asked the guard. The woman was sitting outside the door to the small, square yard, watching Aron hit a ball against the wall with a racket.

"No. What did he do?" The woman watched the game with a careless attitude. A net had been erected over the game area so that the ball wouldn't be lost in a neighbor's yard or the alley. Surely the woman was responsible for this act, this careful measure, though she regarded it with such detachment. Ciceline reached into her pocket and showed the woman the note, and received a nod in response. "I wondered what he was writing."

"But you didn't tell him to write it?"

"No. I did ask him how he thought you felt. I don't think that ever occurred to him before."

Ciceline looked at the note and sighed her reluctant concession. "You're good with children."

"They tell me this." The woman shook her head. "I'm just good at observing people."

"Certainly you're good with your own children."

"I have none."

Words fell out of Ciceline's mouth without giving her time to realize she shouldn't say them. "But you must be as old as I am. How haven't you had children yet?"

She flushed a little as the woman turned toward her. "Twenty-eight?" the guard asked, and Ciceline nodded.

They were the same age exactly. "My life might have been much different," the woman said quietly. "It wouldn't have been by my hand, though."

"What was your name? Elzith?"

They remained in the yard until the sun went down. "Aron can't possibly see that ball," Ciceline remarked as her son continued to jump around the yard. "He'll ruin his eyes."

"Only if he tries to write any more notes in this light," Elzith answered.

Ciceline laughed. "He shouldn't write any more notes at all! Did you see his penmanship? And that grammar—what do they teach him at that school?"

Elzith shook her head, and Ciceline thought she heard her laugh. Then she saw a firefly and looked about the yard, among the obsessively manicured trees and shrubs, trying to find it. It darted at the edge of her vision. It came from beyond the yard, from the alley that ran behind the house.

"I should go inside and check on the servants," Ciceline said quickly. "Supper should be prepared by now." But she didn't go to the kitchen. Instead she went to her chambers, lit a lantern, and opened its shade at her window.

# 25

KERK WAS HIS BEST ASSISTANT. IT WASN'T EASY TO
find good assistants in Rayner's line of work; he'd
gone through at least twenty of them before he'd found
Kerk, and twenty blundering idiots they had been, always failing at their tasks or getting caught. Almost all of
them had been called up before Tables of Justice for
stealing or trespassing, and Rayner had been summoned, grudgingly, out of his blessed seclusion so that
he could testify against them. Two or three of these
worthless creatures had done him the courtesy of getting
killed in the progress of their mistakes, saving him the
trouble of going to court to condemn them.

Then, six years ago, Rayner had found Kerk. The man
was perfection: competent, secretive, unshakable when
confronted. Rayner believed the man could even withstand torture, and in his moments of bored daydreaming he imagined ways to test the theory. Kerk almost
certainly had some connection to the Secret Force, that
pet project of Lord Councilor Muhrroh's that no one
was supposed to know about. Well—Rayner thought—

he doubted anyone did, except those as intelligent and crafty as he. Kerk probably wasn't an operative; he didn't spew words of loyalty to the honor of Dabion or waste any breath on the need to crush her enemies. Kerk bowed sensibly to the ultimate power of gold. Rayner knew he'd found a perfect match at once.

Kerk became, like the misfits before him, Rayner's runner. Rayner himself didn't go out. What was the use, with nothing to look at in this dull town but rows and rows of buildings screaming monotonously about justice? What was beyond Origh—hills? Trees? Rayner certainly wasn't going to filthy Karrim, or to Mandera, where they'd failed miserably in their pursuit of wealth, and the other countries were out of the question. Rayner was too old to bother with the outside anymore. After seventy years of tolerating the world, he felt he'd more than earned his retirement. Rayner rather liked it here, among the countless rows of buried and semisecret passageways below the Great Hall of Justice. The old fools in their Halls couldn't keep track of the tenants of those sunken rooms or what business they carried on there, and so Rayner found it easy to commandeer a suite of rooms in the lower tunnels. When he was called to make those tiresome appearances in the courtrooms, the Justices thought Rayner was coming from far away; they had no idea he was under their noses. The irony delighted him.

The location gave him perfect access to the information he needed for his work, as well. Some of the underground tunnels led to records storerooms, where the lives and crimes and disappearances of the wretched were chronicled. Rayner didn't visit the storerooms himself, of course. He preferred to stay home and watch his ever-growing horde of money, and some of those clerks who scurried around the archives like ants might recognize him, which wouldn't do at all. Fortunately, Kerk was as good at reading as he was at running. Rayner didn't even have to send him off with explicit directions about which records to pilfer; Kerk was bright enough to determine who would be a good target on his own. Of course, this meant there was a danger of Kerk poaching: hitting targets of his own without notifying Rayner or sharing the profits with him. Rayner sighed for a moment and thought of his losses. Then he looked at his ledgers, at the numbers that had grown so impressively over the last six years. As long as Kerk kept him in cash so well, Rayner could let the man siphon a little on the side. It was well worth it.

The first step of his scheme was reading the records and determining the targets. Second was the approach. Since most of the targets had "disappeared" and were rotting in their chains in Dabion's prisons, the second step required a master of disguise and subversion. This was one place where Rayner's previous assistants had failed, and most of them had been locked up in the very prisons they had tried to infiltrate. Kerk never failed. He always came back—from the unpopulated reaches of Dabion where the prisons were built, where no one would have to look at the foul things—with news of success.

Most of the wretched weren't hard to bargain with. Conditions in the prisons were appalling, as Rayner knew. When a criminal disappeared in Dabion he was gone forever. But Rayner knew where to find him, and Kerk knew how to get there. It was easy to get anything out of a prisoner with a simple offer of release. Thieves revealed the location of their stashes, smugglers identified their suppliers, servants convicted of stealing from their employers gave directions for breaking into cabinets and safes. Kerk used this information to easily duplicate the actions, without the bit about getting caught. Kerk was a genius. The payoff was Rayner's.

Of course Rayner didn't actually gain release for any of the prisoners. They were criminals, after all.

Kerk didn't limit himself to the captive quarry of prisoners, either. In the records, he found evidence of even more tantalizing targets, wrongdoers whom Rayner had long suspected but had not been able to access. Powerful men made any evidence of their actions disappear, as surely as the criminals disappeared. Like the criminals, Kerk could find it. Rayner was now on the trail of a prize like no other, his old commander, his old supreme fool, Lord Justice Jannes himself. Rayner grinned like a schoolboy to think of it.

Great prizes entailed great challenges, though, and Kerk was the man to meet them. When the ever-resourceful Kerk was interrupted in his task by the Lord J's wife, he wasn't swayed, didn't give up, and didn't bungle the job. No, he saw the opportunity for an even greater gain, and made the most of it.

And here he was at Rayner's door, his priceless assistant, with new quarry in tow. Rayner stretched out appealingly on the lounge. He cut a fine figure, even if he was an old man. It wasn't often that he entertained a woman in his quarters, still less often the same woman a second time. It was almost a shame she was the faithful sort.

She was a fool, though, wearing that cloak in this heat. It was her attempt at being inconspicuous, of course, the same kind of ineptitude that got so many of Rayner's prior assistants locked away. Kerk knew how to keep the stupid woman out of sight, at least.

"Welcome again, my dear," Rayner said, smiling. "I trust your walk here was pleasant."

Jannes's wife, for all her attempt to be cool and strong, trembled. Rayner had abandoned his jacket and vest and undone the six buttons on his shirt. He laughed to himself, enjoying the game of unnerving her. All this entertainment, and more money as well. Kerk was a jewel.

"I have what you asked for," Ciceline said. So seriously.

Rayner decided to draw a bit more from this delightful new target. "Do you?" he purred, reclining on the lounge. "I think there are things I haven't asked for yet."

The woman's eyes flew wide, amusingly, and she

looked wildly in Kerk's direction for aid. Kerk stood motionless, leaning against the wall in his gray servant outfit, arms crossed, no expression on his face. Rayner knew Kerk was as capable of playing a role as he was, and could easily have joined in with his young man's lustiness, had it been some other woman. Ciceline Jannes had stumbled upon Kerk at the door of her husband's bedchamber, though, bottle of poison in hand as he was about to soak the cloth intended for suffocating the Lord Justice. The woman wasn't very smart, of course, but she wouldn't be convinced that Kerk was anything other than her husband's would-be murderer. Kerk stayed out of the fun.

"Oh don't fret," Rayner said, sitting upright. "Come, show me what you've brought. Come closer!" he ordered as she shied away from his outstretched hand. "Don't be a child! I asked for the agreed amount, and now you owe it to me!"

He expected that ridiculous cloak would be concealing an armload of female things: dresses, lace, things women valued. Someone Ciceline's age wouldn't even have jewels, those relics of Manderan trade that the Justices had outlawed after the economic collapse twenty-odd years ago. But Rayner was pleasantly surprised. Here was a woman who knew her husband's rooms, probably considering herself a good housekeeper. In a shaking hand she extended a purse, filled with perfectly counted coins.

Rayner opened the purse and spilled its contents into

his hand, enraptured. "My dear!" he exclaimed. "This is beautiful!"

Kerk watched the golden cascade with the concealed interest of the professional that he was. A fortuitous interception, indeed. Rayner would give him a generous share of this profit.

The woman spoke then, unbidden, desperation in her voice. "Now you won't hurt my husband?"

Rayner poured the money back into its pouch and smiled sweetly. "No, my nasty assistant won't appear at your husband's door ever again."

Jannes traveled frequently, though, and any number of accidents could happen on the road. Rayner thought of telling Jannes's dutiful wife that, as he watched her pull up her hood and prepare to leave, wondering how much more he could get from her. Better not to push his luck, he decided. The woman might spook and tell Jannes, or more likely, Jannes would discover the missing money and start to investigate. Rayner wouldn't be greedy. He'd have enough cash once Jannes was dead.

Jannes was involved in his own schemes, of course, like so many of the hypocritical Justices, those guardians of law and order. In the storeroom were abundant records of illegal enterprises in the Five Countries, and the most profitable of them were neatly ignored once the reports reached Dabion, buried in the archives by the scheming Justices. One of the most notable of these was a distillery in Karrim, actually a series of small producers that evaded the notice of the incompetent authorities who were supposed to be preventing such stills from operating. Operate they did, though, and produced a formidable amount of liquor and an impressive amount of money. Rayner had seen the numbers in the records Kerk brought him, records that had all been signed and dismissed by a certain Lord Justice. Kerk did some further investigation and identified the go-between who interacted with the manager of the distilleries, diverted the attention of the authorities in Karrim, and collected money that he brought back, dutifully as a little dog, to Jannes.

It wouldn't be long before Kerk could intercept the go-between. He had tracked the man's movements, learned all the details of his interaction with Jannes, and would soon be able to step in and convince the go-between that he was the new collector. Or perhaps Kerk would just eliminate the go-between and take his place, and collect the money directly from the manager of the distillery. It hardly mattered to Rayner, as long as he had Jannes's takings.

The Lord Justice still had to be killed, of course. If Rayner merely intercepted his cash flow, Jannes might investigate. He had a history with Rayner, having been appointed Lord Justice in the last few years before Rayner's timely retirement, and Rayner could not be certain that Jannes would not deduce his involvement. If Jannes were dead, though, no one would come forward. The other Justices would never risk implicating themselves in illegal activities by claiming they knew about

Jannes's misdeeds. Anyone with less status, like the clerks and servants who aided Jannes and carried his reports to their disappearing place, would fear arrest. They would say nothing for fear of disappearing themselves.

But what about the dutiful wife? She knew both Rayner and Kerk now, and could identify them. A foolish little woman she might be, but she had the nerve to steal money from her husband and follow a strange man to a secret meeting place, and she might be bold enough to talk. This would have posed no problem in years past. The words of women never carried any weight before. Women who had brought land or property claims before Rayner's Table of Justice never represented themselves; they had needed a male relative to speak on their behalf. How things had changed. The other day, Kerk brought news from the outside, since Rayner liked to hear such things occasionally, as entertainment. During one of those ridiculous processions that the Justices were so fond of, Kerk had observed females among the guards that formed their armed escort. If Rayner hadn't known Kerk so well, he'd have accused the man of lying. Such a thing would never have been thought of ten years ago, when Rayner was a Greater Justice. His former fellows were going mad. Ciceline Jannes might get her day in court, after all. Rayner might have to do something to prevent that.

He was so absorbed in his thoughts that he didn't notice Kerk's customary scoping of the corridor when he opened the door. He didn't notice that Kerk saw someone out there, fifty yards down the hallway. Rayner certainly wouldn't have guessed that the person was one of those very females who were part of his former fellows' armed escort. Kerk didn't even recognize her for that; he saw a middens-keeper, in dark clothes stained by foul labor, wearing an equally foul-smelling hat that concealed the person's hair and face, and carrying rake and shovel. Kerk turned up his nose and led his charge in the opposite direction down the corridor.

# 26

I KNOW WHAT I LOOKED LIKE, BUT EVEN I HAVE PRIDE. I covered myself in mud; it's only imagination that fills in the smell. Tod looked horrified when I appeared at his door, asking if he had an extra bucket of water.

I didn't answer him at once when he asked what I'd been doing. I told him stories instead. The Thin Man's death was where I left off.

That summer there was a drought in Karrim, and the slim business that sustained the City all but dried up. The thieving that had fed Geordie and me was no longer enough, and Geordie left town periodically to find other targets. He wouldn't take me with him, but left me behind with admonitions to stay put. When the boredom became an annoyance I went out, picked pockets when I could find any that weren't empty, followed the Thin Man's advice about making a fair piece of silver. The local lawmakers were usually good for this, as they were the only ones who had the silver to pay for it. Once, on a day when I was bored with that men's sport, I talked my way into a woman's home, and had her convinced I was a long-lost niece and the sole inheritor of her meager fortune. Then her husband came in, and he recognized me as the urchin he'd given a coin to for a favor under the bridge a few days before. He covered his sputtering red-faced shame by putting me under arrest immediately.

Had Geordie been in town he surely would have found me and smuggled me out of the cattle pen that Karrimian lawmakers called a jail. He didn't have time to do so. Within a few days the embarrassed man who'd arrested me secured a prison transport and sent me to the big house in Dabion.

I didn't try to escape. Tod is surprised. To play the game, sometimes you have to play along. So I went to the prison to see what move I could make there. I was put in a cell with the other women, the prostitutes, the wives who stabbed violent husbands with kitchen knives, the hags who gave out herbs that got rid of unwanted babies, the midwives who warned women not to trust the male physicians. I watched them and I learned their expressions, their emotions, a new range of roles to play.

I wasn't there long before we received a visitor. "The big man," one of the women said, whispering into my ear. "He's looking for crafty ones. I'm too old, but you can get his attention. It'll be your release, if you do." Then the jailers came for me, and took me to play the father of all confidence men. That was how I met Loyd.

He'd devised quite a test for me. He was holding a watch when I was brought in, a bright golden thing that he quickly tucked into a pocket in his coat. Easy enough, I thought. The prison was in the northern part of Dabion, a massive stone building that was cold even when it wasn't winter. We prisoners were treated with no comforts, the cold being part of our punishment, but this administrator's office had a fireplace. No fire was laid, though. I waited to hear what the big man had to say.

"You've an excellent record here," Loyd read from some papers on the desk in front of him. "Compliant, unrebellious. What were your parents like?"

"My mother was a saintly woman," I began spinning, squeezing out fat tears in appropriate places as I listed her qualities. "Even after my poor dad died, and we were paupers. My poor mother worked and worked, and the innkeeper took all her money. He lied and said she broke dishes and had to pay for them. We had no money for food. I had to find money. I had to find"—another tear—"those men." Sob. "We had no wood for fuel, and it was winter." I shivered miserably and gawked at the cold fireplace.

Loyd shouted for a guard outside to bring firewood and a blanket for me. Then, just as I planned, he took off his own jacket and draped it around my shoulders. Now I had to figure out how to get the watch out of his pocket without his noticing. "Do you have children?"

There was a window behind Loyd and he turned to look out of it, but not far enough. He gazed through the glass wistfully, with me still at the corner of his eye. "My children." He sighed. "They're grown now and have no

time for their old father. But they used to play in a
meadow just like this one."

"A meadow?" I sniffed. "I used to play in a meadow,
but they won't let me now."

His expressions were perfect: thoughtful as he
searched my wide-open face, doubtful as he scrutinized
the papers in front of him, then excited as he proposed
his offer. "Come look," he beckoned, and I let him lift me
over his chair, grasping me sexlessly under the arms in
that paternal manner. I crammed myself close to the
window and crooned, and with him at my back I pulled
the watch out of the jacket and dropped it into the
pocket of my shift.

The guard came in and started a fire. Loyd took his
jacket back and replaced it with the blanket brought
by the guard, and I sat in my place again. Then the
prize: Loyd started patting his jacket pockets, his brow
wrinkled.

"Looking for this?" I said, pulling out the watch.

He nodded, without surprise. "You could get in serious trouble for that."

"Sure," I said, and tossed the watch on the table. He
did raise an eyebrow then, at my disinterest. I didn't try
to keep the watch or use it to bargain my way out of
punishment. I stared flatly into his slightly startled eyes,
and saw how shallow the expression was, how carefully
measured. "I don't have a mother, either."

"I know," Loyd replied. "I don't have children. What's
on your leg?"

At first I thought he was serious. I looked down and saw a bright red streak down the side of my shift. I grasped the dress and looked at it. Blood? No. Then I looked up at Loyd. In his hand he held a red wax crayon.

"Looking for this?" he said. I respected him at once.

For two days Loyd interviewed me, fetching me from my cell in the morning, sitting me in the administrator's office in a chair before the fire, and keeping everything far enough away from me that I couldn't reach it or steal it. He questioned me all day, asking me about Big Geordie and the trash heap where I was found, giving me riddles to solve and verses to memorize, testing me to see if I knew my numbers and letters. Geordie had taught me to read—he'd said a confidence artist always had to know more than his target, and not knowing how to read put you at a disadvantage. I solved Loyd's riddles and repeated all his verses back to him, turned them around and said them backward. My mind had passed his tests. On the third day, Loyd put me in a dress and a coat and took me out to a carriage bound for a place I won't name. On that journey, I asked him why he chose me, what else he was looking for with his questions besides my wits.

"I had a sense about you," he answered, and that was all he said about it.

I went to the training dormitory. My lessons happened mostly in isolation. I had individual quarters, and the few common areas—the dining room, the firing range—were supervised. They didn't want operatives communicating, lest we share restricted information. I didn't desire their company, anyway; I wouldn't have even if I'd been able to feel lonely. A competitiveness festered in the dormitory, each operative wanting to prove he was stronger and smarter than the next, trading boasts in euphemisms since they weren't allowed to discuss details. When my two years of training ended and I went out on assignments, I was as relieved to be rid of them as if they were squawking birds.

My first assignment was Tristam. I can say that because Dabion has put their interaction with that seaside Manderan city into official record. They broke down a crime ring there and want to make sure everyone knows it. Dabion is king and no one can hide. I no longer have to conceal my presence there. Dabion sent spies to Tristam and I was one of them.

What they called a crime ring was a union of fishermen, unauthorized by Dabion and therefore illegal. I didn't care about fish or unions. I was there to play a game. The heads of the union—who divided and rotated their roles in an attempt to disguise themselves— were charismatic, energetic, and full of secrets: excellent pawns for the game. It was the finest thing I'd played to date.

I went in posing as a fishmonger, and one of the leaders was so chronically loudmouthed that I heard a good deal simply by scaling fish while he was in the room. That trait, however, kept the other leaders from telling him anything crucial. I did pick up a useful name, though, when he dropped it, and crafted that name into another guise. I took on the role of an idealistic young boy, an apprentice I created for the fisherman who bore the dropped name. That fisherman of the borrowed name was from a village several miles away. He and his colleagues were interested in joining the union but hesitant, and so I claimed to be scouting for them. This got the second leader, the recruiter of the union, to tell me all about its organization. The third leader was the keeper of the greatest secrets, and he was the most taciturn. I got to him with my most audacious ruse, posing as a deaf housekeeper. One of the prison women had told me abundantly of her deaf daughter, enough that I could create a satisfying likeness, and Loyd's training had taught me more of what I already knew: how to react to nothing. I passed all of the third leader's tests of my deafness, all his attempts to startle me with loud noises, and once he was convinced of my ability to keep his secrets, he proved to be in need of a confessor of sorts. I won the games, triumphed over these men, gathered up their secrets, and brought them back to Loyd.

This was what all those early assignments were like, the first ten years. I was playing my game—I was young enough to think it was mine—and I was winning. I culled secrets from across the Five Countries, I broke down men who thought they were infallible, I had ten years of it and a perfect record. Loyd's best. He was proud of me.

Was I loyal to him? I must have been. I didn't care for

the game itself, I only wished to have the victories. I felt
nothing about the people I conned, and I wasn't interested in their secrets. Even winning began to bore me. I
wouldn't leave the Force, though; I began to realize I
couldn't. I began to see that I had made a blind move
into someone else's field, and I had no control over it. I
couldn't have left even if I'd known I wanted to.

But now I'll play their game no more than I have to. I
could have gotten myself into it tonight. I was following
someone, out of habit, I suppose, though I had no reason to. That curiosity, that impulse to search and win
what I could, drove me as it always has before, even after
it should have been burned right out of me. I followed
my target as she was led to some meeting place, dis-
guised myself so they wouldn't suspect me of watching
them, and saw her go behind a door and come back out
a few minutes later. Too little time for any carnal activity,
not with the layers of clothing these proper women
wear, so it must have been an exchange of money. When
she had first come out of her house, when I began following her, I'd heard a jingling with her footsteps, and
after she came out of the meeting place, into the empty
hallway that made every sound echo, the noise of coins
was gone. Judging from what I knew of her position and
status, I guessed it was blackmail.

And there was more. My life is pocked by coincidences, and here was another one: I knew the man who
had escorted my target to her meeting place. He had
been with me at the dormitory, fifteen years ago. He

trained with me on the firing range, and I sat across from him at the dining table. He wasn't there long. I noticed his sudden absence, and questioned Loyd about it. I didn't care about the vanished student or what had happened to him, but I liked to nettle Loyd with my questions. Loyd told me he'd dismissed the student as unsuitable, not loyal to Dabion, or the Five Countries, or even Loyd himself, but only motivated by money. This man's presence with my target supported the blackmail theory. I could have found a way into the room, or followed the man after he left, or pursued the woman more closely. I could have learned what was going on. I could have referred the case to Loyd, if I were too weary to do it myself. But I didn't want to do any of that.

I tried to tell Loyd I was quitting the game. Perhaps I can't, but I won't play any more than they make me. Why should I step into a game that doesn't concern me? Why should I jump like a dog at their command? Tonight they didn't even command me—I'm anticipating their word like a dog waiting to be kicked. I don't care about this woman or why she's being blackmailed or what danger she might be in.

I expect Tod to call me heartless. Fine. When did I have time to grow a heart? Call me dishonorable and you won't anger me, either, since I care nothing for your words. I know my own honor. I've blocked shots aimed at unarmed targets, not because I'm soft for those targets—who might kill me with their own hands if they get the chance—but because it's dishonorable to take gunpowder against an unarmed man. These are rules I will keep despite the orders of the men who call themselves just. Blackmail has its own rules and I don't care to investigate to learn where those rules lie.

Tod didn't call me dishonorable, though, and he didn't call me heartless.

# 27

A RON JANNES WAS SITTING UPSIDE DOWN ON A chair, his back in the seat, his legs extending upward, his head hanging down and his hair brushing the ground. His guard was sitting cross-legged on the floor in front of him. She was teaching him how to cheat at cards.

"I can't wait to go back to school and try this," Aron boasted, gawking at the cards that he could barely see from his reversed vantage point.

"I thought you weren't going back to school," Elzith said.

Aron humphed. "Father will make me. Unless I can be a guard like you!" he suggested hopefully.

"You can't."

He frowned. "Then I'm going back, I guess. But I can cheat everybody!"

"How do you know they haven't already cheated you?" Elzith asked, folding the deck. "That's why I'm showing you this, if you haven't figured it out. People are going to cheat you, and you have to recognize it. I'd advise you to think hard before you cheat someone else, though. There's always a price, and you stand to lose more than you gain."

Aron flipped his legs down and turned himself out of the chair. "So why are you telling me this?"

Elzith looked at him. He liked that; no one else ever did it. Servants and common people weren't allowed to look at him because of whose son he was. They bowed their heads and dragged their eyes on the ground. When his father and his teachers and other men in charge talked to him, to give him rules and scold him, they never looked at him. They looked down on top of his head, they looked around him, but never right at him. Even when his mother looked at him, Aron thought she was seeing someone else. She looked somewhere near his chin, like he was shorter, like he was five or six. "Well, like it or not," Elzith said, straight into his eyes, "and that goes for both of us—I've been put into the position of mentoring you, and this is what mentors do."

"Right," Aron said, and he stretched on his belly on the floor, took the deck of cards, and started stacking them into a castle.

"He *is* maddening," Elzith was saying. She'd picked up a knife and taken the bowl of vegetables right out of Tod's hand, depositing a sack in his hands instead. "But he's not as bad as everyone says."

Tod opened the sack and found a loaf of bread and a cut of meat wrapped in butcher's parchment. "Of course, your idea of bad is a bit different from everyone else's."

Elzith nodded. "Granted. Most people don't have to compare things against getting stabbed or shot at. And I'm told Aron has improved since my arrival. He's gone a whole week now without a fit of any sort."

"He's getting attention," Tod mused. As he emptied the contents of the sack, he saw Elzith looking up at him, waiting for him to say more. Tod tried to put his words together and went on. "He wasn't before, and it was making him angry. Now he is, so he's not angry anymore. I did the same thing, with my brothers, getting angry when they didn't notice me. Then they noticed me only when I got angry, so I got angrier. Now I don't need them. Other people notice me and notice what I do. No one else matters. So I'm not angry." He shrugged. Elzith was still looking at him. Her eyes were sharply focused. He'd said something new, something that commanded her attention, if not actually surprising her. "What? Didn't they teach you that in spy school?"

Elzith's eyes wrinkled at the corners. Tod had learned this was a smile. "We learned types of people. Everyone we deal with is looking for power, and it's either out of greed, or because they think they deserve it, or to gain attention. We only learned how to get information out of them, though, and with attention-seekers that's not difficult. We never cared about why they wanted attention." Elzith nodded consideringly. "But that's interesting. Why does Aron want attention?"

Tod burst out laughing. "Because he's ten! You don't know much about being a child, do you?"

The wrinkles appeared again. "You're getting awfully bold, Redtanner."

Tod fought back a blush of self-consciousness. "Well, I'm right."

Elzith looked down and resumed her efficient chopping. "So," she said, in a reportlike voice. "I'm helping the child merely by listening to his rantings. Well and good. He doesn't require my advice. Also good, since I have none to give."

Tod smiled broadly, turning toward the stove to start preparing the meat. He was content. He felt, for the first time, something he could truly call joy. It was not the mock exhilaration of his brothers' attention, or the dizzy rush of gin. This was different. He had succeeded. He'd given help to Keller, and to Justice Paloman, and to Elzith. He was content. The unknown enemies who were coming for Elzith could burn down his house, and he wouldn't feel the angst of being rushed to his death, or the rage of being cheated out of life. He would be content. That was how his great-aunt died, Tod realized. Though it had horrified him, haunting his sleep and his waking hours with nightmares that he'd risked his own life to blot out, she had passed peacefully, like one who had learned the secret and needed nothing more here.

# 28

How do I describe what changed? Tod wants to know, as he's listening to these stories. The last one I told him was about the game, how I played it, how I was good at it. It's not a game anymore, and he wants to know why. That's how he tells a story, his brothers manipulated him, he let them, then one day he didn't let them anymore. His change is definite—he almost drank himself to death. Almost dying will do that to you. I've almost died too many times for it to matter. And the game began to change more slowly than that.

In 759 I went to Cassile, to Alderstand. It's one of the names I'm allowed to say, that little village with the velvet mills and the managers who weren't really plotting with Mandera. Dabion was wrong, so there wasn't anything for them to keep secret. I was there for a long time, two seasons, the longest I'd been on any assignment until then. Did the game change because I was bored? I recorded all the words that were said around me, nothing about Mandera, many things about religion, then the reconnaissance man came to get me and bring me across the river to Karrim, where the big men waited for their report. And I gave it to them, every word. It wasn't my job to interpret what I'd heard, to decide they wouldn't care because it had nothing to do with the supposed ties to Manderan criminals. I played my move the way I was supposed to, and I told them everything. And then the world changed. I'm the one, then, who brought down the monasteries. What does Tod make of that? *But that's how the* world *changed,* he says calmly, more calmly than any civilian I've ever met. *How did* you *change?*

I didn't know then, of course, what would happen when I gave up this information about the Nanian followers. I knew something would happen, though. That was where I met my first coincidence. There was a certain Justice there in Karrim when I gave my report, someone I didn't expect to see, someone I'd seen before, earlier that year. Where, when, who, this time I can't say. I'd stumbled across him on a different assignment, both of us in a place where we weren't supposed to be. He wasn't happy to see me again. He was so unhappy he could have killed me. I knew it, I saw it in him. I stopped him, I got away, it wasn't much trouble, but he hung on me even as I left him behind. Not the first time anyone had tried to kill me, of course, and not the last, but the first time—the only time I think—anyone wanted to kill *me,* just me, not because I happened to be his enemy or in his way but because he hated me that much.

The work went on, of course. I let the coincidence

drift to the back of my mind, and I went to Azassi in 760. I'm allowed to say so because Dabion has never made their domination of Azassi a secret. Azassi is an inferior race, they say, and the natives must be kept in line. You wouldn't keep it secret that you tied up your dog. The Public Force crawls over Azassi like cockroaches. I can't reveal which houses I had contact with, of course, but the names hardly matter.

In 760 I was twenty-four, and too old to pull off the sad-urchin game. I had been for some time, so the big men started sending me off with firepower. Add another number to my value—I'm a damned good shot. These pistols are notoriously inaccurate, and more likely to explode in your hand than hit their target. I'll never understand why Dabion threw out the Manderan practice of using swords; it's obvious why they made all the Manderan fencing masters disappear, but they could have at least learned something from them first. I had skill with the pistols, though, and more than a little luck. The first time I used one in the field, I shot out the knees of a man who'd been chasing me. Someone with more heart might have laughed with joy.

I didn't kill the Azassian with a pistol, though. I might not have had to kill him if I hadn't been wearing the damned thing. Dressing as Dabionian Public Force was only a cover to get me close to the houses of certain chieftains. There are gold mines in Azassi, and control of them has fueled conflict in that country for centuries. You shouldn't have to wonder why Dabion wants its hands in the affair. After the Manderan market crashed in 742, Azassi was Dabion's only remaining competitor, the only other major power in the Five Countries. If Dabion controls the clan that controls the mines, they've got that power in their fist. So I had to go in and find out who was winning in Azassi's little war.

Dabion is a homogenous country; they made it so by throwing out everyone they didn't want. Other countries aren't like that. You'll see red Azassian heads in Karrim, in Mandera, on the highways, and our brown ones turn up in the households of Azassian chieftains. It wasn't so hard for me to pass as a servant when I was out of my other work clothes. Azassian higher-ups aren't so different from Dabionian or Manderan ones, no matter how the Justices protest. They still don't look at servants, they can't be bothered with drudges, and they're blind to what really happens in their houses. One chieftain told an assistant his battle plans, word for word, while I was in his very chambers, on my hands and knees as I scrubbed his floor. When I left my soggy post and climbed back into my Public Force uniform, I commandeered a pigeon from that chieftain's own gamekeeper, wrapped the secret plans around its leg, and flew it to the household that Dabion wanted to win. I never found out whether the strike was intercepted. As if it matters. They're still fighting over that gold and they will until the mines run dry.

I got separated from the troop while I was writing that message. I was alone, at dusk, behind the chieftain's house. I climbed up a watchtower to loose the pigeon, and as I came down I startled a young clansman who was standing guard outside the tower door. He had come on duty late; he didn't know I was in there. He was that fiery sort of youth, anxious to prove himself, lacking the discipline to think before acting. When I caught his eyes, wide open as he lifted a pike to thrust into my throat, I knew that he saw only my pistol; he did not see my uniform, he was not going to see it, and he wouldn't stop the momentum of his pike until it was thrust home.

I did not kill him with my pistol, though. There was no time for that.

My actions were excused as a necessity by the administration of the Secret Force upon report. I was washed up and sent straight to my next assignment.

A certain official in a certain town in Karrim was suspected of failing to report all his profits from the parcels of farmland he managed. He was believed to have a ring of managers who collaborated and abetted, and I was to learn their names. The official was a frequent patron of a certain brothel. This was the winter of 760. There was never a chance of the absurd coincidence of crossing Tod's path there; he'd stopped going to Karrim years before. A whore is an excellent con, though, more invisible than a servant and able to get far closer, but I had no interest in this game. The names of the official's associates were a prize with no value. I wanted nothing more than to leave.

One night the proprietor sent to my room a drunken

ape of a man, who immediately started smashing furniture. He was so drunk he seemed to have forgotten what he'd come to a brothel for, since every time I got near him he threw me off. I finally got his breeches undone, tangled them around his ankles, and tripped him into a closet. From behind the locked door he started screaming threats at me. I climbed out the window before he could break the door down. The proprietor was guarding the entrance to the building and would have sent me back up to my room if I'd tried to go back in through the front door, so I had no choice but to sit outside until the wood carrier came at dawn. It was snowing. I forced myself to stay awake, watching the snow, watching my bare toes go blue and bluer, wanting nothing more than to leave the place and the official and the assignment. I wanted to give the Azassian youth back his life. I wanted to forget the face of that damned Justice who hated me so much. I wanted to go home. But where was home?

Magus had company again. His solitary vigil on the shore of Lake Azin was broken by another intruder. There was only one this time, thankfully, some peasant, some fool, who had stumbled out of some human city to stare gape-mouthed at a land far too inscrutable for any human to understand. Normally these trespassers came to the lake in ones or twos, being too ashamed of their interest in elves and fairies to let many of their peers know where they were going. Magus could easily handle one or two. This intruder would not see him.

Elves and fairies, he scoffed. That was what the humans thought lived in Sor'rai. They invented stupid tales to explain things that were beyond their pitiful grasp, then told the tales to their children to frighten them. Some of those people had figured out that the Sages—whom they called madmen—came from Sor'rai. It was the Sages that people saw dancing on the Sor'raian shore, when they looked across the lake at night. On this side, the human side of the lake, they would lock the Sages in asylums, not recognizing them as the dancers. The humans never asked any questions about who really lived in Sor'rai. A civilization far older and mightier than any human could imagine was reduced by a world full of idiots to a child's nursery story.

Some of the humans had determined that the Healers came from Sor'rai as well. Such witty little creatures the humans were, stunned by the Healers' great powers. None of us can mend injuries so well, or bring the dying back to life, they said to themselves. These Healers must be great magicians, so they must come from that magic land. The man on the shore scowled as he thought of it, the blind praises he'd heard from the mouths of so many humans. They had no idea who the Healers really were. There were two races of Sor'raians, and the Healers were neither. The Healers were handicapped, mutilated by their own hands. They were not Sages; they were not Magi. They tore themselves, incomprehensibly, from the great race of the Magi, gave up all but a fraction of the power they were born to, to cross into the human world.

They contaminated themselves in the presence of those who could never hope to grasp their greatness. The man on the shore even let the humans call him by the name of Magus, though they could not begin to fathom what it meant.

The man called Magus scowled even more bitterly. The intruder was approaching the lake, with a heavy gait and a creaking sound like a swinging pail, a fat milkmaid or a pimply boy carrying water. Magus wearily lowered himself to his knees and elbows, never dropping his head or taking his eyes off the water. Then he projected his thoughts at the fool walking toward him, and quickly overcame its feeble mind. Where Magus was crouched on the ground, only a hare would be seen.

If only it were someone on a horse, he thought. Horses were never fooled. They knew he was there, he could spook them easily, and they would run off and take their trespassing riders far away.

Once, a year ago, he was seen. Knowing he should have learned his lesson, Magus turned to examine this newcomer, to make sure he wasn't being seen again. This time he had guessed right; a girl with a bucket was sitting on the grass, gazing stupidly across the lake. There was no sharpness whatsoever in her eyes, and as he sniffed the air with his nose—which to her would be surrounded by whiskers—he caught no Sage odor. She was what she had seemed: a simple human female. Such was not always the case. Those Sages who had walked out of Sor'rai, across the rocky land bridge like powerless pack animals, had proven to be promiscuous as the hare that Magus was impersonating. The Magi lived long and bred rarely, but the Sages copulated like beasts, not only among themselves but with the humans, who didn't share the ability to control their fecundity. There could be half-Sages swarming the land like fleas. Magus realized that was an exaggeration; certainly the wise Sages would rein in their fertility, to keep their offspring out of human insane asylums, if nothing else. But Sage wisdom was beyond the understanding of even the Magi. At least one Sage had failed to keep his seed in check, for reasons never to be known, and even an untrained half-blood Sage could bind a Magus if he caught that Magus in the midst of working a spell.

Could the binding be fast, though? Magus had wondered this since the day he'd tried to project the image of himself as a stag over the mind of an intruder on horseback, and neither the horse nor the intruder had been fooled. The man astride the horse had stared at Magus, gasping "I caught you! I caught you!" over and over again. Surely the man didn't know what he was saying, babbling in the weakness of his human half. But Magus had dropped to his knees with all obedience, saying, "I am at your command, o Sage." And so the mixed-blood fool had come to command him for the past year, not often, but insistently. He ordered Magus to remain at the lake, awaiting his word, and there Magus remained. Magus often thought of walking away, of testing that bond, almost certain it would snap. But he was afraid.

He himself was hardly even a Magus, though what he was if not of that race, he did not know. He was the only child of his parents, both revered Magi in the true council, and they had borne him late in life. They had not noticed his failure, as a child, to grasp the household magics that moved like air through their dwelling. On the day of his presentation to the true council, they took him on the long journey from their home, hidden in the forests deep in Sor'rai, through the underground tunnels that led to the floor of Lake Azin. The meeting place was at the bottom of the lake. His father and mother had looked at him with pride, and opened the door to present him to the community of Magi. Then the water flowed in and the unimaginable happened. He began to drown.

Horrified, his mother seized him and swam toward the surface of the lake. It was an eternity away, and the water crushed on his lungs, dragging him ever downward as his mother tried to pull him up. He wished, in his saturated mind, that he was a fish, whipping through the water, free of duty and shame. Then he heard, in the heavy deadness of the waves, his mother's scream. "He's gone! I've lost him!" The hundred Magi launched themselves upward through the water at her cry. By the time he reached the surface of the lake, his head breaking into the harsh air, he was joined by countless other heads, Magi with dripping hair and robes. Beside him, his mother's wet eyes blinked in confusion, as she looked upon her son, no longer the fish she had seen in her hands during her race to the surface.

He could not walk under the water. He had no kinetic abilities, no household magics, none of the great powers of the Magi. His sole ability was in shapeshifting, or rather in causing others to believe he had changed his shape, and even then he could not affect more than one or two minds simultaneously. The elders of the true council examined him endlessly, probing him with powers that stung and scarred in their wake, but they could offer no explanation. He was Magus, yet his only power lay in the ability to cast his mind, like a Sage. He had no trace of the wisdom of the Sages, though, the ability to see things that are not shown to the eye. He was like a Healer who had been born of Magi but sacrificed the best of his powers, only he was not compelled by any sacred calling, such as the Healers professed to, and the sacrifice had not been voluntary. He was nothing, nearly powerless in the land of magic. He went to the other side of the lake though he was not human.

He found some solace in tormenting the humans. Not only were they fools and idiots; the majority of them were dissemblers. Magus detested dissemblers, although—and perhaps because—he was the greatest of dissemblers himself. The humans had built themselves an entire organization on the practice of lying, and Magus worked into it easily. He was admired by its leader, a king of liars. He wandered the human lands, hunting dissemblers, killing a few for spite. At length he bored of it, though. He did not report to the king of liars for his next assignment. He returned to the lake and watched his hidden homeland across the waters he could not navigate. Sickness of heart paralyzed him; he could not go home, he had no place elsewhere. Then the cruel fate that had mutilated him put him in the path of the half-Sage. He was bound. He did not know whether he could free himself, or where he would go if he were free. He remained in service, never far from his master's call, waiting to be commanded. He spent days at the lake's shore, watching the homeland that was never his.

There was a dissembler near him. Magus felt the intruder traveling in the retinue of the Lord Justice, that noisy crowd that harried him with their too-frequent passage, too close to the lake, too many to be overcome. Magus found the smell of the dissembler noxious. If he wished, he could crush that man like a bird. Death was the only other power he'd found he possessed. Could he act without his new master's command, though? He feared learning that he could not. So he remained at the shore, called and neglected by the relentless voice of the water.

# 29

TOD DRIFTED OUT OF SLEEP IN THE WARMTH OF A beam of light slipping through the crack between the shutters. It was morning, a warm and humid autumn morning, thick with heat that yesterday's clouds had held close to the earth throughout the night. His hair, as he pushed it out of his face, was damp with sweat. He heard a voice near his ear, hazy and dreamlike, Elzith's voice. Inside his body he felt his heart pound quick and heavy. Dream scenes still caught him, clinging as he melted out of sleep: breath, sweat, skin.

His eyes snapped open. One of his legs jolted with a cramp, brought on by sleeping in the wrong place, in a chair by the window. Tod stiffly dragged himself out of his slouching position, sitting upright, rubbing his face with his hands. With his eyes closed he could still see the dream. Where had it come from? Oh yes, he remembered, Elzith's story from the night before. It had called back memories of those places in Karrim he had once visited, old and blurry memories that he only had in snatches, a bare arm, the canopy of a woman's hair. The dream wasn't blurry though, it was quite clear, and he had seen perfectly and with generous detail who was involved in it.

Tod shook his head energetically. This was foolish. Elzith would never have him, it was ridiculous to even think of it. Not that he'd thought of it, really—it was just a dream, something that turned up in his sleep. He wouldn't want Elzith like that anyway; the thought of the dream matched up with the brothel story that inspired it made Tod vaguely nauseous. He reviewed her story to get the image out of his mind. He'd be like that unwanted man who stumbled into her room and smashed the furniture. She'd tangle his legs up and lock him in the closet. Tod snickered a little. So much for his dream.

"Tod!" he heard again. Her voice. She was knocking at the door. He plunged out of the chair and rushed to open it.

"A little early, am I?" Elzith said, her head canted at a joking angle, her voice sharp and her eyes bright with something like laughter. Tod smiled, thinking with relief that this was the real Elzith, hard and rough, not some soft and willowy dream image, and trying to ignore how his heart twisted anyway. "I've brought some bread," she added, handing a loaf-shaped package to him.

"How did you get it?" Tod asked, feeling the warmth of it in his hands. "Did you go into town? This early?"

Elzith nodded, giving up on an invitation and brushing past him into his flat. "I got to Jannes's early and they told me the LJ had gone out and taken the brat with him. They want me back at noon." She checked the time on the clock and started rearranging the chairs around the table. "So I picked up the bread before I left town."

"Good," Tod mused, "I ran out last night."

"I know," drawled Elzith. "I was here."

Tod considered it for a second and laughed. He was being silly, and she was teasing him. That's all there was between them. He went obligingly to the kitchen to prepare breakfast.

No, there was something more between them, Tod thought. He could see it in her stories, which he'd collected so carefully, even if she didn't. He filled a need for her. Like the union fisherman in her story about Tristam, she needed a confessor. She had blood on her hands. Tod could imagine how heavily it must weigh on her, like a stone on her chest. He knew how it was. Though he'd had no hand in his great-aunt's death, still he felt responsible because he had known. Guilt had gripped his heart and blinded him. When his brothers offered him their poisoned attention, they also offered him escape. He didn't notice the pain when all he could feel was gin in his blood. He didn't remember the nightmares.

Then one day he let the secret out, before the weight of it burst his chest. He was at Shaan's, having watched Morrn's arrest. He was terrified, he was certain he would disappear himself, but strangely those weren't the words that came out of him. When Shaan returned, after sneaking into Morrn's flat to rescue a last hidden bottle before the Public Force came back to sack the place, Tod spoke. The guilt of his dreams and his knowledge flooded out of him in a rush.

"You're scaring me, lad," Shaan had murmured after a long silence. He'd thrust the bottle toward Tod in a shaky hand. "Drink it up, you'll feel better. Make that stop."

In fact, it did stop, although not until after he'd drunk the bottle and woken up at a Healer's side. Whether it was because of the unnerving company of the Healer or the stress of facing the charges against him, the guilt Tod had felt over his great-aunt's death was entirely over-shadowed. It never regained its former power after his confession to Shaan. That wasn't to say he was free of it. He had to fight off the blackness of it each day, the old guilt and the voice of the liquor. How much darker, he thought, how much more painful the fight must be for Elzith, who'd taken a life with her own hands.

It troubled him in passing, a tremor in his bones that would catch him unawares. His guest, sitting at his table, taking bread from his hands, was a killer. His imagina-tion screamed—she didn't kill the Azassian with her pis-tol. How did she do it? She stopped the Justice and got away. How did she stop him? Tod's mind filled up with a dozen sinister half-formed answers. But he turned to look at her, and there she was, sitting at his table, a figure that was now so familiar, a face that was no longer as hard and impassive as it used to be, her hands draped easily along the table, deceptively thin and frail, capable of death, but not here. There was no tension in her now, no weight of guilt. Tod had helped her.

"What's this?" Elzith was looking at the work spread out on the table, which Tod had left out late last night. He'd fallen asleep unexpectedly in his chair and hadn't put the work away as he usually did. Elzith was looking at his own book.

Tod approached the table a little nervously, carrying the torn pieces of bread as an excuse to come near. No one else had seen his book, and he hadn't even told Keller about it. It was only fair, though. She'd shared her secrets with him.

"It's something I've been making, something the Healer suggested to me. Not the one you reported on, who healed me three years ago, but the one who moved in downstairs after that, who used to live where you do now. He said I should make it. Said it would help me." Tod laughed a little, self-consciously, afraid it sounded foolish, but Elzith was listening seriously. There was no sarcasm in her expression; she even seemed respectful. "I wrote down what he said," Tod continued, reaching for the book, "here, on the first page. As well as I could remember it."

He turned the book over to the front side, gingerly opening the first fragile leaves. They were starting to show wear, since they had never been bound into a cover to protect them. He hadn't looked at these first pages in years, not since he recorded the words that the Healer had spoken to him on the one night he'd invited his former neighbor to sit at his table. "Your heart is good," the Healer had said. "There is nothing I can do to mend it. Let it go. Rest yourself." Tod had written down the rest:

*There is an old custom, very old, from the days when your people wandered these lands whole, before you divided yourselves into countries with laws and borders. Write down your words, your troubles. Live them again in your words, in the ink and paper. Live them for the last time. Then cast them to the fire. Cast the smoke to the wind. The wind is greater than you. Let it go. Rest yourself.*

Elzith read the page, more than once, it seemed. Then she lifted a finger and touched the book, as if trying to appraise it without trespassing on his work. "It's not finished," she said, nearly a question.

Tod shook his head.

"You still have troubles coming," Elzith said, half a question again, half an admission, a trace of wry sadness in her voice.

Tod smiled. If he was her confessor, then he wanted to absolve her. She wasn't responsible for his troubles, no more than he was for his great-aunt's death. "Go ahead and have a look," Tod said, pushing the book a little closer to her. "It's been quite something to bind, pulling all the different pieces together. I think I managed it well enough. What do you think?"

Elzith took the book in her hands, gently turning it and peering at the stitching and folds. Tod remembered that he had put the kettle on and turned back toward the stove.

"I was going to ask you, Elzith," he began. A brief thought had passed his mind last night, and it came to him again this morning. He wanted to preserve something of Elzith in the book, a piece of her stories, perhaps, but he didn't want to do it without asking her. Maybe she would write something in his book herself.

"I just wanted to ask if you would..." Tod repeated, coming back to the table with a cup in his hands. Then he looked away from the steaming cup, up at Elzith and the page she was examining, and stopped short. The book was open to the leaf that the first Healer had woven. Elzith's fingers were on it, as if they had brushed over it as she was turning pages, unintentionally. Beneath her fingers, the delicate fibers glowed with an inner light.

The heat that bled through the clay cup made no feeling on Tod's fingers. Elzith stared at her own hand. She drew it away from the leaf, watched the light die, moved close again and watched the glow warm around her fingertips. Tod realized he wasn't breathing. The leaf, the Healer, the weaving at his bedside. Why? Patience, I've been weaving it since I knew you, a Sage told me—

"You're a Sage," Tod whispered.

Elzith withdrew her hand and lowered it into her lap, below the table. Her mouth was drawn tight. She spoke almost unwillingly, as if enthralled out of her secrecy by the strange force of the light. "They say my mother was."

They were silent, watching the sheet as if it might jump to life like a creature, but the light in it had vanished. Elzith drew a breath and leaned back, away from it. She was going to divert the conversation again. "What were you going to ask me, Tod?"

His mind wasn't working. The woven sheet looked blurry, and he imagined he saw light still. His hands told him they were burning from the steaming cup he still held but he couldn't feel it. His mouth moved without any connection to his mind. "I wanted you to go to bed with me."

The cup dropped out of his hands and smashed on the floor.

Elzith showed no reaction, and Tod thought there might be a chance he'd imagined saying it. But Elzith's face was hardening. She pushed back from the table, leaning in her chair, rapping the heels of her boots on the table's edge as she raised them and crossed her ankles, a sharp and stagy movement. The delicate hands had stiffened. They were not fists, not quite, but those thin wrists were deceptive and he knew it.

"I'm sorry, I didn't mean it," he stammered.

"Yes, you did," Elzith said.

He wanted to protest. He couldn't. She knew, she knew everything he said, everything in his mind.

"It's hardly your fault," she said tightly. "I should have known. I can't imagine how I missed it." Her face was blank and she did not look at Tod. "You can't know why you're a fool. You have no idea." She dropped her feet to the floor with a crash and jolted out of the chair. Tod lowered himself into the puddle around his feet and started picking up broken pieces of pottery, so he wouldn't have to watch her leave.

But she did not leave. She stood at the window, peering through the cracks in the shutters, it seemed. When she spoke again it was in a distant voice, as if she were already on the road outside. Tod did not move, his knees soaked in the thin tea that was going cold, holding the broken pieces of the cup hard in his hands so they did not rattle and obscure her voice. He clutched his hands so tightly that when Elzith finally finished her story, speaking her last words as the clock chimed the hour, and stepped out through the door without a farewell, he could hardly open the stiff joints of his fingers, the palms that were scored by the edges of the shattered pottery.

# 30

WE CALLED IT THE SMYTH ASSIGNMENT. SMYTH wasn't his name, and while I knew his name—you couldn't set foot in the town I was sent to without knowing his name—we never spoke it among the Secret Force. Smyth had a contact in the Dabionian authority, some Greater Justice, most likely, who was able to cover up all the reports against him. Loyd didn't want that unknown Dabionian official to catch wind of our investigations, so we never spoke Smyth's real name.

I won't speak the name of the city, either, because that would identify Smyth immediately, maybe not to Tod, but to anyone who knew a thing about Mandera. Smyth had come from a long line of barons in the days of the Ikinda Alliance—back when barons meant something—and his family name was synonymous with the faded wealth and power of that city. Since then, his own name had become synonymous with the corruption that comes when wealth and power rot. I doubt that name has lost its meaning since Smyth's death. The man had allies, not friends, but associates, all of them nearly as sadistic as he was, and they would be certain to use his name to stoke their own fury if they knew who and where I was. To speak Smyth's true name would be my peril.

It's possible Loyd has found Smyth's Dabionian contact by now, using the information that I snatched unexpectedly from Shaan. Once the crooked Justice has safely disappeared, Dabion will be free to brag about how they shut down the biggest criminal in Mandera. They'll bat Smyth's name around like a child's toy. Mine might be unearthed, too, for Smyth's old cronies to pounce on. But it hardly matters, really.

"I need you to get close to this man," Loyd told me, not long after I returned from Karrim. He wrote the man's name and the name of his city on a scrap of paper, letting me read it before putting a match to it.

I laughed. It wouldn't be easy. The operatives used to talk about their assignments there, even as our masters tried to gag us and keep us from gossiping about such things. There was plenty of information to be had about Smyth; he made sure everyone in his town and the world beyond knew him and knew his deeds, could imagine them in bloody detail. No one could get close to him, though, not successfully. One of the operatives who worked his way into Smyth's company was killed within a few weeks. The next man got too close, drowned in Smyth's lust for money and power, and never came back to Loyd. The Smyth assignment was delayed while another operative was sent to take out the defector.

Loyd tried a different tactic next, attacking Smyth's reportedly massive and lurid sexual prowess. The first woman was a doe-eyed voluptuous beauty, and Smyth completely ignored her. The second one got in but broke. She managed to get her hands on the very dagger that Shaan would later steal, to cut her own throat before Smyth could get any information out of her. Loyd waited for two years before moving forward, to make sure nothing had come out. In that time Smyth sucked up the last remaining businesses in three towns in that part of Mandera, had a dozen or so local Dabionian authorities killed, claimed responsibility for the hijackings of six transports of tax money from Mandera to Dabion, and personally set fire to the office of the Dabionian ambassador to the city, which had long stood vacant, just for spite.

The operatives who circulated on the periphery brought back reports of these actions by the cartload. Nothing was admissible before the Tables of Justice. Someone in Dabion's ruling class was keeping all the official evidence buried. Loyd could wait no longer. I was his last chance.

"So you need me to find out who's protecting Smyth," I asked.

"No," Loyd told me. "I need you to assassinate him."

The city smelled bad from the moment I set foot in it. It was a large city, formerly one of Mandera's economic centers. During the Ikinda Alliance money had poured in and the heads of business there gleefully and smugly shared it among one another. Their houses still stand, though half of them have been gutted by fire or vandals, their sculptures are hobbled by missing legs and arms, and their fountains are filled with mold and seething fungus. I paused by a stinking fountain to look at the city around me and think about how I was going to catch the attention of a madman.

One of his minions found me in a tavern, soliciting drunk men and knocking them senseless, their money in my hand, an instant before they could crawl up my skirts. I was deemed enough of a challenge to entertain the big man. They hauled me to his house and dropped me into a room, where I was locked for at least an hour before Smyth deigned to have a look at me. He entered the room and crossed it in two strides, seized my breast with one hand and used it to drag me to my feet. He waited for a second before seizing my throat with his other hand. He was pleased that I didn't react. He laughed his foul breath into my face, and he kept me.

I wasn't there for Smyth, though. The room he kept me in was a proving ground for his recruits. I was one of the tests for these men who wanted to be Smyth's minions and snap up his table scraps. They'd already been tested for pain and other things, and by the time they got to me they wore bruises on their faces and blood under their nails. They wore nothing else, though, in the room where I was locked. I was there to test their control. Smyth commanded me to seduce them, in that cool, aloof, bait-and-switch way that I was known for from the tavern. He watched the men, their exposed secrets, watching how well or how poorly they controlled themselves.

"Women are the devil," he'd tell them as they stood at my feigned mercy. "They'll tempt you, they'll try to snare you. And men are fools. A woman gets near them and they lose their minds, let them have whatever they want." He'd seize the men by the throat, throw the ones who disappointed him out of the room. "I won't have men who are weak. I won't have them vulnerable to a woman."

Smyth watched me as he said this, taking his eyes off the subject of his test for a moment, fixing them on me. He suspected me. He thought I was the devil, the snare trying to steal from him while he was distracted. I obeyed his orders to placate him, to keep him from having any further reason to suspect and examine me. Those foul orders soured my mouth but I said nothing. I itched at being locked in the room, unable to investigate the house, unable to get near Smyth without the presence of other men buffering him. It was too great a risk to do anything else.

Time passed, two seasons and fourteen days. It was 762. I counted every day of it. There was nothing else to do, locked in that room. I counted minutes. I started to wonder what prisoners did, locked in their walls and chains, watching their years limp past them with no hope of release. In the City I'd watched thieves and batterers scream and tear their hair through the rusty bars of their jail cells. No such anxiety touched me in Smyth's room. I felt little in the empty hole where other people had hearts. The only irritation I felt was in my mind, as I looked at this puzzle I needed to solve and could find no way to do it.

Loyd wanted me to kill this man. I had no weapons. These absurdly thin hands, this small and worthless body I was born in, they had no power in them to strangle, smother, break his neck, even if I'd been able to get close enough to touch him without his minions blocking me. I had only my mind. I could get into him if I could shock him. I could read the truth in his mind when he spoke, and if he could be shocked the barriers of his mind would drop. I could reach in and crack his heart. But Smyth could not be shocked. I read every word he spoke and found no flaw in his mind, no weakness, no splinter in his confidence that I could plunder. Two seasons and fourteen days, and I had gotten nowhere.

Then Smyth brought in a toy. A young man, who could only have been there for Smyth's vicious entertainment. He would never have passed as one of his servants. He was pocked with bruises and fresh scars by the time I got him, and he was sniveling and shivering in his nakedness. His mind was lost, his body unable to tell the difference between desire and fear. He failed Smyth's test before I could even touch him, when I was still a step away from him, hardly close enough for him to feel my breath.

"Weak," Smyth spat, the most damning word that could come from his mouth. He drew his knife, the gaudy, gold-handled, bejeweled dagger he'd inherited from a baron relative or stolen from some wealthy and dead merchant, the instrument of retribution for weakness. Smyth whipped the knife into the space between me and the young man and cut his throat.

The youth collapsed at Smyth's feet, but Smyth's eyes were not on him. He was watching me as I stood motionless, unflinching, with blood staining my face and drenching the scant gauze I wore. I read his eyes. I had an opening, I could reach him. Very slightly, I measured an image of fear and let it creep into my eyes, widened them, let them shine in the light and sweet stench.

It worked. Smyth smiled like a wolf, laughter rumbling in his throat. I was released from the room and sent to his own chambers.

There was a chaise in Smyth's chamber, the foot of it against a wall where manacles were bolted. I was locked into them. I slept there, sitting upright with my wrists pinned. Guards came in twice a day to let me out, feed me and bathe me, since the man who soaked himself in blood detested the stink of the body. Seventeen days passed.

Each day I measured a little more fear into my expression. Smyth brandished his knife at me, that knife I came to know like another hand. He ran it over my feet, my thighs, my belly, my throat, trying to scare me, threatening me with the sharpness of it, taunting me with thin lines of blood. I turned all my attention to the wounds as he put them on me, trying to test their depth. None of them would leave scars; they were too shallow, the knife too straight and sharp. One deep scar and I would be out of the Secret Force, I thought, since they won't have operatives who can be so easily identified. One scar, one flinch from me in the wrong direction, rising up to meet the blade, and my work would be finished. I could not determine what I felt, thinking of that.

Eighteen days and he unchained me. I sat free on the chaise. The door was not locked. He was threatening me still, taunting me with escape. I wasn't supposed to try, I was supposed to stay put, shunning freedom as if it scared me more than his knife. That was his prize in this game. Each day I let him see more fear, and I never tested the door, so that he would believe he was winning. I would have something from him, soon. When? I searched him to see what he wanted from me next. He coupled with me crudely as an animal, rough and painfully, twice a day after I was bathed. It occurred to me that this was his next prize, that I would come to desire it, wanting this abuse like the kiss of the knife, more than my freedom. It would be my next step in gaining his confidence, pretending to turn my body over to him. My mind soured against the thought. I wondered if it was anger. I only lived in the body, after all, this thin papery shell. Its heart did not matter to me. My mind only dwelled at the top of it, and I would not turn over my mind.

Then I looked into my mind. That meaningless heart skipped a beat. I did not know what day it was. My mind had been breached. I looked at the images of fear and could not tell which ones I had created and which ones were real. I stared at the unlocked door and my heart thudded at the thought of going through it. Smyth had to die. I had to do it immediately.

But I did not know how. I had failed to solve the puzzle. I hadn't learned the layout of the house, locked first in one room and then another. I didn't know how to avoid the guards, where to find some lethal tool, or where to find Smyth once I had it. I had no escape route. All my skills, all the moves I had perfected in the game, were useless.

In the end it was dumb, blind luck. The master went out and one of his whelps sauntered into his chambers, playing at being king. He had a pistol in his pocket and a bottle of illegal spirits in his hand. He sat on Smyth's furniture and groped his female pet. I made no use of my higher skills, the ones Loyd valued so much: I did not con the man or twist words out of him or touch his mind. I did nothing better than a common thief would. I picked his pocket.

When Smyth returned I was sitting on the chaise, in the place he made for me. He took me like a habit, then leaned back against the head of the chaise and fell into easy sleep like a man who has no cares. I did not move from where I leaned against the wall, reaching down for the hidden pistol. My mutinous body with its frightened hands threatened to spoil the preparations. Smyth woke, smelling the fear or the powder. His eyes opened to the pistol, primed, cocked, aimed at his head. He was naked and unarmed, too far away to reach me.

Then he laughed. Low, cold, an immortal's laugh. No one had learned his secret, the name of his connection. And though he died his memory was in me, would always be in me, bleeding through the cracks in my mind, living as long as I did. I would kill him but he had won. He laughed. I pulled the trigger and felt my shoulders driven back into the splinters in the wall.

My luck held. I wasn't caught as I escaped from the house. The reconnaissance operative, who'd been lurking at the outskirts of the town for weeks looking for any sign of me, found me and fetched me back to Loyd. The wounds from the blade and the splinters in my back knitted over and left no scars.

# 31

KELLER HAD BEEN WATCHING HIM FOR MAYBE TEN minutes when he finally said, "Well, lad, what are you doing?"

Tod did not take the knife away from his fingers. "Paring my nails," he answered shortly, running the sharp blade close to his flesh.

Keller narrowed his eyes. There was nothing he could say, though, and he went back to work, peering occasionally around the press at Tod. Tod kept at his nails. He hadn't drawn blood yet. Not that scars on his body would mean anything, even if he did flinch in the wrong direction. The knife could slip, or he could hold it steady. Take the bottle or not. He might as well have been sixteen again. Some kind of sense had driven him to Keller's, though, and out of the dangerous solitude of his flat. One more nail and he would be done. He paused, turning the knife in his hand.

The door banged open. Tod didn't look up. It was some Justice; he could see the black figures of the bodyguards from the corner of his eye. Only a few figures came in this time, not the army that the Justices usually dragged around on even their smallest errands. Tod thought he saw three bodies move across his range of vision. Two guards, then, had been spared. The rest were on their way to Cassile, along with Elzith. She'd left Tod a message that the whole Black Force had been recalled to Cassile, on some mission important enough to require even delinquents like herself.

"Good morning, your honor," Keller rasped, and Tod finally raised his head, to find Jereth Paloman in the shop. The frantic expression normally on the Justice's face was different this time, twisted by some new trouble. Tod didn't question it. He dropped his eyes to the knife again.

"Do you have something for me, your honor?" the printer prompted as Paloman remained anxiously silent.

"Oh, yes," the Justice answered, distractedly. He pulled a few coarsely folded papers out of his pocket and dropped them in front of Keller. Glancing up, Tod saw that Paloman's back was turned to the work he'd carelessly handed to the printer, and instead he was looking at Tod.

"What?" Tod mumbled.

Paloman frowned sourly, doubtless offended by this rude and improper response. Tod didn't care.

"I have a request from—for you, Redtanner," the Justice said. His voice sounded as if someone's hands were around his throat.

Tod peered intently at his last fingernail, twisted the

blade over it, cropped the nail carelessly, and folded
Keller's pocketknife. He thought about creeping out as if
no request had been mentioned. His reflexes were more
obedient, though, and his head turned toward Paloman.

"I—I've been," Paloman attempted, seeming no more
eager to make the request than Tod was to hear it. "I have
a certain collection of rare old books." The imagined
hands seemed to tighten. "I can bring them by for you to
see. At your leisure. You live at—at . . ."

"The Barrow," Tod mouthed. He didn't care about the
books. His mouth kept moving, obediently. "Come by,
I'll be home. When are you coming?"

The Justice's mouth twisted. "I'm due back in Insigh,
and I won't be back here for several weeks." Hesitantly he
searched in his pockets, found a calendar, unfolded it.
He peered at it as if he couldn't read his own handwrit-
ing. Finally he selected a date, pointed a shuddering finger at the number seventy-six, and pushed the calendar
in front of Tod.

Tod looked absently at the wrinkled map of the season. "Well," he murmured. "Fine." It was a date well into
autumn. Elzith ought to be back by then.

He noted Paloman's leaving in snatches: a clattering
of guns, the slamming of the door, the Justice's absence.
Tod spun the pocketknife around on the table. Elzith
might be back, if she decided to come back.

Somewhere in his mind, Tod knew he'd made a simple mistake, only a few words, and Elzith's extreme response didn't suit the error. He'd merely been honest,

shocked into being more truthful than he'd intended to be. He couldn't have guessed how she would react to it; he hadn't meant to offend her. He was not the fool he felt like. The thought crossed his mind somewhere, somewhere quiet and buried very deep, below the overwhelming noise of his terror.

Elzith had delivered her last story ruthlessly and left him in the dark of his cottage, his window shuttered against the day. An hour had passed before he even stood and locked the door behind her. The next morning she was gone, leaving a message on his door and shadows in his heart. The story haunted him, horrified him, stole his breath. There was too much of it to think about. He couldn't even form the images in his mind, the men and the scenes and the actions, to grasp them and make them familiar. The pieces of the story loomed outside him, strange and harrowing. When he tried to make up faces for the characters and invent histories for them, he failed. He had no knowledge of that world, he would drown in it. And there was more than that. He knew more now, knew that Elzith could look into his mind, she had looked, she could reach in and do—he couldn't think what. It was too much. He gasped for breath as his hand gripped the case of the knife.

"I don't trust that man," Keller whispered.

Tod jolted. He'd forgotten the printer was there. Keller, who had printed contraband. Secrets were everywhere and there was nothing Tod could reach out for to steady himself. "Who?" he felt himself stammer, pulling away slightly from Keller. "Paloman?" He stared at his hand, wondering how to get it to release its grip on the knife.

Movement drew his eyes away. Keller was shaking his head, frowning severely. "He shouldn't be so interested. There's no reason for a Justice to talk this much to commoners."

Tod let go of the knife. There were creases in his palm from its case, red, like scars. He spun it on the table and careened it away from him. "Maybe," he said shortly. Maybe not, he thought. Maybe this nervous Justice was a threat to him, instead of a harmless, tottering old man. Nothing was as it seemed. Tod could be killed tomorrow. Somehow he didn't care. His heart had run away in fear and hidden somewhere he couldn't hear it. He felt reckless. He heard words come out of Keller's mouth, something about canceling the meeting. He ignored it. "It'll be fine," he said offhandedly, kicked himself off of his stool, and slid out of the door.

Exhaustion struck him suddenly although he hadn't known he was tired. He kicked dust as he walked home, too weary to lift his feet. Inside his cottage he barely locked his door before collapsing at his table. She'll come back, he thought fleetingly as his eyes closed. His mind refused any other thoughts. The story of the crime boss in Mandera drifted out to lurk in the shadows. He forgot about the scene with Justice Paloman. He was asleep.

There was silence for a while, darkness, then muddled images. Skin first, tangled arms, scenes from his earlier dream. He could only see her in patches. He tried to lift her hair to see her face, then she was gone. And he was elsewhere. Running. Someone was chasing him, shadows, pounding footsteps. He ran through a building, turning corners, slamming doors that wouldn't lock behind him. He ran up the stairs, hearing them creak as his pursuer followed, feeling them shudder under his feet. He reached the window just as Elzith climbed out of it. He leaned out, looking for the ground, but the drop was like a cliff. He watched her fall, the white of her gown shimmering about her as she floated into darkness.

Then ice clutched his heart. He reached for her desperately. She slipped away from him. He was running through a field, thick deep grass, soaked with moisture, sucking at his feet. His lungs strained against the hot, wet air. There was water on the horizon. He saw her face in it, then she went under.

# 32

MONASTERY SEVENTY-FOUR WAS ON THE SOUTH-western coast. It was a long trip, hot and miserable, and every day or so it would rain like mad. The driver had seen his fill of water by the time he got to the coast; he certainly didn't want to look at any more in that swirling western sea. He didn't stay at the coast long, though. In no more than an hour his cargo was loaded and he was leaving the monastery, or what was left of it.

Almost every guard in the Black Force had been re-called for the approach on monastery seventy-four. Monks had been steadily trickling out of the condemned monasteries, escaping before they could be arrested, dozens of them, even hundreds. The closures had grown increasingly difficult, the ascetics more stubborn. They blocked the doors with human barricades that had to be shot through. There were reports of some monks taking up makeshift arms, rakes and uncut branches of fire-wood, and wielding them clumsily upon the entering guards. There was reason to suspect the escapees of grow-ing violence, and when intelligence reached Dabion that these runaway monks were congregating at monastery seventy-four, it was considered a sufficient threat to require a larger force than the usual ten or twenty guards with their short-range pistols. Black Force was recalled from all over Dabion to put down the resistance.

The resistance was waiting for the Black Force, but not with the weapon that Dabion expected. The guards and their muskets burst through the doors into a throng of rebels, half a dozen deep, screaming like the fires of hell, surging forward. The guards were treading on bodies before they determined that they were unarmed. Nanian's philosophy of withdrawing from the conflict of the world seemed to have been interpreted by his latter-day followers as a drive to suicide, to throw themselves out of the world literally, at the hands of the guards. These followers were intent on going a step further by taking the guards with them. They were not a match for the greater part of the Black Force, though. The barricade was down before the rear ranks even had a chance to fight. Dabion claimed the monastery.

The entry hollowed out into the cavern of the open sanctuary. The guards marched in to put down the rest of the resistance, those murderous hundreds who were rumored to lurk inside. The guards were dismayed to see no such thing. The sanctuary looked empty. A heavy presence lurked in the outer shadows, around the nave, among the low columns. The guards aimed their pistols at the lurkers. Then they heard coughing, heavy barking coughs, vibrating through the sanctuary, muffled by the mass of bodies piled on the floor. The Black Force had claimed an infirmary.

Guards picked over the monks, looking for weapons. They hefted robed sacks of bones, scowling at cropped scalps and bloody noses and mouths crusted with saliva and vomit. One monk coughed and wheezed so loudly that a guard kicked him in the ribs to silence him. "There's no resistance," someone said. Irritated voices echoed the words. The few monks who had been any sort of threat could have been put down by just twenty guards. The mission was a waste.

From the back of the contingency the supervising Justice swept in to assess the situation. His eyes narrowed; he demanded a glove. Guards scrambled, hot, annoyed. Someone produced the unlikely glove, the Justice sank his hand into it, and thus protected he grasped the jaw of the monk closest to the door. Covering his mouth with a sweat-drenched sleeve, he wrenched the monk's jaw open and peered in. "Out!" he commanded, backing away fiercely. "Everyone out!"

The driver had been told none of this. His only order, other than the traveling directions, was to say he hadn't seen any fire. That much was fair; he hadn't seen it. He was happy enough to have been spared any more heat. He wasn't to make any such remarks, though—he had his orders. "Didn't see any fire." He'd used the line twice already. "Just water for the horses, then on my way. Didn't see any fire." The driver was not to engage the public. Others would come to the villages to convince their inhabitants that they hadn't seen the fire, either. That wasn't the driver's work. His work was only to drive. He had avoided looking at the smoking ruins of the monastery, so he wouldn't have anything else to not see. He didn't look at what got loaded into his wagon. He hummed the tunes of drinking songs as he drove homeward so that he didn't hear coughing.

The news of the monastery's demise would be a disaster. Dabion needed to report a victory, they needed to show strength before the Five Countries. Witnesses could be managed. The victims were hastened to an end that most of them were already within minutes of. When the guards, though, grew feverish, short of breath, a quarantine was impossible. The numbers that had been recalled had to return to their regular duties. The failure of the mission could not be concealed if the entire Black Force continued to go missing. The guards had to be transported back to Dabion.

Those who already showed symptoms were kept in Cassile, in tents that were hastily erected among the still-hot embers of the monastery. The rest of the guards were loaded by twos and threes into wagons dispatched by the Secret Force. They would return to Dabion separately and by various routes, in an attempt to control the spread of disease and rumors. Operatives were arranging to have Healers stationed near a number of crossings on the Cassilian bank of the Great River, so those guards who hadn't died en route could be mended and sent back to their posts.

The driver could have pieced the story together: the rumors of the fire, the guards raking bones among the ashes, the two black-clad bodies loaded into his wagon, the directions to drive to a certain bridge and look for the tents that were so unusual they could be nothing but the dwellings of Healers. He didn't. Piecing things together was the work of other people. His work was to drive. When he made a rendezvous with someone he uttered a code word—that was the bit he enjoyed, whispering the word and waiting with excitement for the correct response—then he drove on. If it was a dangerous assignment, like carrying cargo out of Azassi or Mandera, where the people lurked on the streets with those hungry, bloody eyes, then the driver was given an outrider. That person would climb into the bed of the wagon, making a clattering sound as he went. The driver didn't ask what sort of contraption made that sound, and he never talked to these companions. He hadn't even been assigned one this time, as he drove through the drenched and empty fields of Cassile.

As he approached the River he saw the faint outline of tents on its banks. Another wagon was pulling away, headed toward the bridge. He pulled up his horses, got out and checked their hooves for stones he could say they'd picked up. He kept his head down long enough to avoid acknowledging the other driver. Someone was waiting for him, though, outside the tents. He led his horses forward slowly. He'd driven all over and seen people from many countries, even Azassi, but none were as strange as the Healers. They were tall, much too tall, much too pale, too quiet. The Healer who waited for the driver to drag his wagon forward was a woman, and she was covered in wool robes, despite the heat, that made her indistinguishable from the men. She said nothing as he rolled to a stop. She looked him directly in the eye, but he couldn't meet those eyes. There was something strange about the eyes of Healers, and no woman should look so directly at a man who wasn't her husband. The driver dropped his head and let the Healer walk around to the back of the wagon.

"You have the key?" That voice made him shiver, and he reluctantly joined the woman at the padlocked doors. He pulled out a handkerchief and held it in front of his face as the woman took the keys from his hand, pretending he hadn't seen other drivers and Justices do the same thing back at the monastery. He tried to move away as the Healer swung open the doors of the wagon's covered bed, struggling to think of an excuse about checking on the horses, but he couldn't move.

"Can you speak?" called the Healer.

The voice that answered was faint, hoarse, breathless. It crept up the driver's spine as if it had come from the grave. It drew him unwillingly forward, to peer into the back of the wagon, where a woman was propped up on her elbows, squinting into the light that had been suddenly shed upon her, gasping to speak through a swollen throat. "This one is dead."

The driver watched as the Healer climbed into the

back of the wagon. After a moment she began to back out, dragging the other body by its legs. She showed every intention of carrying the body herself, and the driver was finally shamed into helping her. He did not have to lift the heavy thing far, though, or look into its bluish face long, since another Healer quickly appeared and relieved the driver of his burden. The female Healer turned back toward her living patient, who had pulled herself up toward the edge of the wagon.

"He stopped breathing early this morning," the sick woman rasped. She was looking at the dead man, watching as he was carried away, as calmly as if she were watching a branch float downriver. The driver, who never asked questions, who never made opinions about the things he transported, felt rage bleed into his stomach like a sickness.

"He showed symptoms two days ago. I'm about eight hours behind him," the woman continued, and the Healer hushed her, laid a hand upon her throat. The driver was thankful for the quiet.

"Don't fight me," the Healer whispered. Her hands circled the sick woman's throat. "Let me inside. Let it go."

"I can't do it, not when I'm conscious," the woman answered through gritted teeth. Her face was stony, drawn up like a soldier's. The driver turned away and asked himself no questions about why the woman disturbed him so much.

He walked away, toward his horses, but he found himself in front of the tents. Coughing issued from one.

Another was dead silent. The man who had lifted the body from the driver's arms slipped out of it, his head lowered. Behind him the driver heard a dull scream, a violent retching cough. He turned unwillingly. The sick woman was buckled over at the edge of the wagon bed, dragging in long and jagged breaths. The female Healer was approaching him.

"Her heart has been damaged," the Healer said, as if the driver knew or cared about the sick woman. "She needs to go home, where she can rest." The Healer held out his ring of keys. He was afraid to take it from her, afraid of touching those hands. He didn't want to climb back onto his wagon and drive. He wanted other work.

He hardly realized he had gotten on the wagon and started driving after all until he found himself on the bridge. Karrim lay before him in wide, endless fields. Three days until he would reach Origh.

The Healer's words made him think about his own heart. It didn't seem to beat right. He would go for miles without hearing it, then fearfully put his fingers to the inside of his throat. Then he felt it pounding, far too fast, outrunning his horses. He couldn't slow it down. His hands shook on the reins. *Her* heart was damaged? That woman in the wagon had no heart. No one who had lain with the dead for hours and felt nothing could. When he crossed the border into Dabion he stopped the wagon and flung open the doors. She didn't wake until he'd pulled her halfway out. He jumped away as she started to fight him, and her weight was far enough out of balance that she fell to the ground. He wasn't driving their cargo anymore. He darted to his seat, leaving the doors unlocked, and urged the horses forward. He didn't stop them, limping, worn, breathless, until he'd reached his own home.

# 33

ELZITH'S FACE FLOATED IN THE SEA FOR THREE
nights. It woke Tod up, shattering his sleep into
restless fragments. It lurked in shadows at the corner of
his eyes, when he tried to work, when he struggled to
stay awake through the days. In his fatigue time drifted,
and he would find himself places without remembering
how he got there, at his table, outside Elzith's empty
door. He started off toward Origh one morning and
found himself lost, staring at the hills around him, trying to remember where he was. Finally he realized he
was on the road west, toward Karrim. He'd taken that
road many times before, years ago. Without pretending
he didn't know where he was headed, what was at the
end of that road, he turned and forced his legs to carry
him back home.

"What do you want me to do?" he wailed at the fading
images when they drove him awake on the third night.
He searched blindly in the darkness, as if the face might
be there, lingering in the blackness, solid behind layers

of air and dreams. He thrust the heels of his hands against his closed eyes and stared at the violent patterns.

Then he opened his eyes and saw his great-aunt's face. He was dreaming. He'd tipped his head to the pillow and fallen into a fragment of sleep. The face was hazy and the eyes had no color; it had been too long since he'd seen her and he could not remember these details. He watched her walk, somewhere ahead of him, turn, smile gently, and turn away from him. Tod watched, knew where she was going. He had watched before. She walked farther. Tod could not stop her. At the end of a road he would never see, her hand clutched at her heart, she sank to her knees, and the color of her face drifted like smoke.

Tod bolted upright. His heart was pounding. It labored in his chest like he was filled with water. He stumbled out of bed.

Elzith's door stood ajar. Tod approached it warily as he came around the curve of the hill. It wasn't like Elzith. Someone must have broken in, some unnamed enemy like those he'd been warned of. Someone could still be within. Tod's heart would not stop pounding. He pushed the door wider and plunged inside.

The flat was empty. Almost empty, but for the presence he could feel on the floor. His eyes tracked around the single room to make sure no one else was there before he let them drop. Elzith lay in a crumpled heap, her knees under her and her face turned down. Tod lowered himself to her side. He reached for her wrist, wondering if he knew where to feel for a pulse, but at the touch she stirred and gasped for breath. Tod gasped himself; he hadn't breathed since he'd pushed open the door. He looked at her hand, found it scraped and bloody under a crust of dirt. There was dirt on her leg as well, Tod could see it as she moved and extended it, and the knee of her breeches was torn and stained at the jagged edges.

"You crawled?" Tod murmured.

The bloodied hand seized into a weak fist. Elzith's eyes fluttered open, a reflex, unwillingly, and she forced herself to blearily focus on Tod. "It's you," she uttered between cracked lips. Her eyes drifted shut and the fist loosened.

"How far, Elzith?" Tod persisted, not wanting to believe what he was asking.

"Miles," she slurred. "Last . . . night. Two, three nights? Wagon. Bastard." She gasped again, not enough breath to continue.

He wouldn't have thought twice about moving her. He scooped her up in his arms before he could anticipate her struggle. She had drifted out of consciousness again and didn't know who was lifting her. Too weak to fight seriously, she kicked her legs vaguely and rolled her head against Tod's shoulder. She recognized him and stopped struggling. There was tension still in her body, though, the muscles drawn tight over her birdlike bones. He clutched her close and carried her toward the dangerous steps.

He almost didn't think twice about undressing her,

once he'd gotten her to his room. Her clothes, he saw as he looked more closely, were covered in dirt and grass and stains, and needled through with small and large tears. They needed to come off. As he began searching for buttons, though, he hesitated. Bits of an earlier dream flashed through his mind. He frowned, chastising himself. Elzith was sick. Then he remembered other things. Under the dirty clothes were scars, not like the small needle pricks and cuts he had all over his fingers, but something large and serious and frightening. A hole in her gut. Tod gripped his eyes shut, trying not to imagine it. He pulled a sheet up and laid it over her, undid the buttons with hasty fingers and worked the clothes out from under the sheet, then wrapped the sheet around her and settled her in the bed.

He poured water and scrubbed at her hands, lifted the edge of the sheet to clean her knees. She winced in her half sleep but did not open her eyes. He combed the clotted mud out of her hair and washed her face. He brought a cup of water and set it on the small table beside his bed. She didn't wake up sufficiently to drink it. He sat at her side, watching as the light of sunset faded and her face dimmed. She did not stir. Carefully, Tod bent, lowered his head, touched his ear to her chest to hear her heart.

He woke, not realizing he'd fallen asleep. The sun was bright outside windows he'd forgotten to shutter, and the room was cold from the midautumn night. He reached for a blanket and bumped something unexpectedly. "I'm sorry!" he whispered in a rush, but Elzith did not wake, barely moving the limbs he'd disturbed. The skin on her exposed shoulders was cold. Tod pulled up blankets and wrapped them around her.

After watching for what must have been an hour, Tod left Elzith's side to go about his business. He spent what was left of the morning stitching quarrels in even sessions: ten stitches, check on her, add a quarrel, ten stitches, check on her. She roused enough to drink the water once. Night came and he dragged a chair into the bedroom, leaned it against the wall with his feet on the foot of the bed, and slept facing her.

Two days later she woke fully. Tod raised a neck stiff from sleeping in the chair to find her watching him, eyes wide-open.

"What happened?" Tod asked. The shutters, this time, were closed.

Elzith's voice was still weak, her throat raw with traces of sickness. "Diphtheria," she said, with no effort to hedge or conceal. "The monks are all dead. Half the Black Force as well, probably." She paused, letting Tod hold her eyes. "I've been cured of it. The Healer burned it out of my throat. It damaged my heart before it was done, but it's out of me now. You won't catch it."

"I wasn't thinking I would," Tod answered.

"I know you weren't." Elzith's eyes were full of weary reproach and pity. She doesn't understand, Tod thought. She can't imagine making a sacrifice, taking a risk to care for someone else.

"What is today?" she asked.

"Sixty-two. Third season," he added, as if she could have become so disoriented that she'd forgotten it was autumn. He watched as Elzith calculated the time in her head.

"No one's sent for me? No one's come by?"

Tod had to admit he hadn't been watching carefully for movement around the house. Elzith would know he was thinking that, of course, without his saying it. "No one's knocked, at least," he said truthfully.

"Loyd will have the report from the Healer. I wonder what he did to the driver," she mused absently.

"What did they tell the Lord Justice?"

Elzith shrugged. "Something. He won't worry himself much over me."

"But they don't know where you are," Tod gasped. "You could be dead!"

Elzith's face was very pale, tired and aged. "Yes. And they'll hardly care. Except Loyd. Maybe. But he won't do anything if it would ruin the act. They have to cover up seven hundred monks burned to death and half their best troops killed by disease."

Tod stared at the floor. But I care, he thought quietly. Elzith would never hear it. The voices of the Justices and the big men were much too loud for him to drown them out.

"Tod," she said, interrupting him casually, as if they'd been talking about weather instead of power and hatred. "Why did you come down to look for me?"

He didn't answer. He thought of Shaan, and how Tod had scared him when he told him about his dreams. He knew how it would sound. But this was Elzith. She could reach into minds. Nothing would sound unbelievable to her. He looked up. Elzith was watching him with no impatience.

"I had a dream. You were drowning, you were in trouble. Your heart was hurt." He paused for her reaction. She watched him seriously, absorbing his words, weighing their truth. "It's happened before. I dreamed my great-aunt was dying, the same night she died. I saw it happen, but I was nowhere near her. The next morning my father told me. I was sixteen."

He took a long breath. Other things weren't remembered as easily, buried under years. "It happened earlier, though. When I was a child I used to walk through the town. We'd pass houses where people died and I knew it. I could say, an old man died there, or a girl drowned in a well. I'd tell my brothers and scare them. They started teasing me for it. My father told me to stop. I made the thoughts go away, at least while I was awake. I started dreaming them instead, but I never remembered the dreams. Unless it was someone important."

He was trembling as he finished speaking. The only other person he'd told about the dreams, when they first began tormenting his sleep, was his great-aunt. He'd been a boy of about ten, and she had folded him in her arms until the shaking passed. Tod knew he couldn't expect that again. Elzith sat, her arms thin and cold, watching his eyes without looking at him. She didn't understand comfort.

"Who was your mother, Tod?" she asked then.

He shook his head. "She died bearing me. She wasn't—she wasn't..." He couldn't say what he realized Elzith was asking. "She wasn't a wanderer. She came from a family in town. She must have. Father wouldn't have married her otherwise."

"That could be. But you have the blood, Tod, somewhere, some amount of it. You see me when I do this."

And suddenly she was in his mind. He stiffened with shock and cold. He remembered it as the same feeling he'd had when he'd gone down to talk to her and found her reading the book from Mandera. He'd felt her read him without knowing what she was doing.

"Yes, you did," Elzith answered to the words he hadn't spoken. "Few people can, even when I go that deep. Only two others have. I know one to be a Sage. The other is also, I assume. You have the blood, Tod. At least a bit."

Tod shook his head again. "But my brothers don't. It makes no sense. If I have—if—if I do, then they should, but they don't."

"Maybe they don't. Maybe your mother passed it to you when she died. Or maybe they do, but they can't reach it because they're afraid to."

Tod laughed and shook his head more vehemently. "They're not afraid. I'm afraid of much more than they are."

He was cold again, a thin chill that might have been

the air in the room. His head buzzed with a faint dizziness. Something danced on the edges of his mind, he guessed. Did she know she'd hurt him, and was trying to read him more gently this time?

"You're not afraid, Tod."

It was ten days before her heart was healed from the effects of the illness. She slept for most of that time. Tod watched her often but could do little more than fill glasses of water. Eventually she ate a little and he felt he'd accomplished some great thing, nursing her to health, but she simply fell back to sleep. He watched her face, still worn, still hard. It wore a frown even as she slept, as if angry at being so vulnerable. When she woke she was often tense, speaking in short, fatigued words, but she never showed any temper.

Tod didn't sleep in the chair again. The night after he told Elzith about his dreams, he came in to check on her and found her curled at one edge of the bed, rather than in the middle where he'd set her. Half the bed was free. Earlier that day, he'd been stretching his sore muscles and murmured something out loud about how his neck hurt.

"Why are you sleeping in a chair?" Elzith had mumbled, half-asleep.

She was quite asleep when he came in that night. He stood at the foot of the bed, contemplating and getting nowhere, until his eyes were drooping. Finally he took off his shoes and stockings, and nothing else, and lay down beside her on top of the bedclothes. He coughed and fidgeted, unable to get comfortable.

"Go to sleep, Tod," Elzith slurred. That ended it. He slept there in the same manner until her convalescence was over. When he got cold at night he dragged out his jacket and covered himself with it. As the nights passed he listened to the hoarseness in her throat ease, the irregularity of her breath steady. He slept well.

One day, toward the end, a clerk in a black suit knocked at the door. He carried a clean uniform and a pair of boots. "When the guard is well," he said curtly, "she is expected at her master's post."

Tod felt confused as he carried all this back to Elzith. "Which master is that?"

"Jannes," she said, as if there could be no question.

It was clear she didn't like being helpless. She seemed calm each time Tod saw her, but he had the sense it was an act. As she slowly regained strength and her sleep was no longer so heavy, she seemed more and more restless in it. Tod would turn at night and lean against her, and the jolt of her stiffening would wake him. The early light would show her face contracted and lined. Once as she was combing her hair she caught a tangle and couldn't work it out. She snapped at it and tore it out with a handful of strands and an angry huff of breath.

"I thought you didn't get angry," Tod remarked from the doorway. If he was going to say unwise things he supposed it was better to stay out of reach while he did it.

Elzith glanced up, the fury evaporated, and her mouth twisted, wry and tired. "Damn you," she said, without heat.

He stepped into the room and sat beside her. She wore his jacket over her bare arms, with the sheet wrapped around her breasts. He took the comb out of her hands. She looked at him then, the first time he'd seen an emotion complete in her eyes. She didn't like letting him untangle her hair, letting him touch her, letting him do what she couldn't. But she turned the back of her head so he could reach it. He combed out the snarls.

In two days she would wake and dress for work, and he would receive a message at the end of that day that she would be gone again, for an indeterminate time. Before then, he would listen to her tell stories.

# 34

I'VE TRIED FOR YEARS TO PIECE TOGETHER THE HIS-
tory of Siva. Tod would like me to tell this story neatly,
with a beginning and an end. There's neither, none that
has been written down. The Dabionian histories, the
modern ones that the Force fed me, are useless. They
discount the land as nothing but desert, void of resources, populated by an uneducated, uncivilized people
whose primitive tribes and flint-tipped spears are no
threat to the Five Countries. They tell me nothing about
what's really there. Older histories, those few that the
Justices haven't erased and rewritten, speak of the need
to convert the Sivan barbarians to the state religion.
Those come from the 500s, before Dabion decided Nanianism and its crop-haired monks were a threat. The old
state religion was what the Justices are now trying to
burn out of Cassile.

There are some bland histories of the Azassi-Siva
wars. Dabion wasted little ink on them, apparently
washing their hands of the bloody business between
two primitive peoples. Histories from Azassi paint these

battles with more color: passionate troops of Azassi's hardy sons cut down by hordes of devilish Sivans. I have trouble determining why the Azassians went there. A few accounts exist of violence against the Dabionian missionaries in Siva, and Dabion might have recruited the Azassians for the retaliation, to spare their own blood being spilled. Cassile's holy books actually mention Siva, briefly. A few Nanian houses existed in Azassi at the time of the wars, and they cooked up a prophecy in 553 that called for an end to the violence. Sivan holy men are said to have experienced the same prophecy, as if the spirit of Nanian himself were speaking through both peoples. Thousands were dead on both sides by then, a number that varies depending on where you read it. Azassi grew tired of dying for Dabion. The wars ended. The mission to convert Siva was abandoned.

In the 600s Siva turns up in Mandera's history books. Since there were no material resources for the Manderans to exploit, they took the only thing they could find: the humans. People were bribed, bought, or kidnapped from Siva in what was politely called the Labor Project. Fit ones were sold as slaves to work on- and off-continent. They toiled in factories, stoked fires in smithies, hauled bricks for building Mandera's fine cities. Some got as far north as Karrim's fields, where they broke their backs picking turnips. Woodcut prints in these gilded books show happy slaves hard at work. When the slaves decided they weren't happy they ran away and went home. The kidnappings continued, men and tigers for Mandera's circuses, though the people of Siva were rewritten as being unfit for work. The year of the economic collapse, 742, marks the end of Manderan contact with Siva. It was also the end of Manderan production of glorious history books.

I went to Siva in 762. Twenty years had passed since any known contact between the Five Countries and the desert land beyond the cliffs. A season or so had passed since I'd returned from the Smyth assignment and was tidied up for my next one. I had my training, my lessons in how to survive the climate, a handful of words in the Sivan language. I memorized the instructions for the mission. I still didn't know why I was going there. I searched for history, for some record that would tell me. I've kept searching since I returned, for more than a year, and I've found nothing. Nothing will ever explain to me why I was there, nothing will give reason to what happened, just as I'll never find my memories of that missing year.

It was summer when we crossed the cliffs into Siva. There were seven of us; it was the first time I'd worked directly with other operatives. I've chosen to forget the names they gave me, names that were undoubtedly as artificial as the one I gave them. It would be ridiculous to remember these names when there's so much I can't remember. These spies and I exchanged nothing more than names. The desert has no time for niceties. It must not have rained for a year when we arrived. We lost the first operative within a week, blind and burned and raving from the heat. We hadn't yet seen the unidentified troublemakers we'd been sent to investigate.

We hadn't seen anyone at all. There weren't even any animals about during the day. They must have been sleeping through the heat, hiding themselves in the shade of the sparse shrubs and trees, wiser than us humans who tramped around in the sun. At night we heard the scurrying of small feet, saw shadows of wings against the stars like the ghosts of birds, and heard in the distance the rumbling of tigers. If any of us were afraid we never exposed it to the others, but as we lay in our circle of bedrolls on the dirt we could hear that we all were holding our breath.

After two weeks in Siva we had combed the entire western flank and began to move farther in, away from the cliffs that linked us to the land we came from. We still saw no one. There was still no rain. A second operative collapsed from the heat. We watched as his waterskin dropped on the ground and split, watched as the liquid bled out over the dust and was swallowed by it. We watched each other, wondering who would be the first to dive to the ground and clutch the skin, to suck out the last elusive drops. We stared at each other. Then we dragged the unconscious man into the shade of a wiry tree and kept walking.

Reports of unrest, that was all we were told. A handful of peacekeeping forces had been established at the various crossings into Siva to monitor traffic and activity there. It wasn't uncommon for such outposts to fall out of communication, either due to channels breaking down or the men abandoning their posts out of boredom. The entire southwestern quadrant had gone silent in one season, though. It was suspicious and it would be investigated. We were given no further information.

Cannibals, one of the operatives began saying. That's what happened to them. His eyes were wide and shaking. Another spat that he wasn't afraid of cannibals, he'd killed twenty-four men, twenty-four, and he wasn't afraid of any kind of man. There were no records of cannibalism in Siva, although a series of Karrimian fairy tales threatened wicked children with man-eating desert dwellers. The nervous man stared and jumped at the shadows and dust.

Warring clans, I said. There were many clans in Siva, that much was known. The missing peacekeepers must have been caught in the cross fire. No one listened to me. They had been through the same training. They knew about the clans. They must have forgotten. I tried to list the known clans. Wind clan, Tiger Land clan. There must have been more than two. Or maybe there weren't. Or my memory had lost them. I searched fiercely for the date. Second season, second day, 762. We had been in Siva for eighteen days.

Another operative plucked a fruit from some thorny plant, looking for water. We watched the spikes pierce her fingers as she sucked at the juice. Two hours later she spasmed with poison and fell into the dust. As we left her behind we heard the shrill cackle of carrion birds flying overhead. It was still day. It must have been getting cooler.

There were four of us. We measured the water we had left. Our orders were to split up if our stores dropped to that level, so there was a better chance of finding water. The boastful man went off with the one who had the most water in his skin. The one who was afraid of cannibals was left with me. I looked at my map, read where the known clans had been x'd on it. We're in the middle of tiger land, I said. His eyes widened in fear.

Twenty-three days, and it rained. In the distance. We watched as half the sky darkened like night, as lightning split it into pieces, as it hazed over. We could hear the water pound the ground. My partner started running for it, tripping, kicking up dust, sweating the last water out of himself in the heat. I lost sight of him. The rain stopped. The sun burned off the clouds and the heat became close and smothering. Night fell with a bright moon. I got to my feet and walked. All that was left of the rain when I reached it was a puddle. I stooped and filled my waterskin with mud.

That night Siva's people returned. I heard them singing in the darkness, a chant, or a war call. The lessons I'd had in their language were useless to me. I understood nothing. In my thirst I could imagine it was only my ears ringing, noise with no meaning. When the sun came out I saw them. They were covered in lines. I blinked and realized I was seeing the branches of the bush I was hiding beneath. I strained to focus my eyes on the people I saw. The prints of Sivans in the history books showed elongated stick figures with spots on their backs. The spots were real, not just some artist's creation. The bodies of the Sivans, long and thin and bronzed by the sun, were dotted with birthmarks and embellished with tattoos. When I saw a man, walking close by me, so close I was sure he would smell my sweat as I lay hidden against the dust, and my eyes told me there was a tiger on his back, it was true. Some clansman observing a rite in a religion I never learned anything about had connected the marks on his back into the picture of a tiger.

I saw other things that I pieced together much later. Their simple garments, stitched together from skins of small animals, had been elaborated. The people wore necklaces and bracelets, even the youngest children, and the chests of some men were draped with dozens of them. The jewelry was made of coral and shells. The people had been to the seacoast, far away at the eastern end of the country. We had encountered no one in the early days of summer because they had abandoned their treacherous deserts, wisely seeking water at the coast until the rains came.

The next thing I noticed was something I understood. There was shouting, commotion. In the murmur of foreign tongues I heard a single word I recognized. *Intruder.* The women formed rings around their children. The warriors drew their spears and strung their bows. I sank deeper into the shrub and dirt. They had found the body of my partner.

I crawled through the brush under cover of darkness. I clung to the ground and the sparse shadows. I eluded the hunters and the warriors and their weapons. I heard cries of rally and attack. There was unrest in Siva, its people were fighting. I could not tell who was on which side. I couldn't see the players, couldn't gather faces, couldn't recognize groups. My eyes were full of dust and the birthmarks blurred together. My waterskin crunched with the dried mud inside of it.

One day, or night, suddenly, someone was at my feet. I crawled out of the bush. I drew my knife. His hands were on me. I pushed him and we rolled on the ground. There was noise around us, people gathering in a circle. I didn't know if it was his clan or his enemies. I gained the upper hand. My knife was missing. I could have held him down—to do what then, I don't know—but I was dry and brittle as dead grass. My eyes cleared for a second. The face below me was that of an old man, wizened, gray-haired. He rolled me off, scuttered away. The people around us weren't his people; he ran away from them, hobbled by the injuries I'd done to him. I could not move out of the dust, and the noises descended on me.

I woke with my wrists bound and tethered to a pin in the ground. Water had woken me. Someone stood above me pouring water into my face. The sun blinded me, a scarring halo behind the head that eclipsed it. I closed my eyes, felt the water burn on my face. The eclipse moved away and left me with my scorched throat.

I was in a camp. I saw makeshift tents strung together from skins. I saw the ring of them around me. I saw the people of the tents, and they were not like the clans of Siva. I saw skin pale and brown and burned, hair light and red, clothing that was a tattered mix of skins and worn fabric. I saw tethered animals loaded with packs. I saw other captives, some pinned as I was, some with bound hands but free to move. They did not. I saw but I thought nothing.

There was enough water in me by then that I could count the nights and days. After two nights the camp moved. I was tied in a line of other captives and marched across the desert. There were the noises of birds ahead. The nomads were moving to have better access to game, I thought. We stopped and I was pinned to the ground.

The sun went on. I saw the captives who were pinned, and those who were not. There was a reason, a difference between us. I couldn't think what it was. Then a shell was pushed in my mouth. Water poured clumsily down my throat, spilling across my face. The hands that held the shell were bound. My eyes focused on the face of the old man I had wrestled with days ago. My second coincidence, in the heat of the Sivan desert. The man I'd almost killed was forcing life down my throat.

The nomads were of no clan. Later I would work out that they were the descendants of the Azassian soldiers who were stranded after the wars and the Sivan slaves who returned from the Outside to find themselves with no more family. They must have fought each other for years before resigning themselves to partnership. Anger was in their blood. Everyone was their enemy, the Azassian natives who had started wars and abandoned them, the dark people from Mandera or Dabion—it made no difference which one—who subjugated them, the Sivan clanspeople who were old enemies. They captured whomever they could find and dragged them around on their restless pointless wanderings. They trusted outsiders slightly less than native Sivans, and we were the ones who were pinned to the ground. We were not tortured, we were not killed. They watered us, kept us alive. I heard their pidgin words flung about but understood nothing. I did not know why we were kept.

Days passed. I counted nights but there was no reason. I stopped counting. Time passed and I lost it. It wasn't as it had been when I lost the days in Smyth's chamber. I had no sense of that thing other people call horror, that sudden violent awareness that something is lost, that my mind had been cracked open and plundered. There was nothing in the desert, no horror, no emotion, nothing but heat, dust in my eyes and my mouth and my skin, and the uncaring persistent blaze of the sun. I would wake to the heat, feel it in my marrow, feel it burning out the memories from my battered mind, and watch time drift into other days.

Tod spoke once of losing time to drunkenness. Did I

know what it was like, to have years missing? Oh yes, I knew.

One day I woke unable to move. I knew I should do my best to stretch my limbs, but I wondered how I knew it. After a while I remembered, that being motionless and always in the same position was causing my body to go numb. Slowly I raised a leg, stretched my foot in the air as far as possible. Then I saw that my toes were purple. I couldn't remember if that was normal. I rolled to my side, folded myself, painfully and over the course of some unknown time, so that I could reach my toes to my anchored hands. I watched my fingers probe my toes, feeling neither. My fingers also looked purple, as well as I could see them from my pinned position. Sometime later they began to sting. The sun was bright, it was warmer, thawing my fingers and toes out of the cold that had gripped them. It was winter.

Later I woke and realized winter was gone. The heat was in my bones again. I might have wondered when it had returned, but I didn't.

Then one day, I heard my name. I didn't recognize it. Something buzzed in my head about how I must be dreaming, although I couldn't remember what dreaming was. I drifted back toward sleep.

"Elzith Kar," I heard again. Me, my name. I opened my eyes. A face was in front of me. I saw its strange colors but couldn't name them.

"Where were you born?" it said. Water was pushed into my mouth. I had closed my eyes again. I looked at the face, realized it was speaking my language. It was absurd. It meant nothing to my dusty mind and it drifted out again. My face stung, slapped, I think. I opened my eyes. "Elzith Kar," the voice repeated. "Where were you born?"

I stared as if a lizard had spoken. But my mouth rolled open and some part of me that remembered threw out the words "The City, Karrim." The pin was pulled out of the ground, my arms were wrenched upward, and I snapped unconscious with the pain.

The wagon ride to the border of Siva is in pieces. I remember it as if I dreamed it. There is sun, then darkness, something thrown over me, rain, a crash, the shouting of men at a broken wheel. There is a face, also, one that slipped from my mind over and over before I saw it often enough to fix it there. The face is red, pale in the undertones of its skin but highly colored. The eyes are very deep green and wear an expression of concern, charity, gentleness, which looks strange beside the long scar that runs vertically along the cheekbone. The hair is a mass of curls only partly tamed into a binding unseen at the back of the neck, and it and the whiskers that bristle the chin are brilliant red. It is the face of an Azassian.

I was rescued in autumn 763, carried across Siva's northern breach into Azassi. A tarp covered me, a secret cargo in the back of the wagon, as my rescuer drove me into the courtyard of an old, partly abandoned estate house. The tarp was pulled, I was dunked into a barrel of water, fetched out, clothed quickly with a gown dragged

down over my head; then I was stood up before three of
the big men, Dabionian and strange-looking in their
black suits. They barked official words at me, I uttered all
I could remember, and it was over. I was back in the
world.

The scarred Azassian loaded me into his wagon, long
after the Force officials had departed, and we left for the
camp on Dabion's north coast. He was an operative as
well, of some sort. He was a professional. He asked no
questions and revealed no hint of fear or curiosity. He
crept off the road and waited out passing traffic with the
patience of a rock, and when some huffy landowner
stopped to question us, he spun a yarn I could hardly
have rivaled in my prime. All reality was in the jolting of
that cart. Then we drove past one of the mines. Outside
the gaping mouth of it, some distance from the mountain it was gutted into, was a fenced field. The entry gate
to this yard bore a sign: *Let us not lie forever in the earth.*
Within the yard were man-shaped mounds of rocks. I
pitched backward into the bed of the wagon.

The horses stopped. The Azassian was hovering over
me. I struggled to see him through the visions. I was un-
pinned from the dusty earth, gathering rocks with my
bound hands and mounding them over the body of a
captive who had frozen to death in the unsheltered
desert winter, unable to dig a grave in the hard ground.

"What's wrong?" the Azassian was mouthing through
the noise in my head. I tried to see the green of his worried eyes.

"Keep driving," I rasped. The memory faded as the wagon rolled on, and I had no more of them. I still have not.

The Azassian deposited me when we reached Dabion's border. He was not part of the Secret Force proper, or he wouldn't have been restricted from the rest of the journey along the northern coast, to the site where we operatives are washed up before being sent back on our way. I went immediately to the blind Healer when I got there. I lay unmoving in his tent for three days. Three days and seven hours. I was burned from the sun and dehydrated severely. The Healer rubbed my skin with salve as he worked his imperceptible magic on me. I did not feel the force of that power, you almost never feel it when a Healer touches you; but I felt his hands, worn fingers handling every pore and crevice of my burned skin. I felt battered as if I were still in the sun. I wondered—the nomads of Siva had raped their captives, no doubt, that eternal impulse of rage and power, one brittle and weak human body boasting dominance over another one. If I had been I couldn't remember it. The rasp of hands on me called to mind nothing but Smyth. When the Healer was finished I doubled over the side of my cot and retched.

I stayed on the coast until winter, the longest anyone had ever been on repose, as far as I know. I did little but look at the sea. There are never many operatives there at once, and they are strictly guarded and separated, lest they spill the big men's secrets in their recovery. I watched the distant movements of others as they moved in and out of the cottages scattered along the beach. It was easy enough to imagine they were figments, visions leaking from my troubled mind. They were no more real than anything else.

Then Loyd came for me. He came personally to bring me back to the Insigh offices. I watched his mouth move as he talked. I wondered if he would apologize, offer amends for my suffering. I knew he would not. He sat beside me as we traveled south, chatting idly like that dotard old man he often pretends to be. I was assigned a room in the dormitory, dressed in a weathered skirt, and summoned to a lecture on Manderan terrorists. I was on assignment again.

# 35

I T WAS BUSINESS AS USUAL WHEN I FIRST SHOWED UP on Jannes's doorstep. The servingwoman opened the door, and for an instant her eyes were wide, her mouth open slightly as if she were about to ask a question of me. Her face narrowed into silence, though, and she stepped aside to let me in. Then she locked the door and ran ahead of me to announce my arrival.

Jannes said nothing about my absence. He certainly knew of the disorder in Cassile; he'd probably authorized some of the cover-up, lighting fires with a scratch of his pen. He only looked up from the papers on his desk for a second. "You'll be taking Aron out today, Kar," he ordered, as if he'd been giving me similar orders all week. "The headmaster of his school has scheduled him for an assessment before the upcoming term. Here is the address. He is expected at ten o'clock."

It was already nine and I knew I would need at least that much time to get Aron out of his room. I memorized the address and headed upstairs at once to fetch him, but Aron was morose and unusually silent, and put up no resistance. He followed me wordlessly as I led him down the stairs. Ahead of us his father was putting on his jacket, gathering his papers, and preceding us out the door to climb into a carriage for the short ride to the Great Hall. Aron's face twisted into a grotesque pout as he watched his father leave. "He told me not to ask why you were gone," he said bitterly once the carriage had rolled out of sight. There was more venom in his young voice than I would have guessed of him.

"I suppose he did," I answered. "Say good-bye to your mother."

Sluggishly he turned his head toward an open window and shouted a good-bye at the motherly figure that sat in the rear yard, obscured by the curtain that stirred in the incoming breeze.

By the time we reached the offices of the headmaster, Aron had loosened up enough to start complaining about the school. He talked himself hoarse in the waiting room, and when he finally sat down across an imposingly large desk from an impossibly heavy-browed headmaster, he was almost politely quiet. The headmaster eyed me where I stood in my place against the doorjamb, with a critical expression probably reserved for students he expected of doing something unlawful that he hadn't yet discovered. Aron sat his exams with a minimum of fuss, only ripping up two sheets and breaking one pencil. When the assessment was finished a few hours later, he was even invited to the luncheon with the other students in the rear of the building. He dragged me in behind him with a showy grin on his face, wallowing in the stares of his fellow students, which were fixed on me like I was a tiger in a cage. Aron immediately challenged everyone to a game of cards.

While we were there I was summoned from the crowd of adolescent stares to meet with a clerk. The Public Force had sent a message for me. I was to delay bringing Aron home until evening.

I could have guessed, even then. I did not ask the questions. I was to do my duty and that was all.

Aron was exhausted by the time I had walked him all over Origh. When we finally reached his home, at the authorized time, he went straight to his room, willingly, without observing the Public Force guards in the kitchen or the tormented expressions of the household staff. I took him to his door and closed it, and Jannes appeared behind me, to escort me personally to another small square room.

"You'll be staying here for a few days," he announced. "Do you require anything from your home?"

I answered no, but I sent a message for Tod with the clerk who was waiting to be dispatched.

It would be nothing to sit in that room and wait, counting minutes until I was given further instruction. I'd done it before. It should not have troubled me. When I got hungry I went to the kitchen to find something I might be able to eat. The words I overheard should not have moved me.

"I left for the woodyard at eleven," the old manservant

was saying in a dry, tired voice, as if he'd reported the story many times already. "Pera had left for the grocer's a few minutes earlier."

It was foolish for them to have planned their errands at the same time, when Jannes and I were already out. Had I been there, I could have monitored that. I could have made sure the house would not have been so unattended. I turned on my heel and climbed the stairs back to my room.

Not until the next morning was I told. Jannes ordered me to Aron's room to give him the news that his mother was dead.

I didn't lose time. I was aware of every moment that passed, watching Aron, catching what he threw, getting in his way when he got too violent, holding him when he flailed too much. I counted the few minutes that he was silent, when he'd exhausted himself, when he fell out of consciousness, to measure the time until his next outburst. There was no time to think, only to dab the blood at my mouth, tense my arms, and wait for despair to rouse him again.

He slept part of the night, while I watched without thinking. Before dawn he started wailing, a tortured animal sound, a ghost sound from old stories. It stopped. I tried to blink dry fatigue out of my eyes. I opened them and heard Aron speaking, a crooked trail of words.

"She's really not coming back?"

"No," I uttered. My throat would not open. "She's not."

Aron gasped several times into sleep. When the sun came up he woke and started screaming again.

The doctor was finally summoned after he went half the day without stopping. Aron was dosed thickly with laudanum and dropped into his bed. I untangled his legs and laid them out straight.

"Go home, Kar. Be back tomorrow morning," Jannes ordered, and escorted the doctor out before leaving his son's room, where he had spent exactly six minutes.

"Izith," murmured Aron through drugged lips. I turned back toward him. He was struggling to sit upright, listing from side to side. He flung his arms out unevenly and I reached to steady them. "Don't go." The arms linked clumsily around my waist.

I walked hard, pounding my feet on the ground, disciplining my heart to that steady pulse. My lungs burned as I sucked in reluctant breaths. I felt each one of them, each step, as my swollen feet chafed in boots I'd worn for three days. I felt every minute of that long walk out of the city. I forgot nothing. There were holes in my mind and not a second of this fell through them. In images perfect as crystal, I remembered trailing Ciceline, the shake of coins in her purse, the blackmailer's door, the dark expression of the escort, whose training I knew as well as my own, who could take a life as surely as I could. Thoughts replayed themselves like cards. I know something is wrong, I should report it, I should have it investigated, but no, I will not, I don't want to play, I don't care. Even if it means someone's life, I don't care.

I wondered if I could shock myself by looking into a mirror.

Tod was listening to her breathing. It was even, steady. Her face was chiseled and motionless. It was as if nothing was wrong, nothing unusual. He wondered if her heart was beating. Her ribs shifted very slightly up and down, ghostly pale inside the unbuttoned black shirt. He could believe her heart wasn't beating at all, that the breathing was only an illusion.

Elzith had knocked at his door in the middle of the afternoon. It was so early that he couldn't imagine it would be anyone but Shaan, but Shaan hadn't come by since he'd dropped off the knife. Tod guessed the law was on to him and he didn't want to try and take the knife back yet. Shaan always hollered when he knocked, also. Tod was afraid for an instant that the visitor was someone he didn't want to see, but his curiosity got the better of his fear. He opened the door to Elzith.

She said nothing. She didn't look at him. She didn't respond to his attempts at conversation. She took a chair, and shook her head briefly at his offer of food.

"Too early for dinner," Tod murmured in reply. He tried to remember what he'd been working at. For several minutes he tossed papers around on his table until he settled down at something, but even then he was distracted by Elzith's face, and he looked up at her between every stitch. She did not look at him, her eyes fixed on something behind his shoulder. When her eyes didn't waver he turned as subtly as possible to see what she might be looking at, but as far as he could tell she was looking at nothing.

Tod swallowed hard. "Elzith, what's wrong?" he attempted, but she silenced him with a shake of her head before he'd even finished speaking the words. Her eyes didn't move from the spot of nothing over his shoulder. Tod dropped back to his work. His throat caught and he tried to swallow again. His heart felt pounded thin. He'd been so close, he'd almost thought he had broken through, reached her across her act of coldness and isolation, to a place where he could help her. He thought he'd had an end of days that ended with locked doors. He wanted to stop waiting. There was nothing else to do but wait.

Then Elzith looked at him. Her eyes, he thought for a second, were strangely blank. She hesitated before she spoke. "Is your offer still open?"

He thought in the next few moments that he might not have said yes if he'd seriously thought she meant to take him up on it. He found himself walking to his bedroom, intending to get a lamp or matches or something else unneeded. It was still daylight. When he turned back toward his doorway he found Elzith standing in it. He caught a glance of pale, bare skin, below the hem of her long shirt. She was not meeting his eyes again.

Tod no longer trusted his knees. He sat himself on his

bed. Elzith approached him, still not looking at him. A severe line was growing between her eyes. Tod stared at it, he found it hard to think of anything else. He was surprised when she reached him and pressed him down, his back against the bed. He was expecting that she wasn't really serious, even as she manipulated his clothing with an efficiency that he was too suddenly and traitorously aroused to feel. He looked at her face, drawn and tense. He wanted to stop. He closed his eyes. He could not stop. He tried to lift his hands, hardly feeling them, driven to touch her, reaching at the buttons of her shirt. She pulled his hands away and pinned them down behind his head.

When it was over, he remembered, in a single incongruous minute, the girl in Karrim that his brothers told him he'd mistreated. He wondered if it was true, wanted to find her and apologize. But what could he say? Then his body continued in its rebellion and plunged him into sleep.

With a gasp his eyes popped open. He hadn't slept long; it wasn't yet dark. Elzith was still there. She lay perfectly still, on her back, her eyes closed. He'd undone the buttons after all, down to the seam in the middle, and her chest glowed white within the black shirt. Too pale to be anything but a wanderer. The unknown scar was hidden under the lower part of the shirt. Tod watched her breathing and wondered about her heart. He raised his hand, approached, hesitated, caught his breath. Then he settled his hand on her chest. The movement and the sound of her breath paused for a second. Tod waited. He felt her heart beneath his hand, and she started breathing again. Her eyes did not open. She didn't see the tear slipping across his face.

# 36

---

SHE WAS STILL THERE WHEN TOD WOKE UP. ELZITH
had not moved from the position she had lain in
when she first fell asleep, where she had lain all night.
Tod had slept little, waking frequently and watching her.
She never moved, but her breath had grown deeper
toward the middle of the night. Tod had lain perfectly
still, though his stomach ached from a missed dinner
and his arm was numb from not moving it, but he was
afraid to shift and wake her. He felt her heart still beating. As the sun came up he saw its shadows heavy on her
face. Sleep had eased the hardness of it a little and left it
worn, sunken-eyed, marked with lines. He watched the
lines deepen, the mouth tighten, the eyes draw up as the
light grew brighter and she rose out of sleep. She would
move soon, she'd be gone from him. He wished her eyes
would stay closed but they opened anyway.

She lay still for a moment yet, silent, staring at the
ceiling. Tod sighed. There was no holding back time.
"What's wrong?"

The fatigue hadn't completely hardened out of her

face. She looked old, and Tod realized he didn't know her age. Her voice when she answered crackled like dry leaves. "It doesn't matter."

Tod's hand drifted up to brush the lines around her eyes, but she edged away from him, turning her back. He looked at the back of her head as if he could comb the tangles through with his eyes.

"You should be angry, Tod," Elzith sneered weakly. "I used you like a whore."

Tod swallowed at the lump in his throat. He didn't want to think about whether he was angry. "You're trying to distract me, Elzith," he murmured. "You're playing me. Why are you doing it?"

Slowly she sat up, as if it was a struggle, and her words were forced. "Of course. Always playing a game. It's what I do. It's what they want me to do."

"So stop."

She looked at Tod then, her eyes hard and skeptical. She shook her head. "It's not my choice. There's nothing I can do. Can you stop those people in your dreams from dying?" She turned away again, moving with painful slowness as she did up her buttons and stepped into the other room to get the rest of her clothes. "We take what we get, Tod. We tread water, and when it wants to, it drowns us."

Tod watched her disappear around the edge of the door. He couldn't even hear her any longer. She moved in silence, he realized. She would have to, it would have been part of her training, he should have noticed it before.

He looked away, up toward his window, where light seeped between the shutter slats. He felt worn and strange, his body not quite his own. It was almost like drunkenness, he thought, but he couldn't quite remember how drunkenness felt, not quite. Enough time had passed. It was an effort, now, to remember. And when he did, he remembered something else, something from before all those alcoholic years. His dream about his great-aunt. He hadn't told the story right, when he spoke of it to Elzith. He didn't have the dream the same night his great-aunt died. He had it the night before. She died the next morning. His father gave him the news later that day. She'd been an old woman, and her heart was tired, so there wouldn't have been anything he could do. Still, the dream was different from his childhood nightmares. He used to feel people's deaths after they happened, but that dream had come before. The dream of Elzith, too, had happened early, giving him time to find her before she sickened even more. Maybe the dreams were coming so that he could stop the people from dying. Maybe they weren't simply a fate that he had to take.

He chafed his hands until he could feel them again, until he could recognize his fingers and their patchwork of small scars. He sat up and straightened his clothes. It would be time to speak to Elzith again, very soon.

But she interrupted him. "Tod, are you expecting someone?"

She was standing by the front window, having eased back the shutter enough to peer outside. Tod shook his head, unable to think of anything. "Who is it?"

"A Justice and two guards."

Tod gasped. It was the seventy-sixth day of autumn, the day of his forgotten appointment. "Justice Paloman. He was going to bring me some books to look at."

Elzith eyed him narrowly. "I don't like it. He shouldn't be here." She looked back out the window, where the men were so close Tod could hear their muddled footsteps on the pounded dirt road. "I don't know him. I know one of the guards, though. I'm surprised he survived Cassile." Her eyes darted to Tod's clock. "I need to leave. Don't let him come again without someone being here." She took a few quick steps to the door before the visitors knocked, before Tod could answer. "Playing again," she muttered cynically, an instant before she opened the door.

Justice Paloman stood outside, startled by the sudden swing of the door, and one of the guard's hands was raised, interrupted in the attempt to knock. That guard's face twisted as he recognized Elzith. She spared no reaction for him, but she peered long into Paloman's quaking eyes.

"Why are you here?" she whispered.

Paloman was shaking so hard he almost dropped the bundle of books that he clutched to his chest. He looked up into Elzith's eyes as if snared, anxious and unable to escape. Tod realized Elzith was slightly too tall, even against others who didn't have his habit of slouching, against the Justice and his guards. Her mother was a Sage. "Br-bringing books," the Justice stuttered.

"You don't lie well," Elzith said quietly, turning slightly so Tod could hear. She shot Tod a warning look. Tod swallowed. He had to be on guard for something, and didn't know what. Elzith looked at Tod, then at Paloman, and said, "So show him the books now."

It took ten minutes. That was the longest Elzith could stay, and she bullied the Justice to the schedule. She threw open all the windows and the door, even though there was a snap in the morning air and Tod was shivering. Nothing would be secret. She tried asking Paloman questions but he seemed to lose all ability to speak. The guards were watching her suspiciously. When she finally shut them out she said, "He's spying for someone, but he's useless. I can't get out of him who it is, and I can't work on him any more with his guards around." She shook her head tightly as she checked the clock again. "I *have* to go. I'll find out what I can."

Tod forced himself to draw a breath, more steadily than his lungs wanted to. "I don't care who it is. No one's making me play the game."

For a second he thought Elzith would confront his words, but she only said, "Don't let anyone else in," as she went out the door.

Collin waited eagerly for a quarter of an hour for Loyd to praise the work he'd done. As that time passed and it slowly occurred to him that praise was not forthcoming, the young man's face sank like a mud pit. Loyd thought he might actually cry.

"Of course you did excellent work," Loyd soothed paternally.

"But you're not interested!" Collin cried in disbelief, and hunted around for an explanation. "It's not the answer you wanted, or—or you knew it already." Then his mouth dropped open. "You did know already! You knew who gave the shoot-on-sight order!"

Loyd smiled calmingly. "You have successfully confirmed my suspicions about the man's identity, my dear boy." For an instant Collin looked confused about how to take this, but then he decided to accept it as praise and the black cloud floated away from his face.

"But what will you do now?"

Loyd hesitated. Shocking, he thought to himself. After all these years, to make such a simple mistake as a hesitation. Recovering himself, he said, "Now, Collin, you will go to Barrow-under-Origh. There is an individual I wish you to keep an eye on. You will know who." Still so young, Collin noticed neither the hesitation nor the easy deflection. Loyd neatly turned the question of what Loyd would do into an answer of what Collin would. The young man trotted off to make arrangements.

An expensive choice, assigning Collin to Elzith. Collin would be better spent watching the quarry he'd identified, making sure the man did nothing else violent and gave no more orders. But as Loyd both knew that there was nothing he could do about that man, and how everything would turn out, he was willing to make the expenditure to protect Elzith. She was alive at the end of his premonition and he intended to keep her so.

# 37

THERE'S NO REST FOR THE WICKED. I MUST BE THE wickedest. Fate has outdone itself pricking at the heart I don't have. If I believed in justice, I'd say I was being bled to death for my sins, through the fleshy hole where a heart should be.

I was given four days to ready Aron for his return to school. He woke from his drug-forced rest in a stupor, and over the four days he hardly came out of it. He was quiet, empty of words and hollow of screams. There was no running, no tantrums out of him. He sat in the rear yard, plucking blades of fading grass, planted motionless on the ground as if he'd grown out of it. My services went unused, a guard dog with nothing to chase. I stared out across the yard over his head, listening to the blood pound in my ears as the hours dragged past.

The morning that we packed him up to go, Aron finally spoke to me. "I don't want to go back."

"That's a surprise," my mouth said. "I'd never have guessed."

Aron huffed. "Why does Father tell me I have to go?"

I didn't want to look at him, didn't want to see a face that was as meaningless as a game board, didn't want to see a face that wasn't. "We don't have a choice about these things."

"That's what Mother said."

The pricking stabbed again. None of my flat words came to me, none of my prized skill at deflecting questions or turning other people's words where I wanted them to go. My mouth was dry, like Siva's sands.

"You'll go away and I won't see you again, either." Aron stood at my boots, looking up at me reproachfully. I could hear him breathing. His hands were fists on his hips. This was the time I should speak, spit out some formula of words to quiet him and keep his temper down, time for me to be good with children. The sand was filling up my throat. Your mother is dead, your mother is dead—that was all I could think. Your mother is dead, and I am the reason. I could have saved her but I did not.

The boy shoved at me ineffectually, pushing me with his hands, with no real effort. "Fine," he muttered, and reached for one of his cases that littered the floor.

After his carriage had come to roll him away, I picked up the things he'd neglected, the clothes and scattered baggage, and put them in order.

I waited through the afternoon for my masters to call on me again. The upper floor was silent, its inhabitants gone, and I made no noise in it. Near evening Jannes wandered up the stairs, through the deserted hallway, and was surprised to find me standing by the window at the end of the hall.

"What are you doing here—Kar?" His voice caught over my name, as if he were trying to remember it. He was not wearing his wig, and his hand ran absently over his head, wondering what he was missing. A characteristic of the grieving man, the dry voice of my training recited in my mind, is a vague but pervasive sense of having misplaced something. The pricking twisted in my chest again.

"I have received no further orders, my lord," my voice said, absently as his.

"Well—well," he stumbled, "I'm certain they will be forthcoming."

I was no longer needed. I had to go home. The pain seeped down from the empty place in my chest to the empty place in my stomach. I had avoided Tod in the last four days, returning to the flat only for a few hours of sleep each night, very late when he wouldn't hear me. I couldn't think of him without thinking of what I'd done to him, that foolish attempt to forget, to feel anything other than the pain of Ciceline's death. I was as much a fool as any man I'd conned in the brothel in Karrim. That senseless thing had blinded me to the pain for a heartbeat, for the length of a breath, that was all. That was all I could expect. I knew better, but I had forgotten. Cracks in my mind. And then there was the memory of Tod's hand on my chest, still and resting, which I'd wanted to tear off of me that long night, but now I was cold without the touch of it. That bit of my chest shivered and the flesh pricked deep beneath it.

Jannes still lingered in the hallway, looking at the motionless doors.

"Am I dismissed, my lord?"

He jolted, having forgotten I was there. I watched his mind turn, trying to find an answer. "Yes, you are dismissed," he finally breathed, and ghosted back down the stairs.

At home I met not Tod but Collin, Loyd's handmaiden, the youth who'd played devil's advocate for me. I didn't bother to analyze his presence there or the expressions on his face. He told me in official words that Loyd had assigned him to watch me.

"Watch Tod" came out of my mouth, and I went downstairs to bed.

Orders came the next morning. The Black Force was summoned to the barracks in Insigh for training. The storm on Naniantemple was at hand. I was there at the start of it, the one who brought the report that brought down the monasteries. I would be there at the end of it, the last, bloody end of it.

We were back in Cassile by the twentieth day of the season. Naniantemple, home of holy relics, center of the mystics' religion, sacred ground they were willing to die for, was a sprawling complex of low stone walls shrouded in the forests in the heart of Cassile. The trees had lost their leaves for a winter that the Western Sea blew in early, and they stood like bared skeletons around the eerily silent walls. Fate was mocking us with its fore-shadowing.

"Close combat," Dabion's generals had barked at us in the training barracks, our cobbled masses of green recruits and barely recovered patients. "Use muskets when you arrive, at a distance. When the enemy is too close for loading, muskets will be ineffective." With a metallic clatter, like the music of their absurd marches, short swords were handed out. We dutifully learned to cut the life out of the masses at Naniantemple with our own hands. I was too worn to laugh at the irony, the crude instruction that our clumsy Dabionian superiors were giving us while Manderan fencing masters were dying in their prisons. Our masters taught us to hack and stab, and gave us no shields. The law told them, apparently, that Naniantemple wouldn't fight back.

Nanian, Cassilian monk, born 400-something, was a mystic. He had a prophecy, in 517 the Justices say, that led him and his followers to withdraw from the violence of the time, the controversy stirred up by scholars and scientists, the strife fanned by judges and chieftains to fuel their fights for power. The mystics left it all and boarded themselves up in monasteries. Some mysteries are not to be known by the human mind, their books say, those few written scriptures that outsiders can get their hands on. The work of the monks is to pray and purify themselves and wait for the day when death will carry them to that eternity where all mysteries are made clear. Except for that madman who thinks the mystics work magic, the official word from Dabion was that the monks would be easily overcome.

It's been a long time since Nanian's prophecy. That directive to escape the outside world has had plenty of time to turn into a hatred of outsiders, especially when the fine work of our Black Force has driven the ascetics—those that have survived this long—to desperation. Naniantemple didn't wait for us quietly. Its monks weren't peacefully anticipating the death we were bringing. We weren't even given the distance to use our muskets.

They set on us the instant we were in the clearing. No training, these monks. Only a few had ever held an axe or a rake in their lives. Some had nothing more than sharpened sticks, the tools being too few to go around. It didn't matter. They were on us. We cut them down, trying to press forward to the temple. There were swarms of them, all the survivors who escaped other closures, even peasants in laymen's clothes, people from the tiny villages scattered among the monasteries, those who weren't beaten down by the Justices' threats after monastery seventy-four was burned. There were more of them than us. From somewhere behind orders were given, ranks called back for firepower. Shot rained over those of us still in the front line. A guard beside me fell, the hole in his throat from a monk's stick, the one in the back of his head from a comrade's gun. They should have called me back, I thought coldly. At least I could hit a target. From behind us, I recognized the voice of Geremain, the Justice who had reprimanded me in the summer. He was giving the orders and he wasn't about to spare me my position on the field.

We inched forward. At our masters' call, all of us. I wanted to wonder why we didn't leave. I wanted to think, if the blades and the fire and the blood would stop. There was no time. I aimed my blade where I had been taught and kept moving forward. A storm broke and drenched us in sleet. My feet skidded on the wet and gory grass, and the icy wind tried to push me off my poor footing. My mind woke to the task of keeping me from falling. I realized then what I had been doing, catching the monks as they lunged at me, their eyes wide in fear and rage. I was diving into them, stopping them for a second before cutting through their throats. I had gotten farther than any of the Black Force. I was still alive. I came to a standstill, rain in my eyes. I let my arm fall. A young monk rushed at me. Someone else's weapon cut him down. The Force surged around me. We had gained ground. We were at the doors.

I stood in the rain and imagined myself turning, walking away, out of the clearing, but I could see nothing beyond the bare arms of the trees. The sea was not far away, to the west. The water would take me, I imagined. It would let me into its uncaring depths. It would take me in, cold, huge, empty, give me a place if not a home. Then the water from the sky stopped. Cold wind drove against my drenched body, mercilessly. The short sword slipped in my hand. I looked down at my fingers, crusted still with blood that hadn't washed away. I sheathed the blade and looked up to meet Geremain's eyes.

He said nothing to me. He looked at me for a very long moment. I could not interpret his expression; I did not try.

To leave the field I had to walk over the bodies I had cut down. There's a hole in my mind that no death I have ever caused can fall through. I recognized every face, blue, muddy, blood-spattered, every wound I dealt, every eye I trespassed, staring up reluctantly at the mysteries they'd sought. I saw them still as the wagon dragged me back to Insigh, through the long trek over iced and washed-out roads. The faces were not jogged out of my mind by the stench of the dead guards hauled with me in the wagon, or the miserable complaints of the three deserters who had run from the battle and had been caught, and, like me, sat in shackles as we were dragged to face justice.

I began breathing faster on that journey. I told my body to stop but it would not listen. I measured my breaths to the rolling of the wagon's wheels, two every turn, five every turn, ten every turn. I tried to hold it at ten, and then it was fifteen. I watched it run away from me as if it weren't mine, not even part of my body. The others in the wagon slunk away from me as if I had plague. The clerks who opened the wagon when we finally rolled to a stop—that slowing of the wheels magnifying the speed of my breath so that I couldn't measure it anymore—stared at me. They backed away, stumbling, none wanting the duty of escorting me. When we reached the courtroom I wasn't even called upon. They sent me directly to Loyd.

Loyd, the man who taught me, who shaped me into his best servant, the one person other than Geordie I had ever respected, looked at me in naked shock. He was unable to cover it.

I gasped at the air, opening my mouth in a violent struggle to speak. My hands were growing cold and shaky. My head throbbed. Pain seethed through me. I was angry. I was angry at being unable to speak. "Do—you," I hissed at the taunting air, "know—what—*happened*?"

He neared me, his face all empty with awe, his arms stretched with his palms toward me, like someone either comforting or holding off something dangerous. He knew what happened. He was Loyd. There was nothing he could say.

My ragged breath raged on. The metal of bile or blood burned my throat. "Why?" I spat.

He sank, slowly, impossibly, onto his knees, penitent at my feet. Shock had utterly muted him. He shook his head. His mouth didn't even pretend to search for words.

My breath didn't slow as a carriage rolled me past Origh. Loyd rode with me, watching me with the same bare expression until I could no longer stand it and turned my face into the curtains. I choked on the dust my frantic breathing sucked in. My eyes stung. By the time the carriage came to a stop Loyd had resumed control of his face. The driver summoned Collin to open the carriage and usher me out. They left me inside Tod's door. Tod was there, ready to lock it once I was in, standing strangely upright and stiff. They had briefed him. I could not look in his face. My breath came even faster. I tried to take steps in, away from the door. I lost feeling in my feet. My vision blackened in flashes. Blood throbbed in my ears. The frantic breaths chattered unevenly, catching in my throat. The room skidded sideways. I fell, crouched facedown on the floor. Breath came in huge gasps. I tasted blood and salt. Voice broke out of my stripped throat, uneven cries stabbing the jagged breaths. My ears were blocked and my skin was muffled by numbness, but I felt, far on the outside of me, Tod's body curl around me. The pain strung through my veins broke, piercing, scalding, melting. For the first time I can remember, I cried.

# 38

TOD CROUCHED BESIDE HER FOR A LONG TIME, holding her as she shuddered and gasped for breath. "Elzith has had a shock, and she is unwell," Loyd had told him, in a strange lost voice that sounded different from any Tod had heard him use before, not aged and helpless, not powerful and threatening. Unwell—Tod's heart had jumped. But if she were dead or seriously ill they wouldn't have brought her home, Tod thought, would they? Now he listened to her struggle for breath and wondered if she was actually in danger, if she would die for lack of air. He tightened his arms around her. His mind reeled—he didn't know what to do. Then he felt her body shake in a familiar pattern and recognized that she was crying.

That afternoon when the carriage driver had knocked, Collin had opened the door and slid out, moving casually as he always did. Tod could almost believe Collin was nothing more than a friendly companion, sitting by his fireplace, drinking tea, reading Tod's books. Except, of course, that he canted his chair so that his back was never to the door. Tod was not surprised at all when his door opened again, not to Collin but to Loyd.

"There has been violence in Cassile," Loyd recited in an official tone, so convincingly that it took Tod several minutes to realize that such forced neatness was not like Loyd at all, that something must be wrong. "A very severe confrontation took place at one of the monasteries. You will not be given the details; they are unimportant to you. But Elzith,"—and there the old man faltered, slightly, enough that Tod could tell his guise was cracking—"has had a shock, and she is unwell."

Collin was outside the door, keeping watch as Loyd exited. "Lock the door," he told Tod. "I'll patrol the outside." So Tod found himself stiffly at his post, following orders, waiting for Loyd to bring Elzith in, locking the door again, and watching incredulously as Elzith collapsed in front of him.

He was completely out of his depth. Whatever *severe confrontation* had happened was beyond his understanding, even if he had been told. It was the same as always. He would never understand, never reach her. But he couldn't simply stand and watch, and he dropped beside her, and he recognized what was happening to her. He knew grief, he knew tears. He held her while she shuddered, steady against her trembling, calm. He saw the blood under her fingernails and was not frightened by it.

Time passed. Tod was breathing slowly, listening to

Elzith's breath, feeling her ribs move more slowly against him, hearing her breath gradually come in line with his. He was leading the tempo of her breath, he thought. He wondered if she was aware of it. She was no longer shaking, and when the tension of grief finally left her body she crumpled against him in utter exhaustion. When she spoke he felt her try to tense up, but she didn't have the energy. Her words were weak and thin. "Did you do this to me?"

Tod climbed over her unmoving body so that he was in front of her eyes. "Did I?" he said to her, and let her find out. She could hardly lift her hands, so he raised them for her and set them on the sides of his head. She dragged his head close, gasping with effort. He felt the chill on his eyes and let out his breath, forcing himself to yield.

The ice stabbed him deeper than he could feel. He saw black in her eyes and was smothered underneath it. It was her anger, he thought, his mind slowed by the cold and piercing with pain. It was her anger that hurt. Then, his mind lurching at emptiness, it was over. He saw Elzith outside of him, papery-thin and weak, her eyes half-closed. "No," she breathed. "No, you didn't."

He wanted to touch her, to stroke back her hair and dry her tears, but she wouldn't want it, and she would hate not being able to escape it. "What was it?" he murmured, swallowing his fear. "What happened?"

Elzith was silent, not answering him. Shadows of the battle struggled across her face, she was too tired to keep them hidden, but she still told him nothing. "What happened?" she finally answered, dry and almost soundlessly. "When? In Cassile? Mandera? Azassi? Siva? In the City, when I was born? It doesn't matter. They've been breaking me, bit by bit. Chipping me away. Too long now. I'm too far broken. Doesn't matter. Too far damaged. I'm worth nothing anymore."

He knew, he knew, and he knew she was wrong. "I don't agree," he whispered, knowing she wouldn't listen. "You've suffered so much, but—"

"I've killed twenty-seven men," she broke in. "Twenty-two of them in one day. They died because of me. Because of me. I opened my mouth, told the big men. My report brought down the monasteries. Playing their game. Their game. I don't want to play it. I can't do anything else. There is nothing else. There is nothing. The game, and pain." She closed her eyes and scraped in a breath. "It hurts."

And then he did touch her, just a finger along a strand of her hair. "I know."

She opened her eyes, blurry with damp. She read him very lightly but he still felt it, grazing his eyes dully. She nodded with the truth. When she spoke again it was reluctantly. She did not like to ask things directly. "When does it go away?"

Tod stroked the hair out of her eyes, smoothed it behind her ear. He ran a finger along the shadow under her eye and dried the salt streaks there. "I don't know. It doesn't. It does." He shook his head. She gazed at his eyes, not reading into them, then sighed wearily and closed hers.

They lay on the floor for some time. From outside Tod heard Collin pace in front of the door, tap lightly and call to ask if everything was all right. Tod called back a yes as quietly as he could.

"Don't have to whisper," Elzith murmured without opening her eyes. "I'm not asleep."

"You should sleep."

Her eyes cracked slightly within their heavy shadows. "No," she answered tightly, shaking her head a fraction. "No, I can't."

Tod hesitantly moved his hand to her chin. "Why?" his mouth formed. "You have before."

"Only because I had no choice. I was too sick to stay awake."

Tod frowned. "You distrust everyone that much?"

"I'd be a fool not to," Elzith said, in a voice as hard as she could manage. "Letting my guard down. Anything could happen."

Tod slid down to put his eyes in front of hers again. "You can trust me."

She looked at him, very weary, unwilling to admit what she saw in his eyes. Her stubbornness could no longer hold out. Slowly she tried to push herself up. Tod sat up more quickly, afraid she would try to leave. "I'm not going to sleep on the damned floor," she muttered in a crackling voice. But she swayed and Tod had to catch her.

She let him support her on his arm as she walked slowly into his room, and didn't move away as he helped her fingers that were stalled in the attempt to undo her buttons. He turned to fold her breeches, her muddy stockings, and set them in a corner while she pulled off her shirt on her own. He heard a muffled sigh, her arms in pain as she tried to raise them stiffly over her head. When he turned her scar would be there. He was calm, though. Stronger, strangely, than her. He turned to help with her shirt. The scar stretched at an angle away from her left hip, thick but faded, plain and powerless. He watched it for a moment, calmly, before helping her stretch her limbs and smoothing the bedclothes over her. He took off his shoes and lay down beside her, as he had before, on top of the covers. There was still tension in Elzith's face, and Tod reached to stroke the lines of her jaw. She stopped his hand. He thought she would push it away, but instead she laid it on her chest, over her heart. Tod's heart twisted, his body flooded with heat and taut with sudden desire. He had to let her sleep. Holding to the sweet ache, Tod watched her, and he saw her rest, saw her sleep. When he was sure of it he let himself drift as well.

Sometime after dark Tod rose, went to his kitchen and to his front window. He wandered back to his bed and undressed as if sleepwalking, then found Elzith still there, fast asleep. He pulled close to her, and she flinched at the contact, but did not wake.

In the morning Tod saw tears on her face again. Her

eyes were half-open, gazing, lost, at the ceiling. "It hurts," she rasped.

Tod pressed his hand against her chest, where it had come to rest again in the night. "I know."

"When will it stop?"

He ran his hand upward, to her face, her wet eyes. He caressed her face and she did not stiffen away from him. He could not answer her. His fingers traced the lines of her face, her throat, her collarbone.

Elzith turned her head toward him. He felt her against his eyes, reading what was in them. Her mouth twisted a little. "Are you trying to make me forget?"

"You can't forget," Tod answered, speaking with all truth although he couldn't stop touching her. "Neither can I. I only…"

She watched his words fail him. "You want to make things different now." She breathed out, not a laugh, not bitter. Then she nodded slowly. "I believe you. I don't think you can. But I believe you."

The tension was cold and brittle under her skin, so sharp he could taste it. He watched it tighten her jaw and harden her eyes, drawing her face so taut he could see the play of memories across it. He felt the breath held fast in her chest. He touched the scar on her stomach, ran his finger along the crooked line of it. The tension held. Tod's hands began to tremble. He tried to bring his breathing in line with hers, hers with his, but his breaths darted around unlistening. Hers remained rocky and stiff. Then, suddenly, the tension in her broke. Her fatigued body could not hold it anymore. Her skin softened and was pliable under his hands. The ache overwhelmed him. He hovered over her, slipped inside. Her face drew up with resistance but it passed, and he watched what followed it, fear, pain, helplessness so rare and foreign on her. Tod pulled himself closer, his eyes to hers, speaking in them as openly as he could so that she could read them, until finally her eyes closed with an almost imperceptible sigh: Please. Let go. I love you. Trust me.

# 39

AND NOW I TELL HIM THE LAST OF MY SECRETS. IT happened in Mandera, in a town just across the river from Dabion, a travelers' town of little importance that the Justices passed through on the way to do their business. Always a secret, the names of the towns, so jealously guarded by the big men, as if a name were the winning card. As if it mattered. The town was called Anamaril.

Anamaril was a favorite haven for Mandera's fine population of terrorists. Twenty years of Dabionian rule had trimmed their number to just a few remaining rebels, disinherited sons of barons and merchants who, when they found themselves penniless with the crash of the market, had committed suicide or done worse by signing contracts with the Justices. Few of the rebels were even old enough to remember the collapse, but they had been raised on stories of Mandera's lost wealth, and they felt righteously entitled to their vanished inheritance. They had perfected the act of terror, raining unpredictable violence on the impoverished towns of

Mandera, spurring the already desperate people to chaos, leaving them scattered at the feet of the bewildered foreign governors. The plan might once have been to drive the Dabionians away by drowning them with insurmountable problems. Over twenty years their goal had turned into little more than the chaos itself. On those occasions when Dabion put up an armed force to confront the terrorists, the result was a more perfect chaos than those rebels ever could have engineered themselves. So Dabion turned to a subtler attack.

Years' worth of secret observation had identified the terrorists and the thin pattern that existed in their attacks. Then the assassins were planted. The terrorists were all but blinded by their rage, but they were not fools. They caught on and grew distrustful. They started looking for the weapons designed for use against them. They dodged the kill shots. So I was sent, unarmed. In the skirt of a peasant women I was not to rouse their suspicion.

They struck a customs house, a crude square of a building lined with rows of benches, where travelers waited for the wagons or carriages that would take them elsewhere, where people came to send or collect the post, where itinerant workers spent hungry hours hoping someone would call on their services. These things everyone waited for were few and far between. The customs house was noisy with wordless shufflings and anxiety when the three men burst in.

Two were armed with swords. One of these men

began patrolling the rows of benches, as if anyone would need to be cut into submission. The other rolled a barrel across the front of the building, coming in through one door and going out the opposite one. We heard him pass outside, in a slow path close to the walls, carefully trailing the gunpowder that angrily irritated our noses and throats. The third man stood at the front, his feet straddling the black trail, holding a torch like a standard. We didn't need to hear him speak to know he was the ringleader. We didn't need to hear his orders to know what was coming.

Around the room heads dropped and faces went empty with fear. A few bold voices whispered curses at the men. "I survived the fire in Kysa for this," one uttered near me, in the dead tones of a man who has swallowed so much hardship that he is beyond despair. Behind us the cries of an infant were muffled as its mother pressed it to her breast. *Hush child, this is your last meal.*

Then I looked past the hollowly desperate face of the young mother. Two rows behind me, across the aisle, was a face divided vertically on the cheekbone by a long scar, surrounded by unruly red hair. Coincidences are absurd. I wasn't about to let this one pass.

The Azassian saw me and his eyes widened for an instant. Then he dropped his head to not draw attention. We watched the prowling men until they were both turned away from us. He pointed at the man in back, I pointed at the one in front. He nodded. The rebel with the sword turned to walk back up the aisle. Outside the man with the barrel rolled around the back wall of the building, striking the corner as he turned it to lay fuel on the one remaining wall. The Azassian pointed at me, then sprang.

He was a soldier, a professional; I knew that from the short time I had spent with him before. I had no doubts as I put my back toward him and strode toward the man with the torch. I gave no heed to the Azassian's cry or the rebel's shout behind me. My eyes were on the man at front, who had been utterly stunned by this unthinkable retaliation from the common people. I caught him in an instant, held him until I could come close enough to catch the torch, and snuffed him out. He crumpled facedown in the trail of powder. I snatched a cloak from the shoulders of a gape-mouthed onlooker and smothered the torch with it.

Behind me the Azassian looked up from the subdued body of the second rebel. He raised the sword unevenly in his off hand. His other hand was bloody and hidden among the red of the body lying at his knees. "Can you hold him off?" I called, as quietly as possible, tilting my head toward the pounding of footsteps outside. The third terrorist was running toward the door.

The Azassian turned to follow with his eyes the unseen movement on the other side of the wall. He grimaced with intent, and nodded. I darted out the opposite door.

The powder keg lay abandoned and half-full. I ripped

a panel out of my skirt and plugged it into the opening. The river was not far away.

I could have been born with some other talent. I could have had strength, or the ability to move things without touching them, as another of the Sor'raian operatives was rumored to have. What I had were the arms of a child, a scarecrow, the bones of a small bird and the muscle of an invalid. My suppressed emotions failed to generate the strength to fight, the passion that could move even the frailest woman to throw over armies to save her child. I pushed the barrel with all my meager strength toward the river.

I knew the terrorist was behind me, I heard the pounding of his uneven gait, louder than the rolling of the keg. I knew the Azassian was dead, that he would have put his life between the attacker and the powder. I knew mine was the only life left to put between them. I saw exactly how far I had to push. I knew how much of a chance I had. The terrorist's eyes would be so dampened by blind fury that I could not be sure I could get in to stop him. I couldn't risk it; I had to drown the powder first. It would likely be the last thing I did, with his sword in my back.

For a minute I almost laughed. To die like this. It was absurd. The terrorists would discover their fallen comrade, the one who had died without a mark on him. They would wonder why an unarmed woman stood up to the attack—though they wouldn't think twice about an Azassian's violence—and they would become dangerously suspicious. They would entrench themselves, hide, concoct new and more terrible plots, and return to rain down a fresh terror on the unprepared authorities. I would have ruined the operation. I would have undercut the big men's game, losing them an operative in the bargain. I'd have done it to save the lives of the silent people in the customs house. As if I cared. I almost wished I could have told Loyd about the irony.

The keg tipped over the edge of the bank. My throbbing arms dropped at my side, stripped and worn. No sword in my back. I whirled around and took it in the front. The last terrorist was so close he almost tripped on me as he sank his blade into my stomach, and his eyes flew wide with the shock. He was young, new to the game of terror, someone who had followed the passion of an older brother, perhaps, and signed his life away without knowing what he was doing. He had probably never killed before. He never would again.

I stayed standing for longer than I expected. I wanted to laugh. My tally: five men killed, a hundred saved. Was I to feel proud of this? If I could feel proud of anything, it would be dropping out of the game, making a move the big men had never seen before. I would die. I would win. I should have expected Loyd to have a countermove. I should have known I would wake up on the north coast, with the old blind Healer smiling in recognition as he palpitated my body with his hands, saying, "We meet again, we meet again."

# 40

---

THE BOOK LAY OPEN ON THE TABLE, ILLUMINATED by the light of a single candle within a glass globe. The air was filled with the scent of the ancient, a mood of arcane timelessness created by the old tome itself. Such things were to be mistrusted: power conveyed by mere paper and boards. The mystics claimed there was power in their books as well, not the same power, perhaps, though the mystics were still such a danger as to require extermination. But if the words of this ancient Bioran tome were to be read then it would be done properly, by the dim light of a candle, and in secrecy.

The book had no date inscribed on it, although a study of history could lead one to place it at the end of that Golden Age of Bioran learning, in the late fifth century, before excesses on the parts of various scholars and other men led Dabion to eradicate Bioran science. This book itself could be considered one of those excesses. Only the hubris of the scientist, believing himself the master of the natural world, could drive him into the unnatural land of Sor'rai, through the treacherous mountains that that divided Sor'rai from Biora on its hidden northern border, and to lurk there long enough to discover and observe its secretive people. The author's fellow scholars had doubtless recognized the extremes of this volume as an exaggerated mirror of their own vaulting pride, and they had suppressed it. The book had only come to light through a series of covert investigations and fortunate coincidences. It was quite likely that Dabion's law had been stretched to the breaking point in the acquisition of this small, old book. No matter. The ends would certainly justify the means.

Following several chapters of description of the land and its people, some of which were so outrageous as to not be believed, the book turned to a more noteworthy topic: the working of magic. Spells of every sort were described, with pages of transcribed chants in strange language, and lists of ingredients for dire potions. Every imaginable act was illustrated, both beneficial and deadly, and the method for achieving it duly enumerated. Again, some of these spells—levitation by means of ingesting an herbal concoction, the arousal of passion in a disdainful lover through the burning of a strand of his or her hair—were too absurd to be believed. Some of the recipes, though, were detailed in a sober and unassuming enough manner that they seemed genuine. A number of them bore resemblance to the ointments and tinctures still used by peasant women in outlying areas such as Azassi and the towns of Cassile, stubbornly persisting in their ethnic practices despite the hand of the law.

Magus would have been able to verify, presumably, which passages in the book were accurate and which were inserted by drunkards, storytellers, and copyists over the years. He never spoke of the land of his origin, not of his own accord. He was wise to keep silent, to remain in hiding, in this land of unbelievers who reduced the workers of magic to madmen and locked them in prisons. Those Sages of Sor'rai had their own, unknown reasons for staying within their confines, for if they had chosen to break the walls of the asylums and cast the bodies of their keepers to the wind like so much dust, they had the power to do so. Magus himself had the power to change shape, with such verisimilitude and conviction that none could discover him.

This incredible power was bound to his keeper, the man of Sage blood who had seen him in the act of changing. Magus was bound to do his keeper's bidding, to answer every request. If Magus had failed to respond about the truthfulness of the Bioran book, it was simply because Varzin had not phrased the request properly.

No matter. Varzin had selected the appropriate recipe and had tested it himself, on a wandering band of merchants, who were using the road through District Six without authorization, as they always did. The two eldest and frailest of them did not survive the test; the cloud of spores had pierced them to the lungs and suffocated them irretrievably. It saved the Lord Justice the trouble of finding them a prison in which to die. The other merchants, younger and stronger men, were plunged into unconsciousness by the explosion of particles and were docile for several hours before they regained the fullness of their breathing. Their eyes were damaged by the spores, but their minds and voices were intact. That was good. Varzin had no need for the shapeshifter's judgment on the recipe. Magus would have only one role to play for his keeper, and Varzin had already secured his agreement.

The plan was going far more smoothly than Varzin could have imagined. He had not been so optimistic when he'd first encountered Magus a year ago. If truth were to be told, Varzin had been terrified. For the past five years every step he'd taken had been in fear—though he'd concealed it well—especially in his own jurisdiction, near Lake Azin and the rocky land bridge where the Sor'raian wanderers camped. It was ironic that he should be so frightened there, since his first encounter with the palpable force of magic had been in the center of Insigh, in the corridors of the Great Hall itself.

The year was 759 and Lord Justice Athagar had died. He was not a very old man and there was suspicion of an assassination, though Varzin had never believed that. The Circle had been convened to select Athagar's successor, and Muhrroh had increased security to a stifling level in the wake of the suspicion. It was this extreme caution that had led the Circle to choose such a nondescript and ineffectual man as Timbrel for the post.

One night, after having his every move followed by no less than three escorts, Varzin had tired of the company and went for a walk. He slipped neatly out of an unattended hidden panel and into a barren corridor. He breathed deeply of the solitude and began his patrol. Then he turned a corner and stumbled into a young servingwoman, who was drawing herself up to scream.

"Silence, girl!" he'd hissed. "These are my quarters. I am Lord Justice Varzin!"

She let out her breath as rapidly as she'd drawn it, then looked him full in the eye. Varzin was about to raise his voice in indignation and scold the wench for such insolence, when he was suddenly flooded with the most horrifying cold. His heart lurched to a stop and his blood froze. It was a sensation he had never before encountered, one he could hardly describe, but one he could name. It was magic.

Varzin hated magic. He loathed it, despised it with every breath and particle of his being. He had hated it since he first learned its name as a child; if he'd had sense as an infant he would have hated it then. He hated the wanderers who trespassed through his land, those Healers and madmen with their weird eyes and senseless words. He hated the lake that could be seen from any point in his land, no matter how far or high or low. He hated its fickle waters and the land beyond it that changed and taunted. And then, to find magic, real magic, in its own tangible horrifying icy form, to feel it invading him, seeping through his body and the fibers of his mind—Varzin had spent hours in his chambers, trembling, before he could compose himself.

How he had hated that helplessness, trembling like a child. He had spied himself in his glass and despised the sight. Fear and weakness were greater faults in him, he was certain, than the hateful blood he carried, passed to him by someone beyond his reach. But his fear was under his own control, and control it he would. Though he felt fear each day of the five years that succeeded, he would not show it. Though he wished only to hide in his own chambers in Aligh, he went forth to patrol his lands and keep them free of the foul wanderers. They fled at his approach, all of those invaders from behind the lake, almost all of them. Two great exceptions appeared in those five years. One was a band of dirty mad Sages, and the second was Magus.

The band crossed out of Sor'rai later that first year, in the winter of 759. Varzin tracked them across his District, through Karrim, and into Cassile. He would not enter Cassile himself, that land of mystics, madmen who claimed secrets as the Sages did but lacked even their power. At the time Varzin had regarded them as little more than vermin, and did not want to contaminate himself by contact with them. His men, foolishly, lost the Sages in Cassile, and Varzin was forced to temper his anger in his waiting place in Karrim. Just as he prepared to return to Aligh, though, he was stopped. A clerk pleaded for his presence, as the highest-ranking official on-site, at a meeting of the local authorities. Varzin had tried to think of an excuse to decline, having no interest in settling feuds between farmers or arguments over the fair price of wheat. But then the clerk said something that intrigued him: The meeting was a reconnaissance with one of his—Varzin's—operatives.

No, they were not his operatives, although the Secret Force worked ostensibly for the good of the Five Countries in their entirety. In fact, they worked for Loyd, that interloper, Muhrroh's pet. The Lord Justices were rarely allowed a view of their operations. Varzin did not wish to pass up this opportunity. When he entered the miserable barn where the meeting was to take place, he was so startled he had to grasp at his walking stick to remain on his feet. The operative was the serving girl from the Great Hall in Insigh.

There was magic in the government of Dabion, rot in the very body of Justice. One of Loyd's spies, one of those who were called—terrible irony!—Sor'raian operatives, was a worker of magic. Varzin was enraged. When the girl gave her report and the meeting was ended Varzin demanded a private audience with her, heedless of how the reconnaissance operatives would react to the tightness of his voice. "Who are you?" he hissed at her. "Why are you here? Why are you troubling me?"

She looked at him with insolence and replied, "I don't know. Why *am* I troubling you?"

Any human woman would have suffered for such sarcasm. Varzin was filled with a sudden passion, of a force he had never before known. The woman before him was thin and frail, her neck smaller than the ring of his hands. He stood a head higher and several stone heavier than she. He could crush her. Any human woman would have been punished for contempt, but this was more. Magic stood before him. He could eradicate it. He could rub it out with his hands.

But she knew his thoughts. He had risked too much, he knew, articulating them so clearly in his mind. She was warned to his threat of violence and she responded in kind. No mere touch on his mind, this was a blade slicing through the center of him and casting him to the floor. She threw him down and left him so that she could escape. When the clerks came, finally, to see what had delayed him, they asked whether he was all right, if he'd fallen in a seizure, in voices used for infants and imbeciles. They did not imagine he had been attacked. There was not a mark upon him.

Such humiliation was a greater injury than the touch of the magic. Varzin knew that touch now; it could no longer shock him. To surmount it he would have to control it, as he had controlled the damnable Sage blood in him, binding it up under the study of justice until it was buried, unrecognizable. The woman was gone. He could not control her. But something nearly as hateful remained. The mystics. Varzin reviewed the report that the spy had given. Nanianist tracts were circulating in the villages of Cassile. Mysticism was spreading. The vermin were as dangerous as if they carried the plague. Varzin had work to pursue.

The other Justices of the Circle were difficult to convince at first. The mystics were too far away to pose a threat, they thought. Then Varzin discovered Nanianist writings in Karrim, in Mandera. The disease was spreading. Every rebellion that the Public Force put down on the edges of the Five Countries seemed to have mystics in its ranks. Then the writings were found at the borders of Dabion itself. The Circle was convinced. Nanianism was outlawed. Varzin had succeeded.

And then, the second visitation from Sor'raian shores, in the autumn of 763, one year ago. Magus wandered into the field of Varzin's sight. Varzin was terrified. It had been years since he had seen actual magic, since he had felt the ice-bitter taste of it in his throat. The mystics he had been fighting since then were mere impostors. He called them magicians, indeed, and ordered their immediate deaths as soon as he could create the opportunity to do so, but the wizardry he accused them of in discreetly filtered reports was a fiction, invented to stoke a process that was going too slowly and with too much mercy. Seeing Magus, a true magician, shook Varzin, but he was master now. He knew it, from those loathsome stories he was forced to learn as a child. He spoke the prescribed words and bound the Magus to him. He controlled Magus and the shapeshifter would do his bidding.

At the time Varzin had not known what to do with him. At his hands was a creature that held inside him that which was most loathsome, ready to be reined or crushed, but Varzin did not know what action to take. The world of the magicians was one he had foresworn his entire life. Now that he had crossed into it, though, he was determined to master it. No more would he tremble like a child. Varzin began to question Magus, seeking to learn from him what Varzin did not know how to do himself, but Magus was uncooperative. So Varzin began to seek out books, ancient and suppressed books. He contacted merchants and smugglers, and one Lesser Justice in District Five.

The books that Jereth Paloman had were useless to Varzin, but they suited Muhrroh and his strange new interest in Bioranism. Varzin recommended Paloman to Muhrroh at once; whatever was necessary to further the elimination of the mystics. At length Varzin acquired the book of Sor'raian spells and set to studying it on his own.

Then he had a discovery, unexpected and glorious. After five years, he saw a face he never expected to encounter again. In the ranks of the Black Force who paraded through the streets he saw a woman, thin and frail, her neck smaller than the ring of his hands. At once he went to the barracks and demanded a list of the names of the guards who made up that troop. The captain, anxious to please his superior, gave Varzin the entire file on the guards: their names, their ages, their previous assignments. Halfway through the tedious stack was the record Varzin sought. Elzith Kar, discharged from the Secret Force, first season 764. Residence in Origh, at the address of Tod Redtanner. There was an instant in which Varzin almost pitied the ranks of the spies, so betrayed by their leaders. It did not last long.

He could have sent someone to eliminate her directly. He could have done it himself, had he wished to dirty his hands. But such a feat—the destruction of the thing that symbolized all he hated—demanded more. It was for this purpose, doubtless, that Magus had been put in his path. Varzin would control that which he despised and feared. He would eradicate the woman who had invaded him and purge the last of the Sor'raian influence from himself, fire cleansed with fire.

In this plan, Paloman proved to be useful. He could be manipulated without suspicion. He could be insinuated into Redtanner's services, and with luck, into his confidence. By forcing Paloman to rely on Redtanner to authenticate the Dalanis Black book, Varzin placed Paloman in a position where he was indebted to both himself and Redtanner, and guilt would drive Paloman both to trust Redtanner and to go to great lengths to satisfy Varzin. This would bring Paloman closer to Origh, where he could learn of Elzith Kar's whereabouts and observe her movements. But Paloman also proved to be a fool, a hopeless, incompetent fool. His disastrous reports made Varzin fear all was lost. Varzin was convinced that Paloman had scared Redtanner away by approaching him too clumsily about the Bioran textbooks, that he'd roused the suspicion of Redtanner and the mistrustful printer. But luck blessed Varzin once more. Paloman succeeded in reaching the bookbinder's flat, and brought back more than Varzin had hoped: evidence of intimacy with the spy herself.

The discovery created such possibilities. Varzin now knew precisely how he would command Magus. Even now, Magus was awaiting orders in Origh. He could not approach the flat without being seen, but Varzin would simply send Paloman again to do the work that needed to be done there. Varzin had hired a man called Kerk to track Kar's movements now. Kerk had information about an investigation that was commencing in Origh, into the death of Ciceline Jannes, and Kerk knew Elzith would be called because she was employed in the household at the time of the death. Varzin had only to wait for the proper time. He smiled. Everything was falling into place.

# 41

COLLIN HAD GOOD HUNCHES. IT WAS ONE OF HIS greatest strengths, along with role-playing and his loyalty, which Loyd would praise him for, but Collin was most proud of his hunches. Of course, he always waited until he had the right evidence before reporting them. In some cases, the evidence was embarrassing. One of the things he always had perfect hunches about—probably because he was himself a virgin—was when other people were having sex.

Ordinarily Collin would not let his reaction to such information show. He was very good at playing roles, and he would never break character by letting an uncontrolled reaction slip through like that. He had no role to play right now, though. He had no duty but to watch Elzith, or as Elzith had ordered him, to watch Tod. But since he wasn't seeking any information from Tod, he wasn't sure what to do or what to say. Tod wasn't very talkative anyway, so Collin was rather surprised when the man invited him to dinner that evening, while Elzith was gone to town. The two men had little to talk about, and Collin had nothing to do, so he had no way to conceal the pervasiveness of his hunch and the evidence he'd unwittingly gathered to support it. Elzith hadn't left Tod's half of the flat for the last two days since her return from Cassile, until today when the clerks came to subpoena her to some event in Origh.

"I would have invited you sooner," Tod was saying, "but I didn't really know you were staying here permanently. I didn't notice. I was a bit occupied."

Collin had to tell himself not to giggle.

"Worried, you see," Tod went on, oblivious. "When you first showed up and Elzith went away again, sudden like she always does. I should be used to it but I still worry. So I get wrapped up in my work, to make the time go by faster."

Collin himself hadn't been sure he was staying at first. When he arrived he'd made rounds of the flat and waited for Elzith to come home, intending to coordinate assignments with her. Collin had heard stories about her, rumors at the dormitory about deeds grand and infamous, stories that made her larger than life. He was surprised to meet her the first time in Cassile, astonished that she was so small and frail, and despite her caustic and audacious words, he actually found her quiet and short of speech. He didn't expect her to be terribly difficult to work with. When she arrived at the flat, though, she cut him off quickly, sending him to watch Tod with words that were as unquestionable as Loyd's. Collin stood blinking on the steps around the side of the hill, then went to Tod's door to introduce himself. Tod invited Collin to sit at his fireplace and said nothing else for the remainder of the day. The next morning Elzith gave Collin her key and disappeared for weeks. Collin lived below Tod and waited for anything interesting to happen. Finally she returned, revealed through Loyd that she'd been in Cassile, and vanished again through Tod's door, where she stayed for two days.

"What work do you do?" Collin asked, to be polite, as if he didn't already know. He'd observed Tod thoroughly and learned all there was to know about the man in a day and a half. It had been a dull assignment. Collin was struggling to keep his eyes open as Tod described the process of folding and stitching and cutting, in blunt and clumsy words. Collin actually found himself yawning. He shook his head abruptly. Loyd wouldn't approve of such negligence. Collin tried to pay attention.

"Been doing jobs for one of the Justices, too. Most just come through Keller. Paloman comes himself, though. That's the Justice."

This is definitely odd, Collin thought. There were questions to be asked there, mysteries to solve. Who was this Justice, what was he having printed, why was he bringing it by hand? It was something intriguing, finally. But Tod didn't say any more about it, didn't volunteer any more information. Collin was at a loss as to how to get more out of him. He decided to file the question in his mind and pursue it later.

"Um..." Collin stalled. He needed something else to

talk about. He had eaten all of the meal Tod had served, and sat twisting a fork between his fingers. Tod himself had finished gobbling dinner a while ago, and was busy at work again. Collin watched him thread a needle, spear a fold of paper with it, draw it in, pull it out, draw it in, pull it out. Collin dropped his fork. His eyes started wandering the flat, looking for evidence to prove his hunch. He wanted to ask, but it would be rude to ask about that, not to mention unprofessional. He just needed something to hold his attention. "Why do you love her?" he ventured.

Tod set his head on the side, birdlike, and didn't answer for some time. He pulled his needle more slowly, peering at the thread as if it held his answer, almost about to speak at each stitch. He must have strung up a hundred words before finally shaking his head and saying, "I don't know. I just love her. I have to."

It was a lead, the most interesting Collin had had in weeks. "You don't know?" he prompted.

Tod dropped his work with a shrug. His words came out too fast for his needle to keep up. "Well, of course, I help her, I need to help her, she needs me. When she came back from Cassile, she needed someone, she would have stayed alone, like she's always done, but she needed someone, to talk to, to—well." He looked up at Collin, from the corner of his eye, without raising his head, the way people did when they knew Collin was a spy. "Well. You know how she was."

He picked up his work again and fell silent. Collin

watched the man's quick, sure fingers, making something permanent out of so many flyaway leaves. It was funny, Collin thought, a reminder that he should never be too sure of his own skills of observation. Until then he'd have characterized Tod as clumsy and inept.

"I could go on," Tod said suddenly, surprising Collin when he thought Tod was finished. "I could analyze it, pick it apart. I have. But it doesn't matter. I love her. I need to."

Collin peered at him, the eyes, fingers, face. Collin didn't really need a hunch; Tod's expression was transparent. He was telling the honest truth. It was a shock to see, after the people Collin was used to working with. Having nothing to investigate made him uneasy. "She shouldn't trust you."

Tod smiled a little at the corner of his mouth. "I know. She'd say the same thing. But she has to. She has to trust me, even if she doesn't want to. You have to trust. People need to."

"I don't trust you."

Tod seemed to think that was funny, and he let out his breath almost in a laugh. "No, I guess you wouldn't. But why not? Except that it's your job, of course."

Collin thought about it. He actually came close to answering, though he was quick to stop himself. Still, it got him thinking, and once Tod's words ran out he didn't have much else to do. It wasn't so much that he didn't trust Tod, since if there was anyone who had no malice in him, it was Tod. Collin would never entrust him with anything sensitive, though. He didn't think the man would stand up to pressure, and he certainly couldn't carry an act. Collin was sure Elzith hadn't trusted him like that, either, so there must be something else to it. For a minute Collin wondered what Loyd would say on the subject. Then it came to him. Of course. He trusted Loyd. And just as surely as Tod loved Elzith, Collin did it because he had to.

There's danger in feeling. I always knew it. I watched other people acting out their involuntary emotions, tripping over them; I learned to mimic them, and counted myself lucky that I didn't have them. Now I was falling and I couldn't catch myself.

They wanted to ask me about Ciceline Jannes. When did I see her, where was she, what was she doing, who was she with. Flat round questions tossed out like stones from the black-suited men posed in a row behind their table. Most of them wore wigs. When did that happen, those wigs? I couldn't remember. The answers that the men demanded should have been simple, a list of dates, a description of scenes. I'd preserved these things in my well-trained memory, even though I didn't want them. My throat twisted up and caught my breath and voice behind a knot. I was stammering before I even got to the blackmail scene.

Oh, that got their attention. Here, in the Great Hall? Below us, in the basements? They shifted in their chairs as if someone had lit fires under them. I laughed at that image, I couldn't stop myself. The Justices frowned. Where? Which corridor? Take us there—no, draw us a map. I couldn't be trusted to lead them, as I stood snickering madly like a jackal. They scowled at me in disapproval: me, this dog who wouldn't get her bone that night.

I waited for them to ask the next question, waited for it like the inevitable ending to a melodrama on a rickety Karrimian stage. I waited to play the tragic heroine, that disgusting role. I couldn't help it. My cue: "Why didn't you report this information, Kar?" Why why why. I played the role because I had no other answer. I trembled, my teeth chattered. Tears welled in my eyes like they'd rehearsed it. My chest filled up with molten lead even though my audience couldn't see it. "I don't know," the voice of a sobbing woman said out of my mouth. "I'm sorry."

They sent me away, without asking any more questions, off to investigate a room that had undoubtedly been abandoned by then. They sent me away without even seeing Loyd, who must have come down to Origh to preside over the investigation. They sent me away to wonder what my punishment would be, but I would never find out. The punishment I made for myself was no match for it anyway.

I walked home. The walk was the same, identical to the day Ciceline died. My breath strained against the pain. It would end soon, my body thought, or at least it would pause, for an instant, a breath, a heartbeat. I would go to the door and find Tod. The weeping woman ran to the arms of a man, wanting to hide, wanting him to sweep her up and make her forget, as foolish as it was, as momentary and false. My feet carried me there as if there were nothing else to live for. I watched myself as I'd watched other people, as I'd watched the Thin Man's women at his execution, observing with disdain. But I could trust Tod, I thought. It would be all right. I kept walking.

When does it go away? I don't know—it doesn't—it does. Are you trying to make me forget? You can't forget. I saw Ciceline's face, her glass-scored hands, the coins in her purse. Her son—*don't go*. Small flailing arms bruising my mouth. We're trained to withstand pain. The door opened. I could carry it no more. I dropped it at Tod's feet. He lifted me, shockingly, stripped me, and pierced me against the wall with a jolt of pain, but I didn't care. I cried out the voices that I could no longer withstand. I gave all of it to him and let him carry me into darkness.

It was still dark. Before I had woken far enough to have senses, there was a thought in my mind. Where was Collin?

It was dark, I could see nothing. I heard the sleeping breaths of the man beside me. And there was something else. I breathed it again. It was not Tod's scent.

I slipped out of the bed so I would not wake him, and I was gone.

Loyd was in Origh. I found him in that room in the tunnels below the Great Hall, sitting behind a desk and opening its drawers methodically, checking for scraps that would not have been left behind.

"We missed him by moments," Loyd said as I opened the door. "He can't have known we were on to him at all until yesterday, I'd say."

I would not listen to this diversion. "Where are they?"

This was something new, something Loyd did not already know. He looked up.

"Someone's there. It's not Tod."

"Ah," Loyd said, like he'd found a lost penny. "My shapeshifter. When did you find him there?"

"You know what time your lackeys came for me in the morning," I spat. "You know what time I left the inquiry. He got to the flat between the two. The whole place was covered in some kind of dust." I thrust out my arm, turned my back under his nose so he could see the silt that coated my shirt as it had coated the floors and walls in Tod's flat. I hadn't noticed it, hadn't felt it as the man who wasn't Tod pushed me against the wall while I failed to notice or care how he intruded. "Collin's missing, too."

"Collin?" Loyd's voice was audibly surprised. I looked over my shoulder, at the thoughts cracking through on his inscrutable face. Memory, regret. "So this is how it happened." He sighed, as if I wasn't there, seeing only his own thoughts. "I didn't know they would happen so close together. So this is how the boy died."

I spun, flew at the table, thundered at him. "What?" I shouted, loud enough for him to recoil, to flinch that enviable hairbreadth. "Do you feel guilty?"

Loyd stood then. My lord and master. Whatever thoughts had shaken him, they would not move him from his seat of power. "Elzith," he said, calm and commanding. "I have been summoned. It is the end. It is time for me to go. Come with me."

But I wouldn't have it. Not now. "No," I hissed, fury burning up my throat. "No, I'm not coming with you. You can't steal my confidence anymore. I know better. You've spied on me, you've conned me. I don't know what you want from me but I won't let you take it." I whirled in the dust and my rage blew me out of the room. I didn't look back at the expression I might have scored on Loyd's face.

# 42

THE WHISPERING VOICE IN JERETH'S HEAD WAS growing louder. It had been there all day, quiet and persistent as an itch, since the dawn hour when Varzin had roused him and ordered him into another carriage for another trip to Origh. In the thin cold light of morning, the voice had been barely audible above the chattering of Jereth's teeth as he climbed stiffly into the frost-glazed carriage. His senseless fingers, numb in the early-winter air, were locked around Varzin's latest book, his new assignment. As the day and the miles passed, warming the reluctant air and waking Jereth from his obedience, the whispering voice made itself heard. *Stop the carriage.*

Varzin was sending him on an errand again. Varzin was sending him to see Redtanner, to consult with him about books, an errand he didn't care about, books he didn't want to see. It would be like the last time, when Varzin forced him to take his books, Jereth's own precious Bioran books, to Redtanner. "The bookbinder would be interested," the Lord Justice had said, icily smooth. "He would have an eye for early books, wouldn't he, their binding, their paper, their printer's marks?" Jereth had trembled, knowing Varzin suspected his inadequacy, his failure to complete the authentication assignment on his own. Cowed, Jereth had slunk to the carriage.

Then he'd reached Redtanner's cottage, and found the woman there. Her eyes, her questions, her presence hanging over him as Redtanner's fingers pressed all over his poor books, the awful feeling that churned inside him as she breathed over his shoulder—and Jereth was headed for that again. Because Varzin was sending him there.

*Stop the carriage!* Jereth dragged the curtain from the window, looking frantically outside. Only a few buildings scarred the green of the hills around him. The carriage had reached the outskirts of Insigh, was rolling into the wilderness, and was far past any depot where it could stop. Varzin was sending him somewhere, and Jereth did not know why.

The Lord Justice's face was full in Jereth's mind, the smooth and placid face, the dark and opaque eyes. Not real eyes, those. "Their binding, their paper, their *printer's marks?*" Varzin's unreal eyes had flared. He knew Jereth would fail. He'd known Jereth would fail *before Jereth went!* Varzin had set him up. Somewhere in the back of Jereth's stomach he felt something cold turn. He did not trust Varzin.

But this mistrust was foolish. His ideas were hysterical. Varzin was his superior, the head of the law. His

superior ordered and Jereth followed. He said the words
to himself, again, over again. Varzin was his superior.
Jereth panted fearfully and lost his place. He did what he
was told. He was a man of the law, he obeyed the law. He
opened his mouth to say the words aloud to himself:
obey the law, obey the law. "Stop the carriage."

He'd made his way in life by obeying. The law was his
life. He was a Justice, an unimaginable accomplishment
for the son of a crude farmer. He'd reached it through
obedience. The comforts of his life were due to following
his superiors. Obedience had spared him dirt under his
nails. He'd graduated his school with some distinction,
and had completed his apprenticeship with sufficient
recommendation. As a young man he'd had potential.
He was not always so weak. He would not have trembled
at his superior's voice then. If he were still that young
man, he would have held up his head as Varzin gave him
orders, and answered, clear and obedient—

"Stop the carriage!"

Jereth gasped for air. He hated Varzin's orders. He
only followed them because he was terrified of the Lord
Justice. His hands clenched, seizing the gauze winding
around Varzin's book. He hated the book. It was another
manipulation, this unknown thing he had to carry, this
business of Varzin's, something he didn't know or care
about, but was forced to deliver. Jereth grasped the book
and shook it, strangely light and hollow in his hands.
He almost stripped it of its wrapping and threw it out
the clattering carriage window. But it caught his hands,

holding them fast, as if it were a rope tied around his wrists. He couldn't let it go. He forced it back onto his lap. It was his lead and its owner was his master. He was terrified of Varzin, and the cold at the back of his stomach knew that there was nothing good at the end of the Lord Justice's orders.

How would he explain himself to Piers, Jereth wondered wildly, that old schoolmate who'd once been more foolish than he? Jereth was the one who'd learned not to ask the unforgivable question, and what had such wisdom earned him? Only years of crippling mediocrity, and an empty yearning that had cut him open, turned him inside out for anyone to manipulate, to lead into danger.

Jereth strangled a cry and reached anxiously for his walking stick. His hands slipping, he pounded it against the roof above him. "Stop the carriage!"

The wheels rolled. The horses whinnied and snorted, and abruptly stopped. The carriage jolted. Jereth's stick fell out of his hands and clattered on the floor, and he reflexively clutched the book as it threatened to fly off his knees. A black-jacketed guard appeared outside the window.

"Your honor?" he mouthed through the hazy glass.

Jereth's voice burned out of his throat in a rush. He couldn't speak. He had to speak. He was a man of power and distinction. He was a fool. The guard opened the carriage door. The moment was breaking. Jereth's voice exploded. "Turn the carriage around!"

The guard's eyebrows pinched for a second. "We can't, your honor. We've been ordered by his lordship." He spoke, he was done. He closed the door, he disappeared. The carriage rolled again.

Jereth panicked. Light blinked and whirled in front of his eyes. He clutched Varzin's book against his chest so hard that the corners of the front cover bit into him, but he couldn't feel it. He couldn't breathe. Danger pressed down on his shoulders. His head throbbed. Varzin had sealed him into the carriage. He was sending Jereth to something and it could not be good. Jereth had to get out.

Outside the road tumbled by unstoppably. For a mad second Jereth saw himself flinging open the door and leaping into that motion, rolling on the ground with a cracking of bones. Horrified, he shrank back from the temptation of the door. The carriage would have to stop, he thought. It would have to stop soon. They were due to break travel for the day. Weren't they? It still looked bright as noon outside, in the dizzily passing sky. His memory blurred and he couldn't remember if this was the first or second day of his journey.

He would have to get them to stop again. He would have to get out. He would have to trick the guards. Sweat salted his eyes. He didn't know how. A thin whine crept out of his throat. Then there was a massive cracking noise and the world spun upside down.

Jereth opened his eyes. He was crumpled in the front

corner of the carriage. The door was swinging open with a creak.

He did not remember stepping outside. It took him what felt like forever to look around and determine that a front wheel had broken, that the carriage had pitched to a stop, that one of the guards had been thrown several lengths away, and the other guard was anxiously crouched over him, oblivious to Jereth. That Jereth was free.

Luck is absurd, he thought for an instant. Then he clambered around the carriage's immobile bulk and started running in the other direction, for half a dozen paces before pitching down a hill he didn't see.

When he woke up again and realized he could breathe, it was night. No one had come searching for him. He had escaped the danger. He'd rolled to the bottom of the hill, his arms clutched tightly around him. The book was still clasped in place.

Looking up at the sky, he remembered being a child, watching the stars. He'd been carefree then. He hadn't known that his family's real name was Ploughman. The stars looked old and familiar, and slowly he recognized the constellations. He could determine direction by the stars. He almost smiled as he realized he knew exactly where he was, where all the points of the compass lay.

Then he swallowed hard. He had no idea where he could go. He couldn't go back to Insigh. He would never make it back home, distant in the northeast. He knew no one who would help him in Origh. He only knew one person there at all. He stared at the sky, paralyzed, until the light came up enough to obscure the stars. Just before they vanished he struggled to his feet and started walking to the south.

Someone picked Jereth up before he had gone far. His feet were already hurting unimaginably, and his joints were thick in the cold. The cart driver did not look at Jereth as he climbed in, settling among what he slowly recognized as milk vats, and the driver was silent throughout the morning, his eyes fixed on the road ahead of him. Jereth thought about what he must look like, his wig lost, his cold bare head stinging with scrapes, his jacket dirty and torn. The dairyman was undoubtedly torn between pity and fear. Jereth frowned. But he had acted, he tried to tell himself, he had taken steps like a free man, and he was safe. His hands twisted on the book still bundled in his lap.

They were closer to Origh than Jereth had thought. Before the sun was at its peak, the dairyman stopped at the edge of town and let out his strange passenger. Jereth was on his feet again. He had to walk.

He found the path to Redtanner's cottage before his legs started giving out. His breath was coming short and fast. He reached a hand up shakily to wipe sweat from his cold forehead, and saw a smear of old blood. He was weak, a voice scowled tiredly in his head. He would never make it. He was startled when a door came up before his face.

"Your honor!" Redtanner cried on the other side of it.

Then the man darted away, swimming in Jereth's vision. Behind him was another, younger man, and Jereth struggled to focus on him.

"What are you carrying there?" the young man asked. Jereth wouldn't notice the suspicious look that Collin passed to Tod. "Let me take it."

"Here, your honor," Redtanner was saying. Both men were closing in on Jereth. For a second he panicked, his body straining to turn and run. Redtanner was holding out a cloth, reaching up toward his scraped head. The other man's arms were outstretched, to catch him or something he carried. Jereth tried to take a step forward. His foot, blistered in its broken shoe, slipped out from under him. He tripped. He failed to hold on to the book—still with him, absurdly—this time. It fell from his arms, struck the floor, split open, and coughed out a cloud that choked him before he could berate himself for his failure.

# 43

MAGUS DID NOT LIKE THE MAN CALLED KERK. Everything about him said dissembler: his silence, his composure, the way he held the reins on the cart horse and watched the road in front of him, his eyes scanning smoothly left to right, left to right. He also looked disturbingly familiar, and Magus did not like it at all.

The journey itself was just as unpleasant. The arrogant half-Sage, the idiot master who commanded Magus, had done him the humiliation of dressing him in peasant's clothes, dirty breeches and soot-streaked apron, like a blacksmith, and perched him next to the dissembler Kerk in a tarp-covered horse-drawn cart. It wouldn't do to bring the half-Sage's victims into town, so they were to meet with Varzin at an abandoned workshop outside Origh. Magus frowned and shifted his shoulders inside the itchily dirty shirt. Humans smelled so.

When the cart came to a stop it was beside a hill planted with three flats. Was Varzin mad? Magus was powerful, but it was too much to ask him to disguise himself and someone else in front of the residents of three apartments.

"Don't worry," the man called Kerk said, intrudingly. "The man in the flat next door just went into town for work, and he won't be back until dawn. The woman at the end died yesterday and the gravediggers took her away."

Magus bit back his fury with an acid burn in his throat. He'd let his expression show too much, if the dissembler could read his worries so clearly.

"And Kar won't testify until tonight; they've put her on the late docket. Murder inquiries happen after sunset, but they summon the witnesses early in the morning and hold them all day to break their nerve. You'll have a few hours to learn what you need to and get back here to meet her."

If only he could turn himself into some creature of the air, truly, Magus thought. Then he could escape this condescending lecture. Kerk didn't just reek of deception—he even talked like that king of spies, Magus's abandoned master, with his secrets and briefs and orders. Magus peered sideways at Kerk. Yes, that was where he recognized him from. Kerk had been at the spy-king's training grounds, for just a short time when Magus first arrived there. He was sure of it. He turned his head away and held his breath against the dissembler's stench.

The smell inside the flat was worse. A thick cloud of

dust greeted them when Kerk opened the door. It had settled quite a bit already, and lay in a thick blanket on the floors, walls, furniture, and the three motionless bodies. Magus covered his nose and mouth and looked closely at a sample he gathered on his finger. He might have laughed. Varzin had attempted a spell. The untrained half-Sage had dredged up a household potion from the depths of Sor'rai and used it to poison his enemies. Apparently he'd even had some success.

"This one's dead," Kerk announced, leaning over an old man in a Justice's once-black uniform.

Of course, Magus wanted to say. The cloud stops up the lungs. It suffocates pests, that's what it was created for. It also scars the eyes, even beyond the power of healing spells to mend them completely, and so the less scrupulous among the Magi started using it against their enemies. That's how they learned which quantities would kill and which would simply disable a healthy man. The leaders of the Magi suppressed this potion as soon as they learned how it was being used. That makes it surprising, doesn't it—Magus wanted to ask—to consider how our master got his hands on it. But I can't imagine that you would care, Magus thought seethingly as he watched Kerk drag the old man's body to the cart.

"It doesn't matter," Magus finally answered, halfheartedly. "The one I need is breathing." He looked down at the younger man at his own feet, who seemed, through the blanket of spore dust, to match the description Varzin had given. Magus wondered who the third person was, though. How foolish of the half-Sage not to have predicted his presence, but Magus couldn't expect better. He crouched by the third body and rubbed dust from the face. Again, he could have laughed. He knew that face. It was the boy who had posed as a clerk for Varzin. Magus had known he wasn't what he pretended to be. He was still breathing, but not for long. Next to his unwanted skill at tricking minds, the only other power that Magus possessed was a great strength in his hands. He broke the boy's neck like a straw. He hated dissemblers.

Darkness came early in this late season, so Magus had little time to waste. He sat in the back of the wagon as it rolled away from the hill, a corpse stiffening on either side of him, culling information from his captive. This man Redtanner was starting to revive, clawing at the dust in his lungs. To the dim eyesight that the man might have left, Magus cast an image of himself in a Healer's robes, bristling at the irony. "Breathe slowly, now try to talk, carefully," he uttered in a voice he knew would sound soothing to the man's gullible ears. "Tell me what happened."

In a coarse, shaky voice, Redtanner began to describe the Justice with the books. First this book, then that book, on and on. Magus didn't care about the books, he didn't want to listen, but he had to learn enough of Redtanner's voice and manner that he could project the man onto the woman they were trying to deceive. "And then he came in," Redtanner panted, "by himself, injured, like he'd been in an accident, and then—and then—I don't know. I don't know what happened. But Elzith," and then the man's meager voice caught, and he made a whining noise in his throat as tears stung his damaged eyes. "Elzith. I don't know where she is."

Magus hung over the man like a hawk. He needed more. The wagon was rolling into the meeting place and he had only a paltry imitation and some nonsense about books. Varzin's entire plan would fail if he couldn't find a way to breach Kar's defenses, which the Lord Justice had described as nearly impenetrable. Magus knew the woman's reputation from his brief stint with the spies, and he'd thought Varzin's mad quest for revenge was hopeless. But if Redtanner was so besotted with her, could she be as foolishly in love with him? Magus might have found something, a prize to give Varzin, a trinket for the one who thought he was the master.

"You'll be safe here," Magus said grittily to his captive. "You need to rest. Tell me more about Elzith." He was breathing heavily with the effort of sustaining the spell, forcing the disguise over his face and voice, and he was afraid his hold on Redtanner's mind was slipping. The man's face was creased and closed as Kerk helped carry him into a rear room in the empty smithy, a closet with a door so well hidden he wouldn't have seen it if it hadn't been standing open. Redtanner was suspicious; he wouldn't answer. Magus hastily locked Kerk out of the room when his load was put down, shutting out all the light from the windowless cell. He could drop the vision spell and regain that much power. He needed Redtanner's trust again. He had a lot to learn from him.

But Redtanner wasn't speaking and it was almost dark. Varzin was not yet there, no one to order Magus to stay or go. He could trap the spy himself, break her before Varzin could even get his hands on her. He would win Varzin's game and prove the vastness of his power, prove the half-Sage's foolish arrogance in trying to rein it.

"Where are you going?" Redtanner asked weakly, his hands rising to shield his eyes from the light as Magus opened the door.

He no longer needed to maintain the ruse. He didn't answer.

Redtanner had more of a mind than Magus had given him credit for, and it was showing now, ironically, as his fear was rising. "You're not going to heal me," he said, with certainty in his voice.

Magus locked the door and left to meet the quarry.

He was too late to clean up the spore dust; Kar returned sooner than Magus expected. The woman didn't notice the alien dust, though. She didn't notice Magus's face or his voice, didn't notice whether there were flaws. She closed the door and leaned on it in utter exhaustion. No spy would reveal that to someone she did not trust, and no spy who was wise would trust anyone. Magus had something.

"Elzith," Magus said, holding out his image-draped arms. "What happened?"

She did not tell him. She didn't have to. She flung herself into his arms and Magus knew he needed nothing else to snare her.

He would win; he should have been ecstatic. But he was furious. This was what he was reduced to, playing pawns for humans. The best of them were weak, stupid animals, this one, and Varzin, and the dissembler. He hated them all, and himself none the less. With hatred he hoisted the woman up, and he hated her as she wound her legs around him. He thrust her against the wall like a human would, a stupid animal, worse than the Sages breeding like rabbits. She hung limp on him like a parasite and he threw her down on Redtanner's bed, and she slept. No spy who was wise would sleep where someone could find her. He should have broken her neck when she leapt at him.

But to win he had to bring her to Varzin, didn't he? He was ordered to do it, and he could not disobey. The anger that had motivated him had burned too hot and was now gone. Magus was never one for rage; he'd never had the hope that it would change things. Now he felt only tired. His legs gave out and he found himself collapsed beside the woman. He'd won nothing. He was bound. Despair drowned him like the waters of the lake.

Turning himself into a fish would do no good. He let the guise of Redtanner slip; it only tired him. She would not see. It was dark as the bottom of the lake and Magus imagined the waters closing over him.

He woke an instant after she had left. He went to the window to see her disappearing around the hill. Bitterness flooded him. He'd lost her. He'd failed at the half-Sage's hateful commands. In the early light of dawn he felt the bonds chafe his pathetic wrists and draw him back to Varzin.

"I didn't plan for you to get her yet," the half-Sage said smoothly, when Magus met him at the smithy and reluctantly delivered his account of Elzith's arrival, her weaknesses, her escape. "Now we gather what we need. Later we catch her."

"I could have caught her already," Magus spat.

Varzin turned toward him, his face marble, his eyes fixed with rehearsed composure. It was such a clean act, even Varzin himself believed it was real. This was the extreme in dissembling, Magus thought: deluding oneself. "There is nothing more for you at this moment, servant," Varzin commanded sourly. "These orders are mine. You are bidden to follow them. Now you shall go away until I need you again."

There was nowhere to retreat but the room where the captive already was.

Redtanner was awake; Magus could tell by his breathing. He expected the wounded man to say something, to go on about the pain in his eyes or to curse Magus for deceiving him, but Redtanner said nothing. Magus at least expected him to ask who he was or who the man outside the door was. Irritated, Magus struck a match and held it to the long wick of a rusty lamp he'd found, making a blaze that he didn't shield from the man's tender eyes. Redtanner squinted but didn't flinch or cry out.

"Why do you take orders from him?" the man's voice interrupted, suddenly, unimaginably.

Magus stared at the captive with an incredulity the nearly blind man couldn't appreciate. Why would he ask this, of all questions? "Because I must," he growled. "I have no choice, I'm bound to him." Then he caught his breath. He'd revealed the thing that tortured him the most, his most secret shame, to his captive.

The man regarded him blindly, eerie wisdom in his oozing eyes.

"Ask me something else!" Magus raged. "Ask me when I'm going to kill you and your precious woman."

But Redtanner shook his head with infuriating calm. "I know someone's going to die," he said quietly. "But it's not me. And it's not Elzith."

Magus stormed out of the room, in time to see Kerk entering the smithy through the opposite door. "I tracked her," the dissembler said efficiently, his hand rising in a single motion from the door's latch to Varzin's hand, ready to gather his payment. "She's headed back to the flat."

"I'll meet her there," Magus said, marching out of the smithy before his master had the opportunity to forbid him. His rage was strong; it carried him all the way there without flagging, and when he arrived he was still confident that he could catch her.

# 44

I WAS WALKING, WALKING FOR HOURS, WALKING END-lessly, through streets and corridors and alleys, pathetic creature in a maze, looking for the way out. The words I'd gathered from the people I'd questioned slurred together, until I couldn't remember who said them or where I'd found them. A wagon headed south out of Origh, a carriage due from Insigh that had never reached its destination, new bodies in the common graves outside the city, one definitely an old man, the other—gravedigger couldn't remember, no we can't go look, but just one other, only two bodies. What did it mean, what did it mean? I needed more, needed to search, and I walked more, looking, looking. Then I couldn't remember what I was looking for, I couldn't remember what I had or what pieces were missing. I didn't know where I was walking. I was lost.

The sun was going down, hours I'd dropped and lost behind me. I saw shadows, snatches of light and dark, shapes I couldn't catch out of the corner of my eye. Crowds thinned on the streets, leaving echoes, footsteps

half-heard. I was being followed. Alleys twisted in front
of me, dead ends I couldn't navigate, couldn't find my
way out of. My heart thudded, my feet stumbled. My
ears filled with pounding blood, and somewhere I heard
the rushing of water. Dust filled my lungs, not the dust
from Tod's flat, still clinging to my clothes like cobwebs,
but the dust of a tile I crushed so long ago it had nearly
fallen through a hole in my mind. I looked over my
shoulders, searching for a fluttering of capes, rags, madness. The Sage whom Tod had seen outside his window.
I'd lose my tracker if I turned suddenly; any spy would
be alerted that I was on to him. But the Sages had their
own logic, mad, swirling, and ungraspable like water. I
spun and faced straight behind me. The alley was empty.

Nothing, broken, a broken spy, I was nothing else, I
had nothing else. I sank to my knees in the dead-end alley. They should have taken me, finished me off. I'd wait
here, not moving, for them to come back for me.

Then I saw a glint in the last futile ray of the sun. I
crawled forward. There was a coin on the ground, lonely
like it had fallen out of a neglected hole wormed
through a pocket. Silver, etched with a miniature of the
Great Hall, it was the currency of the Justices. Ciceline
would have carried such coins to her blackmailer. I
snatched it out of the dust. My bones screamed in
protest, trying to weigh me down to the ground, my
malnourished body complaining for sleep through its
scars and dirt. But sleep was not in the game. I was a

player; I had no choice. I staggered to my feet and started running.

I wouldn't find the mercenary, that former colleague of mine who spied now for the highest bidder. He'd know enough to evade me. The Justice, the old man with suspicious errands, was dead. No one was left to interrogate but the man at the flat.

He was there, I heard him inside before I reached the door, and I felt him scrape at my mind. He didn't know I felt him.

"Where is Tod?" I shouted from outside.

The door opened slowly. I wondered if he would still be trying to look like Tod. Stop it, I could say. I know you're not him. Then I could see where the flaws were, the mistakes in his face that should have warned me. But the man inside the door was tall, gray-eyed, his skin blanched like seafoam. And he was angry, baldly, blindly furious, at me.

Angry people are so easily conned. "So tell me, who do you work for? No, even better, take me there." I held out my wrists to be bound. I had nothing more to lose. "Go on."

He didn't bind my wrists, but he tied a blindfold around my head. Someone knew my eyes were dangerous.

There was a smithy in the City, a place I often went to when I was a child and was bored with watching the dramas of people. I admired the iron for its consistency, its hardness, its resistance to the efforts of the little men who struggled to shape it, its unforgiving heat. Once one of the smiths burned his hand on the metal, in a lazy act, as he reached for the bar of iron without gloving himself well enough, without having enough respect and fear for it. The smell of soot, the sting of molten metal, and the stench of burned flesh are forever linked in my mind since that day.

I caught the familiar traces of soot as soon as I neared the building, led blindly by the shapeshifter. I knew by the smell when we entered the yard, though there was no longer a gate in the yard's fence to swing on squeaky hinges and announce our arrival. My boots struck the floor inside the building and I waited to smell whose flesh would burn.

I was seated in a chair with a very high back. My wrists were bound sharply to the chair, and a thick rope was wound around my arms and shoulders to hold me fast. I was bound so tightly to the chair back, hard and painfully vertical, that I could not turn my head. When the shapeshifter was finally ordered to loosen the blind from my eyes, I was unable to see anything but what was directly in front of me.

Someone was evaluating me from the side, where I couldn't see him. I heard him pacing, his hard-soled shoes pounding the floor, slowly, evenly, the unhurried heaviness of power. He gave the order for the shape-shifter to unblind me in a cold, smooth voice. The big men had voices like that; Smyth had spoken in one and still did so in my mind. If there were a king or a tyrant in Dabion he would speak like that.

The pacing man didn't waste words, though. He knew the game, knew not to give himself away by speaking too much, knew how to create fear through silence. He walked with those even paces, echoing steps I could count the measured seconds between, around the back of the chair, in an arc to the side, then behind again to the other side, never letting me see him. The steps were as insistent as heartbeats, and as inexorable.

Then he stopped. He was good; his victim's heart would skip a beat despite itself. He took one precise step forward to place himself in my view, out on the very edges of what I could see. He felt, it was clear, no need to disguise himself. He was a Justice, in his immaculate black robes that were open to the tailored suit beneath, thick black velvet studded with polished silver buttons as costly as the jewelry he and his peers had outlawed a generation ago. He was a very old man, Loyd's age or older, but the kind of age that gathers power rather than loses it. His shoes were polished, his nails were clean, and his shaven face gleamed like polished wood. He gazed at me with the coldest, stillest eyes I'd ever seen. His voice was smooth, as if someone had sculpted it and the throat it came out of. "Certainly you remember me."

My first coincidence, come to visit me again. "Certainly."

He didn't care for my sarcasm; he turned and stepped out of my sight without even acknowledging it. His important steps carried him to the back of the chair, and he stayed there safely behind me. "How long have you been here?" he asked, in the voice of a prosecutor who already knows the answer. "For how long have you corrupted the land beneath our feet with your secret scurrying?" There was a pause, and I drew a breath, but before I could think of an answer he cut me off. "No, you are not to reply. You do not have the privilege."

I would not be allowed to speak, a criminal denied a devil's advocate. This was how low I was to him. I had offended him gravely, somehow. Was it when I read him in the Great Hall, or when I threw him down in Karrim? But these offenses seemed too mild, not severe enough to earn this kind of treatment, or the deaths of Collin and the old Justice. Had I wounded him in some other way, merely by reading him and seeing that he had the blood of a Sage? He was not going to tell me.

"The Sor'raian operatives," he continued, his voice not betraying the slightest waver, "you are without weakness, is that correct? Wondrous in your power? Without weariness, without fatigue? Without need? Without affection?"

From the yard outside I heard the heavy crash of metal, the angry cough of air forced through bellows. The fires of the smithy were being dragged back to life. The Justice intended to test me for those weaknesses. It would be with iron, it would be with fire, and it would be with my body. Or someone else's.

I couldn't see anything but a short stretch of empty

wall in front of me. Blindfolded, I hadn't been able to see the dimensions of the building, to guess from the outside what rooms might be inside. If there was another chamber where Tod might be hidden, I didn't know it. I could assume he was there, though. He'd been taken away and the shapeshifter had copied him, even his voice, so Tod had to have been alive. He probably was still, at least for a while. That was how the Justice would punish me for my offense, I was certain. But I still did not know why. I would have to try his weaknesses before he breached mine. That was the game.

There was another scraping noise, crashing and clattering and the sharp smell of metal, iron bars thrown on the fire. My eyes scratched dry against the fumes.

The Justice stepped into my vision. The sting of the molten iron didn't bring water to his eyes, either. He examined me for only an instant and moved away. He would come back, as the test proceeded. He was curious; behind the stone of his face he would be seething with angst. It would drive him to watch me, to come back again and again, watching for the effect his actions had on me, seeking out the progress of terror. He would watch me; and then I would find a way into him. I would find what I had done to him; and then I would have my weapon.

I would watch him. I would measure my reactions to manipulate him. I would feel nothing.

There is danger in emotion. I had holes in my mind and one in my gut, and a bloody wound where my heart should be. I seized up the torn edges and wrenched them shut. I would feel nothing. I would play the game.

The heavy paces arced behind me, back and forth, unseen. I waited for the Justice to pass before me again. I waited for Tod to be brought out. I could imagine him, see in my mind the torture he would endure. I did not think of it. I would not think of it. I would not recognize him. I would watch and feel nothing. The odor of hot metal stung the air and seared my eyes and nose and mouth. I waited for the smell of burning flesh that I knew would soon accompany it. The Justice passed into my sight. I did not look at him. I would show nothing yet. There is danger in emotion.

There was a noise from the yard, from outside, where the brazier was burning. The Justice stopped in his stride. He was looking up, past me, toward the door.

Once a young boy was playing on the shore of Lake Azin. He had wandered from his camp, left his elders among the rocky flats. Rarely was the boy followed. The wanderers knew something about him; they knew a great many things that couldn't be explained in language. His mother, who had borne him from a man he'd never known, a man the child could only believe was not a wanderer, knew things about him. She knew he was not for their world. And so she let him drift away, along the shores of the lake.

Once he met another boy on those shores, an older boy nearing manhood, dressed in the uniform of an apprentice clerk and the angst of nervous arrogance. This young man's eyes flew wide when he saw the wanderer boy, he dropped the sheaves of papers and official things he was carrying, and he shouted in a voice that caught. "Stop! The law orders you to stop!"

The boy started running toward the water. He was clumsy, made short by his unknown father's blood, lacking the litheness of his country's people. He had never run before. Wanderers knew no reason to. He tripped and fell with his face in the grass.

The clerk staggered forward, filled with wonder, believing his invocation of the sacred law had worked. Then the joy crumbled into rage. The boy climbed to his feet and lunged away again. In fury the older boy sprang after him, flailing his arms, searching for a way to stop the felon. By chance his hand sunk into the pocket where he kept his penknife. The wanderer child tripped again. A droplet of blood flew from his nose as he whirled around to face his attacker, and the tiny quill-cutting blade met him across the mouth.

Suddenly the light was blinding. Fire flashed on the lake and the clerk's hands flew up to cover his eyes. The light was gone an instant later, leaving the clerk to angrily search for the boy who was now missing, to rage back to his town and report the wanderers to his masters, to lead back the guards who would capture and haul away those few wanderers who lingered to be caught. The younger boy would watch it all from within the limbs of a tree, and until his people were taken away he could feel their magic combine with his own fainter powers to shield the tree with opaque leaves that no one would see him through.

"Certainly you remember me," he said now, to the clerk he had met those many years ago, himself no longer a boy, the other no longer a clerk.

Varzin's mouth curled down as he listened to the repetition of his own words to Elzith, but he knew there must be more to the words than mere mockery. "Your obfuscation disgusts me, Loyd. Do me the honor of saying what you mean."

Loyd smiled very slightly. He stood behind the chair where Elzith was bound, but he distracted none of his attention toward her. He knew she was alive and would stay so. "I am saying what I mean," he replied, and his face changed.

Varzin was no longer a boy, and he had trained his emotions as well as any of Loyd's operatives. Still, Loyd could see the fear in his eyes, the anxiety of one whose world has slipped beneath his feet. Loyd dropped the guise he'd worn for so many years, and the air breathed cold against the crooked bump of his nose and the scar that cut across his mouth.

"And you are one as well," Varzin finally said, in a voice that no longer caught. "The eighth limb of the Circle, an arm to my leg. Gangrene in the body of the law." He cast his eyes down slightly to the woman tied motionless before him. "So who is she to you?"

"Who is she?" Loyd murmured. His scarred mouth

turned in the trace of a smile, honest on his naked face. "She is my blood. She is my kin. She is of my homeland, and I found her, and I taught her who she is. She is the only daughter I will ever have. She has blessed me with loyalty I can never deserve or repay. She is the only thing I have ever prized in this dreadful world. She is my life."

Like all men with ice for souls, Varzin soured at Loyd's words. "How touching. You wished me to know this?"

"No," Loyd replied. "I wished her to know. It will not matter if you know. You will not live long enough to repeat it."

The light flared for only a moment. It was the only thing I saw, the only thing I heard. It burned in my head behind my clenched-closed eyes, pounding in the blood in my ears. It swept through me like a storm, a scream, a fire. It echoed in me and pulled me with it, a force and a call that clutched at me to follow it, though I didn't know the way. I ached, I was torn, I felt everything, too much for my body to hold, years, blood, memory, and inheritance. Then it was gone. I was empty as hunger. I heard no screams, no bodies falling. There was only silence, and the burning smell.

Then nothing. The men had left me. There was nothing remaining. It was over, and I was alone. I began to worm my wrists out of the cords.

I had always suspected Loyd had powers, ever since I first read him and saw that he knew what I was doing.

He never told me what they were, never let any clue about them slip. He never even mentioned Sor'rai to me, not by name. He and I were of the same blood, and that was all he said. I knew he must have powers; if I could reach people's minds, he must be able to do something at least as strong. Loyd might have created the flash, wielded some remarkable and untouchable force that killed the Lord Justice. Maybe the Justice had the power to seize minds as well, something hotter and brighter than mine, and he killed Loyd with a grasp or reflected the fire onto him. I had no idea what they were working with. It no longer mattered. There was no need to think of it anymore.

My flesh was raw and torn before I freed my hands. I did not feel it. I peered at the blood and the exposed textures of the skin for an instant, coldly as a hunter. Then I twisted the bindings around my shoulders until I could unknot them.

The two men lay on the floor behind me. I did what was to be done next, I checked their necks and their mouths. I learned they were dead, and I left them. I did what was to be done next, I looked outside for the shapeshifter. He was nowhere. I could assume that he ran at Loyd's arrival, and would return. I did what was to be done next, because it was next, feeling nothing at it. I looked for Tod.

If there was another room it was hidden. I circled the smithy superficially. I had no more time to spare.

The light was beginning to fail. I could search no more without light. The shapeshifter would return, likely before dark. I knew too little about him; it would be unwise to face him.

I had to leave.

I went to the doorway and halted there. I turned back and looked down on the big men. No bigger than any other dead men, now. Loyd told me once, when he was lecturing me needlessly about how to avoid the fear of death, that he had seen the moment when he would die. He lived in the vision of that moment, it steered his steps, he would never escape it. He believed he could not. I remembered the last time I spoke to him, days ago, when I refused his orders. He'd told me to come with him; he'd said he'd been summoned, that it was time for him to go. The moment had come. He came to the smithy because it was time for him to die. He killed himself and this Justice because he knew nothing else.

Who would I go to now? I laughed. Muhrroh was my nominal leader and he would appoint Loyd's successor. My feet were already pointed in the Lord Councilor's direction. I would go because I knew nothing else. My enemies would track me eventually through the paths the big men laid out for me, and one day I would be killed. My life might have been different, but it wouldn't have been by my hand. It was time for me to go, there was nothing else.

I used to wonder if I really believed in fate.

But where? Where would I go, if not to Insigh? Over-seas? Sor'rai? It was madness. I wanted to go nowhere. I cared for none of these things. It was time to go. The light was dying; dusk would obscure my footsteps. I started walking.

# 45

THE DARK, LABYRINTHINE PATH OPENED ONTO A room that was nearly as dark and empty itself. A single candle cast a faint glow on the circular wooden walls. Lord Councilor Muhrroh sat at the head of the table, alone. A collection of books was arrayed before him, volumes as ancient and rare as those possessed by the missing Justice Advisor Paloman. Muhrroh had done a great deal of collecting in the short years since the revival of Bioran scholarship had been officially recognized in Dabion. These were the words that would be used to commit the revival to history, large and impersonal: officially recognized in Dabion. But such a movement required an instigator, and it was Muhrroh himself who gave the order of recognition. He had allowed the Insigh School to operate even under opposition from the greater part of the Circle, he had admitted to the record Varzin's report on the spread of mysticism, he had created the position of Justice Advisor and arranged for the Circle to study Bioran learning. The movement of history was moved by Muhrroh's hand. But few knew why.

The Lord Councilor was not alone in the room; he was almost never alone. Therefore, he had trained himself carefully to maintain a placid expression at all times, in the face of every conflict and dilemma, upon receiving terrible news, even when he scanned book after book and found no answer for the great question in his mind. This was the very day of his birth—a day that put him five years past the age at which his father had died, one year before that at which the cancer had taken his grandfather—and it was known to no one. As he rested his hand upon his stomach none would realize that he was searching for a mass within, any sign that might be given to him that his time was near its end.

"Thank you for coming, your honor," Muhrroh finally said to his visitor, raising his head with complete ease and control. "You have done me a great honor by allowing me to summon you out of retirement once again."

Rayner nodded tolerantly and gave an appropriate measure of a smile.

"As you have responded so quickly, you will be the first to hear the unfortunate news," Muhrroh intoned. He did not mention that the news had been conveyed to him through the dreams of one of his Sor'raian operatives. Men had been dispatched to Origh to retrieve the corpses; only Rayner would be given the news until then. "The body of the law has suffered a great loss. The Circle has been convened to select a new Lord Justice for District Six. Our brother Varzin will be impossible to replace, but I believe a suitable appointment is near at hand. Your opinion will be of value to us, your honor, should you wish to attend our selection."

"As you wish, my lord," Rayner answered. Like a proper speaker, he did not exhibit his boredom with the topic. Justices lived and died; it was no concern of his. He was careful not to yawn.

"We have also suffered the loss of a lesser member of our ranks, Justice Advisor Paloman. He was our representative of Bioran learning; he was instructing us in the old works of scholarship. Our lessons have come to an unfortunate halt because of his sudden disappearance. We are left without a leader in this venue. He will be quite difficult to replace."

Rayner cared more for fever and plague than he did for Bioran learning, and he thought the scholars in the Insigh school were idiots. He'd sooner wear a dress than one of their absurd wigs. For a nauseating instant he feared that Muhrroh would ask him to take Paloman's place, but he couldn't actually expect such a preposterous suggestion from the Lord Councilor. "Surely you will find a suitable appointment for this position as well, my lord," Rayner demurred. "This is certainly not the matter you wished to ask me about."

"Certainly not," Muhrroh smiled. "You are very

astute. That is the quality that makes you appropriate for the third appointment I must make." Gracefully the Lord Councilor drew out a file from beneath one of the books in front of him. "You will recognize the name on this file."

Rayner did not move forward to look at it; he had not been given leave to move from the place where he stood at the ends of the table.

"There are several leaves missing from it, ones I had written personally. They were in regard to a certain member of our brotherhood. You arranged for their disappearance, of course."

Rayner knew it would not be wise to respond.

"I know you have been gathering materials from the stores at Origh. What I do not know is why. You are excellent at secrecy, your honor. You have hidden things even from me." Muhrroh returned the file to its place, keeping his eyes evenly on Rayner. His regal demeanor was untouched by any haste or anger. "You are also highly respected in the body of the law, and in the Circle, as witnessed by your frequent callings to preside over our Tables of Justice. Also, you are one of the last few of our generation." His face softened appropriately, and he reached his hand forth in an almost welcoming gesture. "We are old, your honor. Many of us are long dead, and in these few days we have lost the last of our noble brothers. We have no children, no legacy. These are our final days of power."

It took a moment for Rayner to let go of the brief flash of fear, the suspicion that he had been identified in the murder of Ciceline Jannes and the sense that he would not walk out of this room. Returning to his more composed attitude, he eyed the Lord Councilor and sought for words to test the validity of the offer. "Surely you have considered a younger person for the position, my lord?"

"Only one," agreed Muhrroh somewhat wistfully. "Only one I would trust, and that one is likewise missing."

Rayner glanced at the file again, listening for unspoken words. Muhrroh knew about Jannes, knew about the distillery racket, and had doubtless guessed at Rayner's desire to take it over. He probably recognized the threat to Jannes's life as well, and this offer might be an attempt to keep Rayner closer at hand and less able to do harm to Jannes. If he took the position, Rayner thought, not frowning, he would give up Jannes's money. If he refused the offer, he would call suspicion upon himself. But he would have something rather intriguing to do, at least, in exchange for losing the distilleries. He could seek the identity of Muhrroh's preferred successor to the helm of the Secret Force. Once he discovered it, he could certainly find a profitable way to use it. He smiled humbly. "And do you trust me, my lord?"

Muhrroh sighed, certain that he was allowing his age to show through the placidness. But there was no help for it. The books were empty of what he sought; the scientists of Biora had not found the cure to all sickness. "Does it matter, at this late date?"

Rayner bowed slightly in acceptance of the appointment. It was hardly a late date. He had plenty of time to seize a last few grains of power.

# 46

IF THE PAIN IN HIS EYES AND THROAT SUBSIDED, THE ache of hunger would stab at Tod. When that pain became so old he no longer had the energy to feel it, then the fear would reach him again. He had no idea how much time had passed. A jug of water had been left in the room and he was vaguely aware of the level in it changing, but it was the only sense Tod had of the moving of time. There were no windows, no light, nowhere for the sun to come in. Once Tod wet his lips from the jug, soothed his throat and the pit in his stomach, and with nothing else to worry him for an instant, he felt how light the jug was, and terror knocked him to the floor.

Tears started in his stinging eyes. No one had come to the room since the man who brought him there had left the second time. Even the noises outside the room—crashing things and voices he couldn't decipher in his hunger and fear—had died a long time ago. He had images of himself dying of thirst before anyone came back. While he was unconscious, lying on his floor after the book that Justice Paloman had brought ruptured and spilled the dust everywhere, he'd had a dream. Two men were dead, faces that were blurry and hard to recognize in that dusty sleep, but Tod himself wasn't one of them. Now he wondered if he'd missed something. Maybe one of the dead men was he. Maybe he just didn't recognize himself—how would he appear in his own dream? Any comfort the dream had given him was long gone, in the endless dark with the slowly drying water jug. Tod started shaking again until he felt the pain in his throat return.

After a while he was too tired to feel anything anymore. Nothing was happening, there was nothing he could do, and he had to wait. He could wait, he could. He'd waited a long time already, he could wait longer; it wouldn't be much longer. It didn't even matter if it was. He was calm, he could wait.

Then his heart would skip a beat and he'd roll on the floor with the fear tearing up his stomach.

Sometime later he slept. He felt the exhaustion pulling him into sleep, even if there was too much pain and terror. He was aware enough to wonder if he dreamed, but there was nothing, no message, no word of anyone's death.

Then suddenly he was awake. Light was flooding the room. Tod reached up to cover his eyes, but the brightness didn't come. The light was blurred and shapeless. Tod made a thin cry. He'd forgotten his sight was all but gone.

"She left you."

The voice was almost shocking. He heard it and remembered it, and he felt how much malice was in it. The man who came in, the kidnapper who had brought him here, was trying to hurt him. Tod realized he'd given something away by showing his pain. He'd given the man something to use against him. His breath stung in his throat.

"She fooled you, didn't she? She made you think she loved you, and you'd do anything for her. Dissembling bitch. Then she left you for dead." The man's voice was coming closer, Tod could feel his breath, stale and icy. "I can kill her," he said. "Tell me where she is."

Tod held his breath. Relief ached in his veins. Elzith was alive. The man didn't have her. But she wasn't safe, and though he had no idea how, Tod had to help her. He needed information. "Why do you want to kill her?"

Tod had heard that when people lost one sense their others grew stronger. He remembered watching a blind beggar in Origh, imagining how he lost his sight, wondering what he could hear over the murmur of the city. Now Tod knew. He could hear every furious breath that the kidnapper took, every step as he paced, and the cracking of knuckles as he clenched and reclenched his fists. The kidnapper hated Elzith. He wouldn't tell Tod why, though. "It doesn't matter why I want to," the man finally answered, in a rocky and cold voice. "I have to. I'm bound to my master and I have to follow his order. Even though he's dead."

Tod drew a breath and swallowed hard. He didn't know how to play this game. He wished Elzith was there. "But you hate him. He humiliated you, he treated you like a servant. You despised him. You always wanted to get free of him. Now you are."

He felt the air change an instant before the kidnapper started shouting. "You humans! You think you know everything! You think you rule the earth, that you're the utmost creation, fighting each other as if you were important. You have no idea. You know nothing! You can never understand how I am bound. He is Sage and he has bound me."

Tod reeled from the force of the man's voice. It blew over him like a windstorm, and Tod struggled to catch some of it. There had to be something, something he could use. But he realized he didn't understand a word the kidnapper had said. The man was silent now, withdrawing tangibly. Tod needed him to talk more, but he seemed to have lost all his anger and all his will to talk. Elzith would know how to get him to talk again. Tod thought over the words one more time, bit his lip, and opened his mouth. "He *was* Sage."

The trick worked, in a way. The kidnapper was furious. Tod was almost proud of himself, for the seconds before the kidnapper struck him full in the face and knocked him unconscious.

# 47

THE LAKE IS THE MOST DAMNABLY STRANGE THING in the earth. It is massive; when you try to see the boundaries of it, turning to the left or the right, walking along the shore trying to circumnavigate the thing, it never ends. But across it, looking straight ahead, you can see land. It's empty, wooded, motionless, but when you turn your head to look at that endless shore, you can see movement out of the corner of your eye.

I counted the days it took me to walk there, across Dabion near the thinly patrolled border with Karrim. I begged some bread off a few wide-eyed peasants I passed, a drink of water, but I didn't stop. It didn't take so long to get to the lake. I counted the days, added up the hours, and dropped them out of my memory.

The lake eats time, turns it around, makes it meaningless. I felt it sucking out the minutes as I stood there trying to count them, felt it washing the waves out of my mind as I counted their movements over the surface of the water. The lake played no games. It wouldn't let me.

I knew the wanderer was there before I turned and

saw him. He might as well have told me he was coming. People kept things from each other, hid their secrets, gathered what advantages they could take and viciously guarded what might be stolen and used against them. Wanderers kept no secrets, they took no advantages. This man was no more likely to sneak up on me than he was to tell me lies. Not that I would understand what he did tell me. People called the wanderers madmen, and with good reason. I should have known how mad they were myself; they were my kin.

"What do you want?" I asked. There was no point in using confidence trickery on him. I turned to see whether he would answer. The man was the image Tod had described, the figure lurking outside his window seasons ago. He was very tall, very thin, his wrists narrow and brittle as mine, his skin translucently pale, with strange eyes that might have been green if the light hit them right. The hood of the cloak that he wore over his tattered clothing was dropped down, off of his head, and the wind tossed the irregular braids of his parti-colored, leaf-strewn hair. He wasn't watching me. He looked over the water, with those strange eyes focused as if he were reading something off the waves. Braids blew into his eyes and he paid no more attention to them than he did to me.

I watched while he didn't speak. I could wait.

"Your mother walked through those trees," he said, without preamble.

"When?" I asked.

The Sage didn't answer that question. They didn't think in terms of questions and answers, truth and evidence, Loyd told me once. We see only one thing at a time, points along a line, but the Sages see everything. I was a spy, I told Loyd. I'd look for my answers and evidence.

"She walked through those trees and came upon one of the Magi, the lake-livers, the masters, the wise men. He moves the trees, this is his duty, land-shielder, lake-liver. He moves the trees so that the humans on the other side of the lake can't see within."

"Humans on this side, you mean," I murmured, not expecting him to correct himself. I knew he didn't care about his grammar, his shifting tenses.

"Look at the trees here. When you look away and look again they will be different. The trees stand where they grow, but what do your eyes see? Your mother is called Anazith."

I wondered briefly if she had told me that, long ago when my mind was too young to remember, and if I'd tried to say it to Geordie, and he'd taken the mispronounced name to be my own. It didn't matter.

"She was walking through the trees and came upon one of the Magi," the wanderer continued, circling around in his story. "She saw him working his magic, tree-mover, and she called his name. She saw him. She asked him, Sage in the ocean breeze, she bound him to her. You move the trees, she said, but do you know what moves men's hearts? He was bound, lake-liver, land-shielder, bound to her word. The word is important. She saw him move the trees. She said so, she said the words, I have seen you. He of the Magi answered, I am bound to you, o Sage. They are the blood of life, these words. Men on the other side of the lake value them too little, word-sellers, word-stealers. These words are life.

"Anazith. It means walks far, walks back. You have been here before."

I was too tired to ask what he meant by that. The exhaustion from days of walking was finally taking hold of me, dragging me down, making it impossible for me to stand against the wind from the lake. I looked around me. No one but the Sage was there, no one who could do me harm. I had yet to find out what the Sage meant to do to me. "What if they hadn't said the words?" I mused halfheartedly as I sat down on the damp grass. "Would the Magus still have been bound or not?"

Predictably, the Sage ignored me and launched to another unpredictable part of his tale. "He of the Magi went into the lake, water-walker, glass-gazer. He looked into the glass, the window on the human world. He looked and he saw, he looked long and he told Anazith what he saw. Nothing moves men's hearts, he told her, Anazith, Sage, walker. Nothing moves men's hearts, they only fight their wars and build their hatred. Nothing moves their hearts. They dig their gold and draw their lines, they know nothing but fighting one against the other.

"But Anazith said, look closer. Look in the glass again,

look again, eyes of water. You did not see everything. A flower grows in the battlefield, a child seeks it out, a child plucks it. Now whom does she give it to?"

The Sage had not turned away from the lake. I could lie on my back and sleep, but I knew he was waiting for me—for an answer, for some word. I didn't know what the right response was. It wouldn't really matter. "I don't care," I said. "The flower would have died anyway."

"Zann walks on these shores," the Sage went on, jumping subjects carelessly. "He wanders in the land straits, he watches the people, the humans, the law-makers village-builders. A young woman came out of the village, angry, angry, fighting, nothing to fight at. Zann found her, Zann the Sage. He knew who she was but she did not listen. She was angry, she had no way to fight, she wanted a man the way women do when they have no other weapon. Zann lay with her and she did not listen to his words. He told her her family would curse her and she did not listen. He told her she would come to hate the child she bore and she did not listen. He told her she would fear magic, she would hate the magic in her child, her child would hate the magic in himself, and she did not listen. She ran home to her village. And her family curses her, and she hates her child, and the man hates the magic in himself."

"The man is dead," I said sourly. "It's Varzin, isn't it? Or are you telling me this just because it has nothing to do with me? So why did this Sage do it? I know you can control your seed, I can make myself barren, Loyd told me I could, and that I got it from Sage blood. Why did he get this stupid girl pregnant? Was it you?" I had stretched out on the grass, cold dew seeping into my clothing, and I regarded the Sage's sticklike form upside down. "Was Varzin somehow supposed to be born, so that he and Loyd could kill each other?"

The Sage finally turned away from the water and looked down on me. "You think like a human," he said. "Your mother is dead. Sit up."

When I pulled myself upright I felt a wave of dizziness and I closed my eyes. The last thing I'd eaten had been a day ago. I opened my eyes and saw the wanderer sitting beside me, legs folded into angles like a spider. He held out his hand and showed me a palm full of nuts. Then he closed his hand and pulled it back toward his body.

"Don't play me," I said.

He held out his hand again, the same hand, and uncurled it. A clay tile lay against his palm, carved with three curved lines in the shape of waves.

I looked up at the Sage, searching for the nothing in his eyes. "That was you."

He closed his hand again. "Yes, child, human, that was me." He put his hand out a third time and dropped nuts into my lap. He said nothing else until I had eaten them.

"You'll ask me now why I sent it to you, human, Sage. You have not figured it out. You think it was a spell. You think I tried to harm you. What was it really, do you know?"

I chewed and didn't answer. The Sage's face was wrinkled, showing age uncharacteristically. It hurt him to think like a human, to flatten out his words in a way I could understand.

"Have you spoken to the man?" the Sage demanded absently. "Do you have his trust, do you have his love?"

"I have no love," I uttered dryly. "I have no heart."

The Sage shook his head, turning again toward the water. "You need his help."

"What can Tod possibly do to help me?"

But the wanderer had abandoned the strain of linear thought. He was on his feet, walking toward the lake. "Blood knows the way. A Sage can walk out of the land and back to the land. This is still your home." Then he paused and turned back to me, for an instant. "You can follow me across the land bridge, if that is what you want. If you want to know how Tod can help you, you have to ask him." Then he put his back to me and kept walking along the endless shore until I could no longer see him.

# 48

SOMEONE HAD REFILLED THE JUG BY THE TIME TOD woke up again. He discovered it after lying for what felt like a long time in the half weightlessness of waking up, a time when he thought he didn't feel the pain and might have dreamed the blindness. He realized it slowly, remembering fear like a nightmare that would end. He knew he was awake when the burn that had grown in his throat didn't change. Neither did anything else. Without hope or despair he reached for the jug. The water in it splashed out from the rim and wet his fingers.

It didn't mean anything, he thought. There was no reason to assume anything from the filled jug. What was coming would come. He would remember what he could and deliver it if he was given the chance. He cupped a little water in his hand and wet his mouth. Before he could feel it in his cracked throat, his awareness drifted and he tipped over.

He was hungry, he thought, drifting awake. There had to be food in the building. He couldn't think how he knew, couldn't remember that people had made camp here and must have brought food with them. He didn't remember his vision of the dead men, and couldn't be frightened by the thought of discovering them as he crawled blindly in search of the food. He couldn't remember that the door he crawled through had been locked. Only later did he wonder who had opened it.

Thoughts began to come back to him. Time would keep moving. He would tell what he had learned if he was given the chance. Fear was nothing. There was light. He could see its opaque blur through the painful film of his eyes. The door had been opened and he was out. Something was coming. Time would move him toward it.

He waited, he listened. He could hear everything, his senses were stronger with the failing of his sight. There was silence, a little wind blowing outside. He could smell traces of rain and cold. And something else.

"Elzith."

He could feel the time again, a few minutes, no more, that passed before he heard anything but the echo of his own voice.

"I left you, Tod. Did you hear me leave?" Her voice was very cold, toneless, very distant, although he could smell her close. "Do you know how long ago it was?"

"No," Tod rasped. "It doesn't matter."

"I didn't just leave you," she went on, forming each word hard and bitter, tight and icy. "I forsook you. I sacrificed you. I gave up your life so I could survive. I tore out my heart before it could be used against me."

"So you're saying," uttered Tod, his breath short after not speaking for so long, "that you had a heart after all."

Elzith said nothing. Tod heard, with his sharper ears, something he knew no one else would have noticed, Elzith drawing a deep breath, holding it, pushing it out in the response she couldn't put words to.

"Elzith, I have to tell you something." It was almost worthless, he was sure, but he had to say it, it was time, and he would do what he could.

It was ironic, the way it worked out. All my skills were useless, my power to read, the confidence I could gain, the game I had played so long. Everything came down to chance. Coincidence. Manipulation by the Sages, maybe, for reasons I wouldn't understand. I wouldn't be saved through any act of my own.

But maybe I would be.

I waited in the yard of the smithy. The sky was spitting bits of ice in a temperamental storm, but I wasn't feeling its cold. Feeling still took up no residence in me. Tod was standing outside, behind the brazier, trying to stall his shivering by the heat of a few remaining coals. I tried to tell him to stay inside but he wanted to be here. He had given me the missing piece, the bond between the shapeshifter and the Justice who controlled him, as my mother had controlled the Magus in that story the wanderer by Lake Azin had planted in me. Tod had given me my next move and he wanted to witness the end, as much as he could. He believed that he would help save me. He would give me the opportunity to, belatedly, save him. As if it would save my heart. Faithful, he stood with me and waited.

It wasn't long before the shapeshifter returned.

He was casting magic with all his might, blending into the trees, the earth, the dead leaves. I caught his movement in imperfect shadows passing just outside my vision. I almost saw him when he jumped at my back.

I anticipated him just enough to squirm half out of his grasp. He was heavier than me, he caught my legs and pinned me to the ground, but he couldn't get his hands around my throat.

"Why do you want to kill me?" I gasped, kicking at him.

He dropped his whole weight on my hips in answer. A flash of numbness struck my legs.

"You don't want to kill me. You only think you hate me." My voice was steady even as I struggled for breath. The coldness in my heart would buy me something, even if it damned me. "It's yourself you hate."

His hands clutched at my hair, ripped at it. I pulled out of his fist but his weight kept me facedown on the ground. I couldn't turn over, couldn't face him. He wouldn't believe my words, not yet, and he had to believe them for me to gain control. The words were vital. I didn't understand, but he had to. My fingers dug at frost-crusted ground, and he clung to me still.

And there was a crashing noise. It jarred our bones and rang our ears. The shapeshifter seized up over me.

In a snatch of sight I saw Tod thrown off his feet by the recoil of the rod he had swung crashing into the brazier. Then in that instant of advantage I flipped over and grasped the shapeshifter's eyes.

He froze.

"You're weak," I uttered under his weight. "Bound by a half-Sage. And now you're bound by another one."

His face contorted. "Dissembler," he snarled, reaching for my throat.

"Shapeshifter," I shouted. "I've seen you work magic. I saw you trying to be Tod."

Crying, strangled, furious, his hands closed into their fists, a breath away from my neck. He pushed away from me, hatred in his eyes. Tod said he might challenge the words, that he wanted to get out of his bonds to the Justice. He didn't think the shapeshifter would believe me. But the words were a game, he had bound himself to play it, like all of his kin—my kin, and he would play it to the end. "I am at your command," he spat, "o Sage."

"Good," I whispered. "I command you to leave us, me and him, never to seek us, never to harm us."

The shapeshifter backed away from me, from Tod's half-empty eyes. He held me with the utmost resentment. I read it in his eyes, plain and angry, and I read that he believed there was nothing else he could do. The words were his life. He turned, and walked toward the sky. His form melted into a bird and I let him make me see it. His wings stretched slowly and in time he was gone.

I raised myself from the ground, sooner than my body wanted and far too slowly for my mind. Someone had been to the smithy between the time I left and when I returned; they had taken the bodies away. Since they hadn't found Tod they must have been rushed, and I didn't know when they might come back, or who would come. "We still have to go," I said. "I have no one to protect me anymore, and I'll be tracked. We can't stay here."

Tod sat upright, hardly shivering, not showing the pain he must have had in his arms after striking the brazier so fiercely. "I'll go wherever you go," he said.

"No."

He turned his eyes toward me, trying to see through the haze to understand me.

"You can't go with me." I went back into the building, gathering up the other travelers' abandoned gear. I could not be Tod's. I tried his emotion and failed. I had sought him, ached with him, let him carry me, tried to give the pain away. It didn't work. It was too great a risk, and I paid the price for my mistake. If I'd been someone else I could have returned his love. Maybe. Tod had found my heart for me but it was still a cold thing. It could not change what I knew was true. I could not go with him, and he could not go with me.

Tod was standing in the doorway, reaching out to steady himself in the frame, trying to search for me. "Elzith," he called, blind and hopeful. "I know you left. But you came back."

I walked back toward him, keeping outside his reach.

He raised his head, sensing I was there. I threw my voice and my breath at him. "I would have sacrificed you, Tod. I would have let you die."

His bleary eyes dampened. "I can forgive you."

"But I can't."

I backed away, put him out of my sight while I finished the preparations. I took as long as I could. When I'd finally gathered everything I could use, I looked at Tod again. He hadn't moved. I watched him, feeling I could meet his eyes if I tried, feeling he could look into mine and see more than I would in his now.

"Here," I said, handing Tod a coat, Loyd's, that had been left when his body was taken away. As Tod dropped his arms to pull the coat on, I ducked around him and out of the door. For a long time I watched the wintry sky.

Where would I go? Zann told me I would be welcomed in Sor'rai, and I had no doubt that none of my enemies would follow me there. But could I actually get in—did I trust the Sage? What would I risk in giving away my confidence again? But Sages did not play the game, and I did not matter. I had to see that Tod was protected. I had to trust Zann to find him shelter. Could I look in the Sage's eyes and know whether he would? But I had looked in his eyes, and saw the future that Sages see as all time in a circle, and Tod was already safe behind the mountains of Biora.

"Come on, Tod," I called to him. "We have to go."

"But my book," he protested. "I have to go back and get my memory book."

It was too dangerous, I wanted to say, we had to leave now. But the words I said were "It's not finished yet." I reached my hand behind me. Behind me, Tod met and grasped it.

Over my shoulder I saw him nod. It was not finished yet, and he would follow me. I turned my eyes back to the road before me and led him behind. It was the closest thing to love I would ever do.

## About the Author

Michelle M. Welch has a B.A. in English literature and an M.A. in library science. She works as a reference librarian in Chandler, Arizona. Michelle has also studied music and has played with symphony orchestras, traditional Irish musicians, and Renaissance music groups. Her short fiction has appeared in *Reader's Break*.

Read on for a preview of

# MICHELLE M. WELCH'S

next captivating novel

# THE BRIGHT
# AND
# THE DARK

*Coming from Bantam Books in 2004*

# THE BRIGHT AND THE DARK

*Bantam Books, 2004*

### Part One

# BIORA

"Which side are you going to be on?"

The wind was high, the air drier than the leaves and brambles that crunched under Julian's feet. It was dry as fire, dry as the sun. Over the wind Julian could hardly hear Davi's words.

"I'll be with the Dust," Davi was saying. "They'll choose me, I know it." He was up on the road, swinging a willow wand in his hand, whipping it around like a flail, like a scythe. He laughed, dry and dusty. "You'll be with the Water people," he shouted at Julian.

"Then we'll have to kill each other," Julian answered, not listening, really, to his own words. One of the lambs was caught in the brambles and was calling Julian with frightened, mournful bleats.

Then Julian looked up at his friend. Davi should have replied by now, laughing him off or telling him it wasn't true. But Davi only whipped the branch, back and forth in front of him, cutting through the dry wind.

Branches of the brush caught Julian's knees, bit through the windings around his legs. He wondered what made Davi talk about it, today, yesterday, almost every day for weeks now. Then he remembered, vaguely, like the smell of a rainfall just before he woke, that Davi's brother had gone only a few weeks ago. Who had taken him—Julian wondered. Dust? Water? He reached the lamb and dipped his arms into the brambles, scratching bright blood onto his white skin.

"Or are you staying here?" came Davi's voice, over wind that whistled like the willow wand striking the air, "with the women and the girls? Tending sheep? Will you wear a dress and a shawl with your beard, like Telan?"

Julian spun around, ready to chase Davi, make him take it back. The branches caught his clothing and he couldn't move. He watched his friend stride down the road, distant, taller and broader, his copper-flax hair chopped blunt and short. He was nearly grown now. He would be taken soon. Julian lifted the lamb over his shoulders and began to pick his way out of the brush.

One day, not long after that, Davi put a stick and a skin of water in Julian's hands, and they walked out from Kiela. They were going to see the men.

Kiela was a large town, larger than they knew. Its fields spread out over acres of land, even up to the mountains. Houses, pens with their crooked-ringed fences, fanned rows of plantings, it seemed to go on forever before they walked out of it. They mounted the top of the hills and looked down on it, their home, the world of their childhood. How small it was there, distant in the vastness of the land.

They walked northward, very far, farther than Julian had ever walked. His feet began hurting him, he could feel every stone through the thin leather of his shoes, and he began to sweat inside his woolen tunic, beads of water slipping down his sides. Was it getting hotter? The land around him, beneath its tangle of scrub and brush, looked dry and sandy. It was spring, it should be raining, the clouds heavy and thick. He looked up at the sky. The sun came out from behind the mountain in a blinding swell. Julian squinted, trying to shade himself with his thin hands.

When they neared the village, Julian did not at first see it. He saw only dark spots on the land, piles of sticks, scattered like a child's toys. Only when they came closer, and the spots began to grow, did he see that they were houses. Shacks, rough and broken, and one so far from the next. There were no pens, no rows of grain. The land was unplanted and untended. Behind each house was a tiny scrap of a garden, stuck through with the drooping heads of tired stalks. Here and there an animal wandered, a mangy sheep, a bone-thin chicken. Women stood bent at their doors, and children sat in the shade and the dust beside their walls. Between those walls the dry land stretched out, barren.

"Look," Davi whispered, and the whisper was lost in a distant rumble. "The men are coming."

They swept down from the mountain like a dust storm, like the heavy rains of late summer. They trampled the gardens and flooded the shacks. In the clouded distance Julian saw one of the women, her pale hair flying, swing at the storm with a rake. From the mass of men, one was singled out. He grasped the woman, pulled her into the house, and Julian saw nothing more of them. In the sound of chaos a narrow scream drifted, and was lost.

"They're Dust," Davi breathed at Julian's side. "You can see the marks on their faces."

But Julian did not see the Dust men. He only saw the sun, turned on his back, low to the ground, looking at the sky. The sun stared down at him, hot and angry. Where was the water, he wondered, or Davi said it—where was the Water?

Then, as if summoned, they came. From the south, behind the hillock where the boys crouched, the Water men came, pounding the earth as they ran, tearing the air with their shouts. Their voices were so fierce and loud with rage that Julian would not have known they were human.

And beside him, Davi echoed their cry in a voice Julian had never before heard. He leapt to his feet, thrusting his walking stick out like a weapon, in the path of the Water men.

"Davi!" Julian tried to shout, but his voice was dust in his throat.

He saw one of the men then, heavy with rage, his dark face burning red, his hair like dirty flax. On his face was a mark, painted or cut or burned there, the curve of a line ending in an arrow. Julian wondered who the arrow pointed to. Then the man raised his weapon—what weapon Julian did not see—and brought it down where Davi stood below him.

Julian covered his face and rolled away.

Will I always be a coward? he thought. He did not look out to the field where the men were fighting, and he covered his ears with his hands. He did not know what the sound of it was and he did not want to learn. Then the sky changed. It grew dark, and the air was split with thunder, drowning out the noise of men. Julian opened his eyes. The storm clouds had come, heavy and angry. They opened and the rain fell, striking Julian's face and his arms, pounding on the earth.

In the haze of the rain he could pretend he did not see the men in the distance. The rain washed out all sound of them. Julian crept from his hiding place, going on his elbows, wormlike, until he reached Davi, and he pulled him away into the shrubs. There he hid until the rain was gone and it was silent.

### Part Two

# INSIGH

The School of Bioran Science in Insigh was built on the grounds of what was once the headquarters of the Black Force. Some ten years before, when Dabion finally outlawed Nanianism and the mystical, slightly mad, somehow threatening followers of that religion, the Justices, undertook a massive effort to close the monasteries in the neighboring country of Cassile, the center of Nanianism. The Black Force was instituted to guard the Justices as they went to Cassile to lend firepower to the mission. A rumor had circulated that a little too much firepower had been lent, and monasteries were burned down in several embarrassing debacles that wiped out a good number of the Black Force as well as the offending monks. No troops returned to the headquarters from their stint in Cassile. Those who were still alive after all the monasteries had been destroyed, retired or returned to less colorful police work in the Public Force. The Black Force was disbanded, no longer needed.

By the time the buildings were emptied, Dabion had a new use for them. Lord Justice Marsan of District Six was an ardent supporter of Bioran learning, and soon there was a thriving new population of students looking for somewhere to study. The Insigh school was moved to the larger campus of the former Black Force headquarters, where the barracks were renovated and filled with rows of desks, and the weapons warehouses turned into libraries. Only one building remained unchanged, a small storehouse at an extreme corner of the grounds, where the Dabionian authority kept the few remnants of the Black Force chosen for preservation.

No one would assume that the students would have the slightest interest in the building, being directed as they were toward books and rational things. No one would expect that the locks on the door might be picked.

The small storehouse was packed nearly floor to ceiling with all the things the Black Force commanders saved from their ill-fated missions: old uniforms; broken pieces of wagons and harnesses; masonry pried from the ruins of Cassilian monasteries and confiscated from the guards who wanted to bring back some souvenir; boxes stacked with written records that no Justice decided to read. There was barely a path through the mess, but in the back of the building, almost buried against the furthest wall, was a rack that still bore two short swords, three muskets, a pistol, and a horn of gunpowder.

The metal of the weapons was rusty with disuse, and the parts that someone might test would prove to be nearly immobile. Only one of the muskets still had its ramrod fixed to it. The swords' scabbards were discolored with water damage from a leaky ceiling, and the leather of the belts was cracked and dry. But the horn was untouched, somehow spared by the elements, and the powder inside was as good as fresh.

The powder made a nice line, poured from the plug in the small end of the horn. It could be traced in angles or undulating curves, almost artistic in its sharp blackness. There wasn't much of it, and it didn't make a long fuse, but it was long enough to go from outside the doorway into the building, winding along the narrow path through the refuse, to a convenient pile of broken wood that used to be a wagon. It could be lit and left for several minutes before the fire was touched off, perhaps half an hour before it consumed enough of the mess to become apparent.

Aron Jannes stood at the edge of the school grounds and looked out on the road that ran south from Insigh. It was at this time of the season, every season, that the Lord Justices met, drove into town in their carriages and pristine suits, made their official pronouncements, and then rode back out of town to their home districts. They always left at the same hour, without fail, and in the break between classes Aron could reach the edge of the grounds and watch them go, three carriages starting at first together, in perfect file. They would pass the school, and just before they were out of sight, two would turn to the west on their ways to Districts Three and Four, while the third continued south to Origh in District Two. That one would be his father.

Each season, on that same day and at that same hour, Aron came here, watched the carriages roll out, and tried to distinguish the southbound carriage from the others. The three were identical from this distance, polished black and flawless, as if dirt were an affront to justice, and the horses were always changed lest they look fatigued. Each carriage had the figure of the scales of justice painted on the doors. There were stories, Aron had heard, about carriages in Mandera in the days of the Ikinda Alliance, when the barons and dukes and whatever outdated nobility that existed back then drove around in carriages with designs painted all over them, family crests and granted arms in garish colors. The greatest accomplishment of Justice was that it had outlived the fall of Mandera, said the professors. Aron wondered if the Lord Justices could even see what hypocrites they were. They should be standing here, he thought, looking out over the road at the carriages rolling by.

When he first came here to the edge of the grounds, as a tenth-year student with privileges to leave the dormitory, and then as a tutor who did not need to attend classes, Aron had lurked under tree cover to watch the carriages. Now he stood out in the open, in the clearing between the trees and the storehouse. The Justices in their carriages could see him, if they looked. His father could see him, if he looked. Aron imagined that his father would be looking out the window, that he would catch a glimpse of his face, even this far away, and he would see his father's eyes widen as he recognized him standing in the clearing. One day, Aron told himself, one day he would see it.

But this time, like every other, the three carriages went by anonymously, and the sun glinted on their windows and blacked them out. Aron turned his head as they went south, blurred in the distance, and parted from one another. Even if he squinted he could not see which one of the three remained on the southbound road.

But he did see someone else in the clearing. Kuramin was standing near the doorway of the storehouse.

"What are you doing here?" Aron snapped.

The student raised his eyebrows. There was something wrong with them, Aron thought. They were too dark, almost muddy, like they had been painted on with a shaky hand. His mouth was somehow crooked as it turned in a strange smile.

"Are you following me?" Aron demanded, slowly stepping toward him with his shoulders drawn up, as he did when he approached younger students who needed to be taught more than the usual lessons. He was not used to stalking someone taller than him. "Why are you following me?"

Kuramin stood his ground, still smiling weirdly. "Aren't you going to run?"

Behind him, over Kuramin's shoulder, the glass in the storehouse window cracked and a tongue of flame lapped out.

When Aron was young, he used to fight like a wrestler, lunging out with his arms and legs. He hadn't done that since he was ten years old, not since the only person who had ever respected him refused to respond to it. He had different arms and legs now, ones that had never lunged or struck or kicked. He had taught himself the posture of the student, the clerk he was being trained as, the Justice he was destined to be. It suited him to grow into that body and so he had. But in that instant, standing before Kuramin in the clearing, his arms and legs unlearned everything they knew, and he jumped at the intruder with all the fury his body had forgotten.

A woman was walking toward the Insigh School. She was approaching from outside the city, although she had come from Insigh at first, walking far out into the country before beginning her search. She did not take the road. Somewhere near the school, she'd been told, she would find the person she was looking for. She didn't know where. He could be anywhere in the fields outside the school grounds, and she had been looking for most of the day.

It was getting late now and she was losing light. The search would be more difficult in the dark, and she was getting closer and closer to the school. At least she wouldn't be seen in the dark, even if she had to get right up to the school grounds, right up to the road. That was probably where he was after all, she thought. Idiot. On the road or still on the grounds, like they'd told him not to do. She cursed under her breath. It was always like this, working with him, working with the rest like him.

Her foot caught in a rut in the ground and she almost swore aloud. She bit the inside of her lip to stifle it. Her mouth was full of those bites, puckered bits of flesh that caught in her teeth. She sat on the grass and chewed, like a cow, until she tasted blood. The velvet-smooth fields and hills of Dabion were an illusion. Beneath the carefully groomed grass—so carefully, she knew just how carefully—the ground was broken and pitted. Keep the commoner off the grass, keep him in his place. Only the good people in their carriages who could go on the roads were allowed to come out. The woman stretched her leg out from under her skirts and rubbed at her ankle. She looked at the sky around her, the failing sun she'd had no time to see while she was searching the ground. And in the sky was a thick smudge of smoke. Something on the school grounds was burning. She laughed mutely, spitting blood. What did the man have to do with that, she thought. It had to be something, it had to be.

Dusk brought out the light of the fire, glowing in the windows of some distant building that didn't burn. Masonry, she thought. Filled with something dry. The roof wasn't thatch either, or it would have turned into a blaze that she would have seen even while she was watching the ground. The light brought out the shapes of men in dull gray uniforms, Public Force who'd been called in. The professors in their black gowns and stiff wigs would have been running around like madmen in front of the fire, not knowing what to do. She could imagine it, she could almost laugh. The Public Force had cut down the boughs of trees that hung closest to the burning building, to keep the fire from spreading, and they were standing with their hands on their axes, smug. They did nothing else but watch the last of the smoke smolder out.

"Impressive, isn't it?" a voice said from behind her.

The woman whirled around. There he was, near the road, just like she thought, and he was speaking out loud. She shuffled toward him on hands and knees, scraping her skin and her clothes. "What in hell are you doing?" she hissed when she was close enough to him that her voice wouldn't carry. "Someone will see you."

He was lying in the taller grass at the edge of the road, not easily visible but not caring to hide. His face was mottled with bruises and blood, looking muddy in the poor light. "It was lovely when it was born, bright, golden. Fire. It is not what they think it is."

"Madman," the woman hissed under her breath, not caring to hide it.

The man acknowledged her insult by smiling but kept on with his words. "They teach their children about light, they think they do. But they do not know what it is." He smiled again, his mouth weird and twisted. "You are called T."

"You know bloody well what I'm called." She tugged at his arm, pointlessly, since he refused to move. "Come away from the road."

"He doesn't know what it is, either. I tried to tell him."

She stopped at that, stared at him. She wanted to strike him, to muddy his stained face more. "You talked to him?"

"I tried to tell him. I asked him. He wouldn't listen."

On the school grounds the smoke was dying, and the men were moving around, looking at other things. The woman hissed at her unwanted companion to follow her, and she crawled away toward the slight shelter of a tree, away from the road. Then she waited for him to reach her so she could scream at him. He took his time.

"What did you say to him?" she demanded, when he finally reached her and dropped carelessly to his stomach. "Answer me this time. What the words were. I've had enough of your evasions."

The man lay quietly as if nothing was disturbing him. "I asked him if he was going to run. From the fire."

Frowning, the woman looked back at the traces of smoke. She looked back at the man, and then she pounded her hands on the ground. "What about the fire? Who set it—did you? You're not going to tell me that, are you? Are you, K? I should have left you out here."

The man turned slowly onto his back, letting out a sigh of the pain that did not show on his face. "He did not know, he had never asked. I wanted him to ask." He opened his eyes and spoke patiently, as if to a child. "I challenged him."

"I don't care what you said," the woman muttered. "You provoked him. That's the point. You provoked him.

You risked everything. You could have ruined the entire assignment. You probably did. Do you think you can go back now?"

"I do not have to." He smiled. "That is the point."

The woman dropped her head in her hands. "Madman. Bastard. Idiot. The whole lot of you. Why do I keep doing it?" She waited, watching the sun disappear behind some green hill, chewing the inside of her mouth. On the school grounds the Public Force filed up and marched out, and the noises of professors drew away and died. The school was silent for the night. Then the woman rooted in the pockets of her skirt for the things she had brought. She lit a tiny lamp and opened a vial of a tincture, spilled a little of it out on a cloth and started daubing it at the man's face. She sighed heavily. "I can't see what I'm doing."

The man turned his face toward the light. His face looked dark, too dark, patchy like badly dyed leather. The blood smeared it where he had passed his fingers, and thin blades of grass clung to it where he had brushed the ground. Then his face changed. The pigment bled out of it, draining like sweat rising to the surface and drying into the air. His mouth changed, losing its shape, growing thinner, and his face fell down to its bones like old age rushed to a horrible speed. He breathed out and the flesh on his body seemed to go with it, and his clothes hung on him awkwardly. The light shone through the fine shorn hairs on his scalp and his skin looked red in the light.

"Ah," he sighed. His voice did not change. "I can breathe again." He looked up at the woman, his eyes shadowy with fatigue, one of them sunken with a purple bruise that stood out like it was painted. "It doesn't look so bad now, does it?"

The woman didn't answer. She could see the damage, at least. One blackened eye, a split in the lower lip, a puffy nose that had stopped bleeding and probably was not broken. "What's the matter, K?" she said dryly. "Did he tie your hands up first?"

"Such fighters, all of you. Not for me to stop. I am going home."

"The man won't want to see you yet."

K shook his head. "He won't. I'm not going back to him. I am going home."

The woman stared again. "You can't leave."

"You can tell him." The Sage smiled. "It is time for me to go."

The woman balled her cloth in her fist, tore it out, ripped it. "Time for you to go!" Her teeth sank into her lip as she struggled to lower her voice. "Why do you think you know time? Why do you think you know where to go? Acting so wise, like you know the future." She shoved him with her hands, pushing the side where she thought a rib was cracked, trying to make him cry out.

But he didn't cry out. He sat up and then stood, smoothly and quietly. "But I do not know the future," the

Sage said. "If I did, I could tell you the answer to your question, the one in your blood that you do not ask." Then he climbed onto the road, ignoring her objections as if they were only wind at his back, and began to walk toward the north.